Death in Camera

SR GARRAE

This is a work of fiction. All the characters and events described in this book are fictional, and any resemblance to real events or persons living or dead is entirely coincidental.

DEDICATION

For everyone who supported Death in Focus, encouraged me to write another book and who helped me with this one: especially my family, my friends and, most of all, Joan and Daniela.

CONTENTS

CHAPTER ONE

"Is she ready?" asked the man at the camera.

"Yes."

"Bring her in."

"Stand up straight," another man ordered: the thin, whiny voice already judging the woman and finding her wanting. He ran his gaze over her. "That's not right. Come here." She obediently came closer.

"More tits on show." He moved the fabric of the already revealing bra, so that she was almost spilling out. "Better." He stepped back and scanned her. "That'll do. For now. Follow me." She padded sloppily after him, on to the set: stumbled slightly, eyes dilated, seeming unsure where she was.

It was a bedroom set. The bed was rumpled, as if used; a full-length mirror stood close to a vanity; a nightstand beside the bed. A silvery dress lay crumpled on the floor, as if thrown there. The props made it perfectly clear that it was only one step from BDSM Monthly: a blindfold resting on the dented pillow; a set of metal handcuffs glinting on the nightstand. The drawer was half-open, hinting that there might be more toys inside. Another set of cuffs was insinuatingly draped over the end of the bed. The mirror was quite carefully oriented to expose different angles of the bed and its occupants.

"Perfect," a third man said, from the darkness beyond. "This one is perfect."

"We'll enjoy this one. She'll be just as good as the other girls."

They watched with sharp, lecherous eyes as she wavered further in: mussed hair; smudged, sexy eyes; painted, pouting lips. She was a centrefold dream: everyman's *just fell out of my bed where she did everything I wanted* desire.

"Get the robe off," one ordered. "She'll do anything, won't she?" he checked.

"Oh, yes. Anything we want. She's completely powerless." Their faces were demonic in the shadows, dirty, degrading lust crawling from them.

"On the bed." She slipped, half-falling on to it. The orders began; the camera rolled.

"Now, look a little frightened, but turned on. C'mon, sexy, you know how it feels. Imagine you're pinned down: it's all getting rough. That's it. Pout like you wanna be kissed hard. You do, don't you? Open slightly. Mouth and your legs. Lick your lips. I want them wet."

The three men watched, one through his camera, two with avid eyes.

"You want it. Show me how much you want it. Offer up the cuffs, as if someone's there. He's in charge, and you want it. Make me believe it. That's right. Bite that lip."

The men were openly aroused. "Soon," one said.

"Blindfold on. Cuff round one wrist. Writhe. You love it, don't you? Playing to the camera. Perfect. You're so turned on. Imagine your boyfriend watching you, tied down and ready."

Click. Whirr. Click.

"Now. Take the bra off, slowly. Show me everything. Touch yourself."

One of the other men came out from the shadows, already half stripped. Her drugged eyes barely flickered.

"Now we'll really get the party started," he said.

***

The Klieg lights went out, and the camera whirring ceased. Small, hurting noises quietened.

"We'll need to find a new one soon."

The cold voice might have been referring to a packet of Advil.

"This one's almost done. Even you won't be able to keep her beautiful for much longer."

"Plenty more where she came from."

"There always are," the first man said. "All of them want to be famous."

"They are famous. Just not like they expected." A burst of unpleasant laughter.

"The last one got hundreds of thousands of hits."

"Nice. The variety helps, of course. One for every taste. And every hit is cash clinking into our accounts."

"Ain't social media wonderful?" the clipped voice said cynically.

"Sure is. But..."

"Mm?"

"Maybe we should be thinking about moving on soon? Manhattan's big and all, but someone's going to make connections if we take too many or stay too long. The cops have already gone around to the agency, just for one of them. We don't want to attract attention."

"No. Not that sort of attention, anyway."

"They only found one," a third person pitched in. "Didn't mention any others. If they had a link, they'd be pushing it. Anyway, she left for another agency."

"So she thought." There was a nasty laugh. "Expected something better."

"She got it." Another laugh. "For a few weeks."

"I guess we're good, for now, as long as we're careful."

"Okay. Let's plan, all the same. If they start getting close, we want to be prepared. I don't want to be caught out."

Harsh footsteps left the dim studio. The only remaining sound was the drugged, heavy breathing of the naked girl on the bed.

CHAPTER TWO

"I'm so bored of pop-and-drops," Detective Casey Clement complained to her team and everyone in the Thirty-Sixth precinct within earshot. "What's up with Manhattan? Everyone's killing each other for no good reason."

The other three members of the team grinned unsympathetically at her: the smallest of the group: most of her moderate height in her legs. Her dark eyes held irritation, her dark curly hair was neatly confined in a clip. She wore only a bare minimum of make-up on an arresting face; smart, functional clothing covered a toned body which, despite her best efforts, still managed to be curvy. She scowled back at them, and then at her pristine desk, on which there was no interesting case.

"Stress," Andy replied. "It's everybody realising that they have to see their families for Thanksgiving and they haven't organised anything with only four weeks to go. You know: peace, joy, thankfulness, chaos" –

"Murder," Tyler added sardonically, striding up: a burly contrast to Andy's delicate Chinese features and sparky repartee: tall, black, and brusque. Tyler had been in the Army, and it showed.

"It's all that enforced togetherness. All the family stresses and strains come out and suddenly there's an argument about who got Great-Auntie Yu-Ling's best peacock cheongsam and then there's blood on the turkey."

"Wow," Casey emitted. "Cynical much?"

"What's with you? Usually you're the one who's cynical."

"Awwww," sub-woofed O'Leary's huge bulk, lumbering up. "Casey's happy."

"Say what?" Andy teased, dropping the cynicism. "Casey happy? Nah. No weird cases, no riddles, and she said she was bored. She can't be happy."

"She's happy. Thankful."

4

Casey glared, before O'Leary could carry on the joke. "*She* is right here. I want a proper murder," she groused at her giant partner. "Not you pretending you've just fallen off the hay-wagon and sounding like you ate the haystack. If you carry on with that you'll be the murder victim."

O'Leary merely grinned. "You had one close to a month back, an' got beat up solvin' it, an' you've spent all the time since then bathin' in Icy Hot an' lookin' like you'd been in a paint fight at day care. Bet you're still a bit bruised. How c'n you be bored already?"

She was bored because she wanted to solve cases, not pore over paperwork. She loved the thrill of the hunt, and the sheer satisfaction of cuffing the perpetrator. Five years of being a Homicide detective hadn't dented that rush one iota.

"You shouldn't be wishing people dead. It's not nice."

Casey – and the rest – whipped round to see Carval.

He wandered closer, taller than everyone in the team except the six-foot-ten of massive muscle that comprised O'Leary, sharp blue gaze surveying them and the bullpen to check if there was another shot available. As ever, he had his camera in his hand and had been taking yet more pictures. He was as passionate about photography as she was about catching killers, and her team of misfits was the subject of his current obsession – and his next major exhibition.

"Keeps us in pay-checks," Tyler noted, as sparse with words as ever.

"Keepin' Carval here in photos," O'Leary added.

Casey merely smiled, a touch sardonically. Jamie Carval, she thought. Darling of the cultured elite, who flocked to his searingly honest reality exhibitions; playboy photographer who'd first made his name in glamour shots. And her sometime lover. His panhandler show had cemented his fame, and even the stern Captain Kent had been captured – or his wife had. Kent preferred football to photographs, but he also liked a harmonious domestic life and good PR for the NYPD, so, over Casey's objections, he'd given Carval permission to shoot them, in and out of the precinct.

From O'Leary's approving look, and the spark in Carval's eye, her sardonic expression hadn't hidden her pleasure in seeing Carval's broad form. Fortunately, O'Leary said nothing further. He might be the size of a house, but she had ways of getting her own back.

"What are you shooting today?"

Carval grimaced. "Still messing with the one-way glass. Don't you ever clean it?"

"You want it cleaned, we'll find you a bucket an' sponge. The city pays us to solve crime, not wash windows."

He grumbled. Carval didn't do mundane or domestic: he had Allan, his manager, for that, though he doubted that Allan would wash windows. It might splash his glossy shoes. "No murders?"

"No interesting murders."

"Andy's blaming all these pop-an'-drops on organisin' Thanksgiving. Me, I like Thanksgiving. Lots of food, presents, an' beer. Me 'n' Pete are goin' off to his family. He's got all those nieces an' nephews. It should be fun." O'Leary's moon face beamed. He was a man who loved celebrations.

"Got plans," Tyler said laconically. Casey was sure his plans were centred around the gym and sports, which comprised Tyler's life and were probably the closest he came to religion.

"I'll be seeing my dad," she contributed, "but we haven't planned properly yet."

There was a half-hitch in the discussion. Andy was missing.

No-one asked why Andy hadn't commented before disappearing. Thanksgiving wasn't a great time for Andy. His family wasn't a good memory. Casey didn't like Thanksgiving much either, for different reasons, but within the team no-one would ask any difficult questions.

"Photos," Carval said, filling the gap without knowing why there was a gap. "I always get good shots on the streets on Thanksgiving."

"It's far too early to think about Thanksgiving," Casey pointed out belatedly. "Let's think about the job instead. We've got Hallowe'en first. Always plenty of trouble around then."

Andy wandered back. "Let's get rid of these cold cases, then you'll have space for a messy one, even if it takes till Hallowe'en."

"I'm going back to the studio. I've taken plenty of shots in here. I don't want to take any more if there's nothing new." Carval was halfway to the stairs when Casey's phone rang.

"Clement."

"Yes. Okay. Where?"

"On it. Bye."

She turned round, suddenly alight. "Okay, we got a new one. St Nicholas Park. Let's go."

***

The corpse was a woman: bloody, beaten and, originally, beautiful; though, after being dumped in the park like a sack of garbage, her good looks were much less obvious. A tight, silvery dress gleamed in the remnants of the setting sun, barely covering a messy sprawl of splayed limbs.

"She didn't walk here."

"No way. Too cold without a coat." Tyler tugged his bulky jacket around his shoulders.

"And those heels can't be comfortable."

"Street camera footage." Andy made a note: as the team's technogeek, he would deal with that.

Quietly slipping into the background, Carval calculated the fast-fading light levels and started to shoot the team: their precise movements and focus a contrast to the heap on the dark grass and muddy half-reflections from the sullen sodium streetlights on the black-painted railings. Casey's head was upright, assessing the whole scene: the four cops completely absorbed.

"She's really dressed up," she noted.

"Yeah." Andy smirked. "If you got dressed up, you could look like that too."

"What, dead?" she retorted. "No thanks. Dead's a serious mood killer."

"How would you know? You never go out."

"I do so."

"We don't count."

O'Leary took a hand. "Sure we do. Just 'cause you go to all that fancy cultural stuff don't mean that Casey has to. Havin' beer with us is much more fun, 'less you start tryin' to educate us. That ain't fun."

Andy spluttered, but subsided.

CSU took their own photographs. It was, Carval thought, a little meta: he was photographing CSU photographing a barely-dressed corpse. They finished, and then the team began.

Medical Examiner McDonald's stork-like figure stooped over the corpse, probing carefully: disapproving from the get-go. Carval didn't mind, as long as it wasn't directed at him. So far, McDonald hadn't noticed him, and from the team's commentary, Carval would be delighted if that continued for an extended time. Still, McDonald's pecking posture and elderly-schoolmasterish air was yet another contrast to the life and connection of the team: one he hadn't much focused on as yet. He prowled closer, and centred on the precise, skeletal hands. Back at the studio, he had a single shot of Casey's hands around a coffee cup. Maybe there was another exhibition in there.

"Hell of a looker," Tyler said bleakly, as the corpse was straightened out. He wasn't wrong. She was easily five foot ten, and most of the height came from her legs. Even Casey, a woman in possession of an excellent pair of legs, envied those legs, and the height they provided. An extra couple of inches would have been nice. Well. She would have envied it all, had the legs been attached to a live woman.

"She has been shot through the head," McDonald pointed out, which was entirely unnecessary since they could all see that. "However, she has also been beaten. There are no defensive wounds apparent." His disapproval deepened. "Most peculiar. As is the dilation of the pupils." His thin fingers lifted an eyelid, to demonstrate. "I shall need to perform an extensive tox screen," he directed at CSU. "Furthermore, it appears from my initial appraisal that the assault was post-mortem."

"Huh?" Casey said, echoed by the three cops. That was weird. Beating to death was nasty, but unfortunately common, as beatings often caused deaths – accidentally or otherwise. Beating after death tended to go with beating *to* death, when the murderer forgot to stop whaling on the victim. Otherwise, most criminals were lazy, and didn't waste effort hitting corpses. Shooting and then beating after death was unusual, which meant that this death was likely a properly Casey-flavoured case.

"After death."

"I know what it means, Dr McDonald," Casey clipped. "That's not normal, though."

"No. Hmm." He poked at the head. "Shot at close range. CSU will test ballistics." She knew that, too, but fighting with McDonald was a game she was certain to lose. His prickly fussiness was impenetrable.

"How about you hurry the tox screen through? If there aren't any defensive wounds and the beating was after she was shot, then she didn't put up a fight before death. That says drugged to me."

"I see you have learnt something," McDonald gibed. "Astonishing. The tox screen, however, cannot be hurried. Stop asking for the impossible." He attempted to move a limb. "Rigor has not yet passed off. However, it was cold last night, and it is cool now. I shall calculate an approximate time of death when I return to the morgue."

"This is weird," Andy delicately investigated the scrap of shiny material that called itself a dress. "No ID at all."

"That ain't surprisin'," O'Leary's bass contradicted through the twilight. "Ain't nowhere to keep any ID. That handkerchief couldn't hide a flea."

Casey didn't disagree. "Okay. We've no ID, so" –

"She must be a spy," Andy said dryly. "She could be Jane. Jane Bond."

Tyler made a derisive noise. "No way. Can't fire a gun with those nails."

The nails were long, well-manicured, and decorated with a complex swirl of patterns. Manual work, even washing up, had clearly never touched their perfection.

"It'd take you three hours at the nail salon to get that look," O'Leary quipped. "Guess this girl didn't work."

"Nail salon?" Casey choked. "Me?" She barely managed a clear polish.

"You gotta look cute. It's in the rules."

Casey gave up. She was sure O'Leary had made that up to annoy her, but she couldn't think of a come-back. No doubt it would arrive in an hour or so, too late to be useful.

"No spies, please," she sighed. "We're not spinning crazy theories. Most likely she's a high-end escort who got in with a bad john."

"Boring."

"But most likely."

McDonald and corpse departed in perfect harmony with each other, which was only a tiny touch creepy. The team poked around for several moments, without success. No blood, no shell casings, no purse or wallet. They concluded, again, that she hadn't been killed where she was found.

"We'll get uniforms to search the area and any Dumpsters nearby," Casey said to general relief. "I don't see anything lying around. There's no purse: not even a small wallet."

"She didn't have enough dress to fit a pocket in," Carval pointed out. "She should have had something." He was fussing with the lens of his camera, trying to swap it for another without dropping both or smearing the glass. "Models usually do."

"Models?" Casey queried, a little roil in her stomach.

"Yeah. She's a model. I'd bet on it."

"How do you know?" The roil writhed.

"She's the type. Legs, slender – didn't you see the jut of those collarbones – and that dress" –

"Don't you mean handkerchief?"

"– dress – is a good designer knockoff."

Having dropped that bombshell, he exchanged his lenses to his own satisfaction and took a few more shots, concentrating on the intent expressions of the CSU sweepers and the team's focus, contrasting with the stillness of the corpse. Gradually he became aware of the ominous silence around him.

"Why couldn't she be an escort?"

"She could be both," Carval said absently, still shooting. "Most likely she was."

"Focus *here*, Carval," Casey snapped. "Murder. What we're trying to solve. Not a photo-op. You know something about models, so stop shooting and spit it out."

"Glam shots, back in the day. Every one of them claimed to be a model, but I'm pretty sure half of them were escorts. I didn't ask. They all looked like that. Long, lean, and no real figure. It makes for really good shots. Stunning."

Glam shots? She'd known that. So why did it sting now?

"Hm. You know what's really odd?" Carval mused. "She didn't have a phone. Every model or escort I've ever met had a phone. Surgically attached."

The frozen chill of four cop stares indicated that that was a comment they hadn't wanted to hear.

"You meet *many* escorts, Carval?"

"What? Not like that. I said. They all claimed to be models." His tone hardened. "I also didn't use their services."

"Ri-ight." Andy didn't sound convinced, his face pinched.

"*Really*. I've never used an escort service." He clamped his mouth shut before he could be any further up shit creek by saying *I never needed to*. "I'm not apologising for something I didn't do."

"Mm," Andy hummed sceptically. Carval detected hostility, which he had thought had dissipated after he'd helped to solve the Telagon case. He wasn't impressed by the backward step.

"Okay," Casey said briskly, ignoring her discomfort, which had no place in a respectable homicide investigation. "We all know the routine. Street cam footage; canvassing by uniforms; we've had a good look around to see if we can spot anything, and haven't – no shell casing, Tyler? You usually find those first."

"Yeah," Tyler preened, "but no casings. CSU'll finish the full sweep when we get outta their way."

"We might as well get out of the way now," Casey agreed. "They'll find us anything there is to be found." She frowned. "I wish we had an ID. Maybe prints'll ping."

Back in the bullpen, prints didn't ping, CSU reported that they hadn't found any ID in the vicinity, and the results of the canvass hadn't produced any witnesses. Some unlucky rookies were forced to Dumpster dive, but there was no sign of any purse, phone or small wallet in there either. The team was stymied.

The four of them convened – Carval gone – to stare at the murder board and grumble about the lack of evidence. All they had was an empty timeline – the only data point was when the body had been found – and a shot of the corpse from CSU.

"That was professional," Andy scraped out.

"Huh?"

"That beating. Professional. Or experienced. Same thing, really." Nobody asked how he knew. They didn't have to. Andy had had a difficult childhood, and it hit harder when a case tripped his memories. They all had memories, and demons: they all knew each other's sensitivities. They unconsciously closed around him, shielding him. Had Carval still been around, he'd have been shooting non-stop.

"Why didn't you say earlier?" It wasn't a criticism. "We could've got McDonald on to that. Let's do it now."

"Outsiders," Tyler said. Andy didn't say anything. Casey sent an e-mail to McDonald in lieu of calling him, which intrusion would only provoke an unpleasant reaction.

"I thought you'd been a bit quiet." O'Leary noted, carefully avoiding any implications as to why Andy might have been quiet.

"Yeah. Let's go get a beer. I could use one."

Andy rarely drank any alcohol. His slim body was a temple to daily tai-chi, green tea and a healthy diet. Sure, he'd have a beer – usually only a single bottle – if the team went for a drink, but for him to suggest it was almost as rare as finding a dodo strutting through Central Park.

"Okay."

"The Abbey, then. Seeing as Bigfoot here won't go anywhere else in case he gets picked up by Animal Control and put back in the Zoo."

"Those cages ain't comfy, an' they don't get the sports channels," O'Leary pointed out, to snickers.

Settled in the Abbey, Andy twisted his beer bottle in his hands while the others discussed the critical issues of the day – that would be the football season. They didn't push for answers or excavate his feelings: that wasn't how the team rolled – except for O'Leary, who played Big Brother and knocked sense into heads whenever he felt it was needed. When, or if, Andy wanted to talk he would. If he didn't, he wouldn't. They would be easy, either way.

Casey didn't want to talk either: not about the case, anyway. She was well aware that she was no model: too short and too curvy, and normally that didn't bother her one whit. She'd even prided herself on it, when Carval had first attempted to access the precinct and her team to take shots: dismissed the whole idea with a sarcastic comment of *no, I'm no model.* So being unnerved by a case that featured a stunning model (at least, pre-murder she had been stunning) was dumb. If Carval wanted models, he would find them: quite easily, according to his reputation. But he'd found her.

It was all perfectly logical and sensible. So it was perfectly ridiculous that there was still a small insecure space in her stomach. She was never insecure about men, or her looks, or her body. Never. And she wasn't going to start now.

It was just that having a playboy around a case which featured gorgeous models...well...it wasn't comfortable.

She sipped at her beer, and squashed down her discomfort until it departed, which coincided with the departure of the dregs of her beer.

"Time I went," she announced. "Maybe tomorrow we'll have something to get our teeth into."

"I'm going home too," Andy agreed. "Walk you out."

"Or I'll walk you."

They left O'Leary's enormous frame to spread out a little and talk sport, sparring and shooting with Tyler, and split up at the subway: Andy making for Penn Station and out of Manhattan, Casey heading a little north to her cosy apartment.

As she made dinner – which took no more than five minutes as she zapped a ready meal in the microwave – she thought about calling Carval. It took her less time than it took to heat her dinner to decide that that was a bad plan. She didn't need his wide, warm presence to reassure her. They...weren't like that. No complications. Her dad was complication enough. Carval...was fun. That was all. Nothing more. She didn't need more – she didn't need to be needy.

She hadn't room for more, she told herself, and ignored the small twisting in her stomach. It was simply a final holdover from the beating she had taken on the previous case, or tiredness. She didn't sleep well at the best of times, and the bruises hadn't helped, taking far too long to heal.

She didn't sleep well that night.

***

The following morning, camera footage of the area around St Nicholas Park arrived, just in time to stop Casey exploding with frustration. She wanted to get on with her investigation: eager for a trail.

"Bet that's our corpse," Andy offered, as a van stopped at around the right time and the right place.

"I hope there aren't more," Casey grinned. "One at a time, please."

Their amusement rapidly drained as they watched.

"That's not helpful," Casey growled.

"No."

"There's our body. Can't mistake the dress."

"Handkerchief," Tyler muttered, wandering over. Burly ex-Army types, it seemed, weren't knowledgeable about dresses.

"Whatever. But this is useless. Look at it! Plates so filthy we can't read them, it's a Ford Transit and there can't be more than a million of *those* in Manhattan, and the two guys dumping her are muffled up to the eyeballs in plain work overalls."

"They might not be plain," Andy suggested hopefully.

"If you can pick anything out of that gloom, I'll go to La Mama with you next week," Casey fired back. "I want something to work with."

Andy, and the other two, boggled. "You'll go to La Mama with me?" he squeaked. "You? To experimental theatre? Who are you and what have you done with Casey Clement?"

"I'll put up with it if you can pull anything out of that murk. I think I'm pretty safe." She scowled at the blurry footage. "Two average Joes in average clothes. Useless. I want an ID. Have we got McDonald's report yet?"

"In less than 24 hours? Not likely."

"CSU?" she tried hopelessly, knowing that was too soon too.

"Nope."

"C'mon, you know it's too early," O'Leary rumbled. "Let the techies do their thin', and leave 'em be so's they can read the runes an' throw the bones."

Casey's day wasn't improved by an e-mail from CSU confirming that there were no matching prints on file, even if she'd expected it, nor by Andy failing to elicit anything from the footage. She took out her frustration on cold cases, and left as soon as shift was done, not even suggesting some sparring or range practice to soothe her irritation.

CHAPTER THREE

At home, Casey looked longingly at her current book and her Gaggia, and reluctantly discarded the idea of reading, accompanied by an excellent cup of coffee (or three). She whipped through a shower and changed from dress pants and button-down to a softer skirt and top, loosening the tight clip confining her hair. She'd promised to have dinner with her dad, since she was on a late shift on Sunday, when she would usually see him, and after his reaction to the Telagon case, she couldn't disappoint him – no further than he already seemed to be disappointed, anyway. He'd been really, really spooked by the bruising, but she couldn't have cancelled on him to hide it: that would have worried him far more. So she had thought.

Memory bit hard, still stinging and raw.

"What happened?" he'd cried, as soon as he'd opened the door. "Catkin, what did you do?"

She'd had to explain, minimising as much as possible, but she wouldn't outright lie to him. "A suspect got a little upset," she'd temporised. "I was in the way." Nothing about late-night labs or the ER visit. "It'll all be fine in a day or two. It's just bruising."

"You shouldn't have put yourself in harm's way," he'd insisted. "You shouldn't take risks like that."

"It's my job, Dad."

If only she hadn't argued, maybe it would have been okay. He'd poured himself a glass of whiskey – no point in arguing with that – and downed it.

"I hate you getting hurt, Catkin."

"I'm fine now. Don't worry."

"You're not fine. You got *beaten up*." He'd poured another, and downed that too. She'd tried to change the subject to – well, anything, really: anything except her bruises. She'd even tried to interest him in the architecture of the newer skyscrapers in London, UK, for goodness' sake, about which she knew nothing and cared less, but he'd been an architect once, till her mother passed and the whiskey took over.

Not a single distraction had worked: he'd stuck right with his grievance – and his whiskey.

"Where were your team? Why weren't they protecting you?"

"Dad, they can't worry about protecting me. We're all cops. We all have to take a few licks occasionally. It's only bruises. I'll be fine in a day or two. They're already healing." They weren't, but she had to lie.

It was already too late to try to alleviate his worries. Likely it had been too late from the moment he opened the door and saw her parti-coloured face.

"You shouldn't do this job. It's no job for a woman" – and her heart broke. She'd never thought he'd say that. She'd thought he was proud of her.

"If you think so, Dad, I'd better go home." He hadn't argued, she had said nothing more, and had left: choking back every harsh word she wanted to rain on him. She'd...simply gone home. She hadn't wept. There was no point in weeping when he was drunk: if she once began to cry, she might never stop.

But it was a new level of pain. He'd never hurt her with his words before. He'd never gotten drunk in front of her before.

Despite her hurt, she'd taken his call a day or two afterwards; seen him, as usual, for dinner the following Sunday – and he hadn't remembered a word of his reproaches. Sober, he told her she'd done well when she told him about the case. Sober, he'd been – or convincingly pretended to be – proud of her.

So there she was, another couple of weeks later, walking up to his apartment in Brooklyn for their regular dinner, not knowing whether she'd find him drunk or sober.

"Catkin," he welcomed her.

"Hey, Dad."

"So what new weird and wonderful cases have you had this week?" He loved hearing about her cases. He'd used to love crime shows, but not now. Not after he'd seen his wife autopsied, after the accident.

"We got called to one yesterday. We think it was a model" – she wouldn't suggest *escort* to her father – "but so far we haven't any information at all. No prints, no DNA, no ID."

"That sure is weird. So what will you do?"

"Wait for the ME's report, I guess. There's nothing but cold cases until something turns up."

Her father smiled. "I guess so. Did I tell you I thought we could take a trip to DC to see the new museum?"

Casey's heart dropped like a demolished skyscraper. They'd had that discussion, a mere five or six weeks ago, but her father sounded as if he'd only just thought of the idea. If he was beginning to forget discussions they'd had when he was sober...what was happening when she wasn't there? How much was he drinking when she couldn't see?

Most importantly, how soon would there be that final, fatal call or knock?

***

A week later, the team had found no useful information whatsoever on their dead model. There was still no name or ID: repeated searches of Missing Persons hadn't identified anyone, and McDonald's tox report, though as thorough as ever, hadn't helped. In fact, it had raised more questions than it had answered. The dead woman had been – not that McDonald had put it that way, of course – sky high on heroin. McDonald thought there might have been something else mixed in, but even his brilliance, or the rest of CSU's talent, couldn't identify it.

"Surely *someone* must have missed her by now? Boyfriend, family, anyone?"

"It seems not."

"Checked Missing Persons again. Nothing new."

"Indeed." The team jumped. Captain Kent had appeared behind them. "Until something new turns up, this case is no longer a priority."

Casey opened her mouth.

"*If* something turns up, I will revisit that decision. Not before."

He disappeared into his office. Kent didn't invite, or tolerate, dissent.

"Guess he told us," Andy said.

"Yeah. Early nights all round."

O'Leary looked mischievous. "Haven't seen your boy lately."

Casey glared, which, from O'Leary's grin, didn't have the desired effect, and didn't mention that Carval might not have been around the precinct, but she'd certainly seen him. It had been a handsome sight, and he had equally appreciated his view of her. They'd had plenty of fun: almost enough to take away her worries, and to tire her enough to let her sleep. She'd slept better, while he was there.

"Let's try and clear these cases. I didn't see Kent giving us a holiday," she pointed out, and they got down to it.

***

"Looking good, Jamie," Allan approved, as he glanced at the corkboard covering half the wall of the studio, filled with shots.

"It's not enough," Carval growled. "I need more. One case and a few boring domestics or muggings isn't enough. I need to shoot something *interesting*."

"I thought you had been shooting that dead model."

"Yeah, but that isn't going anywhere. No name, no ID. I need to see the investigation. Interrogations. Going places. If they're just sitting in the precinct slogging through old cases they don't have any expression except boredom."

"And we all know how much you like boredom," Allan jabbed. Carval muttered blackly, not quite under his breath. "Something will turn up."

"When I want Mr Micawber, I'll let you know."

"You recognised that?" Allan asked unflatteringly.

"Yeah." Carval's butterfly attention span flitted back to his woes. "I need them to have a proper case – where are you going?"

"Downstairs. I don't want to listen to you complain. I've got better things to do."

"Like what?"

"I'm going to the theatre tonight."

"Oh. More of your cultural outings?"

"Yes."

Allan's tone didn't invite further inquiry, which was nothing new. If Allan had a private life, Carval knew nothing about it. He had another random thought.

"What happened with the letter you sent to that Marcol cop who stole my photo?"

"Ow," Allan said mildly.

"What's that mean?"

"You changed the subject so fast I got whiplash."

"What happened?" Carval snipped. "You sent it ages ago."

"No, I instructed it to be sent. It takes a few days. I haven't heard anything back, so I had a second letter sent, in stronger terms, ten days ago." Carval's mouth opened. "I have a reminder to follow up this week. You take your photographs, and let me deal with the rest."

"I want him scared, Allan."

Allan didn't feel like repeating all the reasons why that wasn't a fight Jamie should pick. He'd worry about that later. Instead, he moved closer to the board.

"Where's the centrepiece? I thought you wanted that photo right at the centre of the exhibition?"

"I put it away," Carval bit off.

"What? It was brilliant – and you know I don't say that often."

"You should." Allan raised a quelling eyebrow. "I..." – the other eyebrow went up – "look, stop behaving like you're my mom and I did something naughty."

"I'm sure you have," Allan commented aridly, "but why isn't that photo – Oh. Jamie, has your Casey-cop seen that shot?"

Carval coloured.

"She *hasn't*? Why not? Jamie..."

"I don't want her to see it, okay?"

Allan spread his hands in an appeasing gesture. "Fine. But don't blame me when it all goes wrong."

He tip-tapped off before Carval could respond. Allan was merely being pessimistic, as ever. It wouldn't go wrong.

His mind drifted back to Marcol. Steal his photo, would he? Slut-shame *his* girlfriend? No way.

Your girlfriend? a little voice said. *Are you sure about that?* Of course he was. They were just...taking it slow. Easy. No pressure. He certainly didn't want to live in anyone's pocket, or having anyone trying to live in his. They were simply having fun, and that was fine. He ignored the slight twisting in his gut. They'd had plenty of fun in the last couple of weeks, once her ribs could take it, even if there hadn't been anything much going on in the precinct. She'd been a little quiet one evening, but given the hours she put in, being tired was perfectly understandable.

And then his phone rang with Casey's number, and at last there was another new case, which almost allowed him to forget that Casey never talked about anything personal.

***

"What's this?" Casey asked, looking at a crumpled heap of death. "It looks like that one we had two weeks ago."

McDonald looked up. "There are certain potential similarities. However, nothing is certain until I can analyse the deceased properly."

Casey scowled at him. McDonald glared back. "What can you tell me?" she rapped.

"Another apparently post-mortem beating, and dilated pupils. Yes," he emphasised, "I shall run a detailed tox screen. You need not insult me by asking."

"'Nother handkerchief pretendin' to be a dress," O'Leary noted.

"No wallet, no phone."

"No casings."

"Is it another model?" Casey wondered.

McDonald straightened the body out, once all the CSU photographs were done. "I would not know," he said prissily. Of course he wouldn't. That would have involved an interest in live humans, which McDonald didn't have. "Does it matter? The woman has been murdered."

"It *matters*," Casey bit, squaring up to McDonald's angular frame, "because if it is, and *if* the MO is the same, then there could be a connection. Maybe this time we'll get an ID, and then we can find out something on the first one."

McDonald retreated in the face of Casey's passion. "Let us see," he said: almost conciliatory. "I shall provide the results as soon as I can."

Carval watched them through his viewfinder, taking continuous shots to be considered later. The overt conflict between Casey's passionate energy and McDonald's spare, grey, almost wearied age was yet another brilliantly contrasting facet of his cops.

Casey turned away from McDonald, and spotted Carval.

"Hey," she said briskly, with a quick smile. "Do you think this is another model/escort type?"

"Fine, thanks." She stared at him. "Hi, how are you, good to see you?" The blankness didn't lift, as if normal social norms didn't compute.

"This is a crime scene. That is a corpse. She's dead, so she's not fine. I wanna get started on solving it." She paused. "Anyway, I called you so you could shoot the scene, like I said I would as soon as we got something interesting."

Carval shrugged, ceding politeness to cop reality. "Yes, she looks like another model type."

"Okay." She peered sidelong up at him. "Don't suppose you recognise her?"

"No." Why on earth would Casey think he'd recognise her? Her *mother* wouldn't have recognised her, and anyway the models he'd shot had fallen out of his memory the instant they'd fallen out of his studio door or his bed.

"Oh."

"I haven't done modelling shots for years – well, not as my main thing."

Something flickered in Casey's eyes, gone as soon as noticed. "Just a thought," she said. "Maybe this time we'll be luckier with the ID." She smiled again, but Carval, attuned by profession to spot small details in any picture, didn't think it was entirely open. "Go get your shots. We'll do our thing."

Not long later, as the lack of light was beginning to make photography and, Carval assumed, investigating, impossible; Casey came up to him.

"We're done here. Want a ride if you're coming to the precinct?"

"What are you going to be doing?"

"Finishing shift – maybe we'll be lucky and get a hit on prints or Missing Persons – though with that sort of beating it's pretty hard and I don't expect either before tomorrow anyway – trying to start a timeline, requesting street camera footage, that sort of thing."

Carval didn't think that any of that was going to add worthwhile shots to his collection. "No," he said, and caught a flicker of disappointment across Casey's face. "But if you're done in time, call me and come over for dinner."

"Take-out," she corrected.

"That's dinner."

"Okay. I'll let you know."

She strode off, but Carval had the impression that she was as relieved by the invitation as – oh. As he was by her acceptance: as if some unspoken tension had dissipated. He took a few more shots, trying to capture the atmosphere of the failing light drifting across the corpse, and ambled home content with the afternoon's events.

"Carval bored with us already?" Andy asked.

"He doesn't want any more shots of us staring at screens."

"Seems fair," O'Leary chortled. "'T ain't int'restin'. An' it don't show my good side. Iffen I'm goin' to be famous" – Tyler snorted – "an' a cultural icon" – Andy choked – "then I want him to take good shots. Like those ones from the Telagon case. He din't mess around with borin' shots of us fallin' asleep lookin' like we ate too many doughnuts."

"Bite your tongue," Casey flipped.

"Rather bite a doughnut," O'Leary grinned. "Anyway, let's find somethin' so's your photographer c'n get some good shots. I'm gonna be famous!"

Andy made nauseated noises. Tyler just yawned.

Casey growled. "I don't want to be famous. I'll just hide behind you, Bigfoot."

"Not what Carval wants," Tyler pointed out. She growled again. Tyler winced, as O'Leary kicked him, out of Casey's sight.

"Shut up," O'Leary muttered.

"Is there any work being done here, Detectives?"

"Yessir," they chorused, and knuckled down before Kent could call them on the lie.

All their work was in progress at shift end. In the usual, and frustrating, fashion, everything was begun, but nothing had produced results. Kent's beady eye being on them, and Kent being as displeased by unpaid overtime as by anything else which interfered with his well-run precinct, they left on time.

***

"Hey, Casey."

"Hey. Is take-out still on offer?"

"Yeah, sure. Come by."

A short time later Casey appeared at Carval's apartment. Succumbing to his first impulse, Carval had barely shut the door before he'd wrapped her in, her head not quite reaching his shoulder, and simply held her against him. Casey made a contented little noise and softened in. He ran a hand up her neck, and delicately pulled the clip to release the dark curls. Casey looked up, not entirely pleased by his action, which was just what he'd wanted. He leaned down – she was always so much smaller than he expected – and kissed her.

"What was that?" she asked.

"Well, technically, it's called a kiss. See, when" –

"I know what a kiss is."

"Good. In that case you can do it more often. Can't you?" He kissed her again, slowly, and took comfort from her response. He'd thought that they'd gotten somewhere at the end of that first, brutal case, but the last few days hadn't really felt like it. That odd flicker earlier hadn't left his mind.

"I'm hungry," she said, which wasn't an answer, or reassuring.

"Let's get some dinner, then."

Pizza duly arrived, Carval popped a beer, but Casey only wanted a soda. She sat, munching her pizza and sipping at the soda, not communicative.

"What about the case?"

"Uh?"

"You're not here, so I guess you're thinking about the case."

"Yeah. I need to get an ID. I'm sure the two cases are connected but I've got nothing to back that up. It's just a hunch."

"Mm?"

"If the MO comes back the same – and McDonald's almost never wrong, even if he is up his own ass all the time – then there are too many similarities." Casey's voice had shifted to the clipped, professional tone of the precinct. "Dress, body type, no phone or purse, beaten up, likely on drugs." Carval slipped his camera into his hand, and, without consciously realising his actions, started to shoot. Casey, staring out into some far away horizon, didn't notice. "If I had an ID, then I'd get next of kin. If I had next of kin, I'd have a place to start. Interview them, get their job, *something*."

Frustration boiled in her voice. Carval kept shooting, capturing the new aspect of cop work: the sheer difficulty of getting started when there was no information. Casey's expressions shifted with her thoughts.

"Somewhere, there's a family or a boyfriend or a job" –

"Or an agency" –

"Uh?"

"If she's a model, she'll be with an agency. At least, if she's any good."

"Okay, agencies. Something to run with." She humphed. "But I can't do anything until I've got an ID – what are you doing?"

"Photographing."

"*Here?*"

"Yep."

"This isn't the precinct or a case. I don't want to be photographed."

He knew that. Knew the whole damn story; and he'd make certain sure that Marcol suffered for it, whatever Allan thought.

"You were talking about the case."

"Not the point. Do you ever stop with that camera?"

"No," he said bluntly. "I don't. Not when I see something I need to shoot. Just like you don't stop with the case. Your mind's on the case. Mine's on shooting how you're thinking about the case."

Her fingers twisted, until she realised and separated them, taking another slice of pizza. An uncomfortable silence stretched out.

"Why's McDonald got such a stick up his ass?" Carval diverted.

Casey seized on the distraction. "He's always been like that. He gets along just fine with his corpses, it's living people he's got a problem with."

"He's interesting. I'd like to see more of him."

"You'll be lucky. He'll never let you shoot in the morgue."

"Bet?"

"Sure. Ten says he'll throw you out. He'll probably poison you, just to make sure you don't come back."

"That's a little unreasonable."

"Oh, I don't know," Casey teased, deliberately taking the conversation away from any difficult matters, such as photographs or feelings. "It seems pretty reasonable to me."

"You'd miss me." She quirked her eyebrow, but a tiny smile danced on her lips. "You would."

"O'Leary would. He wants to be famous. I don't think he's worked out that he'll be put in the Zoo as soon as he's noticed – as the world's only living Bigfoot."

Carval snickered. "I'll have discovered a new species."

"Yeah." Casey wiped her fingers and glanced at her watch. "Time for me to go."

"Don't go yet. You've barely been here ten minutes."

Casey quirked an eyebrow at the gross exaggeration.

"More than an hour. We start early."

Carval insinuated an arm around her. "I know. It's not very civilised."

"Murder isn't civilised."

"Lots of things aren't civilised," he murmured, "but that doesn't mean they aren't a lot of fun."

"Not very subtle."

"Why be subtle? It just leads to misunderstandings. I don't like those." He smiled rakishly. "I like clarity."

"Clearly."

Carval outright laughed. "C'mere," he said, and tugged her on to his lap on the word. "There. Clarity. As in, I can clearly see that you're messing with me. So, just to be *clear*, can I kiss you again, Casey?"

She didn't answer. Instead, she leaned in and kissed him.

"Guess that means yes."

"Clarity is important, you said," and she kissed him again. Just to be clear. There had been enough talking, and certainly enough photographs. Time for some uncomplicated fun.

CHAPTER FOUR

"An ID!" Casey celebrated, mid-morning. "Daniela Petrovich. At last!"

The preliminary report from CSU, which had prints as well as ID, had popped up on her e-mail. Some focused effort later, there was also a photograph of the woman that didn't include bruises and the damage from the beating up, her age – twenty-two – and her social security number, which meant that there would soon be an employment history. Excellent.

She beamed at her decorated murder board. If Andy hunted down footage, employment history, and social media; and Tyler did some digging to find a phone number and call logs, while supervising (or intimidating) the canvassing uniforms, she and O'Leary could go and talk to the next of kin. She set to work to find them.

Next of kin were Daniela Petrovich's parents, which was always upsetting. Children shouldn't die before their parents.

"Got them," she said. "Ready for a road trip, O'Leary?"

"Sure."

Though Daniela had rented a sublet much nearer Manhattan, her parents lived in a pleasant suburban house in Ridgewood, New Jersey, with a manicured garden displaying pretty, sweet-smelling flowers in neat beds out front, and a clean car in the driveway.

Casey knocked.

"Hello?" said a middle-aged woman: elegant, attractive and bearing an extraordinary resemblance to her daughter. She spoke with a slight accent.

"Mrs Marya Petrovich? Detective Clement, NYPD, and my partner, Detective O'Leary." She showed her badge.

"Oh, er, hello?"

Mrs Petrovich was already paling as Casey began, "I'm sorry to have to tell you," and her colour had drained before Casey had completed the sentence.

"Aleks?" That must be her husband. "Daniela? What's happened?" she interrupted.

"I'm sorry, Mrs Petrovich, but Daniela was found murdered in Manhattan late yesterday."

Mrs Petrovich burst into tears.

"I don't believe it," she sobbed. Through her distress, she gestured them into a stylish but lived-in main room. Casey tactfully ignored Mrs Petrovich's tears, and unobtrusively scanned the space. It contained several photos of Daniela, in each of which she was beautiful: poised and perfect. "How do you know? It can't be." She sobbed harder. "I should have known when she didn't call…"

"I'm sorry. Can you tell me about Daniela?" Casey murmured.

"She was always pretty," her mother said. "She worked hard at school, but then she was spotted by a model agency, in freshman year of college. We looked into the agency: and did all sorts of checking – you hear such awful things – but finally we let her, as long as she kept up her grades. It really helped with the tuition." Her tears flowed faster. "If we'd never allowed it, she'd still be here," she wept. "She'd have listened to us."

They couldn't actually have stopped Daniela, Casey thought, but didn't say. She allowed Mrs Petrovich space to compose herself, with O'Leary looming behind her. She sniffed a few times, blew her nose, and was silent.

"It's not your fault," Casey said, with quiet force. "It's all on the killer, and I'll do my best to find them." She took a breath. "Now, could you tell me who she was working for, and how long she'd been there?"

"Stardance Modelling."

Casey made a note.

"Had she any disagreements with anyone?" O'Leary asked, in a gentle bass lacking his normal bucolic drawl.

"No, nobody. Everyone liked her."

Casey, and, from their single exchanged glance, O'Leary, was deeply sceptical about that. Modelling wasn't normally a hotbed of peace, love and mutual support.

"Did anyone have a problem with her, even if it wasn't someone she knew?"

"No-one. Nobody."

Casey thought. "Anything connected with the jobs she took? Anything new there? Or had she wanted to change agency?"

"No," Mrs Petrovich wept. "She wasn't moving on. Everything was through Stardance."

"What about a boyfriend? Was she dating?"

"No. No-one serious. No-one she'd bring home. She gets hit on so much but they all just wanted her for her looks, she said. She isn't interested in that. She's only twenty-two," she sobbed. "She had her whole life ahead of her."

"Okay, thank you," Casey said. There wasn't anything more to be gained there. "We might have more questions later, so we might need to talk to you again. We'll talk to your husband, too, just in case he knows anything else." She hesitated, but it had to be said. "Please – don't put anything on social media yet. We'll be interviewing her friends, and we'll want to see their initial reactions."

"We don't... I never liked social media. I won't...anything that helps you catch them."

They took their leave, with both Daniela's phone number, to request the call logs, and Mr Petrovich's contact details.

As soon as she entered O'Leary's SUV, Casey called Andy to start him on running down Stardance Modelling, and then gave Daniela's phone number to Tyler. She swiped her phone off with relief that they finally had a trail.

"We better go see Pa Petrovich," O'Leary noted.

"Yeah. More cheery fun for all of us. No matter how often I do that, it never gets easier."

"Naw," he agreed. "An' talking to Pa won't make it any better."

"Guess we ought to do that before he goes home. She's devastated, and he'll want to comfort her, not answer questions."

"I guess so. 'S what bein' married's all about, bein' there for the other one."

"Should be." Casey's lips pinched. She remembered her father consoling her mother after some domestic mishap; her mother hugging her father when his father died.

"Yeah," said O'Leary. "Iffen it ain't, you're doin' it wrong. Hard to watch, though, when we're the ones tellin' them."

***

"What d'you get from the family?" Andy asked, back in the bullpen. Tyler simply listened.

"Just her mother. We'll need to go talk to her father shortly. She's fallen apart, and all she could tell us was that she worked at Stardance Modelling. We'll need to talk to them asap." She thought swiftly. "We need to talk to her father, but we need to get over to this Stardance place too."

"I got an address for Stardance," Andy pointed out, and scribbled it up on the board. "Got a uniform running down Facebook and the like."

"Okay. I'll take the agency, you take the father. Let's see what else we can get running while we're all interviewing. Tyler, you already requested phone records?"

"Yeah."

"Did we get street cameras around where she was found?"

"Waiting," Andy said.

"Okay. Let's add in cameras from around Stardance." She hummed as she thought. "Okay. Midtown, 6th Avenue and W35th Street."

"On it already. Four on 35th, one on 6th Avenue."

"ME's report?"

Everyone looked pityingly at her. "You want that already? You call McDonald. We'll sweep up the ashes after."

Casey groused, but didn't call the morgue.

"So, Stardance. I want to start on them."

"I wanna come along," O'Leary grumped, pouting his ice-shelf lip.

"No. You won't even fit through the door of a model agency, never mind help." Casey looked around. "Tyler" –

"No way." Casey clearly heard the unvoiced: *you're not getting me into any model agency.*

"Andy? You clean up nice, and Tyler can go chat with the father."

"I clean up nice," O'Leary muttered.

"You clean up with the elephants in the Zoo, 'cause it's the only place big enough to shower you."

O'Leary muttered and grumped some more.

Andy regarded Casey as if she'd gone crazy. "You're going to a model agency, yeah?"

"Yeah?"

"Where they photograph models?"

"Yes. What's your point?"

"You've got a photographer on tap who's done a boat-load of shots of models and who's famous. Take him."

Her jaw dropped. "*What?*"

"If they think he's a friend of yours, they'll likely be a lot more co-operative," Andy said extremely slowly and patiently.

"He's not a cop."

"So? You don't want him to be a cop. You want him to be" –

"Expert," Tyler put in.

Casey recovered her composure and put her brain in gear. It had...possibilities. But it was also likely that Captain Kent would disapprove, and Casey had no desire whatsoever to be the subject of Kent's disapproval. Kent didn't like unscheduled departures from the investigative norm, and he hadn't been best buddies with Carval either.

She pondered for a few minutes, as the others got on with the work of checking and warrant-requesting for footage. When she had worked out the best way to approach Kent – more accurately, the way least likely to reduce her to a small pile of scrap with a singed shield on top – she trudged to his door.

She tapped. "Sir?"

"What is it, Clement?" Kent regarded her with an odd look in his eyes: almost worry.

"Our case, sir. The dead model – Petrovich. She worked at Stardance Modelling."

"So? Surely you don't need to have my permission to interview them?" Kent's tone had a sardonic edge, but the tinge of worry had disappeared the instant he'd heard that it was a case matter.

"No, sir. But, well, Carval used to do some...um...glamour photography," she blurted out under Kent's gimlet gaze, "and, er, he might have insights into the business and get us a better chance of co-operation" – Kent stared at her – "and, um, I think it might be helpful to take him with me instead of O'Leary or Andy but I wasn't going to do that without your explicit permission because he's not a cop and we don't want him to get involved but this case" –

"Stop, Clement." Kent leaned forward, hands clasped. Casey stood at the same rigid attention as she had since she entered. "Let me understand you correctly." She winced. That sounded as if flaying was the next action of Kent's day. "You wish to take *a civilian*" – Kent made it sound less desirable than *a sewer rat* – "with you in order to interview a person of interest." He waited.

"Yes, sir," she admitted.

"And you want this because you consider that he may have insights that we, the NYPD, do not?"

"Yes, sir."

Abruptly, Kent – well, he didn't smile. He never smiled – relaxed.

"In fact, he would be acting as an expert consultant." Casey nearly fell over with astonishment. "At ease, Clement. There are, as you should be aware" – *ow*. That had bitten – "precedents for the use of expert consultants. I'm surprised you have forgotten that, since Professor Terrison acted in precisely that capacity in the Telagon case. That was only a short time ago."

Casey winced again. She hadn't connected the matters.

"I shall approve the use of Mr Carval on this single occasion. If his expert knowledge is useful, you will obtain my approval before involving him any further. He is not to take any photographs while acting as an expert." Kent's light, piercing eyes surveyed her.

"Thank you, sir." Casey began to turn to exit.

"Clement."

She spun back. "Sir?"

Kent coughed. If it hadn't been Kent, she'd have said he was almost embarrassed. "Are there any issues which might affect your work that I should know about?"

"No, sir." There was a pause. "Nothing, sir." Her relationship – *relationship*? Liaison – with Carval wasn't relevant. Her father's issues certainly weren't.

Kent gazed at her coldly, almost as if he'd expected a different answer. "I see, Clement. Should anything arise, I expect you to inform me. Dismissed."

She escaped before anything more could discombobulate her. Kent inquiring into her affairs was a consummation devoutly to be avoided.

"Kent approved it," Casey announced, to general amazement, as she returned to her desk and began to dial.

Behind her, Kent regarded the space where Clement had been, and sighed. He wasn't going to push her to admit the truth about her father. He didn't care about her relationship with Carval: it had been crystal-clear at the end of the Telagon case that something was going on – but as long as it didn't affect her work, he was satisfied. Since she'd sought permission to involve the photographer, he was content that she was acting appropriately. However, her father could be a different matter. Still, there was nothing to be done unless and until it interfered with her work.

Since the issues of his team of misfits had come back to his unwilling attention, he considered their current case. Nothing to upset O'Leary. Nothing that would trigger Tyler. Chee...now then. Chee's past might cause a problem. Chee, Kent believed from his earlier perusal of the team's histories, knew more about beatings and abuse than he let on, which had certainly explained his attitude to previous cases where that had been suspected.

He hummed thoughtfully to himself, resolving to keep a close eye on both Clement and Chee, as he turned to his ever-full in tray.

***

"Carval."

"Hey."

"You wanna come along to an interview?"

"What?"

"I need to go interview a model agency. Stardance."

"Oh, yeah. I've heard of them."

"Yeah?" Casey challenged.

"They're legit. I never worked with them, but they've got a good reputation."

"Whatever. Do you want to come along? I got Kent to agree that you'll be our expert." Casey paused. "You can't take photos while you're part of the team."

"I can't?"

"No. Orders. Do you want to come or not?"

29

"Yeah. But it's not fair," he sulked.

"If we bring anyone in for interview, you can take shots then."

Carval grumbled at the phone, but grabbed his jacket and hustled out, a camera in his pocket in case Casey took someone into Interrogation or anything interesting happened.

***

The sign was small; the door unassuming. Stardance, it seemed, didn't wish to advertise. That wasn't surprising to either Carval or Casey, both of whom had separately worked out that the agency wouldn't want hordes of random hopefuls appearing on the doorstep.

The interior was as tasteful as the exterior was discreet. Therefore, the entry of Carval and Casey, and Casey's clear, audible announcement of her status, caused appalled flusterment at the reception desk.

"A detective?" the immaculately groomed woman gasped. "I thought you might be a candidate, even though..." Much of the flusterment had obviously been caused by the disconnects between Casey's photogenic looks, her lack of height, her profession, and the receptionist's automatic and wrong assumption that any pretty woman walking in wanted to be a model.

"No," Casey snapped with strained impatience. "Now get me your CEO."

The receptionist picked up her phone. "Mr Selwyn," she murmured – discreetly – "there is a Miss Clement in reception." Casey didn't correct the receptionist. Nor did she explain Carval's presence.

A narrow, blond man, evidently Selwyn, quickly appeared. He flicked an assessing, rapid, dispassionate glance over Casey and acquired an expression of horrified disgust. Casey instantly bridled.

"What the hell is this?" he fired at the receptionist, who cringed and didn't answer. He whipped a caustic glance around.

Suddenly, he blinked rapidly, and dismissed Casey entirely. "Carval?" he gasped. "Jamie Carval? I thought you'd stopped doing glamour shots? Do you want to use the studio? We're shooting a perfume ad, but you can come through and see if it suits you."

He regarded Casey with another contemptuous look. "We can find you some proper models if you like."

He turned on an expensively shod heel to provide them with an excellent view of a fashionable haircut on an attenuated frame.

"I'm not here for a glamour shoot," Casey said, biting down fury.

He turned back, talking over her. "The perfume shoot's all set up but you're not what I booked. You're too short, too old and at least fifteen pounds overweight."

He twisted round, still in motion, and matched glances with Carval, scowling and clearly expecting Carval to agree with his comments. "She's totally unsuitable. I don't know what she's doing here, but we haven't time to change it now."

Carval winced. He could see trouble heading directly for Selwyn, which his sharp chinos and impeccably pressed designer shirt, sans tie, would certainly not prevent. Casey was wordless, which would *definitely* not continue for long. Despite Casey's ban on photographing, he already had his camera in his hand. Casey, utterly outraged, hadn't noticed.

"Mr Carval...maybe you'd like to take some shots and assess the space while we try and make this" – a variety of unflattering words hung on the air – "*person* into something half-suitable for shooting. If you didn't bring a camera, I'm sure we can find you something for you to get an idea. Anything to help you out."

He opened a door into a studio arranged to look like an up-market urban bar, and turned back to Casey, rapping out orders. "Hurry up. Strip. You – we'll have to Photoshop you. I'm never using that list again if you're the best they can do. Jose!" A small, bright Latino hurried in. "Get her dressed properly. Sexy-expensive. Really high heels to get some height. Spanx. And something to flatten that chest. Then go straight to make-up. Cover up the lines. Yarland – where's Yarland?" Whoever Yarland was, he wasn't there. Carval suspected it was the photographer.

At that point, Casey finally recovered her voice.

"*Stop.*"

It scythed into the room. Everyone stopped dead. The CEO puffed up like an angry turkey-cock. Casey rolled right over him, searingly contemptuous. Carval started to shoot, unseen, from behind Casey.

"You appear to be misinformed," she said with lethal emphasis, pulling back her jacket to show her shield and gun. Selwyn's colour drained. "I am *Detective* Katrina Clement, NYPD. You are *who?*"

The magnitude of Selwyn's mistake dawned on him.

"Timothy J. Selwyn," he stammered out from bloodless lips. "CEO and owner of Stardance."

"We are here to interview *you*," Casey emitted with glacial precision. With every icy word, Selwyn cringed further away from her. "Your office will do. We'll go up there." He didn't move: flash-frozen. "*Now.*"

Even Carval's feet moved, and he wasn't susceptible to orders. Selwyn didn't stand a chance.

One floor up, they entered an expensively decorated office bedecked with industry awards. Carval seated himself on a Charlotte Perriand-style chair, which, astonishingly, was even less comfortable than it appeared.

Casey didn't sit. She prowled the office, leaving the suffocating scent of wholesale intimidation spreading behind her. Selwyn, interestingly, didn't sit behind his expansive desk; instead, he appeared to have been terrified into taking another uncomfortable chair.

When she was satisfied that Selwyn was completely cowed, Casey stayed standing, leaning against the desk. Every inch of her posture emphasised that she owned the room.

"I'll be recording this interview," she said. Her tone did not admit disagreement. Selwyn didn't disagree.

She regarded Selwyn's cringing, narrow form with cold distaste, frigid fury still crackling around her. Carval vacated the uncomfortable chair and, without disturbing Casey, moved to lean on a wall where she couldn't see him. He brought his camera up, and began to disregard everything he'd been told. He'd never agreed he wouldn't shoot.

"Mr Selwyn," she started, with a bite of command which brought his head snapping up and his gaze to hers, "tell me about Daniela Petrovich."

"Dani?" he stuttered. "Why" –

"Answer the question."

He wiped his brow.

"She was spotted at eighteen, nearly nineteen. Still a touch coltish," he adjudged, "but she had enough potential for test shoots to be worth it. Her parents were pretty protective, but after they got comfortable they weren't often here. No problem if they had been, we've nothing to hide. If parents of minors want to sit in, we're cool. She stayed with us."

"What did she model?"

"Clothes, shoes. Once she was twenty-one, lingerie."

"Twenty-one?" Casey asked. "Why?"

"Reputation. I'm not having teens on underwear shoots. Too much chance for trouble. Other agencies can do that if they like. We don't."

"What was her last job?"

"With us?"

"Yes, with you. You said she stayed with you."

Selwyn cringed further. "She did. But she stopped responding to us about three, maybe four, weeks ago."

"Really? So she *didn't* stay with you. Anything else you'd like to lie about? Where did she go?"

"She did stay. She stopped modelling. I don't know where she went. I never saw her on any more shoots. I thought she'd quit. She'd stayed with us the whole time she'd been modelling."

"Would you have recognised her on other shoots? Some of them are pretty well disguised."

Carval said nothing, being extremely keen that Casey forgot his existence while his camera was in his hand. Still, he'd have recognised any frequently-used model in microseconds, so he waited with interest for Selwyn's response.

"Yes," Selwyn stated. "We don't have so many girls on our books that I wouldn't have recognised her anywhere. She just dropped out of the industry."

"Three weeks ago."

"Yes."

"We'll need to get a list of all her shoots," Casey said. "And a copy of her contract with you." Selwyn appeared to be about to quibble. "Or I can come back with a warrant and a few uniformed officers. I assume you wouldn't mistake *them* for wannabe models?" The edge on the final sentence and the flash of her eyes should have sliced him in half.

"It was an easy mistake to make," he muttered. "Cops don't look like you. And plenty of girls think they can model even if they're too" – he stopped before he could insult her further, though *short and fat* hung between them.

"When can I have the information?" Her tone said *it better be soon.*

"I'll pull it today. You'll have it tomorrow."

"Thank you," Casey said, as if instant compliance was the bare minimum that she'd accept.

"When she was here, were there any problems? Anyone jealous of her?" Carval asked, slipping the camera away just before Casey would spot it.

"No," Selwyn emitted, but it wasn't convincing. Carval pounced on it.

"Don't give me that," he barked. "The modelling business is one long bitchfest. We need to know who was on her case about her weight, who she beat out to the good shoots, whose boyfriend was hitting on her, what the catfights were."

"If you don't tell us now, I'll interview every model and staff member on your books down at the precinct at my convenience," Casey bit. "If you co-operate, I might be persuaded to be flexible."

Carval had been more than a little surprised by her aggressive stance. He hadn't previously seen her *start* like that, though it was wholly in keeping with her interrogation style. Of course, having been referred to as *overweight* was hardly likely to begin matters on the right footing. He wouldn't have liked to be in Timothy Selwyn's shoes. The man was withering faster than rice paper in a blast furnace. Carval wished fervently that he'd been allowed to shoot openly, because the sense of intimidation was smothering and he couldn't be sure that he'd caught it.

"Er..." Selwyn stammered. Casey merely waited, allowing sheer menace to taint the air. It took less than three seconds for him to begin spilling his guts almost faster than Casey's recorder could cope with. He barely drew breath for almost fifteen minutes.

"I see," Casey said judicially.

"And freelancers?" Carval added.

Selwyn produced another spate of words, lasting five full minutes more.

"I'll want that list, too." She paused, purely for effect. It wasn't necessary, since Selwyn was regarding her with outright terror. "I'll expect all the information by early tomorrow morning." She paused again. "We might want to speak to you again after that." He shuddered. "Thank you for your co-operation." That didn't appear to reassure him. Carval thought that it wasn't meant to.

She stalked to the door. Carval prowled after her. At the door, he abruptly stopped.

"Portfolios," he said. "She'd have had a portfolio. We need to have that too."

He shoved the door shut behind him and dashed after Casey's hard, irritated stride.

CHAPTER FIVE

"Asshole," Casey fulminated as she started her cruiser. "Why'd he assume I'd want to be a model?"

Carval didn't make the mistake of answering her rhetorical question.

"Why didn't you ask him about that other corpse?" he asked instead.

"Because I don't have grounds for making a connection yet, and when I do, I want to go in and ask him about more than just the name. If they are connected, then I'll need more before I interrogate him again." She grimaced. "Likely he wouldn't be able to tell who the first one was from the photo. Anyway, he couldn't think straight when I'd finished and I want that information asap." She bared her teeth, which wasn't a smile. "We need to concentrate on the death that's current." An acid edge shaped the sentence. "I can't go back to the first one unless I find something."

"Frustrating."

"Yeah. Whoever she was, she deserves better."

"What now?"

"When we get the information from Selwyn, we're going to look really closely at three weeks ago. That's when he said she quit."

"And?"

"I don't believe that."

She pulled up and parked at the precinct. Carval followed her in through the crowded entry, upstairs, and perched on the corner of her desk.

"We got something," Casey said. The team gathered, focused and intent. His camera appeared in his hand, and he slid out of the way.

"Stardance is run by a dumbass, name of Selwyn." Her teeth flashed. "Right now, he's a terrified dumbass."

"What'd you do?" Tyler asked.

"What'd *he* do, more like," O'Leary rumbled. "You got a face that says he rubbed you up the wrong way."

Carval snorted.

"C'mon, Carval. You tell us. What went down?"

"Selwyn mistook Casey for a wannabe model, and he...um...wasn't too impressed."

"What does that mean?" Andy asked, with a nasty grin.

"Not relevant," Casey snapped. The men exchanged glances, agreeing that the story would wait until Casey was elsewhere. "I showed him my shield and gun and he switched his attitude pretty fast. The *relevant* part is that he said Daniela quit three weeks ago, but I don't think she quit. I think that's when whatever happened to her started. Or he's lying about the timeframe, of course."

"That wouldn't be new."

"No."

"Three weeks," Andy said. "Just before we found the first one. I'll get specific footage for a week before that, and then till we found the body, all focused on the Stardance site. I'd asked for it around the likely date she died, but it sounds like that's no good. The techs can try and run facial recognition to see when she was last there, and who she left with."

"I'll go through the phone records," Tyler added. "Bank'll likely arrive tomorrow."

"Tyler an' me went to see her dad," O'Leary noted. "He was pretty cut up." Tyler nodded. "But he did say that she didn't have a boyfriend – or girlfriend."

"Same as her mom said."

"We got the names of her closest friends, though. I wish we had her phone," he mourned. "A contact list makes things so much easier. There wasn't much on social media either, but now we got some times, we c'n mebbe look closer at it."

"Yeah."

"Have we got McDonald's report yet?"

"No."

"Huh. I want to know, *if* Daniela was on drugs, how long she'd been using?"

There was a short silence. Andy got there first. "You think she might not have been an addict," he said bleakly. "You think she might have been forced into it."

Casey nodded.

Carval focused on Andy's face: stony and etched with bitterness, and wondered about his background. The Academy sergeant hadn't known anything, when he'd gone to take shots, hoping to find out about Casey and that thieving bastard Marcol, and only extracted some limited background on each of the team – except Andy, for whom there had been nothing.

"Why d'you think that?" O'Leary asked. "Not that it ain't possible, but that came outta nowhere."

"Selwyn was an asshole, but Carval said the agency's legit, and I think he'd have noticed if the models were on drugs."

"He'd probably have noticed if they were using some things, but not others. Lots of them were on appetite suppressants all the time, but they can't use cocaine or heroin because it'd show up in the eyes. Any half-competent photographer would spot that right away, and that'd be the end of the model anywhere legitimate. Stardance has a good rep."

"The first one was on heroin," Andy reminded them.

"Yeah," Casey dragged out. "Tyler, McDonald doesn't hate you quite as much as he hates the rest of us. Can you ask him to check how long Jane Doe and Daniela were on drugs – assuming Daniela's tested positive for heroin."

"'Kay."

"Is this normal for modelling?" Andy bit out, directed firmly at Carval. "Drugs, beating up, and murders?"

Carval stared at him. He'd not seen smooth, inscrutable Andy less than perfectly calm before. "It wasn't part of my life, if that's what you mean," he flashed back. "I didn't spend my time doing anything stronger than whiskey and I've sure never beaten anyone up."

O'Leary stepped between them. "Andy don't mean that you did, so settle your temper down. You're our expert, so tell us what you know 'bout modelling."

Carval wasn't appeased, but around O'Leary's container-ship bulk he could spot Tyler taking Andy off to one side.

"This is all quite old, you know? I don't really do model work any more, and most of what I did was freelance, not tied to an agency."

Casey jerked. Confirmation that Carval still did any model photography was hugely unwelcome. She'd thought that now he only did reality exhibitions. She returned to the conversation, though she'd missed a couple of sentences.

"So the worst of the so-called agencies were – well, they might not have been running escort agencies but they sure did know how to make introductions. Those girls didn't last too long. You learned to spot those agencies and avoid them. But a lot of the girls wanted two sets of shots: one set a little more...um..."

"Sexy?"

"I guess. I didn't ask why."

"You didn't say no, either," Andy accused. Tyler tapped his shoulder, and he dropped his eyes.

"They were adults," Carval retorted. "And wanting a portfolio isn't illegal anywhere I've worked." He took a breath. "Before you ask, yes, I slept with some of them. So? Wanna make something of it now? I didn't force them – they were all over me – and it wasn't a condition of shooting them." He glared at Andy, who glared right back.

"Cool it," Tyler and O'Leary said together.

O'Leary continued. "This ain't helpin' anyone. Andy, back off. Just 'cause you saw some stuff before, don't bring it to the ballpark now. Carval, it ain't no secret that you catted around – but I ain't never heard that you did anythin' that decent men don't do, so you back off too."

Casey intervened. "So, on that other dead girl, you said some model agencies are more like escort agencies, but you just said Stardance had a good reputation so that probably won't fly. We'll check, anyway. Andy, you go ring your pals in Narcotics to see if anyone's got any gossip on model agencies and drugs, and I'll talk to Vice. Carval, what's the chance of it not being the agency but someone connected – there was a dresser? Obviously there's got to be a photographer. What about any others? You tell O'Leary about that."

Casey didn't want to hear about how model shoots were structured. She'd need to know, but not right now, and Andy definitely needed to be out of this conversation because it wasn't doing anything to preserve his composure. She knew his history, and this case was pushing his buttons. She carefully didn't think that knowing Carval was still shooting models occasionally was pushing her buttons, because that would be ridiculous.

From the corner of her eye, she could see O'Leary steering Carval into the break room, which seemed like a pretty good outcome.

Andy departed to his desk and was soon on the phone. Casey looked at him, worried. They'd had sensitive cases before, but this was shaping up to make the team more edgy than she'd have liked, all because they had Carval in the mix. She'd thought that the men had accepted him –faster than she had, for sure.

She wrote up on her murder board in her cramped scrawl.

"Clement," arrived from behind her. She jumped.

"Sir?"

"Summarise the status of the Petrovich case."

Casey did so, under Kent's minatory eye.

"I see. So Carval has been helpful." She nodded. "He can continue as an expert. Is there anything more you can do tonight?"

Casey grimaced, which had no effect on Kent. "No, sir," she admitted.

"In that case, leave. Overtime will only be authorised if it's productive."

"Yes, sir."

Kent stalked back to his office. Casey looked around for the team. Andy was already packing up. Tyler, from the pained expression, was listening to McDonald, and O'Leary and Carval were squeezed into the break room. When she looked back, Andy had gone. That wasn't a good sign: none of them normally slipped away without a word when a case was live.

"Kent's told us to get out," she said as O'Leary and Carval exited the break room and Tyler put the phone down with a clack.

"McDonald'll run hair tests. Says he'll have results tomorrow."

"When'll he give me his full report?"

"After that."

Casey humphed.

"Won't arrive faster. Least we don't have to go there."

"I *know*. But I want it now. I want all that information from Stardance, too. And whatever we find from her social media. Why couldn't she put her life on Facebook like the rest of the world?"

"Liked her privacy."

"Beer," O'Leary said happily, before anyone could grouse further. "C'mon, everybody, Abbey Pub."

"No, thanks," Carval said. Truthfully, he wanted to get back to his studio and download his camera, to see what he'd managed to catch at Stardance. He couldn't have looked at it in front of the team, and if it turned out that any of the photos were good, he didn't want to risk them being removed. He was also, a little unfairly, annoyed that Casey hadn't stepped in to stop Andy but had left it to O'Leary and Tyler.

"Okay," Casey said, slightly wistfully. "See you."

"Night."

Carval departed. The remaining three looked at each other.

"Beers," O'Leary decided for them all. "An' you c'n tell us what went down at the agency, 'cause it's pretty clear they riled you up, an' Carval's slunk off without even tellin' me the tale."

"Assholes," Casey snarled.

"You mean the agency," Tyler chided.

"Yeah. Assholes," she repeated.

"Tell us the tale over a drink. I always like a good story, an' this one's shapin' up to be some fun."

At the Abbey, Casey bought the beer, O'Leary found a table, and Tyler was deep in thought.

"So this agency," O'Leary enticed.

"Sexist dumbass thought I wanted to be a model and got pretty bitchy, so I tore him apart."

"That's not enough of a bedtime story, Mommy."

"It's all you're getting."

O'Leary left it. Tyler stepped down his nasty smile and sipped his beer. "Guess he's running scared now," was all he said.

"Yeah." Casey relapsed into dire mutterings and dark thoughts.

"Think you should warn your boy," Tyler broke into her thinking.

"What?"

"You'd better warn him that Andy's a tad uptight 'bout escorts an' beatin's," O'Leary amplified.

She wriggled uncomfortably. "He doesn't need to know."

"Thought he was your boyfriend?"

"He's not."

O'Leary's eyebrows lifted, but he didn't disagree.

"Iffen he's hangin' around, he oughta know enough not to upset Andy."

"It's up to Andy to tell his secrets, not me."

The two men regarded her, open-mouthed.

"You ain't told him anythin' 'bout us?"

She shook her dark head.

"What've you been doing with him?"

"Ain't been much talkin', I'm guessin'," O'Leary smirked, swiftly switched off when Casey glared and then scowled. He changed tack. "Does he know 'bout your dad?"

Another shake.

"What'll you do when you stand him up to go get your dad?"

"It hasn't happened." She shrugged defensively. "No need to talk about it."

"Knows I was a sniper," Tyler said.

"Bet you told him."

"He guessed, I told him."

"I'm not sure he knows I'm gay," O'Leary pointed out. "I never said anything."

"You don't make much of a secret of it. You're always talking about Pete. Anyway, Andy's life is his business and my dad's…issues…are mine. Not Carval's."

O'Leary wriggled a bushy eyebrow sceptically. "Don't sound like he's much of a boyfriend to me."

"He's *not* my boyfriend. And I don't tell other people's secrets."

"Fine. I ain't sayin' you should, but we don't need Andy givin' Carval the stink-eye if you c'n stop it, an' it might be an idea iffen you told him 'bout your dad too. Least thataways he won't get all upset if you stand him up."

"My dad's fine right now." Which was an outright lie, which both men clocked. "If you want to talk about Andy you can. I won't." She drained her drink. "Time I went. See you tomorrow."

"What d'you think, Bigfoot?"

"I think we oughta say somethin'. Not a lot."

"Yeah."

"You talk to Andy. You get him best of any of us."

"What about Casey's dad?"

"I ain't goin' there. That's her problem, an' she's made it pretty clear she don't want him to know."

"Won't go well."

"Naw. But it's up to her."

***

Carval downloaded his shots in the company of a large mug of coffee and a finger of whiskey. Fortunately, enough of the shots had caught the mood – and Selwyn's sheer terror – that his irritation largely dissipated, though he was still unimpressed by both Andy's and Casey's behaviour.

He looked at his corkboard, and his eye was caught by the picture of Casey's still hands around a coffee cup. He printed off his shot of McDonald's skeletal fingers, and put it next to the other. Hmmm. That had definite possibilities. As did McDonald generally.

Carval's photographer's instincts drove him firmly down the path of taking far more photographs of McDonald working: he'd surreptitiously taken a few on the previous case, but it wasn't enough to show the man within the surgical scrubs. He wasn't interested in the corpses, only in the actions and reactions of those working on them. He'd try and convince McDonald to let him shoot...maybe tomorrow. He mused for a while on whether he'd need to have one of the team with him, and if so, who?

Tyler, that was who. Casey had said that McDonald hated Tyler less than the rest of them. Maybe he'd find out what was up with Andy, too. It didn't occur to him that Tyler might have work of his own to do; he didn't let himself think that his first thought might more reasonably have been of Casey: all that mattered was taking the photographs.

He looked at the two prints of hands again, and thought that a few more shots of hands might give him a small exhibition and keep Allan from nagging at him for a while longer after *Murder on Manhattan*. He took himself to bed still thinking about hands: hands on bodies, hands on guns, hands against uniforms or arresting criminals. He could really make something of a set of shots of hands.

***

Early the next morning, Detective Benson of Vice called Casey back.

"So we got this corpse," Casey said after some background explanations, "and it's linked to Stardance Modelling. I wondered if you had any information about them?"

Detective Benson thought for a moment. "Not a name that's hit my radar. We've got a few places we keep an eye on, but that's not one of them. I'll check, but it's not ringing any bells. I guess you've tried Narcotics? They sometimes pick up stuff we don't."

"Yeah, we're talking to them too. If anything does pop, let me know."

"Sure will. If it looks like it leads back to us, let me know too."

"Okay."

Casey supposed that that closed off one line, at least for the present. She scrawled on the board, and looked at the two photos again.

"Mornin'," reverberated from the resident mountain.

"Hey," she said to O'Leary, not turning round. "I want the ME's reports."

"Not yet. But we got all our phone records on the way, an' Andy reckons he'll have all his footage after lunchtime. We could go interview the two friends while we're waiting," he wheedled.

"You just want an outing."

"Yep."

"Where are we going, then?"

"Cano Bank. Tessa Colboy. She's a teller there."

"Not very glam."

"Neither pal was in a sexy job. Carlie Davos is a PA at Avocet and Alberman."

"Long-time friends?"

"Pa Petrovich said they'd been pals since before high school. Looks like it stuck."

"Hm. You'd think they'd be envious of Daniela."

"You might think so," O'Leary drawled. "Guess we'll find out soon enough."

At Cano Bank, Tessa was fidgety and fretful as the cops sat down with her.

"It's about Daniela Petrovich," Casey said.

"But what will my boss think? Cops turning up to interview me...I can't afford to get fired. Anything that looks like I might be dishonest...I'll be fired in a heartbeat."

"We'll talk to your boss," O'Leary reassured her. "Just get them in here after we're done."

"Okay," Tessa faltered. "What about Dani?"

"I'm sorry to tell you that Dani was found murdered."

Tessa burst into tears. "Dani? Why would anyone do that to Dani? She was so nice. She shared all the freebies that she got."

"Freebies?"

"Some of the shoots give you perks, like if she was doing moisturiser or make-up she might get some."

"How long had you known her?"

"Since high school. She joined in tenth grade. Carlie" –

"Who's Carlie?" asked Casey, already knowing who Carlie was.

"Carlie Davos. We've been friends since first grade. We were all friends..." Tessa snuffled again.

"Where does she work?" She knew, but it never hurt to check.

"Avocet and Alberman, in Midtown."

"Okay. We'll tell Carlie. Did Dani have any other close friends?"

"No."

"Boyfriend, girlfriend?"

"No...she got hit on so much she said she couldn't trust anyone."

That matched what her mother had said. Dammit. A jealous boyfriend or girlfriend would have been so convenient. Oh well, that was why Casey's team got the weirder ones: they could handle the complicated and confusing.

"What can you tell us about her work?"

"She liked it, but it was tough. She couldn't eat much, she didn't drink."

"Drugs?"

"No..."

Casey raised her eyebrows.

"But if she needed to lose a pound or two she'd get Ex-Lax."

Not quite the drug they'd hoped for.

"What about the people she worked with?"

"It was really bitchy, she said. I guess that's why she liked seeing us. We weren't trying to be models or anything like that, so she could offload."

"What about?"

"Arguments, or which of the dressers or photographers got too handsy, or moping if she lost out to someone else. If it hadn't paid well I think she'd have quit, but she was getting some recognition. She was really pleased about her last shoot."

"What was that?"

"Coronal. Swimwear, beachwear, underwear. It's a huge account, and they're really picky about who they use. Dani was so pleased..."

"When was that?"

Tessa thought back. "A month, maybe? She said they'd been in a hurry to find someone. She didn't know why." Her face crumpled. "How didn't I notice she hadn't been in touch for a month?"

"Easy when you're busy," Casey sympathised. "Time flies." She paused. "Is there anything else you can think of?"

"No."

"Okay." She passed over a card. "If you think of anything, even if you don't think it's important, let me know. Thank you for your time."

"Will you speak to my boss?"

"Sure. Point them out to us."

Tessa's boss left in absolutely no doubt that Tessa had been acting as a good citizen, the two cops made their way to Avocet and Alberman, attorneys at law.

Avocet and Alberman were extremely co-operative, and put Casey and O'Leary in a corporately-smart boardroom, with coffee and cookies.

O'Leary was chowing down on the chocolate ones before Casey could blink.

"Leave me one!" she squawked.

"I'm hungry."

"Didn't you eat your daily elephant already?"

"Naw," he grinned. "That's dinner. It was a small bear for breakfast. Hardly enough meat to feed a chicken."

"You're the largest chicken I ever saw," Casey flipped at him. O'Leary flapped his arms, causing pages on the complimentary pads to ruffle and pens to rattle. Before matters could descend further – and before Casey could snitch the remaining chocolate cookie from under O'Leary's massive paws – a diffident young woman entered, dressed neatly in formal skirt and shirt with a smart jacket.

"You wanted to see me?" she said. "I don't know why the cops want to see me. Don't you want to see one of the attorneys?"

"Carlie Davos?"

"Yes."

"It is you we want to see." – she paled.

"Is it Joe?" Her hands gripped a chair back.

"Joe? No, it's not Joe. I'm sorry to tell you Daniela Petrovich was found dead."

"Dani? That's awful."

Carlie's hands relaxed. She didn't seem to be as upset as Tessa had been.

"What happened to her?"

"She was murdered."

That did shock Carlie. "What?" she gasped, and plumped down into a chair. "Murdered? Why? Who'd murder Dani?"

"You tell us," O'Leary suggested. "Who didn't like her?"

"Nobody. She was nice." The detectives waited. "Joe wasn't so keen, but he didn't *hate* her. He just didn't like me seeing her. He said she was just buying me with the free gifts. He made such a fuss about the last ones that I hadn't seen her for a week or two."

"When did you last see her?"

Carlie counted back on her fingers. "Wow. Must have been a month? I didn't realise it was that long, but we've been so busy here and then I was out with Joe...wow."

"Who's Joe?"

"He's my boyfriend. He's a junior lawyer here. Joe Timpston."

Casey filed that for later follow-up. "Okay. Was there anyone else who didn't like her?"

"No."

"Do you know what she was doing?"

"No. She talked about shoots and stuff but I wasn't that interested. Tessa would know more: she was really into all the stories about what went on."

"Tessa?"

"Tessa Colboy. She's my best friend. We've been friends since forever. Dani showed up in high school. Tessa works at Cano Bank."

"Okay, thanks. Is there anything else you can tell us? Any other friends that might know more?"

Carlie looked completely blank. "Nothing. She didn't have too many friends. No boyfriend."

"Thank you. That's very helpful." Helpful, that was, in the sense that it corroborated a lot of what Tessa and Mr and Mrs Petrovich had said. Daniela seemed to have led quite a simple social life. "Could we talk to Joe, please?"

"I'll need to check. It depends what he's working on."

"That's okay. If he's really busy then he can come to the precinct – I'll give you my card so he can call me." Casey stared hard at Carlie. "If he doesn't contact me at some point today, though, I'll have to come back and interview him. If he gets in touch it'll be at a time convenient for him. If he doesn't..." She let the implication hang.

"Oh...sure. I'll make sure he knows."

"Thanks. Thank you for your time. We'll see ourselves out."

CHAPTER SIX

Back in O'Leary's SUV, on the way back to the precinct, they discussed their findings.

"Not much there. She was pretty quiet, for a supposedly glam job."

"Yeah. Don't like the sound of that there boyfriend."

"No. That's a disaster waiting to happen for Carlie. It would be nice if it was him."

"Yeah. Simple-like. Don't think we're that lucky."

"No. Not liking glam lifestyles isn't a crime."

"You sure? We're all gonna be famous. Bet there'll be some glam there."

"You can have it. Not my thing."

O'Leary thought about Carval's centrepiece, and didn't say a word.

"Anyway, I want a chat with Joe."

"Better rule him out, I guess."

"I want the ME reports more than I want to talk to jealous guys."

"Mebbe they'll be there when we get in."

"I don't see them on my e-mail."

"Still gives you twenty minutes. Thirty, if the traffic's bad."

By the time they were back in the bullpen, nothing had shown up on e-mail. Casey went to make coffee as her computer powered up, in default of calling McDonald and threatening him, which wouldn't work.

A uniform approached Andy, who then signalled Casey. "Social media."

"What've you got?"

"Not a lot, but she says she's going out to a bar – it's the last entry on Facebook."

"What bar?"

"It doesn't say."

Casey slumped. "Crap." She pondered. "Tyler, did Dani's phone have

46

location data?"

"No phone. On it. Might be another route." He strode off to discuss that line of inquiry with a handy tech, and the silence of hard work descended on the team.

"We've got the Stardance data," Casey announced, her bad mood instantly alleviated. "Something more to work on."

"I spoke to Narcotics," Andy said. "They don't have anything linked to Stardance, but if we get a chemical signature from CSU for any drugs in Dani, and if it matches anything they're working on, they'll co-operate. We could always send over the one from that Jane Doe?"

"Let's get Dani's first – maybe they'll match up. Vice didn't know anything either. Looks like Stardance is clean."

"Or doesn't get caught," Andy added cynically.

"Or that," she agreed. "Anyway, let's have a look at all the information we've got from them." She ran down the e-mail headings. Despite his offensive attitude, Selwyn had provided a completely organised set of e-mails, neatly split and properly headed.

"Pretty tidy," Tyler noted.

"I guess he don't want to see Casey again. It sounds like you scared him shitless." O'Leary grinned approvingly. "Small but mean."

"Bigfoot."

"They do say size don't matter."

Casey ignored that with aplomb. "Okay. Who wants the models?"

"Me," Tyler jumped in. "Your boy wants to go see McDonald, and I don't want to."

Casey regarded Tyler with amazement. "He needs to have a babysitter?"

"Nah. Human shield."

"Not happening. We've got work to do." She dismissed Carval's request from her mind instantly, along with the slight sting that he hadn't asked her.

"Other staff? Cameramen, dressers, make-up artists?"

"I'll take that," Andy volunteered.

"I'll split the portfolio with you," O'Leary offered. "Look at the size of that file. Take us a week to read it."

"I think it'll be the photos making it fat."

"Not like the models, then."

"I've got a better idea." She smiled. "You look at the freelancers – Andy, you already said you'd take the guys on the books. Maybe by the time we've done all that, McDonald'll have sent his report through. If there's similarities, we can have a chat with CSU."

"Do we get to go there?"

"Depends if you deserve a treat, Bigfoot." She grinned around them. "Let's get to it."

Shortly the team was head down in data: the inaudible aura of heavy thinking surrounding them.

At lunchtime they sped out to get anything which could be eaten at their desks. With something to do, the team was energised, focused and happy. Kent, casting a supervisory glance around, noted the concentrated atmosphere and mentally applauded. No problems there, or at least none in which he needed to take an immediate interest. He could leave them alone for now, and concentrate on improving the performance of a Robbery team who needed a kick up the ass. He didn't tolerate slackers.

***

Shortly before lunchtime, Carval made his way to the city morgue, in search of ME McDonald. Tyler had declined to come, citing work. Carval thought, based on the short interaction which he'd seen, that disinclination to join him, tending to outright dislike of the ME, had had more to do with it. As usual, when he had shots at the front of his mind, other considerations (such as Tyler's day job, or McDonald's likely reaction to his presence) were a complete irrelevance.

He smiled charmingly at the reception staff at NYU Langone, and...um...might have misled them just a little bit. It wasn't exactly a *lie*. He had a close personal interest in the model corpses, and if they thought that he was a relative, well, he hadn't actually *said* so.

Once in, he followed the signs to the morgue, and then started peering around the clinically pristine corridors in search of offices. Helpfully, the doors had signs and names on them. He took a few shots, hoping to capture the emptiness of the atmosphere: the pall of death and the muted sense of endings. There was almost no noise. He moved on, sobered and respectful, until he came to a small office with the door shut: a plate on the door identifying it as ME McDonald's.

Just for an instant, he wondered if bearding McDonald in his own den was a good plan, but then Carval's total obsession with taking photographs that would make his new exhibition world-class won out. He knocked, softly, in deference to the dead and those who sought answers for, and from, them.

"What?" came an irritated snap. At least he was in, Carval thought, and entered, closing the door behind him.

He took in the austere office in one wide-angle glance: a desk so clear it made Casey's anal-retentively neat workspace seem cluttered; anatomical diagrams on the walls; a framed certificate behind the chair in which ME McDonald was regarding him, his bony form enraged. Carval didn't stop to think, and took four shots, camera fully up, before McDonald boiled over.

"What do you think you are doing?" he enunciated. "This is a private office." His skeletal knuckles whitened around his pen.

"I want to shoot you," Carval said bluntly.

"No."

"Yes. I need to shoot you so my exhibition shows the truth."

"Truth?" McDonald shot back. "The *truth*, whoever you are" – Carval stared at him, astounded: had McDonald not *known* – "is that this is a working facility in which we respect the dead. It is not a place for *photography*." He could have said *necrophilia* in that same tone.

"You don't know who I am?"

"No. Nor do I care."

"I'm Jamie Carval."

"You could be God Himself, and you would have no place – *Carval?*" Carval nodded. "Panhandlers." Another nod. McDonald fixed him with a gimlet eye, whereupon he cringed like a child in front of the principal. The ME perused him slowly and disapprovingly, observing the jeans, t-shirt and leather jacket; the untidy brown hair. "You hardly seem the type to empathise with the downtrodden," he emitted, pecking his head forward. "Privileged playboy. Hardly powerless. Were you simply exercising cultural superiority: as if they were mere animals in a zoo?" His tone bit, sneering.

Carval, riled, bit back. "No. And you know it, because you've seen that exhibition" – a bow drawn at a venture, but the arrow hit home. "They're *humanity*. Just like you, despite your Johns Hopkins medical certificate on the wall. People need to know that they're human. They deserved respect and I gave them it. So don't you dare accuse me of misery tourism."

McDonald steepled his fingers together. Carval shot the pose, isolating the skeletal hands, without apology. A spare, grey eyebrow lifted. Carval met his gaze squarely.

"I see. Humanity is what drives you. How...unexpected." It didn't sound like a compliment. Then again, Carval didn't think that McDonald gave compliments.

"Yes." He barrelled ahead. "My next exhibition is about the NYPD. Your work is part of that – your interactions with the cops."

McDonald's brow creased, as if in search of a memory. "Ah. You were with Detective Clement's team." Another disapproving stare. "Hardly a recommendation."

"Yeah, I was."

"Hmm. You were with Detective Tyler. I assumed you were a part of that team. Dissimulation seems to be your modus operandi." The fingers dropped, and resteepled, folded together, and released. Carval shot it all, since McDonald hadn't – yet – told him to stop. "My morgue" – *his?* Carval wasn't aware that McDonald was the Chief Medical Examiner – "is a place of death."

"That's part of humanity. Anyway, I'm not interested in shooting corpses. I'm interested in you."

Finally, McDonald showed some emotion which wasn't contempt or fury. "*What?*"

"The corpses aren't the point. Sure, they're the reason you're here, and what the cops are working on, but I'm not interested in the gore. I said, I want humanity. You" – he was dead sure of it – "give them your best. That's what I want to shoot. Even when you're disagreeing with the team or telling them they can't have what they want, it's because you're doing your utmost to find the answers. Same as Casey's team." McDonald emitted a *pah*! "That's what I need. I can see it. It's in your hands and face." He locked his mouth shut on further passionate words.

"Hmm," McDonald emitted again. It wasn't actively hostile. It certainly wasn't enthusiastic agreement. He didn't seem to have appreciated Carval's passion in the slightest.

"You may," he pronounced.

Carval gawped. "Huh?"

"Assisting the general populace to acquire some humanity is a worthy aim." McDonald didn't sound convinced of the humanity of the general populace, nor did he sound convinced that the aim would be met. "Futile, of course, but worthy. You may photograph. Do you require my work to be that relating to Detective Clement's cases?"

"No, not really. Like I said, it's not the corpse I'm interested in."

McDonald donned a thin, unpractised smile. "I shall be working on a case from the Eighth Precinct this afternoon. You will return at two p.m. I shall instruct the receptionists to permit you access." He regarded Carval frigidly. "I infer that you misled them to gain entry earlier. Do not repeat that action. Do not return here except when I, personally, permit it. I am sure that you would only be interested in a cell if your camera were with you. Should you arrive here without permission, your camera would not be with you in that cell. Any further mendacity will not be tolerated. If you cannot be honest in your words and actions, your photographs will also be a lie."

Carval gulped. In his own acerbic way, McDonald was as intimidating as Casey.

"I won't," he promised. "See you at two."

"Do not be late. Latecomers will not be admitted to the theatre."

"No. Thank you."

It wasn't until Carval exited the building, in search of lunch, that he thought that McDonald's final sentence might have been his version of humour. He would never have guessed.

At a well-judged five to two Carval returned, gave his name to the receptionist, who passed him through with an air of astonishment that (he presumed) McDonald would allow any living human being to enter his sanctum, and returned to McDonald's office.

"You are prompt," was the only acknowledgement. McDonald vacated his office without another word, clearly expecting Carval to follow, and stalked, stork-like, to the autopsy room, Carval shooting all the way. He'd name that sequence *Death Coming For Death*, he thought, gazing at the skeletal figure in the clinical setting.

"Stay out of my way and sightline," McDonald instructed as Carval entered. "If you wish to be near, you will wear a gown and a cap. There must be no risk of contamination. Touch nothing. Do not lean over the deceased."

Suitably garbed, Carval adjusted his lenses, slipped out of McDonald's sight – and most likely his consciousness – and began to take a series of sighting shots of the autopsy room: the gleam on smooth metal tables, the ominous sharpness of the scalpels and shining viciousness of a pair of shears. McDonald was utterly silent. Not for him, it seemed, the TV trope of talking to his corpses: his concentration was absolute. The camera rose: capturing his intent, lined face; the cool, analytical eyes between pastel cap and mask; and then lowering and closing in on the thin hands, smoothly drawing the scalpel in a perfectly straight diagonal from the right shoulder, mirroring it from the left, the cuts meeting precisely at the sternum and then merging into a single slice to the pubic bone. *Death Inspecting Death* popped into Carval's mind as a sub tag.

Carval was transfixed by the hands in their bright blue nitrile gloves: their exactitude and precision: not a movement wasted, not a cut a fraction longer or shorter than it should be. He'd capture the mastery, the intensity, the searing clarity of a man at the top of his game; the contrasts of the pale, dead flesh and the intimation of movement as the scalpel flashed in the examination lights; then, finally, the black catgut (was it still catgut, he wondered) to stitch the dead man back together, an oddly reverent closing of the eyes, and finally the fall of the shrouding sheet over him as the bright blue nitrile laid for an instant on the white fabric: a benediction and a farewell.

"Are you still here?" McDonald expostulated. "I am done."

"I'm done too," Carval said. "But..."

"What?"

"If there was another case – for Casey's team" –

"I assume you mean Detective Clement?"

"Yeah. Them. If they had a new case, could I come back for that one specifically?"

"Why? You said that was not required."

"Um...because it would link that narrative. The shots have to tell a story as well as show the characters. People like stories."

"I see," McDonald sniffed, evidently unimpressed by such childish needs. "I will consider it. Goodnight."

51

"Bye."

When Carval walked outside, it was already twilight. He'd been there for hours. He checked his phone, and found a text from Casey, sent half an hour previously.

Dinner?

He tapped her number.

"Clement." It sounded like she hadn't looked first.

"Casey, it's me. Is dinner still on?"

"Yeah."

"I'll be over in twenty."

"Okay."

***

"I'm done," Andy said, mid-afternoon.

"Just about," Tyler agreed.

"Me too."

"Okay. Let's go see what we've got."

Once they'd filtered out everyone who hadn't worked for or with Stardance for the last year, they had an almost manageable list. Time to inflict the legwork on others, commonly known as uniformed officers. Tyler normally handled that, his Army background giving him the best knack for command, and in short order a group of apparently enthusiastic officers departed in diverse directions.

"Techs are trying for location data. Takes time."

"Nothing more on social media," Andy added. "This girl needed to join the modern world."

"Prob'ly didn't want the hassle."

"Finally!" Casey exclaimed, cutting across them all. "McDonald's report – dammit, it came in just before two." She opened it up and skim read it. "I was right. Daniela had only been on heroin for less than a month. That fits right in with what Carval said about it being spotted if she was using, and with the point she dropped out of sight."

"Can't he be a little more accurate?"

"He says not." She grimaced. "But it's a start. Now for Jane Doe." She skimmed again. "Bullseye! Same pattern – and the same chemical signature for the adulterants – most likely the same batch or supplier. I need to call CSU. I want them to work up a picture of Jane Doe as she was before she got beaten to death." She looked round the team, the joy of the hunt in her eyes. "We're going to show that to Selwyn. While I get CSU started on that, Andy, will you go back to Narcotics with the tox data, and see if they can be any more help?"

"Sure."

"O'Leary, Tyler, I've got another hunch."

"Yeah?" they said suspiciously. Casey's hunches paid off often enough to be worth listening to, but they also often resulted in a lot of effort.

"We've got two, exactly the same..." She enticed them to follow her thought.

"More," Tyler clipped.

"You think there might be more?"

"I think it's worth someone taking a look."

"I think that's somethin' uniforms were invented for," O'Leary said. "An' I think that the night shift could do it, too, an' maybe we'd have some results in the mornin', seein' as it's already pushin' six."

"Okay," Casey conceded. "You get them started, and then let's see where we've got to and what we'll start on tomorrow."

While another batch of uniformed officers were being instructed, Casey scrawled her view of the team's to-do list up on the board. Tyler added a line or three, and O'Leary, ambling back with an air of profound satisfaction, another.

"Narcotics are working on it," Andy said.

"Write it up, then."

He did. Despite all his claims of taking calligraphy classes, Andy's writing still looked like a drunken spider had fallen in the ink and then gone for a walk. It was lucky that they all knew what it said.

"So, top of our list for tomorrow, calling in and interviewing the jealous wannabes," Casey began. "Good work there, Tyler, so you get to pick which half you want to do. Let's ask specifically what they thought of Daniela winning the Coronal shoot."

"Huh?"

"Tessa told us that Daniela was really pleased about that – it's a huge account and they're really picky, she said. So let's use that. Bound to be some jealousy there, though I bet we find a lot more."

"Fun," Tyler grinned.

"Tears, tantrums and temper," O'Leary suggested. "It'll be like managing the toddlers down at the day care centre."

"When've you ever done that? No baby Bigfoots here."

"I got nieces, an' Pete does. They were toddlers once."

"And after the wannabes, second up is getting that photo from CSU so I can go and interview" –

"*Intimidate.*"

"*Interview*," she emphasised, with a glare, "Selwyn again."

"I wanna go this time," O'Leary wheedled. "I've never seen a modelling agency."

"They're nothing special. Offices with uncomfortable chairs and oversize desks."

"Sounds like I'd fit right in. Oversize, that's me."

"You'd break things. I've got a better idea, anyway. We get this photo and we haul him in. Interview" –

"Intimidate," someone muttered. She scowled.

" – him on my terms and my patch this time. No *misunderstandings* about my role." She turned to her phone. "Right. Let's get that photo started."

She dialled. "Hey, it's Casey at the Thirty-Sixth."

"Hey, Casey. What do you want this time?"

"Don't be like that."

"You only call when you want miracles."

"Shouldn't provide them so often, then. Anyway, I want a photo cleaned up so it looks pre-death and not beaten up. If I send you it, can you tell me how long it'll take?"

"Who do you think we are? Angela Montenegro from Bones?"

"Yep," Casey agreed. The CSU tech muttered darkly at her.

"Okay, send it over and we'll give it a go. No promises, though. Not about results and" – as Casey started to interject – "not about timing either. Give me a chance. You're always impatient."

"I wanna catch the killer. Nothing wrong with that."

"Nope, but I wanna give you something better than the crap you'd get if I did it fast and sloppy."

"Okay. But" –

"Yes, Casey," the tech said patiently. "I'll do the best I can."

"Thanks."

The phone was barely down before she'd sent the photo over to CSU.

"What about that Joe guy?" O'Leary reminded her.

"Yeah." She checked her phone. "Okay, he called. I'll give him a call back and set that up. I don't expect much, but maybe he'll fill in something." She checked her watch. "Might get him now." Another quick call.

"Joe Timpston? Detective Clement. Thanks for getting in touch."

"That's okay."

"If you had time, I could come by your offices now."

"Sure, that would work."

"Thanks. See you shortly."

She started to tidy her papers, looking around the team. "Okay, that's my next move arranged. See you all tomorrow."

On the way to interview Joe, O'Leary's comments of the night before about letting Carval know about Andy's...um...issues nagged at her mind. Maybe...maybe she could say something that wasn't a lie but wasn't private. Something work-related would do. Carval had cleared off pretty quickly last night, and while photos were his life, she wasn't convinced that had been all of it. She thought some more. Dinner. That would mend fences. She tapped out a text, and felt a little better.

CHAPTER SEVEN

Casey having gone off to interview Joe, Tyler and O'Leary exchanged glances in which much was understood and little spoken, and arranged themselves to loom around Andy's desk.

"What?"

"Thought you needed to have a break."

"I'm about to go home."

"Mmmm," hummed O'Leary. "I noticed your chi ain't as harmonious as usual, ever since that first dead girl showed up. Let's all three of us go find somethin' to get your chakras – ain't that the word, or was it tantras?"

"Dance." Tyler muttered.

O'Leary smiled bucolically. "You know I don't remember all this complicated stuff so good. Anyway, iffen I could see those aura things, I bet yours would be all black and outta shape."

"I don't want to have a drink."

"Not suggesting one," Tyler replied. "Chinatown. Noodle bar, beer, or tea."

O'Leary pushed out his lip, ice-shelf-like, at them. "The Abbey's just as good for harmonisin' chi, but Tyler wouldn't have it. Spoilsport."

Since everyone knew that with a modicum of effort O'Leary could beat Tyler on the mats nine times out of ten – something to do with the nine inch height difference – Andy favoured him with a dyspeptic and sceptical half-smile.

"You're not going to leave this alone, are you?" he said with resignation. O'Leary never did, when he had an aim, or the good of the team, in mind.

"Naw. All this disharmonious chi's gettin' my fur all spiky. C'mon. Noodles an' tea."

"Beer," corrected Tyler. He didn't do tea.

Andy, recognising that the others could – and likely would – pick his slender frame up and simply frogmarch him to Chinatown, conceded in order to retain some dignity. "Okay, let's go."

In the noisy surroundings of Tyler's pick of noodle restaurants (chosen to ensure it had a liquor licence) food, tea and beer arrived. After a deep draught of his beer, O'Leary planted his forearms on the table, incidentally protecting his dinner from the others, and sighed, ruffling the napkins and wobbling the spare chair.

"You got somethin' on your mind," he opened amiably, "an' it's botherin' you so's that you're pickin' fights with Casey's boy. D'you know somethin' we don't?"

"Want to run him?" Tyler asked suspiciously. "Before she gets in deep?"

O'Leary looked as if he might say something, and then thought better of it. "Before she finds it out an' shoots him, more like."

"No. You don't need to run him. I already did that."

It was true. Andy simply...hadn't mentioned it to Casey. It wouldn't have gone down well.

"You didn't tell us that. I wasted my time doin' it iffen you did it first."

"Nothing to tell that you don't already know, so I didn't need to." Andy stopped talking, and stared into his tea bowl, steaming delicately.

"So somethin' else." It drifted in the air.

Andy's dark eyes were ancient, hooded and opaque, watching something far away and long ago: his face more than usually inscrutable. The restaurant was bustling and boisterous, but around their corner table there was only stillness and silence: the asphyxiating weight of old, painful remembrance and the knowledge that Andy's demons weren't far from the surface.

"You know my parents died, and I went to live with relatives when I was young." He stared harder into the green tea. They knew this, but gave him time. "They weren't such good people." A sip, trying to wash away bad memories. "A lot of stuff went down. No-one noticed. No-one cared." Another drink. Still, it was a tale they'd heard before, in dribs and drabs, over four years of the team. Tyler refilled Andy's cup, and said nothing: O'Leary's mass blocked any outsider's observations.

"I left." He didn't say – though the others knew it – just before his teens. "Fended for myself for a while. Kept out of the worst stuff on the streets. Saw a lot of people who didn't, and their bodies." He sipped, and sat silent for a while. "Some of them called themselves models. But modelling for them wasn't anything more than being an escort, at best. Down in the shelters, you heard them." His mouth twisted, his voice was bleak and remote. "All the beautiful girls with their pretty portfolios." Tyler drew a breath in understanding, O'Leary's broad fingers tensed. "They all ended up ugly dead, just the same."

"We get it," O'Leary murmured.

"So it isn't about him, but it is...was..."

"Reminder."

"Yeah." Andy searched his tea for answers again, swirling chopsticks through his barely touched noodles.

"Gotta separate it, man," Tyler took point, without asking for more information, without probing feelings. They didn't do that – they didn't need to do that: the whole brutal story laid plain to see. They knew the backing track to that song: the hunger, the beatings, the predators lurking.

"Yeah. But it's not so easy."

"Naw." O'Leary drawled. "He's taken a lot of pretty photos. Stands to reason in a case like this that's gonna trip some switches. But you gotta admit, he ain't done nothin' wrong."

"Yeah, but it's in my face. He's taking his shots and being an expert – and *yes*, I get that we need his input: I want this solved as much as anyone does – and all I can think of is our beat-up corpses and the girls I used to see in the shelters with their bruises and track marks in their arms and their pretty portfolios just like he shoots."

There was an ominous silence. O'Leary shifted in his seat, and disposed of the remains of his dinner in two huge bites. Tyler drew on his beer. Andy simply sat and stirred his noodles, without eating.

"I got an idea," O'Leary said after a moment or two. His contribution didn't appear to fill Andy with confidence. Tyler, on the other hand, clearly knew what was coming.

"What?"

"Problem is, Carval don't know 'bout your sore spot, an' so he keeps proddin' it, accidental-like."

"I don't need you putting on the hayseed accent to hide what you're going to say, okay. Spit it out. Though I know what it's going to be."

"Most likely you do. That don't make it a bad idea."

"Get on with it, Bigfoot."

"I think you should tell Carval the truth. Some of it," he added hastily. "Not everythin'. He don't need to know 'bout your parents, or your relatives. All he needs to know is that you've seen a lot of bad stuff before you were a cop."

"So I get to bare my soul? No. No. Fucking. Way." Andy never used language like that. "You wanna bare your soul, be my guest. I'm not doing it. You're not doing it, so I'm not." He blanked his face. "I don't see any of us 'fessing up our secrets."

"He guessed I was a sniper."

"You're not telling him the rest. And you" – he stabbed a finger at O'Leary – "you're not mentioning the past either, and whether he knows or not you haven't told him you're gay."

"I haven't hidden it, neither."

"Not the point. What about the past? And Casey sure isn't saying anything about anything."

"Never does," Tyler pointed out laconically.

"Not the point," Andy snapped again.

"I don't want you to bare your soul," O'Leary said, suddenly sounding a lot less like a bucolic yokel who hadn't made it to high school and a lot more like the college graduate he was. "In fact, listenin' to you, I don't want you to talk at all. I'll do it, or Tyler will. You don't need to." He looked directly at Andy. "We won't say anythin' you wouldn't like. We've been a team since you got here, an' you're part of that, but it looks like Carval's goin' to be taggin' round for a long time to come." He paused, twitching uncomfortably himself. "I don't want you to be uncomfortable, an' we can blow off Carval if we need to. Casey'll come down on the team's side, not his."

"You think?"

"Yeah. I'm sure." From O'Leary, that had the weight and authority of a tablet of stone. "She wouldn't like it much, but she'd do it. But...he ain't a bad guy, an' he's good for her when we all know her dad's gettin' worse, so I don't want to do that iffen we don't have to. She don't wanna see it, but he's really into her."

"And you do see it? Setting up as Dear Abby?"

"I saw him after she got beaten up."

Andy shrugged. "Whatever. Do what you want, Bigfoot. You always do anyway. I can't stop you, but I won't be there."

"Mebbe you should go down to the theatre with that Allan guy."

Andy frankly goggled. "You what now?"

"You seemed to be gettin' along pretty good the other week. All that culture. Seems to me it'd be somethin' different. Not like we wanna talk about li'l girls' toys."

"*The Doll's House* is great art!" Andy exclaimed. "You're just Philistines." He automatically took a bite of noodles.

"Baseball. Much better."

"Naw. Football's the only game worth playin'."

O'Leary stoked the familiar, good natured argument until Andy's noodles were all gone.

"I ain't goin' to do anythin' just yet. Have a think. Let me know tomorrow, or the next day. Not now."

As they stood to leave, Andy peered the long way up to O'Leary's serious face. "Tomorrow. If I say no, will you drop it?"

"I won't do it iffen you say no. I might keep talkin' at you, though."

"This is a choice?"

"Yep."

"Think it over," Tyler put in. "Your choice. I'll deal with Bigfoot." He punched Andy's shoulder, gently. "Either way's okay. I'll fix Carval, if Bigfoot doesn't."

Andy managed a strained grin. "Okay. Let me think. But" – the grin widened – "if Bigfoot keeps bullying me, I'll take him to the theatre."

O'Leary faked a wound to the heart, and groaned. "Noooooo."

Andy merely smirked.

"Seeya tomorrow," Tyler said, and the party broke up.

***

As soon as the door opened to him, Carval prowled in, caught Casey, and indulged in a long, leisurely kiss designed to reduce her to a melting puddle of receptive warmth. It certainly did that – to him. Casey, while enthusiastically reciprocating, was distressingly unpuddle-like.

"Guess what?" he asked, dropping his jacket on a handy chair and following Casey, who was messing with ready meals in her small kitchen.

"What?" she said, still messing.

He slid up behind her and then spun her round. "Stop fussing with that." He smirked. "I made a new friend today."

Casey's jaw dropped. "Really?" she said, stiffening.

"Yep. ME McDonald."

"Uh?" she squeaked. "McDonald? He hasn't got friends. He hates everyone in the whole wide world."

"Not me. He let me take photos."

"He *let* you take photos? What did you drug him with?"

"He appreciated my charming personality." She made a rude noise. "He did. Anyway, he let me shoot him in the morgue all afternoon."

"Wow," Casey said. "Let's see, then. I need to see proof."

"No," Carval replied without thought.

"Oh."

Carval noticed the tiny hesitation, but, used to that reaction, ignored it. Most people got pissy when he wouldn't show them his shots, but the only one who saw raw shots was Allan, who insisted. He diverted. "You owe me ten dollars."

"Uh?"

"You bet me ten that McDonald wouldn't let me shoot him. He did. Pay up." He didn't want or need the cash, but Casey wouldn't let him pay for anything that wasn't reciprocated.

Casey found her wallet and produced a crumpled ten-dollar bill. "There. But I still want proof."

"You'll see, next time you come to the studio. I don't show the raw shots to anyone till I've played around with them. Anyway, I didn't come here to show you photos."

"Just to show off?"

"Mean," he drawled. "I came to claim my winnings."

"Winnings, huh?"

"Yeah. Ten dollars – and this," and he dipped down and kissed her again.

"I don't think that was part of the bet."

"Doesn't seem like you object." He tugged a little, to bring her closer, where she fit against him so very nicely, and kissed her again, harder. "Definitely not objecting."

She wasn't objecting. She was, however, hungry, proved by the embarrassing gurgle from her stomach. "Dinner." Carval blinked. "I'm hungry," she added.

He shrugged, and stepped back. "Okay. Can I help?"

"Sodas in the fridge."

That was peculiar. In fact, thinking back, she hadn't had beer in the fridge the last couple of times he'd been here. He shrugged again. Likely she hadn't been to the store to get it. It wasn't important. What was important was making sure that his Casey wasn't drifting away from him.

"Andy saw a lot of stuff in Narcotics," she said out of the blue, after dinner, when he'd easily persuaded her into the crook of his arm.

"Uh?"

"He saw a lot of bad stuff as a Narcotics cop. Sometimes it still gets to him. It's not personal."

Carval clapped his mouth shut on an instant, aggravated, retort that it had sounded pretty damn personal to him, and she hadn't done a thing about it.

"Tyler gets it best, so he deals with it. He knows how to fix Andy."

Just as well he hadn't replied. He still didn't like it, but it made sense. He forcibly reminded himself that the team was tight, and he'd only been around five minutes. They knew how to deal with their issues.

Besides which, Casey had just pulled his head down and kissed him, which was a much better idea than thinking about Andy's temper. He responded in kind: running a hand into her hair to release the clip and set all those dark curls rioting. He loved the way that simply doing that took her out of her cool-cop persona: turned her into his responsive, sexy lover. She *was* his lover.

He just wished she'd let him in a little more.

She kissed him again, and he decided that he'd been let in quite enough for now. He gathered her in far more closely, and let his fingers explore, sneaking under her top at the waist to glide over bare skin. Just as the first time, just as every time, touch turned to blaze: hands roamed, mouths crashed, and heat rose till Carval stood and swept her to her bedroom.

They stood, his hands on her shoulders; she even smaller in bare feet, looking up and smiling knowingly, dark eyes dilated, lips red and slightly swollen; his broad form bent a little and arousal obvious. Her pants puddled at her feet, his followed, her top disappeared, and he dipped so she could slide his t-shirt over his head and run elegant hands down over the muscle of his chest.

Selwyn, Carval thought, was a total dumbass. As far as he was concerned, Casey was pretty much perfect: her curves and small size still a surprise to him, such a contrast to the presence she exuded at work. His hands slipped over her back, bringing her in, gradually moving closer to those curves, and she arched to him, encouraging more. More was precisely his plan. She was irresistible.

It seemed as if it was her plan too, and she'd got there first. She shoved: not expecting it, he fell backwards on to the bed, and Casey grinned.

"Nice," she said, and flicked a suggestive glance downward and up again.

"C'mere, then, and I'll be very nice."

She didn't move, teasing him, letting him admire the honed body and the curves which softened it. He couldn't have *stopped* admiring it, and as he did he had the odd impression she was relaxing, more comfortable. He had to be wrong. Casey was totally comfortable in her skin. Which took him right back to the nasty little thought that said she was totally comfortable having sex with him, but wouldn't open up.

On the other hand, right then, sex was *definitely* okay by him. He sat up and reached for her in one rapid, predatory movement, and pulled her down over him, squeezing her neat ass and holding her just where she was most welcome, then pulling her up to kiss her and roll them over so that he could search her eyes and face for her reactions. She'd forget everything but him.

She smiled up at him, slow and sleepy-eyed. "Don't you like being underneath?"

"Sometimes. Not now." He propped himself above her, and swept a hand along her ribs. "See, it's much harder to do this."

"Guess I'll have to cope, then."

"Control freak," he teased gently. His hand moved a little less gently, palming a pert breast and then dextrously slipping beneath her spine and unhooking her bra. "That's better." Shortly, his mouth began to prove how much better it was, lipping at her till she made small sexy noises and arched into his touch, pulling him closer with hands in his hair. She wriggled to reach him – fair was fair, after all, and he deserved some attention too.

Hard hands found damp heat, slim fingers wrapped around rigidity, breathing deepened and harshened, soft moans and throaty groans, and then he rose above her and filled her and each of them touched intimately, driving higher, and then there was only release.

Carval snuggled Casey in with a somewhat possessive hand on her hip, unwilling to leave just yet. He ought to go home and download, maybe mess around with the shots for a while before he slept, but he was content and sated, cleaned up – that had been fun, though her shower could usefully have been larger – and, astonishingly, cosy. He didn't do cosy, before Casey. A few short weeks and his definition of post-sex perfection had been upturned.

She was surprisingly snuggly, off duty, he mused: strokable and pettable, affectionate. But...there was still the niggling doubt that she felt anything more than casual attraction. Oh. Oh, no. Their liaison was *fun*. Not serious. Not...no, no, no. He was not thinking the words *long-term*. He never thought long-term: he had Allan for that, and he certainly wasn't going to involve Allan in his affair with Casey. Long-term was...um...restrictive. Anti-creative. Would stop him going where he pleased, when he pleased.

Oh, hell. He *wanted* long – no, *longer* – term. Longer term wasn't so bad. He still needed months more for the shots for the upcoming exhibition. He needn't worry. She would be with him longer term, and it would give him a chance to be let in. He needed to understand her. He told himself that he needed to understand to add depth to the story told by his photographs, and ignored the small voice that said *no, you want to understand because you're sinking fast; you're six feet under and you've already drowned*.

Casey emitted a small sound in her sleep, and rolled over, away from him. He rolled her back without thinking about it, and didn't realise, as he slid into sleep, the betrayal of his feelings which it showed.

When Casey's klaxonic alarm screeched, she realised that not only was Carval still there, which had never happened before, arm over her in a distinctly *got-you* fashion which she shouldn't have appreciated but did, but that she had slept through the night more soundly than she ever had alone. She never slept well. *Except now, when he's been here*, a small voice snipped at her. She ignored it. Exercise improved one's sleep. That was all. He was uncomplicated fun, for as long as they felt like it. She carefully also ignored the coils of uncertainty about model-girls' figures and looks, and Carval's well-known history of enjoying both. She didn't need to be insecure. She was at the top of her game with a team that was at the top of theirs. History was irrelevant – his and hers.

She slipped out of bed and whisked through her morning routine. When she'd finished, Carval was sitting on the edge of the bed, sexily tousled and scruffily stubbled.

"I've got to go," she said. "C'mon, get moving. I need to lock up."

"Uh?"

Clearly Carval was not a morning person either. How reassuring – if she hadn't needed to get to work.

"Move," she rapped, to pierce his sloth. "I need to go to work."

"Oh. Yeah. Urrhhh." He yawned, but dressed speedily. "Morning?" he queried.

"Yep."

"Oh." Morning? Really morning? He'd meant to go home. How was he still there at Casey's? Why hadn't he woken and left? More pertinently, did he actually care?

No, he didn't, he decided. It really didn't matter if he slept at Casey's: it wasn't as if he had responsibilities. He exited with alacrity, but before he went home – what time? That wasn't a real time. Six a.m.? No, no, no. That wasn't a time he liked from the waking up end of the day – in the gloom of not-yet-daylight and a chill, thin wind biting through his leather jacket, he caught her in and kissed her hard.

"Huh? What was that for?"

"I wanted to." He smiled arrogantly. "You liked it."

She scowled unconvincingly. "Bye."

"Wait!"

"Yeah?"

"What's happening today? Anything interesting?"

"We're interviewing."

"Can I shoot from Observation?"

"If you blur the faces, sure."

"See you later, then," and Carval hurriedly loped off home to wash and change so that he could capture another facet of the team. He'd seen them interviewing suspects, and of course he'd (illicitly) taken shots of Casey ripping Selwyn apart, but witnesses who might not be suspects was something new. He wondered how it might be different, and how it would fit in. That he'd be able to show the difference, he had no doubt. He never doubted his ability to take stunning shots.

Shoot first, ask questions later. It had always worked for him.

CHAPTER EIGHT

"Okay, Tyler. You and O'Leary take the models."

"Why do I get Bigfoot?"

"Stops you getting distracted by all those pretty faces. If we get male models, you get to stop him being distracted."

Tyler scowled, Casey snickered, and O'Leary outright chortled.

"He'll scare them shitless. Dainty little models don't like Bigfeet."

"Too bad. He's going in with you." Casey's tone didn't admit further argument. "Andy and I will take the dressers and cameramen."

"What about your expert?" O'Leary teased.

"We're not a TV show. Cops interview. He shoots."

"Very true, Clement," said Kent coldly from behind them. "I am pleased to see you haven't lost all sense, unlike some others, and haven't forgotten my stipulations." He glared at O'Leary, who, despite his bulk, tried to hide behind Andy. He failed. "However, since you have an expert, I expect you to take advantage of him. Should he have insights" – Kent didn't sound as if he thought there would be insights – "then he is to inform you of them."

"Yes, sir."

"Continue."

Kent progressed towards his office, leaving terror and devastation behind him as his heavy form departed. Sighs of relief were carefully kept below the level at which he might hear them.

Casey tapped her phone. "Carval? You on your way?"

"Yeah."

"Good. We're about ready."

"There in two."

In ninety seconds, timed on Tyler's hi-tech sports watch, Carval dashed in, rather less breathless than any of them expected.

64

"You work out?" Tyler queried, his eyes lighting up. Working out was as close as Tyler came to religion: the gym his church.

"I go to the gym," Carval said cautiously.

"What d'you press?"

"A camera button," Casey flicked back. Tyler on comparative stats would waste a lot of time. "C'mon. First interviewees are already here. Tyler, stop flexing your biceps and start flexing your tongue to get something useful from the models. O'Leary, with him. Keep him focused. Andy, let's start with Jose."

The team began to move.

"Carval, we want you in Observation. Shoot what you want, but also, can you listen up for anything that doesn't match what you know about the business. You might spot something that we don't."

He looked irresolute for a moment. "Can I see both rooms from Observation?"

"Yeah, if you shift from side to side there."

"Okay. I don't think the models are as likely to say much about the business as the others."

"Why not?"

"Turn up, do what they're told, be positioned and photographed, get paid and go home. Most of them don't pay a lot of attention to anything outside the scene, like actors. They need to be in the moment."

"But they look so pretty," O'Leary grinned.

"Like you care."

Carval, knowing that O'Leary was gay, didn't react. It occurred to him a second later that that might have been a mistake, because he was being regarded most peculiarly by all four cops. "What? He talked about his Pete."

"So I did," O'Leary drawled. "Pay attention, don't you?"

"Come on," Casey said, passing over the hitch. "Let's get this done."

Tyler and O'Leary peeled off to their interrogation room. Casey was perfectly sure that she'd heard an admiring gasp from the first witness, which wasn't terribly surprising. Tyler was a finely muscled specimen – and O'Leary a freak of nature.

Carval went on to Observation, and, after a quick look into the Tyler-O'Leary show, in which rather a lot of mutual appreciation and drooling was occurring under O'Leary's gargantuan supervision, he settled back to enjoy the Casey-Andy furnace. Enjoyment was considerably enhanced when he recognised their first victim – oops, person of interest – as the dresser who'd been witness to Selwyn's major misunderstanding.

"Jose Hervalo?"

"Yeah." It came in a slightly incongruous Bronx twang. Jose's small neat person and well-selected clothing had inclined Carval to expect something similar to Allan's precise tones. He raised his camera and began, just in time to catch the moment Jose recognised Casey.

"Detective Clement and" – she gestured – "Detective Chee."

"You were at Stardance," he stuttered, and went pale at the memory.

"Yes," Casey clipped. "Your role?"

"I'm a dresser."

"Explain exactly what that means." Jose did. "I see. And what precisely does 'positioning the clothes' mean?"

Faced with two intimidating visages, Jose was barely hanging on to his composure.

"We...I'd never touch up the girls. Selwyn would fire me in a heartbeat."

"How would he know?" Andy asked sourly. "Not like they'd complain. Not if they wanted another job."

"I wouldn't. *I'd* never get another job. Someone would snitch."

"Really. The same someones who thought I'd want to be a model? That doesn't give me any confidence in their intelligence or observation skills at all."

Intimidation level, maximum, Carval thought, and kept shooting: Andy's hard, cold eyes; Casey's attitude of complete contempt. Something was flickering in Jose's face: he could see it, and he was sure Casey could.

In Interrogation One, Casey could feel Jose on the brink. He was terrified, and it wasn't *all* her patent terrorising technique or Andy's cold dislike. Suffocating silence stretched out.

Jose broke.

"I would never," he babbled. "But there are...there's...I *didn't*."

"Who." Casey was frigidly judicial: demanding not questioning.

"I'd never see another decent shoot – nothing but coffee beans" – Casey wouldn't have minded that, as long as she could drink the coffee afterwards – "for the rest of my life. I couldn't snitch even if I knew anything and I *didn't*."

"So you lied. Actually, *no-one* would snitch. Who was it?"

"I never saw anyone do anything. No-one ever saw anything."

Dammit. That was no use at all. Rumour and hearsay weren't going to give her anything concrete.

Carval rattled off shots, noting the fractional slump in Casey's posture. Jose hadn't said anything that didn't mesh with his memories. Always rumours, but never proof. The models never said anything: they wanted the next job more than anyone.

"Who. Was. It."

Casey's tones fell like the crack of doom.

"Tell us. Otherwise you'll be up on Obstruction charges." Andy's light, icy tenor carried a world of prospective pain. "Or maybe you fancy a night in the cells? Plenty of interesting company there."

Carval spotted a small movement on Casey's part, and Andy stopped. Jose was almost shivering. Silence fell once more. Fancifully, Carval imagined icicles forming on the table.

Suddenly, shockingly, Casey moved. "Look at this," she snarled, and thrust a photo of Daniela's bloodied, beaten face across the table. Jose recoiled. "Look! That's what happened to Dani." His eyes skittered round the room. "Look at her. She's dead. You can help find the killer – or you can go down to the cells. Which is it?"

"Cells," Andy said contemptuously. "This lowlife's more interested in his job than justice. Shame he's obstructing" –

"I *can't* tell you anything solid. There's nothing. Nothing! No-one's ever said anything. It's only rumours..."

"So you're telling us rumours in the hope we'll leave you alone?"

"No! I don't *know* anything more. There's always rumours."

Jose was, in short, useless. He was too scared to string two thoughts together, which might testify to truthfulness – or terror of discovery – but didn't help the investigation.

"Why wouldn't you tell Selwyn about the rumours?"

"There was no *proof*," Jose wailed. "I wouldn't rock the boat for nothing. I'd never get to work on Coronal again if I did. They're a huge account and I can't afford to be offside for them. I'm on their team."

Coronal, hmm? Tessa had mentioned Coronal. Once was coincidence. Twice...might still be coincidence and likely was, since luck wasn't a major component of homicide solving.

They had another couple of go-arounds, but nothing more came out of Jose's mouth that wasn't self-justification or pleading that he knew nothing about anything. Casey dismissed him. He scuttled out like a timorous mouse.

"Ugh," she said bitterly, back in the bullpen. "Nearly an hour, and one maybe-possibly-if-we-really-squint clue."

"Huh?" Andy said.

"Coronal. Coronal was the shoot Dani had got on to – apparently it's a really big deal."

"He said huge account," Andy mused.

"They are." Carval butted in. "They're enormous."

"What are they?"

He stared at her. "You've never heard of Coronal? Lingerie, beachwear, swimwear – pretty high end. All over the magazines."

"Do I look like the sort of person who reads glossy women's magazines?" Casey snipped. Carval clamped his mouth shut on *you look like the sort of person who wears high-end sexy underwear* on the grounds that being dead was not the sort of person he wanted to be.

"I thought that was Bigfoot," Andy snickered.

"Sure I read them," O'Leary drawled as he ambled up. "They got real good tips on fur conditioner, an' how to depilate."

"How are you doing?" Casey switched the subject.

"Got through three. Went quite quick, once they stopped eyein' up Tyler. Who'd'a thunk it?"

Tyler flexed a bicep, which was enough comment for anyone.

"Anyway," the mountain went on, "nothin' much. All wanted to be on the Coronal shoot, all pretty jealous that Dani got it."

"Did they say anything about a handsy dresser?"

"Naw. Thought one or two might be skirtin' somethin', but nothin' to pull on."

"No," Tyler agreed.

"Okay. The other dresser – name of Severstal - is up later. Let's all make sure that we're pushing on the Coronal thread – but we don't know enough to ignore anything else."

The three other cops regarded her with strained patience. "We know that," Andy pointed out. She gave a *sorry* kind of shrug. Just before they dispersed, she turned back to Carval.

"You know about Coronal?"

"Gossip, mostly. I didn't shoot for them."

There was a tiny frown. "Shame. Anyway, can you – later, after we're done interviewing" –

"Intimidating," someone murmured. Casey ignored it, with ire.

"Can you tell us everything you know about Coronal? They've come up twice...I can't ignore that."

"Okay," Carval said equably.

By mid-afternoon, with only a quarter-hour break for a crammed-down lunch, after interviewing the assorted dressers, cameramen (no women, about which Casey raised a cynical eyebrow), make-up artists, set dressers, props people, and so on and so forth, Casey and Andy had learned nothing more. Coronal was a huge account, sure, but there was nothing to tie it to mischief or murder. Everyone wanted to work on it, to make their names. Everyone had heard rumours, but no-one had ever seen anything.

"Okay. Up next, Connor Yarland, photographer."

Yarland was not prepossessing. Unlike most of the others, he was sloppily dressed – Casey guessed he'd had a hot dog for lunch, judging by his t-shirt. He was thin, as was his hair, which should have been washed the night before. His eyes roamed over Casey, assessing her in a prurient, leering fashion. In Observation, Carval bridled, and shot. Instant dislike didn't stop him appreciating and capturing the contrast between Andy's clean, slim neatness and the slobbish man opposite him.

Casey was instantly annoyed by Yarland's attitude, which reminded her far too much of Selwyn's instant contempt for her appearance.

"Connor Yarland," Casey began. "Photographer."

"I'm the main photographer."

"Oh?"

"I'm the first call for all the big shoots. The clients know I can get the best out of the models – I've got the vision."

Really? Casey thought. He'd got the ego, for sure. "So who do you shoot for?"

"Coronal's the biggest account, and they're my priority. Otherwise, I do clothes shoots for all the other accounts." Coronal again, but again, it was because they were the main account.

"Only clothes shoots?"

Yarland looked at her smart, classic blazer and cream button-down with disfavour. "Fashionable clothes shoots," he replied, making it transparently clear that he didn't consider her taste in clothes acceptable or fashionable. (She wasn't fashionable. Designer gear had no place in homicide investigations – and bloodstains were hell to get out of expensive clothes.)

"But only clothes shoots?" Andy reiterated.

"Yes. Second-raters do food, or *products*." That came with contempt. "It takes a pro like me to do clothes. You need to understand people."

"Trying to be Carval?" Andy quipped. Casey let it go, though it wouldn't have been her line. When Andy took a route, there was a reason.

"I'm better than he was."

In Observation, Carval almost dropped his camera. That little toad wasn't even close to his ability. He was still doing lingerie, for Chrissake. Suddenly, he understood. Casey or Andy had a hunch, and were trying to rile this guy.

"He's the one with the global exhibitions and fame, though. Don't you want that?"

"I am famous. The girls'll do anything for me. I make them special. I could make you look good," he leered. "You're too short, but I could do it."

Uh-oh, Carval thought. That was...incendiary.

"Fortunately," Casey said icily, "cops don't need to look good. But since we're talking about looking good – how good do you think Dani looks?" She shoved the worst photo across the table.

Yarland's revulsion wasn't obviously faked. "Uhhh. That's horrible." But he studied it for a second longer. "That's Dani?"

"Sure is. Bet you couldn't make that look good," Andy bit.

Casey switched the subject. "So, you shoot the big accounts. I guess that makes you pretty popular?"

"Yeah." He smirked nastily. "I know what they like – like I said, I got the vision. So I get a say in choosing who'll fit best."

"I see. So you'd know who was testing and who you were going to shoot."

"Sure."

"We heard that Dani was a late replacement on a Coronal shoot. Isn't that rather unusual – it's a huge account, and everyone must have wanted to be on it?"

"Yeah. Previous girl – Melinda" – they'd go searching for that name just in case it was Jane Doe – "fell off the grid, partway through."

"And you didn't report it to anyone?"

"Why would I? She was an adult. Why should I go chasing after her? There were plenty of others who'd step in."

"How was Dani chosen?"

"Portfolio, shots. She looked right."

"Mm?"

"Coronal like legs – really long legs. They don't care about skin colour, in fact they like a range. Legs and someone who can be made to look like she's into more than plain vanilla. Their ads are really edgy. Takes real talent to keep it edgy and on the right side of the line. Same with dressing. You got to get that right."

"Right?"

"Gotta imply what you can't show." *Ugh*, Casey thought.

"And Melinda never turned up?"

"Nope. Dumb of her. If she comes back, no-one'll use her. Unreliable."

"Okay. What about the other big accounts?"

Yarland ran through the other requirements, but nothing much more arrived. He'd last seen Dani on the Coronal shoot.

"Has anyone else gone missing when they should have been on a big shoot?"

"No. But people are always moving around."

"Why?"

"Money, fame, big names..." he said cynically. "Every model wants to be famous. Most of them want to be actresses."

"Mm."

"How far would a model go to get on the big accounts?" Andy asked.

"How d'you mean?"

"Well, you said you'd got influence. I'd have thought they might try influencing you."

"Sure they do."

"What if you heard someone was getting too handsy?"

"Not my problem. I shoot them. If they want more, that's up to them."

"Take them up on it?"

"It's no crime when they're asking."

The unpleasant gleam flickered through his eyes again. Both cops wondered exactly how much so-called asking was involved. Power imbalances were no stranger to either of them. Casey had a fast, sharp memory of Marcol trying it on at the Academy: *I've got contacts. Better be nice.* She'd told him to fuck off, in precisely those words. Andy's tension showed her that he was reliving a vicious memory of his own.

"Did Dani try influencing you?"

"No more than anyone else."

"Okay. Thank you for your time. If you think of anything, let us know."

Yarland was politely escorted out.

"Nasty piece of work," Andy noted. "Saw a few like him before."

"All ego and no empathy. But nothing there to prove anything. Being a greasy lech isn't a crime."

"Should be."

"Yeah. Anyway, let's get someone to start looking for a Melinda something in Missing Persons."

"You really think" –

"Yeah, I do. Same body type, all legs...it's a good shot compared to the nothing we got now. Let's take it."

She hauled in the nearest uniform and explained. He raced off to get going, no doubt speeded by Casey's ...um...*emphatic* instruction. She didn't tolerate slow or sloppy. It didn't make her liked, but she didn't care about that, as long as she was respected – and obeyed. The fact that she had no rank allowing her to give orders didn't affect that in the slightest.

"I think we should take a look at some Coronal shots. Don't remember any in Dani's portfolio, do you?"

"No – that's weird. You'd think she'd have them right at the top, if it's that important."

Another uniform was briskly summoned and instructed to obtain as many Coronal shots from Stardance as he could. He jumped to, though Casey thought that the way his eyes lit up indicated a considerable desire to go stare at models rather than any terror of her. She supposed that that was a nice change, though not one she wanted to happen often.

"Last one," she said, after a truncated break. "Severstal. Dresser."

"Rumours," Andy hummed. "No smoke without fire."

"Let's not make assumptions here. Open mind. No-one's mentioned a name."

Andy grinned at her. "Sure. Glad he's last. That Yarland – I want a shower."

"Me too. My skin itches."

Kyle Severstal was nothing like they expected. He was...pretty. Boyish face, blond, artfully arranged hair, designer clothes. He looked like a model himself, until they got to the ragged, bitten nails.

He was also pretty unpleasant. It wasn't unusual for persons of interest to be scared, annoyed or both, but Severstal was just plain angry.

"Why am I here?" he opened. His pretty face wasn't nearly as pretty when it was contorted with anger. Anger didn't faze either Casey or Andy.

"Daniela Petrovich was murdered," Casey grated. "This is a murder investigation and you are being interviewed as a possible witness."

"Never heard of her."

"Really? So you never heard of a girl who you actually dressed for the Coronal shoots?" *Liar* hung over the Formica table.

"I never listen to the names. They're all the same. Dress them, send them out. They're interchangeable. All that matters is who the shoot's for."

Casey pushed a photo of Dani – before she got dead – across the table. "Maybe you'll recognise the face," she rapped.

Severstal flicked a bored glance at the photo. "Yeah, so? One of many. Nothing memorable about her."

"Is this more memorable?" The post-mortem photo slid forward. Severstal jerked. "That's not so pretty, is it?" Another jerk. "Do you remember her *now*?"

"Yeah," he dragged out. "Yeah. She was a real princess about getting dressed." That didn't sound like a compliment. "I knew what the shoot needed, and that precious little snowflake thought she knew better. Bitched about it non-stop, like she had any say."

The cops exchanged glances. Those rumours were suddenly sounding pretty well-founded – on this guy.

"What was she upset about?"

"Coronal likes edgy. So they want tits, lots of legs. She didn't like having her tits plumped." Casey translated that as *felt up*. "Didn't wanna show it off. Too bad. That's what they pay for." He smiled unkindly. "Didn't stop her acting it up for the cameras on set, though. She loved that."

Or she was a damn good actor, Carval thought in Observation. He wondered why Severstal wasn't modelling, though. His camera liked him, unlike Carval, who'd pegged him accurately as a control-freak of the bitchiest kind within half a second.

"When did you last see her?"

"When she walked out of the changing room after the Coronal shoot. No loss. Snowflakes like that are more trouble than they're worth."

"You didn't like her."

"I don't like anyone making life difficult."

"Who else didn't like her?"

"No idea. Why would I care?"

They went around a few more loops, but pretty-boy Kyle couldn't have cared less about Dani or her death. Everything came back to how difficult she'd made his life, and they couldn't crack his sulky self-absorption. Eventually, they let him go.

CHAPTER NINE

The team, plus Carval, who hadn't bothered asking permission and didn't intend to seek forgiveness either, convened in a handy conference room to discuss the full suite of interviews.

"Waaallll, that was a waste of a day," O'Leary grumbled. "One possibility an' that was that."

"Just 'cause they admired me not you."

"'S okay for you. I coulda swum outta the room, there was so much drool on the floor. Ugh."

"Enough," Casey said wearily. They were already an hour and more past shift end, and she was tired from the egos and unpleasantness. Too many leers never improved her day. She wished Carval weren't shooting from the corner, because the last thing she needed, or wanted, was reminders of photographers. "Tyler, stop baiting Bigfoot or take it on to the mats and come back when you've worked it out."

Both men blinked at her rebuke.

"Now, what was this one possibility?"

"One girl. Cassandra. Flat out jealous she wasn't picked for Coronal. Said it was 'cause she wouldn't play nice with the dressers and photographers when Dani did."

"Yeah?"

"Yeah," O'Leary took up the tale. "Said the others were always makin' up to the main men, an' it wasn't fair. She was real big on fair."

"Weird," Andy chipped in. "I didn't get the impression that Dani was making up to the dresser."

"Or the photographer."

"Could it be that simple? Rivalry?" Andy mused.

"Could be. D'you wanna bring her back in?" Tyler looked like he wanted a go-around.

"Not yet. Let's check out her alibi, and put some of this in order first. I'm not feeling jealous rivalry here – and what about Jane Doe?"

"Why not? Plenty of it around." O'Leary was definite.

"Drugged, shot and beaten? It's pretty hard-core for jealous rivalry. Strangled by a scarf, I'd get – or stabbed with a mascara wand. Not this."

"Put like that..." Andy agreed.

"More likely she'd sabotage her somehow," Carval said from the corner. "Times altered, messages not passed on, itching powder in her lip-gloss."

"Kidding."

"No, I really saw that done."

"Wow."

"So you're saying she'd be mean but not murderous?" Casey clarified.

"Yeah, most likely. It's bitchy."

"Okay. So possible, but not likely. Let's not rule it out."

"What about your guys?" Tyler asked.

"Mostly useless. Two I want a better look at."

"Why?"

"I didn't like them and I'm mean like that," she flipped. The men merely waited. "Because they were key to Coronal shoots."

"So?"

"So Coronal's popping up everywhere I look and it's the only connection I've got between Dani and anything at all."

"What about that Joe guy?" O'Leary queried.

"Useless. Scared in case his girlfriend got a taste for the big time that he couldn't afford."

There was a trepidatious tap on the door.

"Yeah?"

A uniform sidled in. "Detective, I went through Missing Persons like you asked, and I got a hit on a Melinda."

Casey beamed. "Great. Pull the details and get them in here."

"Here," proffered the uniform, handing over a slim file.

"Good work," she said, and opened it up. The team crowded around her.

"Waaallll, ain't that just peachy," O'Leary drawled. "All-American girl, an' don't she just look the same type as Dani?"

"Yeah. Right. Melinda Carnwath. Twenty-three. Reported missing by her ex-boyfriend about six weeks ago. Mm. Jane Doe's about three weeks dead. That's about the same time gap as Dani. Let's get CSU on to this overnight to try and tie Melinda up to our Jane Doe. Finally, we caught a break."

"Sure did."

"Okay. We'll get CSU going, fill in the board, and then we're done for the day. We're two hours past shift end already."

She marched out purposefully. Behind her, Andy held O'Leary back for a second, stretching to whisper something in his ear.

**

"Come for a beer," O'Leary suggested to Carval after all the interesting happenings, such as interrogations and the like, had finished. It didn't sound like a suggestion to him, so he   reluctantly parked the idea of downloading his camera and then sharing take-out with Casey. "Me 'n' Tyler want a chat."

"Do you?" he challenged. "This isn't another intimidation party, is it? Because I thought you were past that and I'm so over it."

"Naw. No intimidation. Just beer 'n' a chat."

"I guess that means the Abbey," Carval sighed. "Now?"

"Give us a few minutes to pack up, an' now, 'less we catch a break. Iffen that happens, I'll holler."

Carval wandered off to a handy chair to consider what O'Leary's game might be this time. His short experience of the NYPD's mobile mountain didn't exactly fill him with confidence, but he'd thought that they were pretty square with each other after that first case. On the other hand, Casey'd been a little off with him, and Andy had a problem with him that Carval surely didn't get.

He shrugged it all off, since there was no point speculating. If he'd really screwed up, he'd have known about it in seconds – likely looking up from the floor with broken limbs. The team weren't shy about making their feelings known.

**

"So what's this all about, then?" Carval asked, settled with beer in the Abbey.

"Andy."

"You're actually going to tell me something? Thought you were on the "we don't know you" kick."

"We had a chat. Andy okayed it."

"So why's he not here explaining why he's pissed at me when I've done nothing to be pissed about?"

"Just listen," O'Leary said. Carval bridled.

"He knows it ain't what you do or did, but he don't like the memories, an' this case is bringing them back. So mebbe if you watch your words for a while..."

"And what about Andy, huh? He's the one making trouble. Doesn't he have to watch his words, or is that just me?"

"We'll deal with him. Like earlier when Tyler calmed him down."

"That's it?"

"That's all you need to know 'bout dealin' with it. You leave it be. We'll handle it."

"And where's Casey in all of this?"

"Not interfering."

"Not interfering or not informed?"

How amazing, Carval thought. Tectonic plates could cringe.

"Not informed. Waaallll...we told her she should tell you, an' she said it was up to Andy what he told. But she don't know we're here."

"Really? 'Cause she told me he'd seen some bad shit in Narcotics, and it wasn't personal."

O'Leary cringed again. Before he could speak, Tyler did, leaning forward aggressively.

"Rest of it wasn't her story to tell. Sure there's more, and if you button your lip and listen we'll fill you in a little more. We're only telling you 'cause Andy said it was okay, so don't get pissed because Casey didn't say squat. None of us talk about stuff. Nobody else's business. Got it?"

Carval met his eyes squarely. "Got it. Don't have to like it."

"Up to you. But for my money, someone who doesn't respect privacy doesn't belong."

Ow. That was a raking down if ever he'd heard one. Even the amiable O'Leary was nodding sternly.

"We don't blab our business."

"I remember," Carval said, more placatory than an instant before. "You don't know me."

"We know you better now. You did good when Casey got beat up. 'S why we're talkin' to you. So don't mess up 'bout this, 'cause Casey'll stick by the team."

"That sounds like a threat."

"Naw," O'Leary drawled. "'T ain't a threat. 'S a fact."

Carval hadn't doubted that for a minute. He knew exactly how tight the team was: he reinforced his knowledge with every shot of them. He tipped down the last of his beer. "Want another?" he asked, and they all heard the apology and acceptance of their point within the offer.

Further beer supplied, the normally taciturn Tyler continued as point man.

"Andy's parents died. Went to live with some uncle. Didn't go so good. Ran away, lived on the streets and in shelters. Saw some seriously bad shit before he was a cop. Street girls. Pretty when they started. Thought they'd be modelling. All ended up ugly dead."

Carval stared. "Just like these girls," he said quietly. "I get it now." He pulled on his beer bottle.

"Yeah. But you took photos of pretty girls – no-one thinks you did anything, not even Andy," Tyler said quickly – "we don't, or you wouldn't be here – and Andy remembers all the pretty girls with their portfolios, thinking they'd be models and ending up drugged and dead. Case is just the same. Like we said, bad shit."

The men were quiet, for a while, until talk turned to the much easier matter of sport. Emotions weren't for cops.

***

Halfway through the next morning, CSU's miracle magic-workers had come through. Jane Doe was indeed Melinda Carnwath. Even better, there was some basic information in the Missing Persons report.

"Waall, waall, waall. Lookee here," O'Leary said happily. "Boyfriend said she worked at Stardance. Hoo boy."

Casey grinned viciously. "Better still, I got a cleaned-up photo too, and it looks just like the one in the file. Shame we don't need it any more." The nasty smile widened. "Shall we have some fun, Bigfoot?"

"I do like me some innocent fun," he rumbled. "I'm guessing you don't mean Parcheesi, though?"

"How about some nice terrorising?"

"Sounds good to me. We gonna terrorise that agency-man?"

"We sure are. In here, so you fit through the door and don't collapse the chair."

"Don't guess that fallin' on my butt would give the right impression."

"Nope."

Selwyn was summoned, and agreed – no doubt remembering Casey's scalpel-sharp evisceration of a few days ago – to arrive forthwith.

***

"Mr Selwyn. Thank you for coming in."

Selwyn didn't look as if it was a treat to be there. He regarded O'Leary as if he were Grendel: looming and ready to attack. He couldn't meet Casey's eyes at all.

"We want to talk to you about Melinda Carnwath."

"Melli? I haven't seen her for…um…two months? She stopped testing."

"Did you try to find out why?"

He stared, astonished. "Why would I?" Obviously that had never occurred to him.

"She dropped out of a Coronal shoot. We understand that's the biggest shoot going, and everybody wanted in on it. Didn't you think it was odd that she would miss it, or drop out part way through?"

From the blank expression on his face, he hadn't. Casey's opinion of Selwyn dropped another notch, passing through the earth's core on its way to the Indian Ocean.

"Is this Melinda Carnwath?" O'Leary growled, sliding their CSU mock-up of Jane Doe across the table.

"Yes," he agreed. "Why" –

Casey watched as ghastly knowledge slid across his face.

"Oh God. She's dead, isn't she?"

"Yes."

To give him some – limited – credit, Selwyn was genuinely shocked and even unhappy at the news.

"Tell us about her?" Casey asked.

"She was the quintessential all-American girl. Tall, blonde, legs to Delaware. Preppy, you know. But she tried out for the Coronal shoot. I guess she was wanting to broaden her portfolio, but that's not my problem."

"If she was that preppy, why'd she want to go for Coronal? I thought they were edgy."

"Right dress and make-up, you can make a teddy bear look edgy. We'd seen what they wanted from other shoots, and we could make her look right."

"Others?" Casey asked.

"Oh, we only do their New York shoots. They use other agencies in other areas, but they want the same theme across all the shoots. So we look at what the earlier ones did."

Casey made a note. "Is that unusual?"

"Not really. They might be a huge account but they're as hot as anyone on keeping costs down. They don't want to pay the travel/accommodation for the whole shebang."

"But – Yarland said he was their main man."

"Photographers, you know? Go where they want, when they want. No idea where he was before us, or even whether he shot for Coronal before he came here. Yarland's freelance, but he's stuck around for six months or so, and the clients love him."

"What about the rest of you?" O'Leary rapped. They'd noticed the evasion: Selwyn hadn't mentioned co-workers. That was always suspicious.

"He's an acquired taste. Likes a pretty edgy atmosphere, and he likes to talk a lot. Some of the models don't much appreciate his conversation."

"Don't you clamp down on that?"

"He's talking them into the scene. He doesn't touch. Anyone touching is fired."

Casey and O'Leary exchanged a cynical look. "How long have the dressers been with you – Jose and Kyle?"

"Jose, about the same as Yarland. Kyle, a little longer, maybe seven, eight months."

"Don't stay long."

"They all move around. Wherever they think'll get them more work, faster, or awards. Modelling's not for the faint-hearted. They're all ambitious."

"Any complaints?"

"No. Kyle's a bitch, but no-one's complained."

"I see. Thank you."

"Can I go?"

"One last question." Selwyn's narrow shoulders drooped. "Are there any other girls who've suddenly dropped out without a word? Not just ones who've worked on Coronal, anyone?"

He stared at the table, and then around the room, frantically thinking. All his contemptuous confidence and dislike of the non-beautiful people had fled when he entered, and now he was only a thin, scared little man, in deep water without a lifejacket.

"Maybe," he offered.

"We'll want names."

"Yes. Um...Angelita Herrados. Callie Donbass." His eyes skittered away from Casey's dispassionate gaze. "Valetta Merguado." He shook his head. "I can't think of any others. Models are always moving on."

"Okay. Can you send us their portfolios and details?"

"Are they dead?"

"I don't know."

"Then...I need to see a warrant. I can't give their information out without a warrant."

"We'll get one."

"I'll get it all ready for you," he stuttered desperately, "but I can't give you it without the warrant."

Casey muttered under her breath, but she couldn't criticise Selwyn for that. "Is there anything else we should know?"

"I don't know."

"If you think of anything – anything at all – tell us." Her face was cold. Stardance were up to their necks in whatever was going on, and Selwyn owned Stardance.

"Yes. Of course. Of course I will."

"Thank you."

Selwyn outright fled.

"Let's work out where we are," Casey said. Strangely, O'Leary was scowling. "What?"

"You didn't let me terrorise him."

"He was already terrorised. He looked at you like you were an axe murderer waiting to chop him in half. We want him to talk, not faint."

"Still not fair."

"Oh, shut up, Bigfoot. You'll get more chances. Stop messing with me and let's go see what more we've got. I'm not liking this timing or the way they all moved around every ten minutes."

"You need to drink a coffee."

"I *always* need to drink another coffee." She grinned up at her partner. "You won't like me when I'm decaffeinated."

They hit the break room, to be joined by the others.

"Anything new?" Andy asked.

"I got a whole series of shots," Carval enthused, appearing out of nowhere as they exited with their drinks.

"On the case."

Clearly Andy wasn't exactly cool with Carval yet.

Casey, ignoring Andy's tone, finished scrawling on the board. "There. Everything we've got mentions Stardance or Coronal or both."

"'T ain't enough. Coronal was their big account. Ain't surprisin' they all wanted a piece of it."

"Every model wanted in on it," Tyler added.

"Everyone else wanted to be working on it, too," Andy reminded them.

"Yeah, but these guys actually were."

"So why ain't they dead like the models?"

"You thinking someone's looking to make space?"

"Could be. Can't rule it out. Ambition's a big motive."

"Surely is," O'Leary drawled.

"That's an interesting line," Casey agreed. "So we got two lines now: someone – more than one – looking to be the stars; and" –

"And the nastier one," Andy said flatly. Tyler lurked not far away from him. Carval took a surreptitious shot of the instant of reassurance.

"Yeah."

Nobody needed to elaborate on the nastier one. It had been in their minds since moment one.

"Still most likely. Beaten up girls, dead, recent drugs."

A chill fell around the group. Carval, shooting from a corner, noted the harder faces, an impression of old pain, the distaste. Indefinably, they were collectively older, bruised by life.

And then Casey shook her head and they were themselves again. "Right," she said briskly. "There's another line to close off. Sure, they look similar, but there's always coincidence. Melinda had a boyfriend. We'd better make sure it wasn't him."

"You don't really think that." Andy stared bleakly at her.

"No. But I'm not taking chances, either. We don't know that her boyfriend wasn't dealing." She grinned. "Andy, Tyler? It's your turn to interview. Can't let me and Bigfoot have all the fun, can we?"

"Nope. Where's that file?"

"Here." She handed it over, and turned to O'Leary. "I want to work out the timings. When the girls joined, when the other ones did, when heroin happened" –

"That's vague."

"Yeah, but it's all a picture – when they dropped out. C'mon. Let's go draw pictures."

"Just as well you got a ruler."

"Uh?"

"You can't draw. I've seen you tryin'. Seen better down in the day care centre."

Casey made a rude noise, and picked up some wide paper, coloured pens and a ruler. "Like you're any better."

"Bigfoots don't draw."

"Cave art?"

"You got it," he grinned, unbreakably amiable. "Gotta have somethin' on the walls. Gets borin' otherwise."

Casey conceded the point. "C'mon, then. Let's do this." Quiet fell, broken by occasional rumbling.

Carval watched the two mismatched pairs and took a few more shots: trying to capture the odd similarity in O'Leary and Tyler's positions: both subtly protective and encompassing. Of course, O'Leary's bulk couldn't be anything else other than encompassing, but somehow there seemed to be a little more to it. Tyler's posture was entirely explained by the previous night's discussion.

He sat back and thought. Mostly, he thought that Casey was oddly off-beat where all those models were concerned. That was a touch insulting. If he'd wanted models, he'd have got them, he thought with unconscious (but justified) arrogance. He didn't want models, he wanted Casey. More pertinently, he wanted Casey to open up: talk about something that wasn't the case. A memory of her reaction to his careless mention of her mother sneaked into his head. He'd wondered if there were something more, but, not wanting to hurt her or pry – and certainly having no opening to ask – he'd not pursued it.

He had another sudden recollection: a night in the Abbey when she'd upped and left unexpectedly, and the others had made sure he couldn't enquire. Tyler saying *she's dealing with some shit.* But that couldn't be her mother, because she had passed. So what was she dealing with?

He waved a goodbye to the team, and left. Somewhere in his photos, he might have some more information: a look, or an expression.

He'd work out what lay beneath the odd reactions, and...and then they'd have a little more than a casual, fun affair.

CHAPTER TEN

"Detective Clement?"

Casey looked up from her pristine desk. "Yeah?" she said coolly.

The large officer regarded her nervously. "Um...I found a Jane Doe that matches your criteria."

"Show me." Her momentary irritation at being interrupted dissipated immediately.

He tapped on the keyboard, fingers tremulous – Casey's badass reputation, and ability to deal with people wasting her time, were well-known in the Thirty-Sixth – and a cold case came up. Casey scrolled through swiftly, analysing. The officer became more nervous the longer she took. Finally, she sat back.

"Good work. Looks like a match."

He sagged with relief.

"Can you pull the file, please." Despite the cool courtesy, it was an order expecting immediate compliance. He scuttled off and returned a few minutes later with the file.

"Thanks," she said absently, already sinking into the details. "If you find any more, let us know asap." The officer departed, and Casey absorbed herself.

Fifteen minutes later, she looked unhappily up at O'Leary. "Got another one," she said.

"Three? That ain't good."

"No. And worse, it's one of ours."

"Ours? We don't got no open Jane Does."

"Not us the team, us the Thirty-Sixth. It's Feggetter's."

"Oh. That really ain't good."

It wasn't. It wasn't good for bullpen harmony for Casey's team to be finding clues on other people's cases. She sighed heavily, knowing that she'd have to manage the information as if it were a primed grenade to avoid offending Feggetter. There was no chance that she could avoid Kent with this latest discovery, and even worse...

"And this is the third. Kent isn't going to like that. Three the same..."

"Lookin' at a serial, ain't we?"

"Yeah, unless Tyler and Andy come back with something from Melinda's boyfriend. And that likely means profiler. Ugh," she said gloomily.

Ugh was right. Profilers might spot things that the team really didn't want spotted, and worse than that, might tell Kent about them. The team did not need to have Kent looking too carefully at them. He might decide to discuss matters with them, or try to fix them. They could fix themselves, thank you very much. Kent was far better left in blissful ignorance.

Casey shuffled unwillingly off to Kent's office – she led the team, she got to beard Kent in his den – and tapped.

"Sir, may I talk to you about the model case?"

"Yes." Kent raised his eyes from his desk. "What is it?"

She collected herself to deliver the brisk efficiency for which she was renowned. "Fremont – uniform - picked up a third similar murder in the cold cases."

Kent nodded, not only because she'd given credit where due.

"Firstly, it was Feggetter's case, originally. If you approve, sir, I'd like to take it up because it matches with my two. More efficient to have them all together. Secondly, though, we have three cases, spread over approximately three months, and I suspect that this may indicate a serial, although we're not discounting other options. If that's the case" – she grimaced – "then we might need to consider whether – if we find or have another – a profiler should be brought in."

Kent frowned in return. He didn't like outsiders much, and FBI outsiders less than that. At least it wasn't Homeland Security, he supposed.

"And thirdly, if we find any more from other precincts, would you support bringing them into my team, sir?"

"Do you expect to find more?"

"Not from cold cases or Missing Persons. That's all been reviewed."

Kent acquired a look of mild approval.

"New ones, then."

It was Casey's turn to nod. She stood at parade rest and waited. Kent didn't appreciate his considerations being interrupted.

"Okay, Clement. You may take on Feggetter's case. You can inform him that I have ordered it."

That was helpful.

"We'll leave the profiler for now, but I will keep it under review. If there is a fourth case, we will find one."

"Yes sir. Thank you, sir."

"Dismissed."

Casey scooted out, pretty happy with the outcome: that was to say, she had escaped alive.

"Okay, guys, we got the case. And we don't get a profiler, so we're two for two." She smiled, got herself a coffee, and buried her dark head in Feggetter's file. Half an hour later, she re-emerged, still smiling.

"It's good, and we can build on it. I'll go talk to Feggetter as soon as we've got some lunch. When are Tyler and Andy due back?"

"Dunno. When they're done, I guess."

Lunch done, Casey strode across the bullpen towards Detective Feggetter: a stocky, dark haired man who claimed Scottish ancestry and had, therefore, attempted to inflict Robert Burns and haggis on anyone who couldn't run away fast enough on Burns Night. He regarded her warily.

"Hey," she said.

"Hi." Suspicion laced his greeting.

"You know we've got two dead models?"

"Yeah. But I got plenty of work of my own to do." He gestured to his desk, which had a tidy pile of papers on one side and a file on which he was clearly working in the middle.

"Yep. I wanna take some of the work away." He gaped. "Your cold case – Carissa Ndbele – matches up with our models. Kent ordered me and my team to take it on because of the similarities, but can you give me a heads-up?"

Feggetter's gape snapped shut. "You're taking *my* case away?"

"No, Kent's consolidated it with the two similar cases that I've already got." She tried a smile. It didn't really help. "Easier for us to do the work on all three at once rather than both of us doing it separately." She tried a different tack. "Not like we'll be allowed any overtime for it."

That had a slightly better effect. "Guess not," Feggetter grudged. "Okay. What do you want from me?"

"Just – anything that isn't in the file? Feelings, or anything that didn't have any evidence but you thought about?"

"Nah. She broke up with her boyfriend, but we looked into him pretty thoroughly and there was nothing there."

"And was she at Stardance?"

"Yeah, but she'd left a few weeks before and that pompous prick knew nothing."

"He sure is," Casey said with venom.

Suddenly Feggetter was a lot friendlier. "You too? Said she'd left for another agency, and looked at me like I was a gorilla 'cause I wasn't some heroin-chic pretty boy."

Feggetter wasn't bad looking, in a stocky sort of way.

"Can you imagine what he thought when he saw Bigfoot?" Casey sniggered.

"Surprised he survived the sight."

"Me too." Casey bared her teeth in a not-smile. "He never mentioned your visit to me."

"He was so far up his own ass he could eat his dinner twice. I reckon he forgot me as soon as I was out of the door – he barely remembered Carissa, and she'd only been gone three weeks. That was nearly three months ago."

"He remembers me," Casey growled.

Feggetter, now thoroughly comfortable with Casey taking the cold case away, bared his own teeth. "Yeah? Good. Would be nice if it was him. So anyway, I moved on to her new shop and they said she'd just stopped turning up. Gave me her portfolio after I waved a warrant at them, and the trail went cold. Kent told me to move on after a while. Is Selwyn looking likely?"

"If he is, we'll all get a go, okay?"

"Sounds good to me. Let me know if there's anything more you wanna talk through."

"Thanks."

Casey whisked back to her own desk congratulating herself on managing that conversation without any head-butting or territory-marking. Taking someone's case – even a cold one – didn't usually go well.

"We got it. Feggetter's okay with us."

"He likes me anyway," O'Leary pointed out.

"Or he's not dumb enough to get on the wrong side of you."

"Waalll, mebbe so. Don't make no nevermind to me."

"Lose the hayseed, and let's have a look at this. Feggetter was all over the boyfriend."

They reread the file and Feggetter's witness notes.

"Not surprised," O'Leary mused. "They'd broken up, couple of weeks earlier."

"How'd you know that?" came Andy's tenor from behind them.

"Andy? We were talking about Feggetter's case – uniform picked it up as a cold case while you were out looking at Melinda's boyfriend."

"Melinda had ditched her boyfriend a couple of weeks earlier too."

The four cops stared at each other.

"An' Dani din't have one," O'Leary reminded everyone.

"So when each of them were shooting on Coronal they didn't have a boyfriend?"

"Nobody to notice straight away."

"Waaallll, ain't that int'restin'?" The mountain shrugged. "Where'd you put that pretty coloured time-line?"

"Thought you'd had enough multi-colouring for the month," Andy

86

teased.

"I missed the colours," Casey flashed back, "and none of you volunteered to be face-painted. My inner child" – there was a derisive squawk – "needed it."

"I told you, you should come to calligraphy class with me."

"I'd rather stick pins in my eyes. Ugh."

Andy merely smiled.

"Anyway, how did Melinda's boyfriend go?"

"Punching above his weight," Tyler said. "Didn't approve of the Coronal shoot. Ditched on the spot. Wasn't impressed. Didn't get a second chance."

"He tried to tell he didn't like her posing for shots in sexy underwear," Andy expanded. "She told him to get lost, not nicely, and when he tried to make it up she told him she wasn't interested."

"But he reported it?"

"Yeah. Wanted to get back together, couldn't even get a brush off, then she wasn't at home anytime he called. Got worried."

"Claims an alibi."

"New girlfriend?" Casey asked cynically.

"Naw. Night shifts. We'll check."

"That won't prove anything. We don't have an accurate time of death or even a certain date. We've only got when she was found and McDonald's best estimate." She thought for a moment. "You two do what you can with him. I'll get CSU on Feggetter's one."

"Ain't it in the file?"

"Yeah, but I want that hair test for heroin done, and I want them to try and match it to Melinda and Dani."

She put in a brisk call to CSU, and then looked around in the manner of a stooping falcon. Her eye fell upon her prey.

"Larson!" she called. He whisked over. "You get those Coronal shots?"

"Yes."

"Give them here, then," she said impatiently. He handed them over and hurriedly retreated. Casey dismissed him from her attention.

"Wow."

"Edgy ain't the word."

Andy's face was tight and his lips pinched hard. Tyler flicked an unimpressed glance over the shots, and didn't waste his limited stock of words on comment. He didn't need to.

"That's..." She couldn't find a word. They weren't *actually* indecent. But they implied...eurgh.

"Looks like it oughta be in an adult magazine," O'Leary disapproved.

Casey stared at the photos, with Andy.

"They're cruel," Andy said.

"Huh?"

"Look at them. They're not just edgy, they're cruel. She's an object." Casey's stare transferred to Andy's set expression. "Ask your boy," he bit. "Bet he agrees."

"Good idea." She tapped her phone.

"Carval."

"Hey. Wanna come over and look at these Coronal shots? Andy thinks your expert opinion" – she smiled, and knew he could hear it – "would be interesting."

"*Andy* suggested it?"

"Yep."

"Okay."

Casey heard the slight relief in Carval's voice, and was herself relieved. She didn't want the tension between Carval and Andy to continue any longer.

"I'll be over in a little while."

"See you then."

She turned to the case, and began to try to put together further timings, all the while tapping her fingers until CSU should come through. After that, she looked at Feggetter's good work round social media. Unlike Dani, Carissa had shared.

"Carissa's mentioned a bar up on the Upper East Side – Felice 83."

"Pretty plush," O'Leary offered.

"Did we get anything from Dani's location data?"

"Still looking. Techs are overloaded."

Nothing new there, then.

"What about Melinda?"

"No-one's looked yet."

"Okay, I'll take that till CSU come through."

Melinda Carnwath, she typed into Facebook – and up came the public page – pages, and pages, and pages. Melinda had put a lot on Facebook – and the final entry, unusually badly spelled (maybe typed in a hurry? she wondered), was gold. *Of to a bar uptown. Van. Culd b big brake. Cd use wine. Cornal fab.*

She scrawled *Van* down and then skimmed through the previous few days' entries. All of it was about how Coronal would kick-start Melinda's career as a supermodel: how much she wanted to be picked, her dress, her make-up, her hairstyle: how she was making herself look exactly like the shoot would want; and then the delight of winning the gig. Desperation, to Casey's cynical eyes, permeated every entry. She pulled up a photo of Melinda. Tall and beautiful – and twenty-four. Getting older. A pack of fresh-faced newbies nipping at her heels. No wonder she was desperate – and desperate models would be especially susceptible to being given a break.

The others weren't quite as old – relatively speaking – even though Dani was already twenty-two. So it couldn't just be that. She pushed it to the back of her mind and tapped *Van* into Google. Nothing helpful came up. She leaned back in her chair, and pondered.

She was deep in thought when her phone rang.

"Clement."

"Is that Katrina Clement?" The voice and number were unfamiliar.

"Yes."

"Miss Clement, this is Officer Marlson of the Port Authority Police Department at JFK. We've taken a David Clement into custody."

"I'm sorry?"

"David Clement has been taken into custody for drunk and disorderly behaviour to airline staff and attempting to assault a police officer. You're listed as the emergency contact."

The colour drained from her face. That was a whole new level of problem.

"We'll release him to you, but he will be charged with disorderly conduct."

"Thank you," she managed. "I'll be there as soon as I can."

She swiped the phone off and looked around her team. "Guys, I got a problem." She winced. The team closed up around her desk. "Dad's been arrested at JFK. I've got to go get him." She glanced at her watch. "It's only an hour till we're off shift. Can" – she winced again, because she'd never asked this and she'd hoped that she would never have to – "you cover for me? Say I've gone to interview Carissa's boyfriend? Something?"

"Sure we will," O'Leary confirmed, echoed by the other two. "Shouldn't be an issue."

She hightailed it out of the precinct. Behind her, O'Leary gathered the other two. "I'll give her the download tomorrow on what we do tonight. She'll be in hours early."

"'Kay."

They set to. She'd do the same for them, after all.

***

Carval arrived in the precinct to look at the Coronal shots, and indeed to see if he could collect Casey, or the whole team if that was the way it fell out, for beer or food or both.

"Hey," he bounced in, and only then realised that Casey's desk was clear and her jacket missing. "Where's" –

"Shh!" O'Leary whispered. "She's gone to interview Carissa's boyfriend," he said more loudly.

"But..."

"Shut *up!*"

Carval suddenly noticed the ominous figure of Kent looming behind O'Leary, and, a moment too late, clamped his mouth shut on his query. "So where are these shots Andy wanted me to look at?" he said, trying to recover the situation.

"Here," Andy said, ghosting up.

"Precisely what are you doing?" Kent enquired. His eyes fell on the shots. "Ugh. At least yours were nothing like that," he directed at Carval. It didn't sound like a compliment.

Carval took a good look. "No. These are technically excellent," he said dispassionately, "but they haven't got any humanity. The girl's just another prop."

"Objectified," Andy grated.

"Who took them?"

"Dunno. Larson!" O'Leary bellowed. Larson came trotting over in time to watch the mountain picking up the papers which had blown from the desk and straightening the chairs.

"Yes?"

"Who took these shots? They tell you?"

"Uh..."

"C'mon. I don't bite."

"In public," Andy whispered. "Bad for Bigfoots, that." Carval tried not to snicker, and didn't quite succeed.

"Just said their main photographer."

"That'll be that asshole Yarland, then."

"Mm. The one who thought he was better than me?"

"Is he?" O'Leary grinned.

"No. Well" – Carval made a face – "technically he might be, though these are posed so it's not the same as reality shots where you take them on the fly: he's got all the time he needs to set up his focus, lighting and lenses but I only have an instant" –

"So no, then."

"Like I said, maybe technically, but I don't really think so – but he's got no feeling for the humanity of it. None at all. She might as well be a sex doll. It's edgy, sure, but it's not...um...welcoming. Display, not a relationship."

He stopped. The three cops, and Kent, were staring at him.

"When'd you do your psychology course?" Tyler asked, not at all nicely.

"More to the point, Detectives, where is Clement?"

That was not a question they had wanted to be asked. Nor did they want to answer. O'Leary, being the one most likely to distract effectively, and because the others could hide behind him, stepped up.

"She went to interview Carissa's – the third corpse, sir – boyfriend."

"Alone? How surprising. That is not precisely usual. Especially since the expert is here."

There was a long silence. *Never admit, never explain* hung in the air.

"I see," Kent said, and stalked away, leaving fear and loathing in the bullpen behind him.

"Aw, *shit*," O'Leary emitted. "'T ain't your fault, but now we got a fuckup."

"Where *is* Casey? She's the one who called me, why's she not here?"

That was greeted by three stolidly blank faces.

"Dealing with some shit," Tyler said.

Carval's face twisted. "Don't ask?" he said bitterly. "Because you won't tell me, and she sure won't."

He marched out, leaving the others silent.

"She needs to tell him," Andy said.

"You tell her that. I tried. Coulda been talkin' to a haystack for all she took in."

"Won't go well."

"For sure."

***

Casey hurried out of the precinct and was shortly on her way to JFK. This was a whole fresh level of hell. What had her father been thinking? Well, clearly he hadn't been thinking. He'd been drunk. So drunk, he'd tried to assault someone – not just someone, a Port Authority police officer.

Far too soon, she was striding through the airport, flashing her badge to get to the holding room. She introduced herself at the desk, and tried not to show her wince at the looks of pity in the faces of the desk officers.

"Detective Clement," she said calmly.

"Better come through. He was lucky. Too drunk to hit us. If he'd connected, we'd've gone for assault."

"Catkin, Catkin. You come t' get me home?"

"Yes, Dad." She turned away, not wanting to look at the mess. His clothes were – mostly – clean. The holding room...wasn't. Whether that was her father's fault or not wasn't something she cared to contemplate.

"Do you want to take his desk appearance ticket, or will he?"

"Look at him," she said. "I'll take it. Safer that way."

The officer wrote it out and handed it to her. She tucked it away. Her father didn't notice, and wasn't grateful to have his possessions returned.

"I only wanted to go to DC and see the museum. They wouldn't let me buy a ticket. Nothing wrong with me." He was still belligerent and highly offended. "If you'd been there it would have been fine. You should've been there. Why weren't you in the airport?" And, obviously, he was still sodden drunk.

"You didn't ask me," Casey pointed out.

"Did so. Called you."

"No, you didn't." She pulled out her phone and checked. "See, no calls. I couldn't have come anyway, without requesting leave," she added, which she knew had been a huge mistake as soon as she said it.

"You shouldn't be doing that job. Should be here for me. Should've been a lawyer, not a cop." In his slurred tones Casey heard disappointment, and her gut twisted. So they had been disappointed in her choices. She blinked, and steeled herself to get her father home. She'd deal with that bombshell later. She'd suspected – but there was the proof.

"Let's get you home," she said again, through her choked throat. Her father, lost in his grievances, didn't hear the edge on her words.

At his Brooklyn apartment, she guided him upstairs, brusquely took his keys and opened the door for him after he'd fumbled for a moment, then steered him to a chair.

"Sit there," she ordered, too tired and upset to soften it, "and I'll get you some water."

"Don't want water. I'll have whiskey."

Her tight-strung temper fractured. "Fine. But I'm not staying to watch. Deal with it yourself."

She dropped the desk appearance ticket on the table, stalked out, and in a matter of minutes was back on the road to her own home, trying desperately to focus on the traffic and not think of the last three hours in any way at all. She would have gone to the precinct, but someone would rat her out to Kent, and then she'd be several miles up shit creek and heading for shit bayou without a paddle. She'd just go in early. Less noticeable.

Home was silent, and should have been soothing: her warm-toned decor, comfortable furniture, and mellow light. It wasn't, though, long-buried fear hitting the surface: the worms of doubt about how her parents had regarded her, for surely if her father was disappointed in her then her mother must have been so too? She made coffee, but for once it didn't help. She wouldn't drink: she'd just seen where that led. Still, tomorrow she'd be with her team and that would help. She firmly ignored the small voice that said *you could call Carval: he'd distract you.* He might have asked questions. She couldn't deal with questions.

CHAPTER ELEVEN

Carval left the bullpen feeling ridiculously rejected and not at all ridiculously angry. He was sick of Casey and the team still treating him like some sort of alien afterthought and never telling him anything. Whatever they said, they didn't trust him. He'd thought he'd paid his dues; he'd thought that when they'd told him about Andy it meant he was part of the team.

His annoyance intensified when he realised that he'd never previously been the slightest bit interested in his girlfriends' histories or deeper feelings. Casey should be more...well, just *more*. He'd never had to work on a relationship before, and that didn't make him happy either. She *should* need to talk to him.

He turned to the happier thought of his corkboard and the growing number of photos there, and suddenly realised that he hadn't yet taken many shots of Kent. He needed more of Kent: adding authority and age to the story.

Unfortunately, arranging his shots, plotting how best to convince Kent that he should take more shots of him, and adding new ones, didn't cure his annoyance, it only postponed it; and realising at dinner time that Casey hadn't bothered with so much as a quick text didn't improve his mood. In a small outburst of common sense, he didn't call or text her. Instead, he regarded all his photos of her, trying to find any clue to the matters she was dealing with. He failed. All he found was frustration that the damn woman couldn't even be bothered to call. Well, he wasn't going to call her either. Her turn to make a move.

***

Casey didn't sleep well. That was nothing new, but the night was worse than usual: restless and waking, plagued by her father's accusations. She sped through her abbreviated morning routine and went straight to the bullpen, where her coffee was stronger than usual to deal with the earliness of her start. She loathed mornings. It was simply that today, she loathed her thoughts and nightmares more.

Under a concealing sheet of paper was a short note from O'Leary, in his untidy, broad scrawl. They'd always assumed it was because he could only fit his hands around crayons. *I'll be in early*, it said. *Brief you then.*

Fortunately Kent was absent that morning. Unfortunately, that likely meant a meeting at 1PP, which invariably left him bad-tempered. Even more unfortunately, Casey had no good excuse to absent herself for an interview or to following up a lead. She felt guilty about the hour she'd sneaked the day before, and being at her desk early, which would more than cover that hour, wasn't helping. She just hoped that the team had managed to keep Kent well away.

She'd been there for well over an hour – four espressos' worth of intense work – when O'Leary tromped in.

"Mornin'," his bass reverberated.

"Hey." She didn't sound cheerful.

"Bad?"

"Could've been better," she tried to shut down. She absolutely could not think about her father now. She shrouded cold calm around her. "What happened?"

"You look like shit," O'Leary said flatly. "Better put another layer of make-up on before anyone else sees you. Don't want them blamin' me."

"Lend me some, then. You know I don't keep a cosmetics counter in my purse."

"Naw. That's Tyler, ain't it?"

Casey laughed, weakly. "C'mon. What happened yesterday?"

"Waal, your boy turned up like you asked" –

"Oh, hell." She turned suddenly shielded eyes on O'Leary. "And?"

"And, he wasn't too pleased that you'd run out on him." Casey cringed. "But he looked at the photos – that guy Yarland took 'em" – she nodded, she had expected that – "an' said the girl was just an object. No humanity. Technically great, but, um, no soul, I think he meant."

"Mm." She thought for a second. "That's interesting. These murders, the drugs and the sexy dresses: that's all the same feeling too."

"Feelin'? We don't do feelin's. We do evidence."

"Yeah. But the evidence right now is that the girls were drugged and dressed like dolls by whoever killed them, and here we've got a photographer who shoots them like they were dolls too. Question is, though, is he part of it or just that they've spotted them by looking at the shots?"

"How'd they look at these shots? They haven't run those ads yet."

"Back to Stardance again. All we ever run into is Stardance and Coronal."

"Yeah. Or the ex-boyfriends, mebbe. The girls might've showed 'em the shots" –

"That might have been why they broke up. Some guys might not like shots like that."

"Some girls might not like their boy bein' all possessive like that."

"Yeah."

"*Some* girls," O'Leary said meaningfully, "might talk about thin's with their boyfriends."

Casey ignored that with perfect aplomb. O'Leary dropped the point. No question that Carval would turn up at some point – especially if he called him – and then there'd be some fun. He briefly considered whether locking them in a conference room, or a cell, would be sensible, or just picking them up and banging their lips together; but then he remembered Kent's likely reaction and thought better of it. Even Bigfoots were wary of some things.

"I want CSU's heroin results," she grumbled. "If it matches it's going off to Narcotics too."

"While we're waitin', I remember that Selwyn stick-insect said Coronal did shoots in other places, with other agencies. I'm thinkin' we oughta have a look at that."

"Huh?"

"Waal...we got three. So far. An' every time we turn round it's the agency an' Coronal comin' up in conversation. So...I think we oughta make sure there ain't nothin' the same elsewhere."

"You want a profiler to play with, don't you? How're we going to do that without one?"

"We could...just see where else Coronal shot, yeah?"

Casey, little as she liked the suggestion, trusted O'Leary's instincts as much as she trusted her own. "Okay, but let's get a uniform to do it. Grunt work, for now. If we find anything...."

"I think," O'Leary said heavily, without his yokel tones, "that we're going to end up with a profiler pretty soon anyway. Might as well get something started. This don't feel good to me any way up. I think we're going to have another one, pretty soon." His huge frame shuddered. "I don't like this one, Casey."

"Me neither," she said, and patted his ham-hand, then swiftly withdrew. "But it's ours – they're ours now – and we're going to solve it."

"Yeah."

"Do you want to find a uniform or will I?"

"I c'n manage that."

"Don't scare them, okay."

"I never scare anyone," O'Leary said with massive and mendacious dignity. He did scare people, just as soon as he forgot to smile.

The morning passed. CSU's results came back, with a short cover e-mail extolling the virtues of patience, which might have been prompted by Casey's third call to them. The results were just the same, and were sent to Narcotics, just the same.

Casey, trying and failing to bury her fears in the case, kept flicking glances at her phone. Nothing came up. No-one called. Under the guise of making more coffee – it would be her eighth, but she couldn't stop chain-caffeinating – she went to the break room and stared at the screen. She ought to call her dad. Her fingers went to the speed dial, and withdrew. She put the phone on the counter, started the coffee, found the speed dial, withdrew.

She couldn't bear to call: to find him still drunk, still spitting anger and disappointment at her – if he even answered. She couldn't bear to call, and, maybe, have her call declined. She blinked, hard, and concentrated on finishing making her coffee, and didn't try to call. He, after all, hadn't called her.

One day, she thought bitterly: she'd thought that one day it would be that final, fatal, knock. She'd – well, not been prepared, but considered that likelihood. She hadn't considered that before that knock came, he'd.... Face it, Casey. *In vino, veritas.* In whiskey, the same. The truth: that he was *disappointed* in her. She blinked again, downed the coffee in one, hammered down her feelings and returned to her work, from which she didn't look up once, declined any offers of lunch, and ignored her silent phone.

O'Leary watched from a safe distance, and, after lunch had been missed, tapped out a small text. He thought that Casey could use a little cuddling, and there was a convenient candidate for that. Carval might have been pissed at Casey, but O'Leary would cure that: forcibly, if required.

***

"Clement, my office," Kent rapped, late afternoon. She complied at speed. Kent sounded furious. "Shut the door." She obeyed.

"Explain your unauthorised absence yesterday."

Silence. Casey was frantically trying to think of anything that might save her from Kent's wrath. How the hell had he found out anyway? The team had covered her.

Kent stopped speaking and fixed her with a pitch-black scowl. "You will recall that I ordered you to inform me if there were any issues which might affect your work. Did you not consider whatever removed you, without obtaining my permission to leave, to be such an issue?" His tone bit. Casey shrank.

Oh, shit.

"What was it?"

"My father was arrested, sir," she confessed miserably. "I had to go get him."

"Had to." It wasn't a question. "Why can't your mother deal with it?"

"She's dead."

Kent's mouth opened, and then snapped shut. He'd forgotten that, and the sharp remembrance chastised him. "How often has this happened?"

"It never has before, sir."

"Before." Kent's voice was as heavy as the tones of doom. "Do you mean that I haven't noticed before, or that you have never taken unauthorised absence because of your father before?"

"The second, sir."

Kent's anger diminished, but certainly hadn't departed. "I see. So this is the first time that he's been picked up drunk?"

That was a particularly nasty question. Casey shrank further. She couldn't lie – not least because she was pretty sure that, before hauling her in and over the coals, Kent had checked up – but she really, really didn't want to tell the truth about her father's state either. Her gaze skittered around Kent's office and didn't find a good solution.

"No, sir," she admitted through a choked throat. "It's not. But it's never been in working hours before."

"I'm relieved you didn't try to lie to me." So he had been checking up. What else had he been checking up on? "You should have informed me of this issue yourself." An ominous pause. "*Before* you left to bail him out."

By that point Casey had shrunk so small she could have exited Kent's office without opening the door.

"Now. Explain how long your father has been...ill."

"Five years."

"And this is the first time in which it has affected your work."

"Yes, sir."

"How are you intending to ensure that it doesn't affect your work next time?"

"He'll just have to wait until shift's over," Casey said caustically. "He won't notice anyway." Kent raised his eyebrows. "He'll be drunk. He won't remember."

"That is your solution, is it?"

"Yes," came back baldly.

"It didn't occur to you that you might request an early end to your shift, and make up the time later?"

Casey goggled at him.

"Clearly not. Nor did it occur to you that I might listen to any request for assistance. Instead you assumed that I would deny it without checking your facts. That is not how I expect a detective to behave in this precinct. Next time, you will refer to me if you are requested to collect your father in working hours. Dismissed," he snapped.

Casey crawled out, feeling approximately two inches tall.

"What was that about?"

"Yesterday. He noticed."

"Aw, shit."

Nothing more was said. Nothing more needed to be said, between the team.

Unfortunately, Carval wasn't part of the team. "What happened yesterday? You just disappeared."

"It's fine."

Casey's tone was deliberately nothing-to-see-here. Carval looked entirely dissatisfied with the comment, but she simply couldn't face that discussion. As ever, she turned to work as a guaranteed route to cover up.

"What have we got?" she asked generically.

"Nothing more than half an hour ago."

"Which was half an hour after your shifts ended, Detectives. Therefore, you should be gone. Make it so." Kent was implacable.

"Do you want to get a drink, or dinner?" Carval asked. If only she'd come out, he could find out what was wrong and help to make it better, even if that were simply a hug and some cosseting. O'Leary's text had been pretty uninformative: simply *Come by, Casey could use a pal.* When O'Leary suggested that, Carval had already learned that it was as well to obey. Besides, O'Leary was on the side of love and romance, so even if it was her turn, O'Leary had spotted an opening for him.

"No, thanks," she returned wearily. "I'm too tired. I'm just going to go home and sleep."

She was heavy-eyed and pallid, the adrenaline of the investigation and leads draining now that shift was over. Even the wisps of curls leaking from her clip seemed to have drooped.

"What's wrong?"

"Nothing." His raised eyebrows gave her the lie. "Nothing you need to worry about."

"That's it?" He stared at her. "That's all you're going to say? None of my business?" He'd be happy to provide comfort, but if she wouldn't confide, he wasn't going to be shot down. She needed to make a move here.

Casey's strained temper flared as soon as Carval's irritation showed. He had no right to be irritated. Her dad's *issues* weren't his problem and she didn't want her dad's problems interfering in their relationship. "Yep. Not your problem."

Carval stepped back, expression closing down. "I see."

"Look, this isn't your problem. Let it be. It'll fix itself in a day or two." But oh, she knew far too well that it wouldn't be fixed. It wouldn't ever be fixed, this side of a cold grave. "We're fine as we are. It's not important."

"It's not?" he bit. "So something that you're really upset about isn't important between us? Or do you mean that *I'm* not important enough to you that you want to talk to me?" Silence. "Okay. Guess I'll see you when I'm next taking shots or when you want an *expert*. Bye." He stalked off, vitriol in every movement.

"That wasn't smart," O'Leary said in a quiet sub-bass.

"Shut up. This isn't your business either."

O'Leary's raised eyebrows and focused regard said much more loudly than words that he disagreed. "Don't you pull that on me. Who covered for you?"

"Fat lot of good it did. Kent found out anyway, and ripped me a new one."

"You blamin' me? 'Cause iffen you are, you 'n' me are gonna have a long chat." His gaze was sharp. "Or you c'n get your dumb head out your dumb ass before it starts pokin' out your dumb mouth."

Casey coloured hot scarlet. "Go away. I'm going home. I don't need to listen to this, or to you."

The exceedingly rare sight of O'Leary losing his famously amiable temper would have transfixed what was left of the bullpen, if they hadn't been taking cover.

"I don't take that crap from you. I've been your pal since day one and I don't care iffen you think you ain't gonna tell me what's up, 'cause I ain't leavin' you alone till you spill the whole damn story." He placed a meaty hand on her back and pushed her out of the bullpen.

"Get your hand off me!"

"Naw." O'Leary was totally immovable as they reached his SUV. "I'm takin' you home." He glowered. "You c'n get the subway tomorrow."

Since O'Leary could have – and in the mood he was in, would have – stuffed Casey into his SUV as easily as if she were a doll, Casey begrudgingly accepted reality and climbed in; after which she turned a glacial shoulder and didn't say a single word all the way into her apartment.

O'Leary followed her in and started to make coffee with the same forced calm as might overlay a volcano before it erupted. Casey went straight to her couch and kept her back to him, fidgeting with her phone.

Shockingly loud in the tense silence, her phone rang.

"Clement," she rapped, without looking.

"Catkin? Catkin, I found a desk appearance ticket on the table for Queens County Criminal Court on December 13. I don't get it. I haven't done anything but it says I was drunk and disorderly in JFK. I haven't been to that airport for months. How could I have a ticket? What do I do about it?"

Casey didn't say anything for a moment. O'Leary, sensing the change in the atmosphere, turned around in time to gain the full benefit of her frozen, pallid face.

"Dad," she started. O'Leary covered the floor in two huge steps and openly listened in. "You...I was called to pick you up from the Port Authority Police at JFK yesterday." She gulped.

"What?"

"You were arrested at JFK yesterday."

"No..."

"Yes."

"But...what did I do?"

"You got into a loud argument with the airline staff and then took a swing at the cop who tried to break it up," she said flatly. There was no way to shade the truth – and she didn't want to. He needed to know that he was in real trouble.

"I did what?"

"Argued with the desk staff and tried to slug a cop."

"No. I don't do that."

Casey only just stopped herself saying *you don't do that sober. You did do it drunk.* From O'Leary's sudden start, he'd heard it anyway.

"If you really think that, we can request the CCTV. Do you remember anything about yesterday?"

There was a horrible, protracted silence. "No."

"Nothing at all? I can't request CCTV without a really good reason – and you'd need to get a lawyer anyway, to help you with this. I can't do it. I don't know enough."

"You won't help me?"

"I *can't* help you as well as a lawyer can. I don't know enough."

The point took her right back to her father saying *you should have been a lawyer,* and in his pause she heard his disappointment all over again.

"You need to get yourself a lawyer, Dad. I'll come with you, but you need a lawyer too." O'Leary shifted on his seat, meaningfully. "I'll book leave."

"I need you there. I can't go to court without you. You've got to come with me," he begged.

"I said I would, Dad. Listen to me. Get a lawyer, and tell me who it is so I can talk to them too."

"Okay." He hesitated. "You will come on Sunday, won't you?"

"I'll come on Monday. I'm on shift Sunday."

"But.."

"Dad. I'm at work. I can't. I'll come on Monday."

"I wish..." he trailed off desolately.

"Monday. I'll see you then, and you can call me with the details of the lawyer as soon as you've got them." She managed to sound breezy and confident, but underneath she was pretty sure that the hearing was going to be make or break time. "Love you, Dad."

"You too, Catkin."

CHAPTER TWELVE

She put the phone on her coffee table and buried her face in her hands. Worriedly and tentatively, O'Leary patted her shoulder.

"Okay, Casey," he said gently. "How's about you tell me the real story?"

"You don't like sad stories."

"Just tell me. C'mon. Pals. Just 'cause we had somethin' of a set-to earlier, don't mean we ain't still pals." He turned her face round to him, examining her through sympathetic light eyes. "Have a good cry an' get it out."

She sniffed. O'Leary stretched out and put a Kleenex in her hand, then patted her again. "I'll go finish makin' some coffee."

He did just that, and returned with two mugs. Casey downed hers without regard for the lining of her throat, and sniffed again. O'Leary simply sat and waited, quietly comforting.

"Dad got arrested at JFK. Not just picked up and left to sober up, but arrested. He took a swing at a Port Authority cop. They gave him a desk appearance ticket for Queens County Criminal Court on December 13. I'll have to go."

"Why was he at the airport?"

"He wanted – he wants to go see the new Museum of African American History in DC. We talked about it a few weeks back. He said he wanted to go a couple of weeks ago, again – but it was like we'd never talked about it before. He'd forgotten." She looked at her hands, unmoving in her lap. "Guess he decided to go. He must have been drunk already. He thought I should have been there with him." Her head fell. "He said...he said I should have been a lawyer, not a cop. Again."

O'Leary didn't say anything. He simply curved an arm around her: the only person she'd ever allowed to hug her outside of boyfriends or family, and sat, carefully ignoring the shuddering of her shoulders.

"Sounds like he's always been disappointed in me," she dripped.

"Can't argue with drunk or dumb," O'Leary pontificated, after a pause. "They don't know what they're sayin'." He patted her some more.

"Yeah. Well. He said it."

"Mmmm," hummed the world's largest bumblebee. He left a long space before speaking again. "I'm your pal, but why ain't you leanin' on your boyfriend?"

Casey stiffened instantly. "I don't want him to know about this. It's too complicated. I don't want things to be complicated, just to be easy. Dad isn't *easy*. And I saw the photos of the panhandlers. They looked just like Dad did yesterday. Wouldn't that be a fine contrast?" she asked acerbically. "The drunkard and the cop?" She scowled. "He hasn't respected any limits so far - he thinks I don't know he was shooting Selwyn" -

"Thought you wanted to shoot Selwyn?"

"Yeah, but not with a camera."

"Mmmm, guess so."

"Anyway, I told him Kent said he wasn't to and he did, so how'm I supposed to believe he wouldn't just take pictures of me and Dad?"

"You could try askin'."

"Yeah, 'cause that worked *so* well the first time round." She remembered perfectly Carval's commentary on his photography. *I can't not shoot you...I can't – I won't – change that.*

She slumped. "Anyway. I don't want to tell him. I don't want him to get involved."

O'Leary changed tack before Casey could follow that thought to its logical conclusion: telling him not to talk to Carval. "He had to deal with knowin' 'bout Andy. Tyler got Andy to agree to us tellin' his story, though he wasn't there. "

"How the hell?" Casey squawked. "Did you dope him?"

"Naw. Just...It was gettin' a little edgy. I don't like edgy. Tyler don't, neither. So we all three had a chat, an' then we had another chat."

"Your funeral."

"Nearly was. Took a lot of talkin'. An' talking to your boy ain't a picnic." He drooped. "He ain't too pleased 'bout Andy treating him like some lowlife who beats up the girls."

"Neither would any of you be too pleased about that," Casey pointed out tartly.

"True enough." He shuffled on the couch, which creaked. "I'm hungry. C'n we get some food an' a soda or three? Pizza?"

"Sure."

That was the end of it. Nothing more was, or needed to be, said. Behind his light eyes, O'Leary thought the more, however, all the way through industrial quantities of pizza of which Casey had almost one whole slice.

"Anyway," he said, "time I went home. Pete'll worry."

"Thanks," she said. O'Leary bear-hugged her, and left.

Casey cleared up the detritus of dinner, had a hot shower, which didn't soothe her at all, and tried to sleep, in which she was notably unsuccessful. She had no idea how to help her father, and she would have to ask for leave from Kent, who would pity her. She'd rather he didn't. At least she could rely on Kent to sound acerbically unsympathetic, whatever was in his eyes.

Eventually, she gave up, got up, and spent some quality time in the precinct gym punching the hell out of the speed bag. It didn't help.

***

Carval went home in a cold rage. Casey had simply shut him out without a blink. Just like when she'd slept with him the first time and run away, this time she'd run away emotionally. He'd been totally right to be suspicious – she just wanted the sex, she wasn't interested in a relationship. (*Since when have you been interested in a relationship?*, a nasty little voice said in his head. *You don't want relationships, either.* He ignored it.)

Well, if she didn't want a relationship, then he sure didn't. And since she didn't, then he would just do whatever he liked. He made a call, and sure enough there wasn't a problem at all. There never was. Never had been. Plenty of women wanted his talents. Plenty.

And if Casey wasn't one of them, then that was just plain *fine*.

***

The next morning, Carval collected his camera and lenses, took himself off to a hired studio – not Stardance – where he would spend the day taking easy, slick shots of a novice model who needed to improve her portfolio. He ignored the discomfort in his stomach with extreme ease and too much coffee, and prepared to spend some time with someone who'd be nice, pleasant, friendly and appreciative.

"This is so great!" Alejandra-call-me-Allie, the newbie, squeaked. She was gorgeous: tall – easily five-foot-ten – slim, legs halfway to Texas, dark eyes and long, curling dark hair, loose around her shoulders: Hispanic in the best possible style. "Thank you so much!" Her voice was high, little-girlish and breathy. Carval had known a lot of models like her, and had a lot of good times with those who wanted them.

He didn't feel the slightest twitch of desire. Not one. Objectively, she was just his type. Subjectively – she was all wrong. She was also too young. Neither realisation improved his mood one iota.

"Happy to help," he said smoothly, and started to shoot.

Shooting soothed him. He sank into his own expertise, knowing that the shots were good. Easy, but good. Every shot he took would make this

Allie-child happy.

If only every shot he took didn't remind him that his camera loved Casey better: the snap and snark, the authority and intensity that she projected. Ridiculously, photographing a beautiful model felt like betrayal, even though he wouldn't touch this girl.

"They're wonderful!" she enthused. "These'll really help me! You're such a sweetie, Jamie!" She planted a kiss on his cheek. "If you know of anything I could do...." She handed him a card, looking like she might try to kiss him again. He stepped back.

"I'll just put them on the flash drive, in case you need to show them before I can print them. I'll call you when they're ready." He copied, and handed them over.

"Thank you! Byeeee!"

He put his camera and lenses away in their cases, and trudged home, not at all soothed or eased now that he'd stopped shooting.

"Where have you been?" Allan asked, as he passed the office.

"Shooting."

"What's wrong? Wouldn't the cops co-operate?"

"Wasn't at the precinct."

"So what were you shooting?" Allan asked suspiciously.

"Model. Portfolio shots."

"What? Why? And since you didn't do it through me you probably did it for free too. Why me? What did I do to deserve this? You need to focus on your exhibition, Jamie, or at least get paid."

"Shut up," Jamie snapped. "I know what I'm doing and I don't need to listen to you fussing. Leave me alone."

"What's happened?"

"None of your business." Jamie stormed up the stairs. Allan, after an astounded stare, followed him.

"Jamie," he placated, "what's up?"

"Nothing," Jamie said, sounding like a sulky, cross child. Obviously something was wrong: it always was when Jamie started to sulk. His hands were automatically downloading his camera, and, as Allan scanned the screen, there was nothing there but shots of some pretty girl. Good shots, but nothing of which Allan approved.

"Very nice," he dismissed. "Now, what's wrong? Why are you doing portfolio shots – for free – when you've been spending every hour you can with your cops?"

"They don't need me."

"I hate to tell you this, but that's been true since moment one. You shoot them, not solve crime."

"I'm an expert consultant this time!"

"Sure you are, but that's not what's put the burr up your butt. What you actually mean is that your Casey-cop doesn't need you except as an expert."

"Shut up."

"So I'm right."

"Stop analysing me."

"Stop sulking, then. What's up this time?"

Jamie hunched his wide shoulders and turned away from Allan.

"I told you not to get involved."

"You didn't."

"I must have misheard. Didn't you mean *I didn't*? Every time you get involved it gets complicated and I end up having to sort it out. Remember that female panhandler? If it wasn't for me she'd be living in the stairwell, and you didn't give her a hint of encouragement, you just bought her some food."

"I'd have dealt with it."

"You didn't deal with it, though. I had to. Now you're chasing round after a cop who isn't interested."

"She is *so* interested."

"Oh, for Chrissake. Already?"

"What's that meant to mean?"

"I knew this would happen. You've fallen into bed with her and now you've had a fight and you're sulking because she isn't treating you like God."

"That's not true!"

"Isn't it?"

"No! She just won't talk to me about anything."

"You've known her for what? A month, nearly two? Why do you think she'd bare her soul?"

"I saved her life!"

"No, you called the ambulance when she got beaten up. She wasn't dying."

"I didn't know that then. She should" –

"Be grateful? Really? Jamie, don't be dumb."

"She should talk to me."

"And you said so, didn't you?"

"Yeah. She's treating me like an escort service."

"Why does that bother you? You never want to get involved, so what's so different this time?"

"It just is. How about some sympathy?"

"I think it's amusing, actually."

"Do you? Just because you don't have any problems because you never" –

Jamie stopped his tirade in his tracks at Allan's look.

Allan turned on his polished heel and clacked irritably down the stairs.

He'd known Jamie was after the woman, but he'd hoped that there would be at least enough shots for the exhibition before it all went wrong. He knew he should have put him in a cell. Jamie's idiotic behaviour had quite spoiled his otherwise good mood.

Fifteen minutes later, a rather shamefaced Jamie clunked down the stairs. "Allan?" he said in a small voice. "I'm sorry. I didn't mean that. Are you mad at me?"

"No," Allan sighed, disarmed by the sincere apology. "I'm just not interested in trying to fix your love life. Whatever you did" –

"But I didn't. That's what I'm trying to say. All I wanted to do was help, and she just shut me down and shoved me away."

"Jamie, you can't make her talk to you. I bet you had a fight about it, and now you're sulking and she's sulking. Give it a day or two, and just shoot someone else till it's straightened out. From what you've said about the team, they'll get involved pretty quickly."

"I guess," Jamie said, mollified. "Thanks."

"Thank me by going and taking some shots that fit this exhibition." Allan was desert-dry.

"Okay. Tomorrow."

"Fine."

***

"Mornin'," O'Leary rumbled to the bullpen at large.

"Hey," Casey managed, not looking up.

"Hey, Bigfoot," came from the tenor-baritone harmony of Andy and Tyler. "Where've you been?"

"Went to have a chat to Larson about findin' out where else Coronal shot. What've you been doin'?"

"Chasing down my warrant for those other models' portfolios." Casey tapped her fingers impatiently. "It should be here." She finally looked up from the screen, which wasn't showing her a warrant no matter how many times she refreshed her e-mail. "Anything from Larson?"

"Some. He ain't the sharpest saw in the toolbox, but he's methodical."

"And?"

"So far, Coronal did shoots in San Francisco, Chicago, New Orleans."

Casey hummed, with an edge of irritation.

"An' London, Paris, an' Berlin."

The hum abruptly changed to an infuriated buzz.

"We're going to end up with a profiler an' the FBI like it or not, Casey. If there's anythin' outside New York, 'cross state lines...'"

"I *know*," she said exasperatedly.

"I ain't goin' near Kent. You get to do that."

"Chicken."

107

"Awwwkkkkk," O'Leary squawked, flapping his elbows.

"Got it!" Casey said to her screen, stopping the clowning flat. "Warrant for all those portfolios. Let's go get them."

"We gonna get Carval to have a look?"

"Why?"

Tyler raised eyebrows. "Might know if it was the same photographer."

"Selwyn can tell me that. We don't need Carval." She started for the stairs. Behind her, the team exchanged glances. No-one called Carval. No-one wanted to suffer Casey's wrath. "O'Leary," she called. "You coming?"

He hurriedly pulled himself together and lumbered after her, not having expected to be asked.

"Why're we doin' this, 'stead of a uniform?" he said, on the way to Stardance.

"I need to see it myself. I want a look at Stardance's set up. And while we're at it, we'll go after that asshole Selwyn for why he didn't tell me about Feggetter dropping by or Carissa."

"Mm," O'Leary hummed sceptically. "An' avoidin' Kent's got nothin' to do with it." Casey flushed. "You're gonna have to tell him 'bout the hearin'."

"I know." She drooped. "That's going to be fun. FBI and 'can I take a day's leave' in one go. I won't need to worry about my future after that, 'cause it'll be about ten seconds long."

O'Leary guffawed. "Naw. It won't take that long."

"You're not helping."

"I'm cheerin' you up."

"Stop trying. It's not working."

O'Leary said nothing, and said it at full volume, audible at Battery Park. *Talk to your boy* hung in the air. Fortunately, before he could attempt suicide-by-Casey, they pulled up at Stardance.

"Mr Selwyn, please." It was an order, given to another glossy receptionist, lips and nails perfectly colour-matched.

"He's very busy."

"Detectives Clement and O'Leary. He'll see us."

The receptionist complied. Extremely rapidly, Selwyn appeared, and even more rapidly whisked them out of his stylish reception area. Perhaps he thought they spoiled the image.

"We have our warrant, Mr Selwyn." Casey extended it. He barely read it.

"I've got your information all ready," he offered. "Here you are." He produced a large pile, which O'Leary took.

"Thank you. Now" – Selwyn cringed – "what about Carissa Ndbele? Detective Feggetter came to ask you about her. You didn't mention her to us. Why not?"

"Carissa who?" He looked completely blank.

"Carissa Ndbele. Detective Feggetter came to see you about her murder."

It took some moments before understanding and recognition dawned on Selwyn's face.

"Carissa? She's another one? Why didn't he say? She left weeks before that detective came round. I never connected it with you."

Casey regarded him sceptically.

"I didn't, okay? Models come and go, and she said she was going to Parfaitil. I wasn't going to stop her. She didn't leave me with a gap to fill. The others did. When I said she'd gone off to a new agency he went to see them and never came back. He didn't show me any photos or tell me anything about how she died – not like you. I just forgot about her."

"I see." Casey could, reluctantly, just about believe it. Selwyn was so self-absorbed it was probably true, though she thought Feggetter had missed a trick by not returning to Stardance. "Could we have a look around?"

"What? Why?"

"I want to know how it works. Is there a Coronal shoot?" She didn't give any further information, though she was thinking that since the models had been dumped, she'd like a good look at the layout in case they might have been killed here. She didn't have nearly enough evidence to get CSU to do a sweep. Yet.

"A tour?"

"Yes."

He stared at her, worry creasing his face, fingers twisting the knife-sharp crease at the seam of his chinos. Casey held his gaze, while O'Leary became mildly menacing.

"Okay. There's a Coronal shoot going on now. But you have to be quiet. No disturbing the shoots."

"We won't."

They followed Selwyn back down to the studios, and, having toured the dressing rooms, seen some makeup being applied, and decided that there were a lot of places where murder might be done, watched in complete silence as Yarland shot for Coronal.

They stood it for fifteen minutes. After that, Casey made a sharp gesture to Selwyn, and they exited the shoot.

"Does Yarland do all the Coronal shoots?"

"Yes."

"What about other shoots?"

"Some of those, too. The high end ones. He's my best photographer."

They left, with chilly thanks.

"That was ugly," Casey said.

"Sure was. Could've been a porn shoot."

"Ugh."

"Andy called it. He said it was cruel. Your boy" – Casey hissed inadvertently. O'Leary pretended not to notice – "said they had no humanity. Objects, Andy said, too." His hayseed drawl was entirely missing. "They were right. That was like watching dog training. Do this. Do that. Do what you're told."

"And the treat is the next job," Casey added, acid-etched. "He's got all the power and he knows it. He doesn't have to be nice, or treat them like people. They're all just dolls to him."

"Even the guy that was in it was a doll. Yarland didn't discriminate. He didn't care at all."

"No. But we've got no evidence that it was him. None."

"Shame."

"Yeah."

The remainder of the journey proceeded in thick silence.

***

Throughout the rest of the day the team waited for anything to turn up from Narcotics, who singularly failed to oblige, and went through endless hours of camera footage, which was equally disobliging. There was hardly anything helpful at all.

About the only thing that went anywhere close to right was the location data on Daniela, which arrived. It said she'd been on the Upper East Side – but anywhere between First, Madison, 58th and 96th. There couldn't be more than, oh, fifty bars in that space. The best they could do was send a uniform up to Felice 83 to see if anyone recognised Daniela, Melinda or Carissa.

Worse, Casey couldn't put off seeing Kent any longer. The day just got better and better. She rammed down any thought that she could improve it simply by calling up Carval, going round to see him, and sharing her troubles. Sharing her father's *issues* wouldn't help anyone. It didn't stop the thought sneaking back into her head every chance it got.

Finally, she gathered up her nerve and went to see Kent.

"Sir?"

"Yes, Clement?"

"May I have a moment, sir, please?"

"Come in. Shut the door." She did. "I assume this is about your father?"

"And the case, sir."

"Start with your father." Kent thought that that might be the quicker matter, and he wasn't wrong.

"His hearing is at 9.30 on December 13. He wants me to go with him."

"I will approve the leave request. Put it in by tomorrow."

Kent would not allow Clement to use him as an excuse to avoid dealing with her father. His assumptions did her a disservice, which he realised when an expression of relief flickered across her face.

"Now, the case."

"Sir. We still only have three deaths – thankfully. I have no evidence, but every thread I pull mentions Coronal or Stardance. But Coronal only use Stardance here in New York: they use different agencies around the country and internationally. I'd like to see if there are any similar deaths related to Coronal's other shoots."

"You want to play a hunch."

"Yes, sir."

"What makes you think it might be connected with Coronal?"

Casey managed not to squirm. "I haven't anything solid, sir. Just – all three models worked for Stardance. All of them were on the Coronal shoots. All of them were single. The style of the shoots is impersonal and objectified, and the corpses were dressed and drugged so that they weren't anything more than a puppet." Her face twisted. "The dressers and photographer move around a lot, and the Coronal shoot moves around too. It's all conjecture, sir. But I think that if I could investigate whether there are similar deaths in other places where Coronal have had shoots, I could try to eliminate that possibility."

"Or confirm it," Kent said, distaste in his voice. "However, I follow your reasoning. We'll need to get assistance." The distaste exited his voice to twist his face. "I'll request a profiler, to begin tomorrow."

"Yes, sir," she said tonelessly.

"Dismissed."

He was dialling as she left.

CHAPTER THIRTEEN

"We're getting a profiler," Casey announced bleakly. "As soon as I said that Coronal had shoots in other states and overseas, Kent went straight there."

"Ugh," Andy emitted, which pretty much summed up the team view.

"And..." she trailed off, unhappily.

"Mm?"

"I need to take leave on December 13."

Three pairs of keen eyes regarded her, and three mouths didn't open.

"'Kay," Tyler said, and that was the end of that. They knew.

"Is there anything more we can do?"

"No. Narcotics haven't gotten back to me yet, there aren't any new bodies" –

"Good," muttered O'Leary.

" – and we've gone through all the footage and there's nothing useful at all. Sent a uniform out with a photo of Daniela, but nothing there yet either."

"Must be beer time, then," O'Leary grinned.

"Not for me," Casey said.

"Sure?" Andy asked. "Looks like you could use a little time out."

"No. I just wanna go home."

"You need to get your beauty sleep," O'Leary teased. "You're lettin' down us sharp-lookin' men."

"Yep," she said lightly. "I do. Can't let the team down. Night, guys."

"Night."

As soon as Casey was gone, O'Leary grabbed his phone and dialled.

"Hey. Team's havin' beers in the Abbey. Wanna come?"

"Seeya there."

He smiled beatifically upon the other two and the bullpen. "There.

Now we'll get somewheres."

"I" – Andy began.

"You're comin'. I don't like fuss an' fightin', an' I don't like it when people don't get along. You liked Carval fine up till this case, an' if you don't make trouble neither will he. I ain't havin' trouble in the team. We got enough trouble with Casey's dad an' this profiler comin' by."

Andy conceded with a small nod. Casey might lead the team, but when Bigfoot put his size fifteens down, even Casey backed off. And Bigfoot had certainly put his foot down, which meant there was a reason.

"Okay," he agreed, slowly. "But I'm not doing any touchy-feely-all-pals trash."

O'Leary faked a shot to the heart. "What d'you think I am?"

"Trying to be Dear Abby."

"Mean. I just want everyone to get along."

"And you'll hit them over the head till they do."

"Iffen that's what it takes," the mountain boomed happily.

The Abbey was quiet, which was helpful. The team found a table and disposed themselves around a large quantity of beer (mostly in front of O'Leary). Shortly, Carval turned up, appearing less than perfectly contented with life.

"Have a beer," O'Leary gestured. Tyler grunted in greeting.

"Hey," Andy said, neutrally.

Carval sat down, and took a beer. "So what's this about?" he challenged. "Are we on intimidation, we don't know you, or let's have a drink even though we won't tell you anything?"

"Aww, don't be like that. We're pals."

"No, I'm your *expert*," Carval spat. "I forgot that one. Maybe this is a case discussion?"

"Enough," Tyler commanded. "Okay, you're pissed. Leave it at the door."

"We're good with you," O'Leary said. "Pals, like. An' you're useful. Win-win. So like the man said, leave the pissed at the door an' have a friendly beer."

Andy notably said nothing. Tyler nudged him.

"Okay. We're cool."

"Yeah."

"See, all pals. Let's have beer an' talk about sports." Andy winced. "An' culture. I c'n do culture. I went to the theatre once."

"You did?" Andy said with unflattering amazement.

"Sure I did. I went to see this comedy show. Think they called it...um..."

"Stand up?"

"Naw, that wasn't it. Um...Shakestick?"

"Shakespeare, Philistine!"

"Gotcha," O'Leary grinned. Andy groaned. "Anyway, it was quite funny. Girls bein' boys an' boys bein' girls an' misunderstandin's all over the place. An' it all ended happily with everyone in love." He favoured three deeply cynical faces with a sappy expression.

"Right."

"I like happy endin's. I don't like all this bein' pissed with each other. So we're sortin' it out now." The last sentence carried all of O'Leary's considerable weight.

Tyler drew on his beer. "If Bigfoot's decided, best just to go along."

Carval was sharply reminded of their original meeting, after Casey had departed in a swirl of triumph and ire, when it had been clear that O'Leary had had the final say.

"Now," the Titan said to Carval, "you know where Andy's comin' from. An' he knows that you ain't one of the bottom-feeders. But seems to me that you're both still pretty antsy with each other, so we're goin' to have a nice sociable drink an' make everything easy again."

Andy and Carval stared at him. Tyler simply had another glug of beer, and sat back.

"Seriously?" Carval said.

"Sure I am. You did good on the last case, an' likely you'll do good on this one – a lot more official-like. Though iffen I was you, I'd not let on that you were takin' shots when you were bein' an expert at Stardance. Cap'n won't like that, 'specially as you were told not to."

"How did you" –

"Casey ain't dumb. She saw you shootin'."

"Oh," Carval emitted, deflating. "That why" – he stopped.

"She's fed up an' not talkin' to you? Naw."

Carval clamped his mouth shut on *then what is the damn woman playing at?*

"Bigfoot..." Tyler warned.

"Nuthin' he don't know already, 'kay?"

"Okay."

"So, you might remember that Casey said her mom had passed."

Carval dragged up a memory of a coffee bar near the CSU lab. "Cancer, she said." He also remembered that O'Leary had taken the emotional lead then, and sent Casey away on her own. It dawned on him that O'Leary was the team's stability. Now, how to show that in his photographs?

"Yeah. Well, her dad needs a bit of help 'bout it every so often, an' she's it. She don't talk about it."

But, Carval thought, the three cops clearly knew a lot more about it than that, which they weren't telling him.

"Doesn't want it known," Tyler added. "No need for scuttlebutt in the bullpen."

"Anyway," O'Leary emphasised, "that's the deal. She don't like us noticin', and she won't like you noticin'."

"So don't notice," Andy put in. "If you don't make a big deal of it, likely she'll say more." He fidgeted uncomfortably. "Same as me," he pushed out. Tyler blinked. O'Leary sat, watchful, to see what would happen. "I saw all those pretty girls die ugly." He swallowed. "But if you can help us find this killer, I can..."

"I get it," Carval said, cutting off the rest. "Sure I'll help. As an expert."

O'Leary raised his hedgerow brows. "Don't recall as we asked you to be anythin' else."

"Good."

"Works for us," Tyler said.

"Iffen you were thinkin' we'd got you out to put the hard word on about Casey, we ain't. Not this time."

"Nope."

"Good," Carval said again.

"Leave her be. Good for her."

"We're pals," O'Leary repeated. "That'll do fine. We don't need to go talkin' about emotional things. It's not manly."

"Talk about sports, instead," Tyler said, and the conversation remained on sports, despite Andy's complaints, all evening.

On the way out, Tyler held Carval back for a moment. "Might wanna be around tomorrow. Got a profiler joining in."

"Okay."

"Said you sparred?"

"I've done a round or two."

"If you want a go-around, say."

"Okay."

It wasn't until he got home that Carval realised that Tyler's offer of sparring had been a statement that he was part of the team. The men's view of the team, anyway: Casey hadn't contacted him at all. Fine.

***

"This is our profiler, Dr Julian Renfrew. Luckily, he was immediately available." Kent introduced a tall, spare sixty-something; silver hair and — what? *Pince-nez glasses?* The team exchanged glances.

"Hey," Casey offered up.

"Good morning," the man said formally.

"I'm Detective Clement. Casey."

"Delighted to meet you, Detective Clement."

Casey was slightly daunted. "These are Detectives O'Leary, Chee and Tyler," she continued.

Dr Renfrew regarded them all critically. "I am pleased to meet you all." If he was pleased, it didn't show on his face.

"Dr Renfrew trained with ME McDonald," Kent said. That piece of information didn't endear him to the team.

"What in?" Andy whispered. "The school of sticks-up-asses?"

Casey required considerable effort not to snicker. O'Leary's face was purple. Tyler was impassive, except that his fists were tight.

"I will brief Dr Renfrew, after which he'll review your information." Kent and Renfrew departed for Kent's office. The team stared at each other. From the corner where he'd been unobtrusively shooting, Carval joined them, carefully avoiding being close to Casey.

"Wow."

"How did we get so lucky?" O'Leary mourned.

Carval, in stark contrast to the cops, was delighted. Another cadaverous, older subject was yet another brilliant contrast to the life and intensity of the team. He was absolutely certain that this pompous profiler would annoy Casey, and likely the rest of the team too, shots of which would go beautifully with his earlier shots of Casey squaring up to McDonald. Perfect. He supposed he'd better talk to Renfrew to obtain permission, before Renfrew tattled to Kent.

***

Kent briskly brought Renfrew up to speed, not without a feeling of being watched, reviewed, assessed and found marginally wanting. It didn't improve his view of Renfrew. He'd heard of him, but never come in contact, and frankly, he was already wishing that Renfrew hadn't been the only available profiler, no matter his top-class reputation.

"Thank you, Captain Kent. That was exceedingly comprehensive," he said, a touch patronisingly. "May I ask some further questions?"

"Of course." Kent expected some queries relating to the case. His hopes were immediately dashed.

"Could you explain to me Mr Carval's role in this affair?"

"He is an expert consultant," he explained. "Photographs seem to play a major role in this case."

"I see. Quite an odd role, for such a famed photographer."

"Yeah."

"One might almost have thought he was photographing your teams. Is he to be present for substantial periods?"

Kent's immediate, inchoate dislike of Dr Renfrew's prim prissiness hardened into a definitive annoyance at his disapproving tone.

"Operational matters are my affair. He is here with my permission."

"I see."

Kent, by this point, would dearly have liked Dr Renfrew to see the exit,

116

assisted by Kent's boot to his supercilious, skinny ass.

"You are, of course, aware that there is some tension between Mr Carval and Detective Clement." It wasn't a question.

"I am." He hadn't been, but he was now. Kent had had enough. "This is my precinct and I am in command. I think we're done here."

"Of course," Dr Renfrew said courteously. "You are a busy man. Thank you for your assistance."

He left, leaving Kent wondering what in hell the man meant by the last sentence. He was sure that he didn't mean the case.

Dr Renfrew exited Captain Kent's office with well-concealed, but considerable, curiosity: not about the case, which was interesting but was unlikely to present him with inordinate difficulties, but about the team investigating it and the inclusion of a famous celebrity photographer. Dr Renfrew had not missed Mr Carval shooting the group, and intended to deal with the discourtesy of not asking permission in short and quelling order, after which he would graciously grant consent. He had also not missed the sidelong glance Detective Clement had given Mr Carval, nor the mismatched nature of the team. Really, it would be most interesting to study their interactions. He anticipated his discoveries with pleasure.

"Detective Clement?"

"Yes?"

"Could you provide me with more detail on your findings to date?"

"Okay. Let's use one of the rooms."

Dr Renfrew approved of the privacy. Detective Clement stood up, but before she could show him to a room suitable for the forthcoming discussion, there was an unwelcome interruption.

"Hey." Mr Carval had approached. Interestingly, Detective Clement was exhibiting signs of tension and discomfort. Mr Carval was not: he was bypassing her entirely. "I'm Carval."

"I am aware," Dr Renfrew discouraged. Mr Carval, regrettably, was not daunted.

"I'm shooting the precinct and this team for my next show." How intriguing. Detective Clement had winced. "Since you're going to be working with the team, can I shoot you too?"

Dr Renfrew was not, naturally, dismayed that his intended reprimand had been forestalled. It was always pleasant to raise one's opinion of another person. He became aware that the entire team was awaiting his response.

"You may," he consented.

"Thanks."

Mr Carval took a few steps back, and, to Dr Renfrew's astonishment, began to photograph immediately. He had not anticipated that. From their expressions of resigned amusement, however, the detectives had.

"Detective Clement? Shall we begin?"

"Yes."

Mr Carval began to follow them. "I would prefer you not to be present during this discussion." Good heavens, the man had grimaced at him. How astoundingly childish. Of course, it would have no effect whatsoever. It was far more important to understand the situation in full than to pander to the ego of a celebrity photographer.

"So, Detective Clement," Dr Renfrew began, "Captain Kent has provided me with an overview. However, I should like to understand the case in greater detail, and in particular why three murders in Manhattan should lead you to believe that there might be more elsewhere or in other countries. Please elaborate."

Casey picked her way through the thicket of pompous prolixity and arrived at the much shorter: *gimme all the detail*. She explained her reasoning as she had done to Kent the day before.

"I see. It seems exceedingly tenuous." She bridled. Renfrew continued. "However, I consider that the 'hunches'" – she could hear the quotation marks – "of an experienced detective should not be discounted. I will request one of our technicians to run searches and to contact the relevant police forces and countries."

He peered at her over his pince-nez, tapping at his laptop as he spoke. "I take it that this will be acceptable? I should have preliminary results from some of the American forces by this afternoon, and from overseas by tomorrow."

"Er...yes. Thank you." Casey managed to recover some game. "Tomorrow? How will you get results from overseas by tomorrow?"

Dr Renfrew smiled patronisingly. "I have been working with the FBI for many years."

Yeah, Casey thought. *About two hundred years, and it shows*.

"I have strong relationships with many agencies overseas, and I shall be able to 'call in favours' from my acquaintances."

"I see. Thank you," she said again.

"You are welcome. Now, I should like to speak to Detective O'Leary. Please send him in."

Casey only just didn't stomp out at the dismissal. She wanted to, though.

"He wants to see you." She jerked her head at her partner, whose face fell.

"What'd I do?"

"Something terrible in a past life," Andy gibed.

O'Leary drooped off, casting a miserable shadow over at least half of the bullpen. Fifteen minutes later, he drooped back, and indicated that Andy should take his place. Another fifteen minutes passed, after which

Andy stalked out and Tyler marched in. Another precise fifteen minutes later, he marched back out.

"Lunch," Casey suggested.

"Not yet. Carval, you're up."

"What?"

"He wants to see you. Go."

"Enjoy," Andy said dryly. "It's only fifteen minutes."

Carval trudged off with a sceptical expression. An exact fifteen minutes later, he stalked back, clearly riled.

"Man's a human clock," O'Leary noted. "C'mon. Lunch, before he comes with us."

"Fuck that," Tyler said, uncharacteristically angry. "Move."

They departed as a group. Fortunately, they couldn't see Dr Renfrew, watching them with considerable interest. His sojourn in the Thirty-Sixth was already proving to be most interesting. He could not imagine a more disparate team, but he was already convinced that it was their disparity that held them together. He looked forward to studying them in detail. In his spare time, he took a close interest in team dynamics. He might start with a discussion with his old friend, ME Dale McDonald, whose acerbic opinions would be fascinating. He would decide after the case was solved.

***

"How did we get landed with that poker-up-the-ass profiler?" Andy asked the gang. He didn't get an answer, mainly because everyone else had a mouth full of lunch.

"Dunno," O'Leary eventually managed. "He was askin' me about the team after the case."

"And?"

"Didn't tell him nothin', just made like I was a dumb cop."

"He didn't ask me about the team," Casey said.

"Asked me," Tyler noted.

"And me," Andy added.

"And me," Carval said, to general astonishment. "I said I didn't know you well enough to comment." He received four approving nods. "But he asked about the case first."

"What's he playing at? He's here to help with the case, not profile us." Casey glared around from her corner seat, squashed into the wall by O'Leary. Four men nodded. They would have nodded whether they agreed or not, with Casey in that mood.

"Doesn't matter. We don't talk about it."

"Yeah," rumbled O'Leary.

Lunch done, the team, trailed by Carval, returned to their work.

They were collectively unimpressed to see Renfrew smiling, skull-like, at them, late on in the afternoon. Couldn't he have retreated to some FBI profiling cave, elsewhere? His general demeanour and critical eye made them nervous about exactly who or what he might be profiling. They didn't need to have poke-noses poking their pointy patrician noses into the team's history.

"I have obtained information from San Francisco already, relating to clusters of murders of women of a similar bodily type. I shall supply further details from Chicago and New Orleans as they arrive. Owing to the time differences, I do not expect to receive results from overseas until tomorrow. The information which I have has also been sent to your e-mail."

"Thank you," Casey gritted, and turned to the team. "Let's have a look."

Annoyingly, Renfrew's access was considerably better and faster than Casey could have managed. Everything they needed to start with was there. She wasn't nearly as grateful as she knew she should have been: Renfrew's stiff superiority hadn't gelled with her at all.

And, of course, Carval was walking wide around her and making it pretty damn clear he wasn't going to make a single move until she did. Which was just plain *fine*, because she had a case to solve, which was far more important than a sometime affair. He could just stay sulking in his corner and shooting. The fact that she was sulking at her desk was neither here nor there.

"Okay. Andy, you take the tox results, since you're already into Narcotics."

"Sure."

"Tyler, you take the rest of the autopsy results – McDonald might be more reasonable about it if he's talking to you. Maybe ballistics might match?"

"An' us?"

"We'll take all the rest."

O'Leary waggled his eyebrows. Casey scowled at him.

San Francisco had yielded four similar corpses, but unfortunately hardly anything in the way of supplementary information. Specifically, there were no portfolios and no details of the victims' careers.

"Useless," she muttered blackly, and began to make a list of what she would need. About halfway down, she realised that it would be most efficient to share her list with Renfrew, which caused her pen to dig in almost hard enough to tear the paper. She swallowed down her dislike.

"Dr Renfrew," she said briskly, "I've reviewed the San Francisco data, and I've got a list of the further information we'll need to be able to match up with our victims – or rule any similarities out. Since you can get it faster than us, could you request it, or get one of your guys to try to obtain it?"

"Certainly. I will instruct an agent" – Casey thought she heard a tiny stress on the last word, and ignored it – "to start immediately."

"Thank you." She turned to leave.

"I should like to ask you a few more questions." Renfrew halted her. "Since you require further information, now appears to be a convenient time."

Casey preserved a calm countenance, while wishing for an immediate murder. Renfrew would be the perfect victim.

"Allow me to request your data. Please sit down."

It was *her* precinct. How was this overly-formal ass giving her permission to sit in her own precinct? Still, she sat. No point in standing if she didn't have to. Renfrew tapped for a few minutes, and then turned his gaze on her. She leaned back, studiedly relaxed.

"Having spoken to each of you, I wish to understand the method of killing better. I have Dr McDonald's autopsy reports here. It appears that the women were drugged, shot and then beaten post-mortem."

"That's right."

"Do you have any hypotheses which might account for these facts?"

"No. It's overkill." Renfrew frowned at the inadvertent pun. "If the victim was dead, there was no reason to beat her. If she had died of an overdose, there was no reason to shoot her. Unfortunately, we can't tell if the drugs or the bullet killed her, or any of the victims."

"Mm. There were four deaths in San Francisco. The modus operandi was similar. I hypothesise that the killer was, at least in part, driven by a need to destroy beauty."

It was Casey's turn to frown. "Why?"

"In large part, because of the post-mortem beating."

"Destroying their looks," she said flatly. Renfrew accorded her a look of respect. She thought for a moment or two. "We interviewed the two main dressers and the photographer who does most of the Coronal shoots. Both dressers looked good, though Severstal's" –

"Mm?"

"The dresser Coronal likes best. Rumour has it he's a little familiar when he's dressing the girls."

Renfrew's mouth pinched disapprovingly. "Another man who treats them like objects."

"Yeah – yes. Of course." She smiled brilliantly. "That's why he and Yarland – the photographer – work together so much. Same nasty attitude." She returned to the first point. "But Yarland wasn't good-looking at all. He was a slob, and even if he'd cleaned up he wouldn't have been handsome."

She stared into space for a second. "If you weren't beautiful, you might not like beauty all around you... We need to know a lot more about

Yarland," she rapped. "Can you do a deep dive into him?"

Dr Renfrew blinked at the change in tone, and at the speed of Detective Clement's comprehension and analysis. "Certainly," he agreed.

"How long will it take? And the two dressers. I'll give you all the names."

"I will find out for you."

"Thanks." She left, anxious to brief her team.

CHAPTER FOURTEEN

"Renfrew's got a theory," she announced.

"Already?"

"Yeah. He thinks it might be to do with destroying beauty." The team regarded her with collective blankness. "Like, the killer isn't beautiful so he's ruining beauty in other people."

"Or she," Andy said.

"Yeah, maybe, but McDonald's report said the beating was hard. It's less likely to be a woman."

"Might not just be one person."

"True. Anyway, he's going to do a deep dive on the two dressers and Yarland."

"Most of the dressers and photographers do it to be around beauty," Carval's baritone announced. "And the chance of getting lucky, of course." He looked around the unreceptive faces. "Look, it's not nice but it is true. You already know that – and yeah, I did. Consensually. How many times do I need to say that?"

"You don't," Tyler said. "We know. Wouldn't keep you around otherwise."

O'Leary closed his maw on a similar comment. Andy nodded, and Casey, after a slight hitch, followed.

"Anything more from the rest of the US?"

"Not yet."

She humphed. "Okay. What do we know?" The board was pulled across, to consolidate the team's thoughts and findings.

"I've sent the heroin signatures to Narcotics. They're all busy, but they said they'd give us any thoughts tomorrow."

"Ballistics matches," Tyler said tersely.

"That's major. Don't suppose there was a hit through the databases?"

She looked hopefully at him, head cocked like a baby bird. Unseen, Carval shot it.

"No. Would have said."

"Bigfoot?"

"MO's the same, the girls all look the same type, all in tiny little handkerchiefs pretendin' to be a dress. Same sort of fabric: shiny silvery stuff. It's lookin' awfully similar."

"Yeah. Those ditched boyfriends aren't looking very likely now."

"Saves some time."

"I want the portfolios," Casey groused. "And the deep dive on that sleazy slob Yarland. And" –

O'Leary sang a few lines from *I Want It All*, in a basso profundo which evoked Freddie Mercury in no way whatsoever.

"My bones hurt," Andy complained. "Stop that noise."

"Aw," mumped O'Leary. "I like singin'."

"And I like my eardrums intact."

"Save it for the Bigfoot choir."

"He sings?" Carval asked.

"When we don't stop him in time," Andy flipped back.

"No fair," the world's longest windpipe grumped.

"He does am-dram musical theatre," Casey explained. "Don't you, Bigfoot?"

Carval gaped. "As what?"

"Frankenstein's monster," Andy grinned. "Or he stands in for the mountains in the scenery."

O'Leary emitted dark mutterings which didn't dent the team's grins in the slightest. "'S not fair," he sulked. "They never let me be the hero."

"Nope," Casey said briskly. "So c'mon and be the hero here and find me something I can work on."

"It's after shift end. Let's go work on a beer."

"Again? We were out last night."

"So? Beer's always a good thin'. Fundamental human right, ain't that so?"

"That's chocolate," Casey grinned. "Don't we have anything to carry on with?" she added. Her desire not to go home, where she would have nothing to think about except her father, easily outweighed any considerations of Kent's reaction to extensive overtime.

"Naw. Everything's out there, but nothin's comin' back."

She made a horrible face at them.

"You can go swap theories with your new pal."

"No, thanks."

"So are we goin' for beers or not?"

Carval flicked a look at Tyler. "Want to try a round or two?" he asked.

Tyler blinked, and then acquired a thoughtful expression.

"Sure."

"Guess we're all watchin'?"

"No." Tyler was firm. "No watching."

No-one made a move to join O'Leary for a beer.

"Guess I'm goin' home, then. Mebbe Pete's made meatloaf."

The gang dispersed. Carval followed Tyler to the precinct gym, which wasn't prepossessing. It didn't stop him taking a few shots of the dingy walls, moth-eaten mats and grim metal lockers. The equipment was limited to heavy bags and speed bags, with much newer protective gear.

"Got some gear?"

"Brought it," Carval said as laconically as Tyler, and rapidly changed.

"You work out," Tyler noted.

"Yeah."

"Why'd you want a session now?"

"Felt like it."

"Mm," was all Tyler said, sceptically.

Twenty minutes later, the two men regarded each other with considerable respect.

"Wouldn't have guessed that," Tyler said.

"You won."

"I work out with Bigfoot. Nobody else is much of a challenge."

"Mm."

"You put me down a coupla times."

"You put me down a lot more."

"Wouldn't be much of a cop if I couldn't." Tyler grinned. "You didn't do so badly. Up for a return match?"

"Not for a few days." Carval stretched, and creaked. "I'll have to work out these bruises first."

"Wouldn't recommend a go around with Bigfoot, but you'd be a good match for the others."

"Uh?" Carval said intelligently, halfway to the showers.

"Casey and Andy. They spar together. 'Bout your level."

Carval suddenly discovered a deep desire to shoot the team in its various sparring sessions, which was chased by a primitive desire to spar with Casey. Whoever won, he'd win.

"Good for frustration." Carval shot Tyler a penetrating glance. "Part of the team. We look out for each other. If you hadn't asked, I'd've suggested."

"Suggested with a side of ordered, more like."

"Whatever. Beer? Cures bruises."

"Sure."

***

The following morning, Casey arrived far too early, again. Helpfully, information from Chicago and New Orleans had arrived overnight on her e-mail. She buried her nose in her coffee and began: comparing the new data to her existing information, San Francisco, and her all-important list. Nothing new had arrived from San Francisco, annoyingly.

Not annoyingly at all, Chicago and New Orleans had sent portfolios. She flicked through them. They looked almost identical in style to the New York portfolios, but she was no expert and she already knew that Coronal had a house style. She grimaced. Her lonely evening and self-protective backing off didn't incline her to think that Carval was going to be pleased to receive contact from her. Too bad. She needed his input. As an expert. Which was just *fine*.

It wasn't fine at all. *Damn my father*, she thought viciously, and tried to push it away as soon as she had thought it. She didn't mean it. It wasn't her dad, it was the alcohol. Spoiling everything, faster and faster.

She took a short break, and returned by way of the coffee machine. She could explain her reddened eyes by claiming a burn from her coffee making, if she had to. Of course, the team would know it for a lie, but no-one else would, which was all that mattered. And thinking of no-one else, she tapped out a text to Carval requesting his expert opinion on the new portfolios: specifically, whether it was likely to be the same photographer.

Carval was woken by the chirp of a text arriving, and didn't appreciate either the early hour or the painful effort of staggering to a hot shower. He worked out, but hitting the mats with Tyler was a whole new level of effort and subsequent aches. He didn't much appreciate the content of the text either.

More portfolios. Need expert opinion, pls. C.

Great. Not so much as a greeting or farewell. He was tempted not to go, but then recalled Renfrew. He didn't bother replying, though. He wasn't a dog, to be called to heel.

Some forty-five minutes later Carval showed up in the precinct, eyes barely half-open. It wasn't yet seven-thirty. He carefully didn't ask himself why he'd bothered to arrive so soon, especially when he knew that shift started at eight-thirty today. The rest of the team wasn't there: only Casey, head bent over a file and a peculiar slumped tension in her posture. He didn't announce his presence: instead shooting until he was a few feet from her desk.

"Hey," he greeted her, blandly neutral, and didn't really smile. She startled, and her head jerked up. Carval just about concealed his shock. Her eyes were shadowed, and the dark rings below them required more make-up to cover them than she wore, if she was wearing any. It looked as if she hadn't slept for three days, which, he realised, rather neatly matched up with their fight. Well, he wasn't going to offer to mend matters, if she wouldn't.

"You've got portfolios."

There was a tiny hitch. "Yeah. Can you tell if it's the same photographer? It's the same style, but you might spot something I won't."

Carval was abruptly dead certain that wasn't what she would have said if he hadn't opened his mouth first.

"I can try. Why?"

"Because Yarland moves around. I want to know if he moved with the Coronal shots and I don't want to ask him till I've got an idea of the answer. Right now, if he was going to lie, I wouldn't know."

"Okay." He stood there.

"Yeah?"

"They're on your computer."

"Oh." She coloured. "There. I'll go work at O'Leary's desk," she added awkwardly.

"Fine. Any other expert work you want done?" He didn't try to hide the edge.

Her face pinched. "No," she replied, and turned away to drop her files on O'Leary's desk, after which she stalked in the direction of the break room. She didn't say another word to him.

As each of the team arrived, they glanced between Carval and Casey and didn't say a single audible word about the tension between them, until O'Leary tromped in.

"Why're you stealin' my desk?" he asked plaintively. "You got a nice desk of your own."

"Yeah, and it's all tidy. Yours is a mess."

"Works for me. Why're you here, anyway?"

"Carval's looking at the portfolio shots and had to use my computer." She smirked, but it wasn't convincing. "Seeing as you won't tell me your passwords."

"You could've shared your desk, 'stead of disapprovin' at mine."

Casey didn't dignify that with an answer. "Let's get on with the case," she said instead.

"Where are you goin' to sit?"

"Conference room. There's no room once you sit down."

"You can have your desk back," Carval interjected. "I'm done."

"And?"

"Best guess is that it was the same photographer. There's no certainty, though. It's not like they sign it, but there are a lot of similarities."

"Okay, thanks." She paused, uncomfortable. "Want a coffee? I'm getting one."

"No, thanks." He stood, collected his camera, and disappeared in the direction of the interrogation rooms.

"I guess I'd better start making a list of questions for Coronal." Casey's voice was brittle. "Anyone else want coffee?"

"I would be grateful for a cup of coffee," Renfrew's patrician voice greeted them. That hadn't been the *anyone else* Casey had meant. How long had he been present anyway? They hadn't noticed him.

She couldn't refuse without being blatantly rude, and if she were to be blatantly rude Kent would have her head, though it might be worth it if it got the profiler out of their business. Everyone else – cowards! – declined coffee, and stayed super-glued to their desks.

"You have a coffee machine?" Dr Renfrew was surprised. In his extensive experience, the police forces drank a hot liquid that resembled coffee only in name. In certain forces, he had considered utilising the truth-in advertising laws to establish the precise composition of the liquid provided.

"Yeah." Renfrew's expression forced her to elaborate. "The dishwater from the old machine was undrinkable, so the team clubbed together and we got this." That should hold him.

"The team?"

"The four of us."

Dr Renfrew raised an intrigued eyebrow. "Not Mr Carval?"

"No." This wasn't a conversation she wanted to have.

"When did he join your team?"

"He isn't part of the team. He's shooting cops for his next exhibition." Neither statement was a lie. They were merely completely misleading.

"Really?" Dr Renfrew asked sceptically. "He appears to be photographing the four of you, and I understood him to be acting as an expert. Is not an expert part of your team, at least temporarily?"

Casey flung Renfrew a searing glance. "Temporarily, yes," she gritted out. "Have you had any results from overseas yet?" Renfrew's return gaze told her that he'd understood exactly why she'd changed the subject.

"I have already forwarded them to you and your team," he said calmly. "It appears that there are clusters of deaths in London and Paris, but not Berlin." He regarded her over the top of his prim pince-nez. "I have requested an assistant. Agent Bergen. He will arrive shortly. He is fluent in French, should that be necessary to interpret the file from Paris."

"Does Captain Kent know?" Casey asked unwillingly. It would be much nicer to allow Kent to explode all over Renfrew, but the bullpen might get messy and cleaning blood from the walls was an unnecessary distraction from solving cases.

"I have informed him." Dr Renfrew had indeed informed Captain Kent – by e-mail, an hour after he had expected that the Captain had left the precinct. Dr Renfrew did not believe in borrowing trouble, nor in seeking permission for actions that were quite clearly necessary and for which, in any event, permission was not required. His authority in this matter was unquestionable. "Agent Bergen will assist with the data matching and further searching. He is particularly skilled in data analysis. I believe the term is 'technogeek'."

"He and Andy" –

"Andy?"

"Detective Chee – should get on well."

"I shall ensure that they are introduced at the earliest opportunity," Dr Renfrew said smoothly. "One would not wish to duplicate effort."

Casey had a momentary desire to expend some effort in duplicating several kicks to Renfrew's skinny rear, and would, for once, have found herself receiving total sympathy from Kent.

"I'd better get on," she said, planning her escape.

"Indeed. However, I consider that it would be profitable for us to reconvene, with Mr Carval in his capacity as an expert, later this morning, when you have had an opportunity to assimilate the new data and Agent Bergen has been briefed. He will also have been able to begin any further searches which we may consider appropriate."

We? We? This was *Casey's* investigation, not Renfrew's. *She'd* decide what were appropriate searches, not Renfrew. After *appropriate* consultation, naturally. She left, with her coffee.

Dr Renfrew watched her leave, with gentle amusement. Detective Clement, it was clear, was not used to sharing leadership. Nor, he noted, had she any enthusiasm for discussing Mr Carval. Dr Renfrew readily concluded that this reluctance stemmed from romantic complications: it was, after all, the most logical explanation. No doubt it would resolve itself in due course. He put it from his mind. Romantic complications had no place in pursuing an investigation.

***

"Okay, we've got more data. Same split as yesterday. Renfrew's bringing in another guy – Bergen. Technogeek, so, Andy, you can be pals with him." She made a face. "When he's up to speed, and we've got our heads round this new info, he wants a sit-down. All of us, Carval included."

The news wasn't universally popular, judging by the grumps, grouses and grumbles. Casey ignored them all in favour of reburying her head in her data and cross-matching all the points of similarity. There were more portfolio photos. She supposed, unhappily, that she should find Carval and ask him to look. She simply didn't want to do so.

It was case-related, and necessary. She could do case-related, and necessary, and to ask any of the others to find him would be cowardly. She wasn't a coward, despite the twisting in her gut.

Eventually, she ran Carval to earth in an interrogation room, still messing with the one-way glass and reflections. He'd talked a couple of the other cops into helping him. Not her problem. The impatient, irritated glance at her interruption wasn't her problem either, and being hurt by it would have been stupid and unjustified. Therefore, since she wasn't stupid and didn't go in for unjustified emotions, she couldn't have been hurt. It was simple logic.

"We've got more portfolios," she clipped out. The two officers, picking up instantly on the tension, departed with alacrity.

"And?"

"Could you come have a look?"

"As an *expert*?" he tossed back acidly.

"No, as a chocolate teapot," she retorted. "*Yes*, as an expert."

"When I've finished here."

"What?"

"I'm busy. This is my real job. I'll fit you in when I'm done." He paused. "Just like you do to me." She turned white. Abruptly, Carval realised that it wasn't upset, it was sheer rage.

"So you'll delay a murder investigation because your feelings are hurt? Fine. What we *had* was some casual fun. Didn't mean anything. You take your *snaps* and when you think you can act like a professional you can see Tyler. He'll have the pictures. Don't bother coming near me."

She spun on her heel. Carval moved even faster and shut the door before she could exit.

"Didn't mean anything? So that's why you look like you haven't slept since *you* wouldn't tell me anything? Well, I'm not a mushroom to be kept in the dark and fed on shit. If you don't want a relationship that's fine with me, but don't behave like it's my fault when it's not. I don't need you either."

"You're the one who was trying to make something out of a casual bit of fun. I don't *need* you" –

"Who pulled your unconscious ass out of Havemeyer Hall? You were plenty happy to need me then."

"That was work."

"The hell it was. You were in my bed all curled up like a kitten" –

"What's that got to do with anything? So you're good in bed. So?"

"So *you're* the one who's making this into a big deal. Fuck it. I don't care. You keep your secrets and your life. Go solve your murder. Work's all that matters to you anyway."

She yanked the door open and stormed out. Carval stayed put, defiantly taking a few more shots till his conscience kicked in sufficiently to prod him out of the interrogation room and to Tyler's desk. He didn't look at Casey. She didn't look at him. In fact, as he was walking into the bullpen she walked out.

"I've come to look at the new portfolios," he said.

"'Kay. Get a chair." The matter-of-fact response was calming. Tyler shifted his chair along to allow Carval access to his screen, and didn't say a thing, even when Casey returned and ignored Carval as assiduously as he ignored her..

CHAPTER FIFTEEN

"Did we get anything from Narcotics yet?"

Andy looked at Casey with a *how-did-you-guess* expression.

"Just called me." She heard an odd note in his voice. "Um..."

"Tell me they've got something for us."

"Yeah. They're sending someone over."

"Why?"

"They say they've got links, and it'll be quicker if their detective explains it in person."

"Great." Casey put her head back down to comparing the files from each location.

"Casey..." Andy said.

"Yeah? What? We've got what we wanted."

"The guy they're sending..."

"Yeah?" But she already knew something was wrong from Andy's hesitation.

"It's Marcol."

He simply couldn't help it. Carval, who had been able to hear everything from Tyler's desk even if he'd pretended he couldn't, raised his camera, and began to shoot her pale face, the hard brown eyes, the changes in her expressions from shock through an instant of scalding hatred to cold blankness.

"What the *hell*?" She didn't need that. She absolutely did not need that. She took a slow, deep breath. He didn't matter. Eight years on, he wasn't relevant. He was just another cop. She hadn't thought about him from the moment she graduated from the Academy, and she didn't have to think about him now. He was just another cop.

A sheet of paper crumpled under her hand.

"Yeah."

"Now, no shootin's in the bullpen," O'Leary drawled.

"No," Tyler, joining the group, added. "Mats are up there." He bared his teeth in a not-smile of feral joy. "Bigfoot and me, we could use some practice." They locked eyes, and for a moment danger and violence sparked. The team closed in to surround Casey, whose fingers were shredding the innocent sheet of paper. Carval kept shooting, hoping to capture the team bond: the sense of protective camaraderie tinged with the hard edge of anger and dislike – which wasn't only emanating from Casey.

"I see," she said tightly. "When's our evidence turning up?"

"Didn't say."

"Okay. Let's get on with the other leads. I'm not holding up anything else waiting for Narcotics." The men simply stood there. "What are you waiting for?" she snapped. "Christmas?" O'Leary covered her shoulder with one span. She didn't shrug it away, though his hand surely didn't linger. "We've got work to do. Our victims won't walk up and tell us they're connected, we've got to prove it."

"Zombies would make our life a lot easier," O'Leary grinned. It didn't lighten Casey's mood.

Andy hung back as the other two ambled away. "You okay?"

"Yeah. He's just another cop." But her fingers were still knotted and white, and there was a little pile of shredded paper on her otherwise tidy desk.

Carval took a few shots of her hands, unseen, and slipped his camera away as her hands relaxed.

"Who's Marcol?" he asked disingenuously. He knew perfectly well who Marcol was. He *also* knew that he'd better not be around when Marcol showed up, because around two seconds after Marcol heard his name, Marcol would let the photographic cat out of the bag and most likely start a fight about it. Carval had no desire to explain his actions to Casey, and still less to be raked down and undoubtedly banned by Captain Kent.

Still, he badly wanted to see the enemy – enemy? No. Not enemy: he couldn't think like that. Bastard, certainly – but Marcol couldn't hurt her now. He should go, and leave it to the team to deal with him. It wasn't like Casey wanted him around to support or help her.

"Narcotics cop," Andy said.

"'Kay." Carval wandered in the direction of Observation, but once out of sight, switched to the back stairs. He couldn't stay.

He really, really wanted to stay.

With astonishing self-discipline, he forced himself to leave the Thirty-Sixth. Much as he'd have liked to, he even managed not to loiter in the entry area. He could have been there for hours, and he wasn't allowed to shoot there – not that it had stopped him, but if he was there for a while he would be noticed, which would land him in trouble, which would be dumb.

Halfway home, he remembered his shots of hands, which totally distracted him from Marcol, the team, Casey's coldness and Casey's tension.

"Allan, Allan!" he hollered as he bounced in.

"What is it *this* time?"

"You'll like it."

"I will? Tell me you've grown into a mature adult overnight. I'd like that."

"Mean. You will like this. I've got us a mini-exhibition."

"I'm dreaming. I'm asleep and dreaming. You're telling me you've got another exhibition theme?"

"Yep. Look."

"No."

"What do you mean, no? You're always complaining that if I don't do more I'll fall out of the cultural public eye."

"No. You have to concentrate on the main event now. You don't have nearly enough shots yet."

"I'm getting more every day. *And* I've got this other one." He sounded offended.

Allan sighed. Jamie was difficult enough to keep in order when he had one exhibition theme in mind – actually, the problem then was usually to keep him focused on the essentials of life, like looking both ways when crossing the street. Two themes would mean that Allan's orderly existence would soon resemble the management of a day care centre, and there being only one Jamie to manage still wouldn't make it easier than managing several toddlers. Jamie's attention span, once away from his viewfinder, was considerably shorter than that of the average toddler.

"What is it?" he asked.

"Hands. Look. See those three shots on the edge of the corkboard. They don't fit with the main theme. But they're really good" –

"How modest" –

"Stop it. They are. Anyway, *while* I was taking shots of the cops I took some more of hands. We can do a small exhibition that's all about hands."

He was downloading the camera as he spoke.

"Let's see, then."

"See, you're interested. We'd only need a small space."

Allan was the only person who ever got to see raw shots, and that was only because he insisted he had to do so in order to plan the exhibitions. Since Allan imposed order, neatness, organisation and a constant flow of royalties upon Jamie's chaos, Jamie had to put up with it.

"Be quick, then. I'm busy tonight."

"That's twice in a week. Are you seeing someone?"

"Unlike you, I don't cat around with anyone who takes my fancy."

"That's unkind. I haven't been doing that lately." Jamie growled, which wasn't a good sign. "Never mind," he gritted. "Who're you seeing?"

Allan didn't like the sound of that. Jamie was bad enough when he was happy. When something in his life was going wrong – and it sounded like his Casey was still wrong – he was hell to deal with. Best to keep him focused on the happier track of a small exhibition even if that would mean that Allan's life was even more complicated than usual.

"If I were seeing someone, it wouldn't concern you, as long as your life wasn't interrupted. But no, I'm not. I'm going home." He looked at his watch. "I'm leaving in an hour."

"You have to see these before you go." Jamie pulled up the shots of hands.

"Oh."

"Oh? Is that all you've got to say?"

"Where were you thinking of showing them?"

"No idea. You do all that."

"Usually I have an idea – from you – of how big it's going to be. This one, I have no idea. So where were you thinking of?"

"Don't know yet." Suddenly Jamie's eyes lit up. "You do like it. You know it'll be another good one. Stop messing with me."

"How many shots do you think it'll be?"

"Not many. One room. I said, just a mini-exhibition."

"One big room, or one little room?" Allan asked patiently.

"I don't know yet. Stop asking questions I don't know the answers to. Depends how many more I get."

***

"Detective Chee?"

"That's me."

A tall blond, handsome in a boyish way, walked over to Andy's desk with arrogant confidence. This was clearly a man who expected to be going places.

"Hi. I'm Mark Marcol. Narcotics. You've got a case that connects?"

"Yeah." Andy was chilly, which didn't dent the confidence but did cause a slight hesitation. "You can brief the whole team at once."

He flicked a glance around, and collected Tyler and O'Leary. Marcol looked a little undersized as the big men crowded in, and didn't appear to like it.

"Let's get a conference room for this. Tyler, you wanna get the senior detective?"

"Sure."

O'Leary raised an eyebrow at Andy, but got only his best inscrutable expression.

"Sit down," he invited. Coffee was not offered. Marcol sat. A small expression of worry lurked in his eyes: he could sense something was awry but couldn't place it.

O'Leary's normal amiability and bucolic cheerfulness wasn't in evidence.

"Here's the senior detective," Tyler announced.

Casey strode in, face blank and cold.

"Detective Marcol," she said, just as if he was a total stranger. She didn't show as much as a blink of recognition.

Marcol's jaw dropped. "Clement? Well, hello. Long time no see."

"This is Detective Marcol," Casey directed towards Tyler and O'Leary. "Narcotics have evidence which connects to our cases."

"Hi," Marcol tried, with a smile which would have been instantly attractive if they hadn't all known the history. "Good to see you again, Clement."

He became the recipient of three hard stares. Casey didn't react to his attempt at familiarity at all.

"Marcol..." O'Leary mused. "Now, seems as I might have heard that name before."

Tyler nodded. Both of them everted lips in an expression that didn't waste time pretending to be a smile.

"Captain Travers asked me to bring over the drug information about your victims," he said.

"Thank you, and Captain Travers," Casey said formally. "Okay, let's hear what you've got." Marcol bristled at her note of command, then stood down.

"Yeah. Mebbe by the time he's finished I'll have remembered why I've heard of him."

That didn't improve the atmosphere either.

"The heroin signature" - he looked as if he might explain, though any half-competent detective would know what that meant.

"We know what that is," Andy cut him short. Marcol mansplaining wasn't going to go down well in an already tense room. Not that Casey would make the point, oh, no. Tyler or O'Leary would.

" – is the same as one we picked up a couple of months ago."

"When exactly?"

"I'm not sure. It wasn't my collar."

"Can you let us know? It might correspond to our murder dates." The tone could, if someone had wanted to interpret it so, have carried a *why-didn't-you-think-of-that* implication.

"Okay," Marcol said, disagreeably. "We arrested the dealer. He's in a cell, but he wouldn't spill where it was from."

"We're more interested in where it went to. Did he say anything about that?"

"That wasn't our problem. We were trying to get the source."

"It is ours, though. Since it was used to murder three girls." She collected her thoughts. "Okay. Tyler, you get the rest of the details on this lowlife from Detective Marcol. Andy, you're the liaison with Agent Bergen. He should be here by now. Make friends. I'll get on with the results of the cross match for the US. O'Leary, you get to follow up on the files from overseas. Let's see if we can come up with a list for Renfrew and Bergen. Let's get to it, guys." She stood up. "Thanks for your time."

"But.... You'll want me in on the interrogation. He's our collar, and we know enough to help you."

"I don't think that'll be necessary. If our Captain thinks it is" – Kent wouldn't – "then he'll contact yours."

"Okay." Marcol manufactured a pleasant smile. "Still, always good to see old friends. How about we catch up sometime, off the job?"

Casey regarded him icily. "No. Thank you."

"I remember now, " O'Leary announced with an air of happy realisation, which conveniently stopped Marcol trying to hit on Casey again. "This here's the guy who came second."

Marcol scowled.

"O'Leary!" Casey snapped. He winced. "The overseas information." O'Leary scuttled out. Marcol didn't look grateful for the intervention. "We can handle it ourselves, thank you." Pause. "And since you've been unprofessional enough to try to arrange a social event during a homicide investigation, here's your answer. No. I have no interest in catching up with you. Ever."

Casey exited in pursuit of O'Leary. She didn't look back.

"My boss said if your Captain wanted any extra help..." Marcol tried yet again, and then trailed off as Andy left, also without a backwards glance. Tyler closed the door quietly and deliberately.

"We all know who you are," he said, dangerously softly, his sniper's stare piercing. "You're the asshole who couldn't take being beaten to the top by a woman. You know that between our team we own every Academy record going. Casey's ours, and she leads this team for a reason."

"You're as pussy whipped as the instructors," Marcol spat. "Guess I know who's trying to put the frighteners on me now."

"Why'd we bother? We don't worry 'bout second raters. If it hadn't been you they sent we'd never bother thinking of you."

"Don't give me that crap. One of you sent a letter from some asshole lawyer claiming I'd stolen some sexed up photo of that bitch" –

"Who?" Tyler demanded, all his military rank and authority to the fore.

Marcol looked at Tyler's face and saw a promise of retribution. "Detective Clement," he forced out.

"Oh, we know you did that. Or you got someone to do it for you. Weasel," he added contemptuously. Marcol spluttered. "So which was it?"

"I had nothing to do with it."

"Liar," Tyler contradicted. "Not that it matters, 'cause if we wanted to know who it was we'd have found out. See, we don't care. Just like we don't care if assholes like you try 'n' insult us by calling us pussy whipped. We just don't care. We know we're the best team around, and crap like you're spouting doesn't change that." He regarded Marcol coldly. "I think it's time you left. Don't bother coming back. I'll expect the details of your lowlife by e-mail. Today, Detective, please."

"My Captain" –

"If you're about to say that he'll have you inserted into our team, you're wrong. Next place I'm going is *our* Captain. He's a helluva hardass, but he'll listen to the tale. You won't be coming here." The air of menace intensified. "If you go near Casey, you'll be dealing with me and O'Leary."

"Can't she fight" –

"That's if there's anything left of you for us. We'll give her first go. Only polite." He bared his teeth. "Now, leave. You're not welcome here."

Marcol stood up with stiff fury and marched out. Tyler watched him all the way to the stairs, and didn't trouble to be subtle about watching him from the doorway all the way down and out into the entrance hall. His solicitude didn't seem to be appreciated. That was almost a slam. Would never have been tolerated in the military. Asshole.

Tyler, whose relationship with Kent was rather better than that of the other three largely because he never normally came in contact with him, decided to head any inter-precinct cooperation off at the pass. He didn't much like doing it, and he was pretty sure that Casey wouldn't be impressed, but it wasn't like she could outshoot him or out-spar him, so the worst that could happen was that she'd hide his Gatorade every day for a week.

He rapped on Kent's door a few moments later, carefully timed for a moment when Casey was absent. There was doing the necessary, and there was being a dumbass. Tyler was no dumbass.

"Come in."

"Sir?" Tyler walked in smartly and shut the door. "Got a matter to discuss."

Kent blinked. That was unexpected. "Do you have a problem I should know about?" he queried.

Tyler assumed parade rest. "No, sir. But we might have."

"Explain," Kent said wearily. It had been a long day already, and problems with his best team were not something he wanted to deal with. If they were coming to him – voluntarily, dear God – it was going to be complicated. Why couldn't they just have dealt with it themselves, like usual? He consciously smoothed his face.

"We were provided with information from Narcotics, sir. They sent over a detective – Marcol. He wants to be part of the investigation."

"What? No. I'm not having that. If I require extra people I'll arrange it."

"Thank you, sir." Tyler exited.

Kent relaxed. That had been remarkably simple. He stopped. Suspiciously simple. In fact, that shouldn't have been necessary at all. Therefore there was more to it than he knew. Marcol, huh? He'd known a Marcol – good guy, but older. Must be close to retirement now. He'd had a son.... More worried than curious, he tapped. Ah. Son. Same age as Clement – same class, he saw. Uh-oh.

He stalked out of his lair. "Detective Tyler," he rapped. "My office."

Tyler stood, miserably. Aw, *shit*, he thought. He'd really thought he'd got away with it when Kent had cut it off at the neck. His instincts for superior-caused issues were hollering. Tyler, in fact, had the horrible suspicion that Kent knew more than the team would like. Superior officers shouldn't do that. It wasn't the natural order of things.

"Who'd you shoot?" Andy teased.

He trudged off without answering.

"Detective Tyler. It was entirely unnecessary for you to approach me about a simple matter such as temporary additions to the team. Therefore you have some reason why you don't want to include Detective Marcol, which you didn't disclose." Kent's tone bit. "I am disappointed."

Tyler stood straight, and watched strips of his skin decorate the floor.

"Now. Explain. Properly."

"Don't want him."

Kent regarded Tyler beadily. "Why do you not want him?" There was a squirmingly uncomfortable pause. "Well? I require an answer, Detective Tyler."

"Marcol and Detective Clement have a history, sir."

Kent raised his eyebrows. "And why should an affair and break up worry you? Clement is, as far as I'm aware, a professional."

"Not an affair. Marcol didn't like coming second at the Academy."

Kent stared. That was *not* what he had expected to hear, nor was it anything he wanted to hear. "Carry on."

"He tried to get it on. Casey wasn't interested. So he tried to sabotage her with that photo."

"What photo?"

Oh, *shit*. Kent didn't know or didn't remember about the photo. Oh, *fuckit*. Now, unless Tyler was really careful, Carval was going to get dragged in too. Clusterfuck Mark One.

"Begin at the beginning, *if* you please. A full report, in better order than you've managed so far."

Tyler wished he could be elsewhere. Even Afghanistan would be better than being in front of Kent. He collected himself, and wished fervently that he'd left this to Bigfoot. Or even thought of leaving it to Bigfoot. Or never thought of talking to Kent at all. Never volunteer, dumbass!

"When Detective Clement was at the Academy, someone found a college photo of her at a party. It was hot – not indecent. It was used to make it look like she was easy."

Kent's face was a picture. An extremely ugly picture. "And what has this to do with Detective Marcol?" It suddenly seemed that memory had hit him hard on the back of the head. "Are you suggesting that a fellow officer started those rumours about Clement?"

"Marcol didn't like that Clement was better than him and he sure didn't like that she wouldn't date him. Widely known, sir. And now he's tried to ask her out when he should have been telling us about the model case, earlier."

"And?" Kent's suffused face was a shade of reddish purple that Tyler hadn't seen on the angriest sergeant in the Army.

"Shut him down."

"Hm. However, I meant, was he responsible for those rumours?"

"Maybe it was him or maybe it wasn't – we don't care enough to find out, though I'm sure he knew about it. But Marcol's still got a problem with Clement, and he isn't going to work well with us."

"I see. You should have informed me of this the first time." He scowled. "Is there anything else within this mess which concerns my precinct?"

"No, sir," Tyler assured him.

"Dismissed."

Tyler had told the absolute truth. Whatever Carval was doing – and Tyler was certain sure Carval was behind the legal letter about stealing the photo – his actions didn't involve the precinct. Nor were they going to, though Tyler intended that he and Bigfoot were going to have a friendly little chat with Carval – and that Allan guy, in which case he'd better get Andy along to deal with any cultural crap – about it. Casey...better leave her out of it. Involving her might be explosive, and not in the good way. He hadn't missed her behaviour, or Carval's, this morning. Anyway, he'd quite like to know what Carval was doing keeping secrets from her, without her there to argue.

Tyler groaned. He was getting as big-brotherly as Bigfoot. He'd got to stop getting into this interpersonal shit. A good session at the gym should do it.

"What's up?" O'Leary asked.

"Want a word, later."

"Okay. Lemme know."

They turned to their work.

CHAPTER SIXTEEN

Casey was only too delighted – so she told herself – that Carval wasn't there when she'd finished with Marcol. Her day was just chock-freaking-full of over-testosteroned men who couldn't keep their dumb male relationship issues out of her precinct. Men, she decided grimly, should all be shot or neutered, like tomcats.

"Detective Clement?"

Oh, *fuck*. Renfrew probably wasn't on the neutered list, since she couldn't imagine *anyone*, male, female, gender-fluid or for that matter an alien from the Sagittarius Whorl, putting up with his prissy, prating pomposity for more than half a second. She couldn't imagine why someone hadn't already shot him – maybe she could get crowdfunding to meet her bail? She'd surely get off on the provocation defence, especially if the judge had met Renfrew.

"Yes, Dr Renfrew?" she said as primly as he.

"I appreciate that your meeting with Narcotics had to take priority, but may we now schedule our meeting?"

Dr Renfrew had been assessing Detective Clement since he had arrived that morning, and was not reassured by his conclusions. There had, he had deduced, been – in the vernacular, which he normally scorned to use – a stand-up fight between Detective Clement and Mr Carval, which had resulted in (he further deduced) a bout of enraged tears on one side (he was unsure which side, given Mr Carval's childish behaviour the previous day) and prolonged sulking on the other.

To add to an already emotionally toxic mixture, Detective Chee's announcement of the Narcotics detective had triggered a primal, protective response in the three male detectives, who had closed around Detective Clement in a way strongly suggestive of an army's defence of its general. Three of them had exited that meeting, but Detective Tyler had spent longer with the detective, and had obviously and overtly made sure that he had left. Dr Renfrew did not use the emotive word *fled*.

However, despite his professional interest in the team dynamics, a meeting to discuss the case had been agreed and would be helpful.

"Yes. When do you want to meet?"

"This afternoon, if you please."

"Okay. Three?" Dr Renfrew nodded. "Do you have to have Carval back?"

Ah. Mr Carval had vacated the precinct? How surprising. Dr Renfrew would have expected him to wish to shoot the Narcotics detective. He had certainly tried to shoot everything else. There must be a deeper reason surrounding his departure. Really, this team was as full of mysteries as their cases.

"Indeed. His presence is also required."

Detective Clement did not appear to find that statement to be pleasing, which was exceedingly irritating. The case would not be assisted by interpersonal strife.

Casey grimaced at her phone and then, yet again, pulled herself together, reminded herself that the only matter of any importance at all was solving her case, and dialled.

"Yes?" Carval snipped.

"Renfrew wants you at a case meeting this afternoon. Three. Okay?"

Despite his own chilly words, Carval was – fuck it, this was not him: he never reacted like this – *hurt* that it wasn't even Casey's idea to call him. He could hear her reluctance to be speaking to him, and her obvious desire to cut the call short, in every word.

"Why does he want me there?"

"No idea. Does three work or not?"

"Yeah."

"Okay, bye."

And she was gone, before he had a chance to say anything else. Carval swore horribly at his studio, and then went to the gym to hit things as hard as he could for an extended period, which relieved his angry frustration but didn't help him work out what to say to break the ice with Casey. If he even wanted to break the ice between himself and Casey. Who was he trying to kid? He wanted Casey just as much as ever, but he wasn't prepared to be a live action sex toy.

Casey cut the call and took a short break to clear her head. When she returned, she was no happier but was focused on her case.

"So we've got all the initial reports, but we're still waiting for follow-up?"

"Yeah. Why don't we go talk to Agent Bergen?" said Andy.

"Okay."

Agent Bergen proved to be a totally forgettable figure: medium height; unremarkable mixed-race face; neutral voice, neither high or low; not overly muscled nor particularly thin. He'd be invisible ten seconds after he'd been seen, even when looking straight at him.

"Hi," he said.

"Hey. We wanted to talk about the follow-up searches."

"Okay," he said. "You wanted deep dives into Yarland, Severstal and Hervalo, and you wanted further information from London and Paris."

"Yep."

"The deep dives are running. Should have them by end of today. London and Paris are out there, but it's coming up to evening so I can't promise anything. London's more likely to get back to us tonight than Paris, in my experience."

Casey grimaced at him, and Bergen's forgettable face became sympathetic.

"I know," he said. "I want it back too. I've got some neat software that'll do all our data matching for us – um...can I have your original files, too, so I can input while we're waiting? That way we can run all the fingerprint and CSU matches, and the heroin signatures, and I can get them started now."

"Sounds great," Casey said much more happily. "Sure." She swung off to find them, leaving Andy and Bergen to talk tech and the search and match parameters. She didn't understand a single technogeek word that floated after her, but she didn't have to. That was Andy's game, and all she had to know was that he would get the results. With nothing to do but wait, she claimed that she was going out to find some lunch, even though she was anything but hungry, and declined any company.

Behind her, the team exchanged amused, cynical glances.

"Reckon we should lock 'em in a holding cell till they see sense?" O'Leary grinned.

"Only if you take Casey's gun away first. It won't do us any good if she goes down for Murder One."

Tyler simply snickered. "Man can spar. Your level, Andy."

"You put him on the mats?"

"No shame in how he did."

O'Leary raised eyebrows. "You don't do that often," he said.

"Team."

O'Leary's eyebrows met his buzz-cut. "Yeah?"

"Yeah. If he's going to be running around when Casey's getting beat up, then we better know he can handle it."

"Okay." Massive shoulders shrugged, and a breeze spread through the bullpen.

***

Casey, ignoring such culinary attractions as McDonalds and Starbucks, wandered down to Sakura Park and planted herself on a bench, under bare trees. A thin, whining wind gnawed through her coat, though there was no rain from the gloomy sky. She wouldn't have cared if there had been. In the course of the week, her life had turned into one long alcohol-soaked disaster. Her dad was a mess, and *that* wasn't going to get any better, and she couldn't even have some mindless fun because Carval wanted to *talk*. Why did she have to get involved with a man who wanted to *talk*? It wasn't a notable feature of men where relationships were concerned.

She hunched into her coat, and tried to disentangle all the different issues. Maybe, she thought, maybe this would be the shock which would stop her father drinking.

And maybe she could see a flock of pink pigs flapping through the sky. The wind whined, and she shivered. No matter how she told herself she couldn't fix her father, guilt chewed at her: guilt that she hadn't been the lawyer he'd now admitted he'd wanted her to be; guilt that she couldn't save him; guilt that her mother must likewise have been disappointed in her. Worst of all, guilt that she couldn't change any of it now, and more, didn't want to. She loved her job.

But then there was Carval. All she'd wanted was some easy, fun, undemanding affection. He was just right: big, broad, and interesting. And good in bed, of course. Why couldn't he just have stuck with that? She could even put up with the photographs if he'd stuck with that. Instead he wanted *talking*, and something deeper. Ugh.

If only her father hadn't been the barrier to something deeper, and to talking; the thought crept through her mind. If there hadn't been that...

If her father hadn't crossed another contour line down the slope of his descent, she wouldn't be in this position. Back to her father. Everything came back to her father.

She stood up, not eased by her break, chilled to the skin by the thin November wind and chilled in her soul by her thoughts; ignoring the thought that if she shared her father's issue with Carval, she'd probably feel better. She didn't want to see pity in his eyes. She'd rather see nothing.

Plodding back to the precinct, she felt no better than when she'd left.

***

Dr Renfrew steepled his fingers, pushed up his glasses, and swept an avuncular gaze around the assembled team. He had found that such an expression produced a more relaxed discussion. Behind it, however, he was considering the arrangement of personalities. Agent Bergen and Detective Chee appeared to have reached a professional accommodation and tentative friendliness. Detective Clement was as far away from Mr Carval as she could be, with Detective O'Leary's immense bulk and Detective Tyler's taciturnity between them. His avuncular expression required some effort to maintain.

"Thank you all," he began. "I should like to consolidate the different lines of investigation in order to explain the reasoning behind my initial conclusions. I have reviewed the work of Detective Clement's team, and the searches which Agent Bergen and Detective Chee have conducted on the potential clusters from other states. It appears to me that, as Detective Clement had originally surmised on considerably less evidence, we do indeed have a serial killer or killers." He paused, and took a sip of water.

"From the portfolio photographs and my initial discussion with Mr Carval, I am inclined to agree that both the style of photograph: objectified and puppet-like; and the sexualised nature of both the Coronal advertisements and the manner in which the victims are dressed, give support to the theory that there is a connection. Whether that connection is tangible or a so-called 'copycat' is as yet uncertain."

He sipped again, entwined his fingers and then released them, pushed at his pince-nez.

"It is my preliminary hypothesis that the killer or killers – we cannot rule out the possibility that there is more than one person involved, and indeed I consider that it is most likely to be more than one person – are driven by a desire, ultimately, to destroy the beauty which they have taken."

Dr Renfrew allowed that to sink in, expecting a significant pause in proceedings.

"The Collector."

Everyone goggled. Dr Renfrew blinked.

"You mean that horror movie?"

"Waaallll," O'Leary drawled, "actually I meant the book, but I guess the movie'll do too. The first one, though. Not the remake."

"You *read*, Bigfoot?"

"Sure I read. An' as long as my paws c'n turn the pages without tearin' them on my claws, it's fine."

"Bigfoots read?"

"Nothin' else to do above the snowline."

Dr Renfrew surmised that this was an in-joke with the team, and smiled thinly.

"Cliffs Notes version?" Detective Clement said.

"Ugly man stalks and kidnaps pretty woman, keeps her prisoner, kills her, goes after another one," Carval said heavily.

"Has everyone seen this movie but me?" she grumbled.

"You don't like horror movies," Detective O'Leary reminded her. She settled back.

Dr Renfrew surprised an odd expression on Mr Carval's face: almost affectionate, which swiftly departed; as if he had realised and evicted it.

Detective Clement grimaced. "So what you're all suggesting is that we've got someone out there who's stalking beautiful women, keeping them for a while – I think we can guess why, but Tyler, can you get McDonald to find the rape kit results on them all or hustle it through if it hasn't been done – and then killing them."

"Casey," Detective Chee ventured, "If they were all on heroin" – his face was pale – "they probably wouldn't have resisted. Too doped to care – or to know."

Detective Tyler whispered something which Dr Renfrew was grateful not to hear.

"Kit anyway," Detective Clement said tightly. "Maybe there was DNA, hair, or semen residue." Her lips pinched together. "Okay. Take a quick break while Tyler gets that moving. And Bergen, can you get a rape kit run for everywhere else, if it's not there already? Long shot, but let's see."

Dr Renfrew waited for Detective Clement to remember that he had called this meeting, and that Agent Bergen was not, in fact, part of her team. He was rapidly disappointed. Agent Bergen had jumped to his feet as quickly as Detectives Tyler and Chee. Clearly, Detective Clement expected instant compliance with her orders. That was not surprising, but the immediate response, in a team of equals, was.

"Perhaps we could reconvene in fifteen minutes?" Dr Renfrew asked, mildly chiding.

"As soon as the searches are going," Detective Clement agreed. "While they're doing that, have you seen anything in the interviews that suggests any of the people might be involved?"

"There is nothing substantive: although the attitudes displayed by Mr Yarland and Mr Severstal are suggestive, there is no clear evidence. I also wonder to what extent Mr Hervalo is affected by their attitudes. In the words of the Bard: 'he doth protest too much'."

"He's exactly the sort of pathetic jerk that hangs around lingerie shoots and pretends he isn't getting off on it," Mr Carval said vulgarly. "They get in the way and spoil the mood."

"If he's hanging around Yarland, nothing could spoil the mood," Detective Clement said caustically. Detective O'Leary patted her shoulder.

"We'll get them."

"Sure we will, but how soon? We've found three. All these other places had four. We're missing one."

Dr Renfrew's view of Detective Clement's intelligence rose further. He had expected to have to point that out. Perhaps he should consider whether this ill-assorted team were, in fact, considerably more intelligent than they showed?

"Iffen we find a fourth, then they'll be done, most like."

"And move on."

"We could find out where Coronal are planning to shoot next."

"Yeah, but how can we do that? We haven't contacted them for good reason – if they're involved, I don't want to spook them; if they're not, I've nothing to ask them – yet. Maybe when Bergen's searches and matches throw up something that links them to the other places with more than just some adults-only photo shoots I can start on them."

"Selwyn didn't mention anyone else that we found missin'. We cleared up all them others."

"No. But there should be." She frowned. "Do we know when the next shoot is? Or when the last one was?"

"Course we do. We watched it."

"Oh. Yeah. Okay. We'd better follow up with Selwyn how many Coronal shoots there were compared to how many missing models. If they've done ten shoots, and we've got three, they haven't picked their fourth just on the Coronal connection. There's something else."

Detective Clement turned a piercing gaze on Dr Renfrew, who merely looked calmly back. "What's the other link?" she asked. "In the clusters. There's got to be another similarity."

"They're all different ethnicity," Detective Chee said, re-entering with Agent Bergen, who appeared to be somewhat disturbed. "One white, one African-American, one Slavic, one Hispanic. Every single time."

"And we've got three – but not Hispanic. That shoot we were watching, O'Leary: what was she?"

"White. Hadn't enough clothes on to mistake that."

"Okay. So" – Detective Clement turned back to Dr Renfrew – "we should be looking for a Hispanic model. We've been through Missing Persons and we haven't found any other missing model types." Her eyes were hard. "We might just have a window here."

"McDonald'll run them," Tyler said, returning.

"Okay."

It was clear to Dr Renfrew that he was no longer in command of his meeting – if he ever had been. At this stage, he doubted that.

"We're going to do it this way. Andy, Bergen, you try and find out anything that matches Yarland, Severstal or Hervalo – or Selwyn, for good measure – to the crimes. Can we track their passports to see who went abroad and where? Does that match the Coronal shoots? Partials, DNA, names? Let's get to it."

Dr Renfrew watched everyone disperse except Mr Carval, who, Dr Renfrew now noticed, had a camera in his hand and had clearly been taking photographs. In fact, he appeared to be taking a photograph now, of Dr Renfrew's steepled fingers. He met Dr Renfrew's gaze, completely unembarrassed.

"Supplementary exhibition," he said. "The main one's in five months –

Murder on Manhattan. But I've got some good shots of hands, so that'll make a small exhibition of its own. Allan'll sort it out for me."

Dr Renfrew seized the opportunity. "The main exhibition?" he queried. "How did that come about?" Mr Carval appeared delighted to expound upon his activities.

"I couldn't find anything to shoot after the panhandlers" – Dr Renfrew nodded. He had visited that exhibition, and been impressed by the depth of emotion uncovered in each photograph – "and I needed to get some stuff at the store so I went out and there was Casey's team with a corpse. I had to shoot them." He smiled. "They weren't too impressed, but after a while they let me tag along."

"How did you achieve that?"

Mr Carval coloured slightly. "Um...it turned out I'd shot Casey for a poster, when she was at Stanford." Dr Renfrew blinked. Detective Clement's fierce intelligence was no surprise if she had been at Stanford. "So when I brought in my crime scene photos in case they were useful, I brought that too. We had a chat, and the gang agreed that I could tag along."

Dr Renfrew was entirely sceptical that Mr Carval had revealed the whole story. He determined on a path to follow.

"And in the process, you and Detective Clement began a romantic relationship," he stated. Mr Carval did not appear to appreciate the comment.

"We're not in a relationship," he spat out. The door slammed behind him.

***

"How long will those cross-matches take?" Casey asked.

"Running now, but we don't have the data from Paris yet. London's here. Deep dives are still running – they'll cover overseas travel for the three of them. You said Selwyn too?"

"Yeah. Timothy J. Selwyn."

"Okay. Got him from the briefing. Let's throw him in and see what it spits out."

Bergen tapped happily at his tech for a few moments and smiled. "That's in now. We'll just have to let it think."

"How long will it take?"

"That depends."

Casey growled.

"It depends how much data is in the system. If there's a lot, it'll take longer, but we'll get much better results."

"I know that," she fretted. "I just want to get on with it. Every moment there's a chance they're picking up some new victim."

"I can't make the searches run any faster," Bergen apologised.

"You could go harass McDonald," Andy suggested. "I mean, it's not like finding or running three rape kits would take him more than twenty minutes."

Casey made a particularly childish face and improved her looks not at all by sticking the tip of her tongue out at Andy.

"Shoo," he said. "We're working, and you asking for results every five seconds won't make it happen faster."

Casey humphed out. Why couldn't results be instant, like on TV shows? It wasn't fair. She needed those results. She had an ominous feeling about the whole situation, although that might simply be the whole of her life. She resorted to the old-fashioned solution of simply reading the London file, and pretended she wasn't impatiently tapping her fingers and checking the time.

The remainder of the afternoon wasn't improved by the way in which Carval was managing to bypass any interaction with her while still shooting everyone, including Bergen and Renfrew. She didn't get so much as a smile. Even Renfrew got a glare. She got...indifference. She hunched her shoulders again – she'd hunched so much that she'd need to see a chiropractor by the evening – and concentrated on the case. Work never disappointed her. (*Only your father*, whispered a nasty little voice.) Never.

CHAPTER SEVENTEEN

Finally, Andy relieved Casey's attempt to wear off her fingerprints by telling her that the searches were done. Her yelp of satisfied joy brought the whole team, plus Renfrew and Carval, to loom over Bergen's computer and try to elbow each other out of the way. The net effect, to Casey's pleasure, was that she was at the front and Dr Renfrew was entirely blocked by O'Leary and Tyler.

Carval didn't even try to get in on the game, preferring to shoot the shenanigans. He'd seen cleaner tackles in an ice hockey match.

"So what have we got?" Casey demanded.

"Well," Bergen enticed, "we got something rather interesting." Andy smirked.

"What?"

"We tracked all the passports, and they went to London, Paris and Berlin at the right times for our clusters. A little set of boys' holidays."

"Thought we didn't have matches in Berlin?"

"No, we don't. But I've suggested they take a look, though likely they'll not get my email till tomorrow. Anyway, obviously he doesn't need a passport for San Francisco, New Orleans or Chicago."

"You don't?" O'Leary said with faked amazement. Everyone groaned at him, except Renfrew, who couldn't prevent an irritated *tut*.

"The names are different in each place, but everywhere had a Coronal shoot, every shoot is in the same style – thanks, Carval: you really helped there" – *Hold on*, Casey thought, *when did he get hauled into that?* – "and we've just had a partial match on fingerprints, and guess what?" Bergen said with more emotion than Casey had thought that the FBI allowed.

"What?"

"Half a chance at matches for all three of them. Only partials, and it won't hold up in court, but it's suggestive."

"Yeah? None of the case files had matched any prints to anyone," Casey said.

"No," Andy agreed. "But we've got all of them, so we – well, Bergen – ran it all through his smart tech with the prints we got" –

"How'd you do it? We didn't take any prints."

"But they all had cups of water," Andy smirked. Casey smirked right back.

"What a shame," she said insincerely.

"And because we had them, we could match them."

Bergen took up the tale. "Yarland in San Francisco – no-one else pinged. Severstal and Hervalo in Chicago. Only Hervalo in New Orleans. They're trying to be careful, but occasionally they get a little sloppy. I gotta say, that shiny stuff the girls are wearing holds a print well."

"Hervalo's in it too?"

"Looks like it."

"Wow. He deserves an Oscar."

"Don't think you get parole from Rikers for the red carpet."

"Now what?" Tyler asked.

"Sting," said four voices at once.

"A decoy operation," Renfrew said, which amounted to the same thing in far too many prissy-voiced words. "I agree." As if it were his decision. "That is undoubtedly the best way of luring these killers into prison."

"We'll have to have co-operation from Selwyn and Coronal," Casey pointed out. "And we haven't ruled them out yet."

"There's nothing to tie Selwyn to anything."

"You said all of them."

"Not Selwyn. Sorry."

"We have to be sure. Get his phone records. And all theirs. Cross-match – Bergen, your tech is faster than ours" –

"Can Andy help? He's faster than me."

"Sure – and make sure they weren't chatting to each other. Or that they were." She smiled nastily at O'Leary. "I think it's time we had a friendly little chat with Coronal, don't you? We want the guy who sets up the shoots. Let's find him."

O'Leary strode off to start that line of investigation.

"I'll get results from McDonald," Tyler said briefly. His burly form disappeared towards his desk. Tyler didn't speak technogeek, nor did he want to. He wasn't stunningly keen on creative types either. The nearest Tyler got to fashion was a pair of jeans, un-ripped, and an un-logoed t-shirt.

"Is there anything more you can tell us?" Casey directed at Renfrew.

"Not yet. Agent Bergen's searches will assist."

"Okay."

It was unpleasantly clear that he had fallen from her mind the instant he had nothing useful to add. Dr Renfrew was not used to such treatment. He ought to find it refreshing that he was not being used as a source of affirmation or approval. However, he found it both disconcerting and unpleasant.

"You won't get anything from her till she's wrung every last drop out of the case."

Mr Carval, of course. Dr Renfrew endeavoured to repress his irritation.

"She doesn't see anything else."

"Including you?" Dr Renfrew snipped, with a remarkable lack of courtesy for which he upbraided himself almost instantly. He realised, with considerable consternation, that Detective Clement's automatic assumption of authority had left him irritable. He was no longer used to being merely a part of a team, rather than its leader. "I am sorry. I should not have said that."

"Doesn't make it less true."

Dr Renfrew concluded that Mr Carval was unimpressed by Detective Clement's reluctance to pursue a romantic relationship. He altered the course of conversation.

"I should like to discuss your thoughts on the style of the Coronal photographs. The case notes are not as enlightening as a discussion might be."

"Me?"

"Yes. I deduce from your previous exhibition that you endeavour to discover the humanity of your subjects, and to provide a visual narrative to those who are visiting. Therefore, it appears to me that you have already considered that there may be a narrative behind the Coronal shoots. I wish to understand your conclusions, and then share with you my own."

"Let me get a coffee," Mr Carval said. He did not sound as flattered as he might have done. It was certainly not everyone from whom Dr Renfrew would seek opinions. "Would you like one?" he added, after a noticeable pause.

"That would be very kind. Black, without sugar, thank you."

Mr Carval returned with coffee and the photographs of the Coronal models. Dr Renfrew regarded them with distaste, and became aware that Mr Carval had taken photographs of his expression. Despite having given his consent, he considered that Mr Carval's constant photography was excruciatingly irritating.

"Please tell me the inferences you have drawn from these photographs."

Carval put his annoyance at Dr Renfrew's pomposity and arrogance to one side, mainly by remembering the immense number of shots he'd taken today and the possibility of some, or most, of them being good. It was also flattering that Renfrew had sought his views and wanted his presence. Casey hadn't exactly given him the sense that either was desirable.

"Technically they're pretty perfect. The lighting's right, there aren't any unattractive shadows or highlights – though the make-up artist should avoid those – the lighting focuses on the subject and her dress, which is what I'd expect for a clothes shoot." He paused. "The exposures are right, the focal length is right. As I said, technically, they're really good."

"As good as you might do?"

"No."

"Oh?"

"I can show you what I can do in the same circumstances. Give me your laptop."

Carval, whose pride was thoroughly pricked by Renfrew's doubting *Oh*, tapped forcefully for a moment or two and pulled up his cloud storage.

"This is what I can do," he said, and flipped the screen round to show Renfrew.

For several seconds, there was absolute silence in the conference room.

"I see. Although I am not acquainted with the technicalities of photography, I can detect a considerable difference: not in technique but in style."

"He doesn't care about the people he's shooting. You can tell." Renfrew nodded. "There's no real life or emotion in these: it's vacuum-packed sex, as sterile as a lab. There's no attraction, no attempt to show the lingerie as something you might enjoy in a relationship or even friends-with-benefits. It's just a transaction. Wear this, do what I tell you, get paid, done. IVF, not lovemaking."

"Prostitution, without the physical interaction."

"I guess."

"Mm." He steepled his fingers. "Your thoughts match my assessment." He pondered for a moment, in which Carval took another batch of shots of the expressions playing across his face. "I think we must consider the history of each of these persons. I shall speak with Agent Bergen."

He went out. Carval wandered after him, shooting all the way.

"Agent Bergen, as part of your detailed search, would you investigate the early backgrounds of our four significant persons?"

Bergen seemed a little embarrassed, in Carval's viewfinder. "Er...we're already doing that, Dr Renfrew. Andy suggested it." Renfrew blinked. "I don't know how long it'll take."

"It is begun. That will suffice."

***

At her own desk, Casey and O'Leary were racing each other to find the right contact at Coronal.

"Got it!" they said, almost simultaneously.

"Who've you got?"

"Bothwell. John Tucson Bothwell."

"Me too." She squinted sidelong at O'Leary. "Go ask Carval if he knows him."

O'Leary gazed at her until she squirmed. "Okay," he rumbled. "But you gotta sort this out."

"I'm not talking about it."

He shrugged, straining his shirt seams. "Up to you. But I think you oughta." He ambled off to find Carval. Shortly, a subsonic boom reverberated through the bullpen, its desks, chairs, floor and the fillings in the cops' teeth.

"We found a John Tucson Bothwell. Looks like he commissions the shoots at Coronal. Know him?"

Carval, who had no issues with O'Leary since the men had said they weren't going to put the hard word on him, grinned. "Sure I do. He rejected me as a photographer six times, years ago. He's sorry now."

"So iffen you wanted a chat with him, likely he'd want to chat with you?"

"Yep."

"Waaallll, as our expert, here's what we'd like to do." O'Leary's grin lit the room. "We're runnin' searches on these guys' background – includin' Selwyn. We're thinkin' about a sting, you know, but we're gonna have to get Coronal on side. Now, iffen they ain't involved, they'll co-operate" – he stopped hard. "Had a thought. Would they know how old their models were?"

"Not really."

"Mm." He strode off, poked his huge head into the room where Bergen and Andy were companionably technogeeking, and returned. "Asked them to check ages. Bet at least one's under age."

"It's not their responsibility." Carval abruptly caught up. "You're going to blackmail them."

"Naw. That's not a nice word. It's just...persuasion. Somethin' to help them see the right path, you might say."

He suddenly took another two strides back to the technogeeks. "C'n you cross-check phone records from this Bothwell to the others, too?" And back again. "That'll give us an idea if Coronal are likely in on it or not."

The flurry of activity died down as the computers took over.

"I think we're done till the searches are finished." Casey gathered the gang together.

"Yeah. We'll park it till tomorrow," O'Leary directed at Carval.

"We're supposed to be off-shift tomorrow," Andy reminded them.

"We're on a live trail." But Casey made a face. She'd have to go and ask Kent to approve the overtime for them all to work tomorrow – oh, *shit*.

Her father was expecting her tomorrow night. She flicked a quick glance at her watch, and found that it was still before five. She could change it and go tonight.... She *should* change it and go tonight. It had been a pretty crappy day already, why not deal with the rest of the crap too? It wasn't as if it could get much worse. "Okay, I'll go ask Kent."

She trudged off to Kent's office, and tapped.

"Sir?"

Kent looked up. "Yes, I will approve the overtime." He looked straight back down, and thereby missed Casey's dropped jaw and muffled gasp. She'd expected argument.

"Thank you, sir."

She hurried back to the group. "We're good."

"Uh?"

"He said it's okay. So let's finish up tonight and start bright and early tomorrow when we've got the searches."

Everyone was on board with that idea.

With considerable reluctance, Casey found an empty room, and called her father.

"Dad, is it okay if I come for dinner tonight, not tomorrow?"

"You are coming tonight. It's Sunday. You always come on Sunday."

Casey swallowed. "Dad, we discussed this. I wasn't going to be working tomorrow so I said I'd see you then, but now I have to work tomorrow and it's worked out that I can come tonight."

"You always come on Sunday," he said stubbornly. "I even got us an apple pie for dessert."

She dropped it. "See you later."

"See you later."

She could only sit, slumped, in Interrogation One. He'd forgotten. He'd been stone cold sober when she told him about the change. Another thing he'd forgotten.

It took her a few moments to pull herself together. She'd have a lot to do tonight, because now she was sure that he would have forgotten to call a lawyer – oh, hell, she had to do that leave request too – and probably forgotten the hearing. She'd have to take him. She crumpled again: sniffed hard, blinked harder, straightened up and left the room, to all appearances perfectly composed. Her leave request took less than two minutes.

From Observation, Carval had shot it all. And then he slipped out and waved a generic goodbye before anyone could ask him where he'd been for the last fifteen minutes. He wanted a really good look at those shots, because just maybe they'd tell him something. It wasn't like Casey would.

***

"So what's this chat you wanted?" O'Leary hummed at Tyler.

"Put the hard word on Marcol."

O'Leary's hum became approving, in much the same way that an elephantine bumblebee might approve of an open flower.

"Didn't take it well."

"My surprise is killin' me," O'Leary said, and smirked. "He's a li'l touchy, that man."

"Yeah. But."

"Mm?"

"Someone put a scare into him about that photo" –

"Waal, there's only one suspect there."

"Yeah. Should have another chat with him, and that Allan guy."

"We'd better take Andy. He c'n keep Allan calm. Talk about culture, or somethin'."

"Yep."

"You c'n tell him. I don't guess he'll argue."

"Casey doesn't have to know."

"Naw. Not yet. She might get a tad tetchy."

"Like fire's a tad warm?"

"Yeah. Tetchy."

They grinned. Casey wouldn't shoot them, and there wasn't much else that would have an impact.

"Okay. You get Andy on side, an' I'll tell Carval we're comin' to visit later on. There's another guy who's tetchy right now."

"No playing Cupid."

"Everybody should be happy," O'Leary said sententiously. "I don't like it when people ain't happy. Makes the bullpen soggy."

"Yeah, you're a weeping mess."

"Exactly. So people should be happy."

They drained their drinks, which made them happy, and wandered out of the break room in perfect harmony, to find that Carval had left and Casey and Andy were packing up.

"I'm off," Casey said, and didn't offer any further information.

"Got an issue," Tyler told Andy.

"Huh?"

"Carval's been puttin' a scare into Marcol without tellin' us. Oughta have a little chat with him, before anythin' more, um, interestin' happens," O'Leary picked up.

"Don't you think it would be a lot simpler just to tell him not to get involved?"

"Yeah, but the man's gotten involved, so now we gotta deal with it. 'Sides which, it was his photo an' he got pretty riled when he found out."

"Why do I have to come?"

"You're goin' to keep that Allan guy calm. Use some of that culture for somethin' useful, y'know?" after which helpful comment Andy grumbled, mostly under his breath, all the way to Carval's apartment.

***

"Hey, guys." Carval got a good look at their faces. "What's up? Didn't expect to see you tonight."

Allan was ushered in by Andy, who'd stopped off to collect him. "Yes," he said prissily. "I'd like to know too. I don't imagine this is a coffee meeting to discuss modern culture."

"Naw," O'Leary confirmed. "Though some coffee or some beer would be good." Everyone glared at him. "Anyway. Today we got one of them blasts from the past." Allan winced at the grammatical atrocity. "Guy called Marcol. Detective Marcol."

"And?" Carval said. Allan shuffled backwards, and found Andy unobtrusively in the way.

"You don't seem surprised."

"I was there when you said he was coming from Narcotics."

"Yeah. But the funny thin' is, every other time you'da been in there askin' for permission to shoot him. Or not askin', like usual. This time you snuck out before he could get there, an' we had to get you back for the afternoon to be our expert."

"Man said he'd got a lawyer's letter saying he stole your photo," Tyler said. "Only one person we could think of."

"We're a little upset by it," Andy added. He didn't sound upset in the slightest.

"But mebbe not as upset as you were about him takin' your photo to mess with Casey."

"So spill," Tyler finished.

"He stole my photo," Carval bit out. "Nobody steals my photos and gets away with it."

"If we allowed one theft to go unpunished, then we wouldn't be able to pursue it as aggressively if somebody stole a more important photo," Allan explained.

"All my photos are important."

Allan threw Carval a quelling glance, and, much to the cops' amusement, Carval shut up. "You can't let any of it go," Allan noted.

"What did you do?"

"Found out who it likely was" – notably, Allan didn't say how – "and got our usual attorney to write a standard letter about breach of copyright. When we didn't get an answer, he wrote again, more strongly."

"And if you still don't get an answer?"

"Court papers usually have a galvanising effect." Allan bared his perfectly white teeth. "What happens if a cop gets served at work?"

157

"Waaalllll," drawled O'Leary, squashed into a too-small chair, "it ain't usually too good. 'Course, it's normally divorce papers, so mebbe it won't make much of a stir."

"Our process server has a very loud voice, and likes to announce the allegations."

The three cops blinked.

"Play rough, don't you?"

"He stole *my photo*," Carval repeated.

"Must've missed that," Tyler said dryly, "first few times."

"Okay, he stole a photo, an' you got a commercial interest in keepin' that from happenin'" –

"But," Andy chipped in, "it wasn't public. It wasn't used for business or profit, so what loss did you suffer?" Allan stared at Andy. "I did a basic tort course. Carval here doesn't seem to have suffered a loss. If anyone did, it was Casey. And *she* doesn't know about this, does she?"

An indistinguishable mutter arose from Carval. Allan's mouth opened, shut, opened and slowly shut again.

"She don't know, on account of Carval here's still alive. She ain't gonna like this."

"Not going to find out," Tyler said.

O'Leary gaped at him. "Huh?"

"Not telling her. No point. Can't change what's done."

"But" –

"We got enough issues. Up to Carval if he tells her." Tyler turned. "Think you should. Up to you." He shrugged. "Not our problem if you get dead. She doesn't like secrets."

"Only her own?" Carval snapped.

"Up to her."

"Casey'll be told too. Ev'ryone in this team gets the same deal."

Allan was still imitating a stranded codfish. Carval scowled blackly at everyone.

"We're done," Tyler continued. "Any chance of a beer?"

"You guys are really something," Allan managed. "Really...something."

"Does that mean we get a beer?" O'Leary hoped. "All this fixin' matters makes me thirsty."

"You're always thirsty when someone else is getting the beer in."

Andy noticed Allan's dumbfoundment and patted him on his sharp suited shoulder. "You'll get used to them," he said consolingly. "I did. I just keep taking the tablets."

CHAPTER EIGHTEEN

Late that evening, after he'd shooed out the cops and Allan, who had been getting along surprisingly well with Andy, based on experimental theatre and ballet; Carval added beer to the scrawled shopping list. He relaxed from the implied telling-off at the start of the evening, which had been wholly unfair, and finally had a chance to examine the photos from the interrogation room.

He didn't know why he'd followed Casey. Maybe he'd thought he'd talk to her, maybe he'd simply been spoiling for another fight. At any rate, she'd pulled out her phone before he could say anything, so he'd slipped into Observation before she could spot him, glanced at her reluctant form, and instantly started to shoot.

He gazed at the results. Something had been said to her during the call which changed her stance from reluctance to worry, and, the call done, outright unhappiness. It couldn't have been case related, because she wouldn't have sought privacy, and anyway, he knew her moods. Misery wasn't one of them where cases were concerned.

Contrary to Allan's opinion, Carval did have a brain, which he occasionally used for something other than photography. Presently, he was applying it to Casey. Based solely on O'Leary's comment that her father *needed a bit of help*, he decided she'd been talking to him, and it hadn't gone well. His brain cranked into gear. Casey had disappeared, and then said...*this isn't your problem. Let it be.* That must have been about her father. Hm. His Casey-cop had definitely been keeping secrets. It stung. Surely she could have told him something? It wasn't like he hadn't seen pretty much every form of degradation along the way: he'd shot it all.

It didn't occur to him that that was precisely the point. He shot it all.

***

Casey went home to change before she went to her father's: ensuring that her appearance contained nothing that would make her look like a cop. She used a little more make-up than usual, covering the evidence of sleepless nights and worry; and chose a smart, office-wear skirt and cream blouse. She even put on some jewellery. When she checked her appearance in the mirror, she resembled any of a thousand identikit female professionals in a hundred Legal 500 firms. She didn't look like herself at all.

Still, if it kept her father happy, for long enough that she could deal with dinner and the logistics of finding a lawyer for his court hearing, she could do it. She rammed down her feelings and simply...got on with it. What else could she do?

"Hi, Catkin," her father said happily. "Ready for dinner?"

"Sure."

She let him fix dinner: mac 'n' cheese with bacon; apple pie with ice cream. She didn't bring up any cases, and her father didn't ask, which was another unwelcome change. He'd been interested, up till...up till she'd been beaten up. And then he'd had a drink, or several, and all the truth had started to come out. She wondered, suddenly, if he'd ever been interested at all, or if it had just been pretence: humouring a child.

Dinner done, she couldn't put it off any longer.

"Did you find a lawyer?"

"Lawyer?"

"For your hearing."

"What hearing? I don't have a hearing. Why would I be in court? I've never even had a traffic ticket."

"Dad," she said hopelessly, "you have a ticket for a desk appearance at Queens County Criminal Court on December 13."

"Catkin, this isn't funny. Court isn't a joke."

"It's not a joke." She hunted around, and finally spotted the slip on the table, half-hidden under – oh, *hell* – brochures for the tourist sites in DC. "Look."

"But I didn't do anything. It's a mistake."

"It's not a mistake. You were *arrested*, and I had to come bail you out at JFK."

"Don't be ridiculous."

"It happened. You were sodden drunk and you don't remember any of it. You tried to hit a cop and abused the check-in staff, so they arrested you. Look at the appearance ticket." He didn't. "You need a lawyer."

"I..." – she cut him off.

"Unless you want to go to jail, you have to get a lawyer. I *told* you that. Did you do anything about it?"

His silence was its own confession.

"You forgot," she said, heavy as cannon-shot. "You didn't remember what I told you on the phone, you don't remember what you did. You forgot I told you I couldn't come tonight, till I called to change it."

She didn't bother looking around, or searching the trashcan. She knew why he'd forgotten. Sometime in the last three days, he'd drunk enough to fog his memory. No point finding proof.

"Don't talk to me like that, Katrina. I'm your father."

"So act like an adult, then." He bristled, but she ran right over his protest. "You have to deal with this. You can't shove it under the rug and hope it'll go away. You have to get a lawyer or you'll be in jail."

"Why won't you" –

"Because I'm *not* a lawyer. I never wanted to be a lawyer. I get that you're disappointed about it, but you have to get over it and deal with the situation. You. Have. To. Hire. A. Lawyer."

Her father sat, open-mouthed. "Disappointed?" he said. "How" – but Casey had had enough of the whole thing.

"Because you *said so*. You told me I *should have been a lawyer*. When you were too drunk to lie. How long have you hidden that? Did Mom think the same?"

"Catkin, that's not *true*. We weren't disappointed."

"Really? So why'd you say it, then?"

She couldn't stop herself: all her terror and pain that he was getting worse; that she'd have to keep bailing him out and picking up the pieces; that her whole life was breaking on the wheel of his disease; that he didn't respect her choices.

And that he didn't love her.

"I...I don't remember."

"No, because you were drunk. Again. You're getting drunk more often, and it's getting worse. You need to get help, Dad, but you're not doing anything about it. You're losing your memory. Do you know what that means?"

He was silent under her anger.

"Do you? It means you're not coping. You're not just drinking to take the edge off. You're blacking out, and you're hurting people. You have to fix it."

"I'm fine. It was a one-off. It won't happen again."

But it would. Of course it would. Whatever he said, this wouldn't be the only time. The bottle was right there on the dresser, a cut-crystal glass beside it.

"I'm going home," she said wearily. "I can't help you. I can't help you with the court case and I can't help your drinking. It's up to you. I'll see you next Sunday."

She pulled her coat on, and left. Behind her, her father reached for the glass, his face lined and his hands shaking. He didn't call her to come back, and she didn't turn her head.

As soon as she got in the door she fell apart. She hadn't meant to lose her temper; to say any of what she felt. She didn't have the excuse of alcohol for her loss of control. She didn't have any excuse. She didn't even try to sleep: the nightmares had come while she was awake; no point in adding more. She read for a while, absorbing nothing, drank coffee, and then, heedless of Kent's likely wrath, dressed for work, and went.

At least she didn't disappoint her team.

***

Kent had arrived that morning at his usual hour, cast a swift glance around and noticed his misfits hard at work. He also noticed that the photographer wasn't present, which was pleasing. The man might not be disruptive but he was around far, far too often. That hadn't been the plan at all, although at least he left Kent alone.

He closed his door, and considered his precinct. Clement seemed to have managed Feggetter quite nicely – no complaints about moving that case, and the profiler wasn't annoying him, which meant she'd managed that nicely too. She hadn't managed her father's issue nicely, though. Not at all. In fact, she'd made a fine mess of it. Kent was more than a little irritated that she hadn't simply requested an hour's leave, which he would have granted. He hoped she'd learned her lesson. He scrawled approval over her leave request and shoved it into his out tray.

Unfortunately, that was the only simple matter of which he could dispose. Now he had another problem. He didn't think that Travers of Narcotics would be pushing Marcol on him: Narcotics needed every cop they had to deal with their own cases – but he wasn't at all sure of it. Marcol's family had pull. He definitely wasn't going to ask for Marcol: he didn't want to pay someone else's wage bill from his budget. However, he also wasn't going to allow problems to arise between his team and Narcotics, where their case looked like it might have Narcotics implications.

He tapped out a number.

"Sergeant Carter, please."

A moment later the senior Sergeant at the NY Police Academy replied. "Carter."

"Sergeant," Kent said pleasantly. "Kent here, from the Thirty-Sixth. Good to talk to you."

"Nice to hear from you, sir. What can I do for you? Looking for a sneak peek at the latest batch of recruits?"

"That on offer?"

"No, but it doesn't stop any of you asking."

"Can't blame us for trying. But no, that wasn't why I called. I was hoping for some information."

"Yes, sir?" Carter queried.

"Detective Clement."

"Sir?" Carter was intrigued.

"I hear she had history at the Academy with Detective Marcol."

"She beat him to top spot, if that's what you mean. Thought he might've been interested, but she sure wasn't so I didn't have to get involved. They fought it out for the first few weeks, then she turned up the engines and that was that."

"I see. Did you hear anything about photographs?"

"No, sir. Some guy came to tour a few weeks ago, to take photos – had a great photo of your team" –

"What?"

"Some photographer came round" –

"Carval," Kent said heavily.

"Yeah, that's the name. Said he was doing an exhibition around New York's Finest, showed me this shot of Clement and the team, took some shots, I cleared them, he went. Chatted about the team – couldn't believe they gelled like he'd shot. How'd you make that happen? I'd never have believed it if I hadn't seen it."

"I had a hunch," Kent said, flattered. "So, nothing about photos, no nasty rumours."

"Rumours? No sir, not a thing."

"Okay, thanks. Now, anyone I should be looking at?"

Carter laughed. "Not yet, sir."

Kent sat back, irritated. He had no evidence, but a bunch of hunches and a complicated problem, all centred round the misfit team and Clement specifically. As if her father wasn't bad enough. Worse, Carval was mixed up in it, which Tyler hadn't mentioned. Tyler had chopped his words like a barracks lawyer. Technically, Carval wasn't part of the precinct.

There was nothing he could grill the team about, and he couldn't kick Carval to the kerb for shooting at the Academy. Kent merely wished that he couldn't see trouble with Marcol heading straight down the track, with no real way to head it off. If Travers did try to push Marcol on him – which he didn't want: Kent wasn't going to be pushed around in his own precinct – he'd better have a good reason to say no. Which he didn't.

On the other hand, Garrett at the Third might have a better view. He'd rated Clement high, and he'd brushed it away when Kent had mentioned the rumours. Mm. Yes. A friendly chat between Captains.

He picked up the phone, again.

***

"Okay, where did we get to with the searches?"

"We didn't match Selwyn to anything. Occasional calls to the others, in business hours, on weekdays. Calls to Bothwell at Coronal, same again. No history of going to any of the places there were other clusters, and nothing in his past to indicate anything that Dr Renfrew would want to know more about – we did ask him," Bergen added, before Casey could ask.

"Hm. Sounds like he's off the list." Casey was a touch disappointed. It wasn't that his commentary on her appearance still stung, but...okay, yes, it did. She told herself firmly that ruling someone out was as important as ruling them in, and refocused.

Andy took up the tale. "The other three talk all the time. We expected that, though Hervalo is a lot more involved with the other two than he let on. They're not talking to Coronal outside normal hours either, though. Again, it's not proof, but it's directional."

"We're trying to run down a lot of other numbers that they've called, too."

"Berlin?"

"Still nothing."

"Anything that would definitely tell us that these three are the same three all around the game – apart from the partial prints?"

"Nope." Faces fell.

"What about the models' ages?" O'Leary asked.

"You were right," Bergen admitted. "Couple of them – not the ones who got dead – were too young for those sorts of photos."

O'Leary bared his teeth. "Guess they'll want to co-operate," he said.

"Nice."

"And the early history?" Renfrew queried.

"That was pretty interesting, too. Turns out Yarland had some relevant history." All attention locked on Bergen. "Even at school he was a good photographer, but he didn't make friends and he wasn't much liked. Got into some trouble for annoying the pretty girls, but that stopped when he started shooting them. On camera," he added hastily. "Funny thing was, some of the pretty girls found that there were some, er, interesting photos of them available. Coincided with the trouble stopping."

"Or anyone reporting it."

O'Leary and Tyler were suddenly either side of Casey, whose fingers were locked, white-knuckled.

"Severstal had done some modelling, but never hit the big time. A few complaints, but nothing ever followed up – they all got withdrawn. Hervalo – nothing to speak of. Always been a dresser. No history."

"I see." Renfrew steepled his fingers. "The Collector seems to have been an accurate analogy."

"Unfortunately, it hasn't got us any solid evidence to pull them in as suspects," Casey said bitterly. "We're going to have to go with the sting."

"I agree. I believe that we should begin to plan it."

There was an ominous silence.

"We will require a decoy," Renfrew said. Everyone looked at Casey. "Detective Clement is entirely unsuitable. Not only is she not Hispanic, but one could not mistake her for a model of the type Coronal use."

That was true, but, Casey thought acidly, Renfrew didn't have to be quite as unflattering as that.

"We shall have to seek out someone more appropriate." The team looked blankly at each other. Model types didn't figure in the NYPD's recruiting requirements.

"We don't know anyone else," Andy said, "and I guess Vice don't, because we'd already have tapped them up, but" – his face twisted: not everything was totally cool yet – "I bet Carval knows someone."

Casey felt her stomach churn. She hadn't seen Carval outside the bullpen since he'd told her that, if he wasn't important enough to talk to, then fine, he'd stick to photographs and being an expert. She simply did not want to explain. She couldn't stand the pity, or worse, proposing solutions. Or, still worse than that, photography.

"We'll need Kent's approval."

"No, we will not. This is now an FBI operation, and only my approval is required. I will inform Captain Kent myself."

"Carval!" O'Leary boomed through the bullpen. Casey was conspicuously silent.

"Yeah?" He ambled up, having listened in and then wandered off to take candid bullpen shots, and smiled generically around, cooling when it reached Renfrew, and disappearing entirely at Casey. "What is it?"

"Got a question for you?"

"Yeah?" he said, looking around with his camera half raised.

"Focus," Casey rapped. He scowled at her.

"We want to find someone to act as a model."

"Uh? Why?"

"'Cause Casey here's the wrong type for a Coronal shoot an' we're settin' up a sting to see what shakes out."

"Oh, okay, yeah, you said. Yeah, I know someone," Carval flipped out, without apparent thought. "Alejandra Despero – Allie – would do it, if you paid her. She's the right type."

Casey stared for an instant, then blanked her face. That had been horribly quick.

"How d'you know?" Tyler asked, curiously. Unseen, Dr Renfrew observed the exceedingly interesting reactions of the various team members.

"She wanted some portfolio shots, so I took some. I gave her the shots and printed them for her" – the fifty-degree temperature drop from Andy and Casey hit him – "What?"

"Thought you didn't do that nowadays."

Carval met O'Leary's gaze with a hard stare of his own. "Then you thought wrong, didn't you?" O'Leary flicked a glance at Casey, who was rigidly quiet, and back to Carval, and said no more.

Tyler stepped in. "How do we find this Alejandra Despero?"

Carval flipped him a card. "Tell her it's me, otherwise she'll think you're an agency – or a john. That won't start anything off well."

"I got a better plan," Tyler replied. "You come with me to call her." He swept Carval off. O'Leary raised his eyebrows at their backs. Casey sat down, then stood up and aimed for the break room and the coffee machine. When Andy looked like he'd follow, O'Leary indicated that he shouldn't, and did so himself.

"Waaallll, that was interesting," he drawled.

"I don't think so."

"Just talk to the man."

Casey fussed with the machine, which was producing perfectly fine coffee without any fuss whatsoever.

"You're miserable. He's mad – an' he's got a right to be, 'cause you're treatin' him like a one-night-stand when we c'n all see it ain't."

"Why are you always telling me to make up?"

"'Cause it's you who's screwin' up," O'Leary said bluntly. "I get that you don't want your pa mixed up with your boyfriend, but you could say somethin' without goin' that far." He patted her head. "Think about it."

He ambled out. He could rely on Tyler to have a preliminary chat with Carval, now or later. Fact was, he himself intended to have a chat with Carval, which he didn't intend Casey to know anything about. She'd only get cross and fuss at him, and he didn't like fuss and fretting. Though...something else had gone down.

He re-entered the break room. "Did you see your dad last night?"

"Yeah."

"Guess it didn't go well."

"No."

***

"So," Tyler said, conference room door firmly shut. "You still do glam shots."

"This is your business how? But no, I do *portfolio* shots."

"Depends. Portfolio for Hustler, guess that's a level or five below your pay grade. If you're getting this Alejandra girl something to get her a better chance, that's different." Carval said nothing. "No shame in helping someone." More silence. "Where's Casey in all this?"

"You tell me."

Tyler merely regarded him, which had no effect, and then dialled Alejandra's number.

"Miss Despero?"

"Hi!" bounced a little-girl voice. "This is Allie Despero."

"Miss Despero, this is Detective Tyler of the NYPD. I have Jamie Carval here, who gave me your name. We'd appreciate your help on an investigation."

Carval hadn't heard Tyler use that smooth tone before. Normally he rationed his words like they were cut diamonds, and was as harsh as on the battlefield.

"Yes?" she wavered.

"Allie," Carval said suavely, "Detective Tyler and some of his colleagues are looking for a model to help them with an operation. You'll get a chance to be shot for *Coronal*."

"*Coronal?*" she shrieked. Tyler winced as his ears bled. "Jamie, you mean it?"

"Sure do."

"I'm there! Where? When? Now?"

"We'd like to brief you," Tyler said. "Could you come to the Thirty-Sixth precinct now?"

"You bet!" she squealed. "Jamie, are you shooting for *Coronal*?"

"No, not me."

"Oh," she drooped. "You made me look so good!"

"We'll explain everything when you get here."

"On my way! Byeee!"

"How old is she?" Tyler asked, face pained.

"Twenty-one. Sounds like she's a teen."

"Shit."

"You'll live," Carval said callously. "Just let her get over the excitement and she'll be sensible."

Tyler grunted. "Casey doesn't like this."

Carval shrugged.

"Don't you care?"

"Better ask her."

"Asking you."

"Not your business."

"You got a face like someone stole your last dime, Casey's got a burr up her ass, something's wrong."

"Ask her."

"Likely I will." Tyler shrugged himself, and changed the subject. "Better tell Renfrew."

***

"Doctor Renfrew."

"Yes, Detective Tyler?"

"Alejandra Despero will do it. Here as fast as she can get here."

"She's expecting me to be here," Carval said.

"I had anticipated that. I consider that to be the most effective strategy. Your presence will reassure her, should reassurance be required."

Casey came in on that statement. "I hope not," she said, briskly. "She's not a suspect or a witness. She's doing us a major favour and all of us will treat her accordingly."

Tyler flicked her a look. Casey wasn't going to be best buddies with Carval's baby model. Professionalism wasn't the same as kindness. Wasn't like Renfrew was warm and cuddly, either. He'd better stick around..

CHAPTER NINETEEN

"We need to get the next one." It echoed darkly in the dim space of the empty set.

"No hurry. Views are sky high."

"We need to keep it that way. They expect variety." The words slithered out.

"We can't afford to raise any flags. The cops are still out there."

"They haven't found anything."

"They're looking. Just because they haven't got anything doesn't mean they won't."

"We took care. There's nothing to see."

"Phones?"

"No way. We're supposed to speak to each other – setting up shoots and all that."

"We are." A sneering laugh.

"They're not dumb."

"No. But we're smarter. There's nothing that can't be explained. So they track us? We were shooting. We're Coronal's main team, and we go where they want us."

"But..."

"Even if there's evidence, we shot those girls for Coronal. Of course we were there. There's nothing that's not circumstantial." The men relaxed. "We have to find a new one. We've only got a couple more weeks here, then it's on to somewhere else."

"Rome. We haven't been there."

"That'll be nice. Warm. It's too cold here."

"Can't have goose bumps on the girl. Spoils the party."

"They're all hot."

"Hot for it. They all love it. Anything for the next gig."

"No problem getting a new one, then."

"No. But keep your hands to yourself, this time."

"Why? They like it."

"Last one was complaining, all the way up to the bar. I don't want you to get a reputation. They won't come out if they think you're gonna be there, and someone'll be prepared to blow their future to get you if you go too far. That dumbass Selwyn'll fire you if he finds out, and then it'll be a whole lot harder to keep you with us."

"Selwyn wouldn't dare. He needs to keep us."

"There are plenty of dressers almost as good as you. Tone it down. Selwyn whines about his agency being totally clean, and that's part of the reason he gets the best ones. If you wanna keep this going, dial it back, okay?"

"Okay."

"Now, we better get this place ready for the next one."

"Sure. All the props are ready." Dark satisfaction swirled. "They love all those toys. Can't wait to play."

"Just how we like them. All ripe and ready.".

CHAPTER TWENTY

Dr Renfrew regarded Captain Kent with professional aplomb, having determined that he should inform him of the forthcoming operation, and in the process understand a little more about the team with which he was working. He discussed the key details of the operation, and then moved on.

"You have assembled an exceedingly interesting team around Detective Clement." A hint of curiosity was permitted to infiltrate his voice.

"They do good work," Kent said sharply. He wasn't inclined to allow some high-faluting FBI profiler, who'd swallowed a dictionary and allowed it to meet the stick up his ass, to mess with his best team.

"So I observe," Dr Renfrew soothed. "However, I also observe a number of fragilities. Were you aware of Detective Clement's dislike of photographs?"

"I was. I don't need you to tell me about my team. They're fine. They don't need my input."

"Is that always the case?" Dr Renfrew inquired delicately.

Kent flushed. He had dealt with Clement's issue with her father – not that she'd been grateful. Nor had it appeared to him that she had thought that it had been necessary for him to assist her, although he couldn't have overlooked an unauthorised absence once he'd become aware of it.

"Yes," he said.

Dr Renfrew considered Captain Kent to have been mendacious in making that statement. He did not consider that saying so would be helpful. "Mm."

"Let's go back to the sting operation. You intend to use a civilian? That's not something I would allow."

"How fortunate that it is not your decision, but mine. There are no suitable candidates among your teams," Dr Renfrew rebuked Kent, who coloured like an angry turkey-cock. "Detective Clement is entirely unsuitable – physically," he added swiftly at Kent's fulminating gaze. "She is perfectly competent otherwise. However, the agency and the majority of its employees would undoubtedly recognise her. I would be extremely surprised were her original interaction with Mr Selwyn not the subject of considerable comment. I gather that she made a strong impression."

Kent couldn't argue with that. If Selwyn wasn't still cowering in a corner, he didn't know his Clement.

"Mm," he said, imitating Renfrew's irritating mannerism.

"We have selected a model who will fit the profile perfectly."

"How?"

"Mr Carval suggested her," Dr Renfrew said calmly. "He appears to be a man of resources, if arrogant."

"Wait till he asks to shoot you," Kent growled.

"He already has. I had no objection. I find his exhibitions to be extraordinarily interesting, and I am quite content to be included." Dr Renfrew smiled smoothly. "In any event, our model will be well compensated."

"From whose budget?"

"Mine."

Kent relaxed.

"I shall ensure that Coronal co-operate, and also that all the staff at Stardance remain unaware of the operation."

"You suspect their involvement?"

"I cannot rule it out."

"And if your civilian is injured?"

"That will be the FBI's issue. No blame will attach to the NYPD."

Kent was thoroughly sceptical about that, but, having called in the FBI, he'd lost the ability to control the decisions. It didn't improve his mood.

"I see."

"No doubt we shall," Dr Renfrew condescended. "Thank you for your time." He began to leave.

Yet again, Kent wondered why he had ever involved the FBI. If he never saw Dr Renfrew again, he would be an extremely happy man.

Suddenly he replayed a part of the conversation.

"Dr Renfrew," he said, "Can you come back for a moment?"

"Yes?"

Kent shut the door. "Has Detective Clement actually discussed her dislike of photos with you?"

"No. I inferred it from her behaviour during a discussion of Mr Yarland's history, from which we deduced that he was spreading embarrassing photographs of non-consenting girls." Dr Renfrew paused. "But surely you are aware of her views?"

"Of course. It'll make no difference to her excellent work at all."

Kent re-closed the door, and added up everything he knew about Clement, photographs, and Tyler's truncated explanations. The total was exceedingly unpleasant, but it contributed nothing more than he already knew. Sufficient unto the day, he thought, and decided to leave the team alone until he'd talked to Garrett. He had an uncomfortable sense that he might be opening a bigger can of worms than he'd like. He'd do the right thing, but, as he'd thought earlier, Marcol's family had a lot of pull, and if he was going to wade into a mess he'd better have his big boots on.

***

Less than an hour later, a wave of gasps and gazes announced the arrival of Alejandra. The bullpen was, for the first time in its collective life, struck dumb. That, Casey thought tartly, was likely because the tongues that might have talked were trailing on the floor. Alejandra was gorgeous. Tall; long, dark hair and huge dark eyes; full lips and legs from here to eternity. She didn't walk, she sashayed in four-inch heels, and, when she shrugged her coat from her shoulders in one liquid movement, wore a dress which emphasised both her astonishing legs and her slimness. Even O'Leary's jaw had dropped, and he wasn't interested in women.

"Jamie!" She undulated over to Carval and planted a kiss on him. Casey's pencil broke in two. "The lovely man downstairs sent me up! Wasn't that sweet? He was so nice to me!" Somehow that wasn't a surprise.

She smiled round the bullpen. Naturally, she had perfect teeth. Thousands of dollars had hit the pockets of the orthodontist who had carried out the work. The gleam hypnotised otherwise tough cops, who were reacting like kittens to catnip.

"Who is everyone?" she asked. The little girl pitch of her voice was already giving Casey a headache.

To Casey's mingled astonishment and irritation, Tyler whisked up to Alejandra.

"I'm Detective Tyler. I spoke to you earlier. Thanks for coming in so fast. Let me introduce you."

Carval, cut out, blinked at Tyler's instant reversal of his earlier opinion, gazed round, and caught Casey's eye. An odd expression flicked across his face, and he strode over.

"Something wrong?"

"Nothing. I'm really glad Alejandra is prepared to help." She manufactured a smile. "Tyler's smitten. I've never seen him like this." An equally manufactured laugh arrived. "It's cute. We'll tease him for months about it."

"Did you actually sleep this week?" Carval asked, which had nothing to do with anything, as far as Casey was concerned.

"Yes, not that it's your business."

"Really?" His disbelief was patent.

"Yes. Shouldn't you be introducing Alejandra to the team?"

"Tyler's doing it." He watched her carefully. "I'm sure she'll be delighted to meet you."

"That's nice."

"You're upset."

"Don't be ridiculous. I'm just tired."

"Thought you said you were sleeping just fine?"

Casey clamped her mouth shut.

"Or you're jealous."

"That's even more ridiculous. Why would I be jealous?"

"Oh, I don't know. Maybe because Allie can do something you can't?"

"I wouldn't want to kiss you," she snapped.

"Interesting that your mind went straight there. I meant, take the lead role in this sting operation. But since you went there, let's just talk about that."

"No."

"That's what you do every time I say something that's true but you don't want to hear. Shut it down and try to shut me up. It won't work. You are *so* jealous but you won't admit it because you won't admit it was your fault in the first place."

"Get out of here!"

"No. I'm shooting and everyone else invited me."

"Yeah. We all know that all you care about is the photos. You don't give a flying *fuck* for the real people behind them."

"Hey!"

Carval's furious face instantly transmuted to a fondly resigned expression.

"Allie," Tyler said, "this is Detective Clement. She's in charge of our team."

"Call me Casey. Everyone else does." She managed a semblance of a smile. "Thanks for coming to help out. We really appreciate it."

"Everyone calls me Allie!" Alejandra said. "Only my mom ever calls me Alejandra!" She pouted, adorably. "It makes me feel like I've done something wrong!"

Next to Alejandra-call-me-Allie, Casey felt short, fat, and over-endowed in the cleavage department. She swallowed down her envy, and the sour knowledge that *this* was what Carval liked. Tall, super-slim, and beautiful. Everything that she wasn't.

"I'm totally happy to help! I'd do *anything* to get on a Coronal shoot! That's really hitting the big time! I'm so glad that Jamie remembered me! He's so sweet!"

Sweet wasn't the word Casey was thinking of using, especially as she could see him taking yet more freaking photos. She wanted to tear the camera from his hands and jump on it, and only her unwillingness to show the bullpen what a full-on tantrum looked like was stopping her.

"His portfolio shots of me are fabulous! Do you want to see them? I can get them."

"Maybe another time. Right now, we'd better brief you so you know what we're suggesting – and make sure you're totally happy with it. If you don't want to do it after you've heard everything, then that's okay."

"Oh, I'd do *anything* to get on the Coronal shoot! And to thank Jamie, of course!"

Casey just bet Allie would.

"Tyler, you want to get the team together?"

"Can I go with him?" Allie asked breathlessly. "I've never been in a police station before, and it's so interesting!" She – good grief. She was giving *Tyler* the eye. Oh, wow. Casey's anger took a back seat to evil amusement. *Tyler* getting hit on by a model? This was going to be good. They'd get *weeks* of ragging out of that.

"Sure you can," she said. "It'll just take a minute or two."

Allie sashayed off with Tyler. Casey wasn't at all sure that she wasn't thinking about taking his arm – or vice versa.

A few minutes later, the team had assembled in Renfrew's annexed conference room, pursued by longing looks and several suggestions that if extra help were required there would be plenty of volunteers.

"We've never been so popular," Andy smirked.

"Never will be again."

"I'm popular. Ev'rybody's my pal."

"I bet you're just the biggest teddy bear out!" Allie said. Andy and Casey choked. "And Tyler here is just so sweet!" She only seemed to have one adjective. "You all must really work out." Tyler flexed, and preened. "It's really cute!" Preen changed to wince. "I really love fit men! I mean, I meet a lot of models but they're all real skinny." She batted her excessively long eyelashes in Tyler's direction. Annoyingly, Casey was sure they were all natural. Life was not fair.

"Miss Despero" –

"Call me Allie" –

"Miss Despero," Renfrew said, and her face fell like a kicked puppy. Tyler unconsciously growled. "Thank you for agreeing to assist. Detective Clement and I will explain the operation to you. When you have heard our strategy in full, you will have the option to decline. Should you decline, you will be paid for your time today. Should you accept, you will be paid for the entire operation. I will advise you of the relative amounts in private, after the briefing."

"I get paid too? That's amazing! Anything you want!"

Renfrew, Casey noted, was almost as pained by the little-girl voice as she was. Casey hadn't known there were that many exclamation points in the *world*.

"Detective Clement, if you would explain the case to Miss Despero?"

"Okay. About a month ago, we were called to a dead body. We later found out it was Melinda Carnwath, but before that happened we got another one: Daniela Petrovich."

"Dani? Dani's *dead?*"

"You knew her?"

"Not, like, best buddies, but yeah, we'd tried out for some of the same shoots. She was really sweet: didn't bitch like some of the girls." Allie looked like she was about to cry. Tough-guy Tyler patted her hand, and passed her a Kleenex. "Poor Dani."

"Anyway, we caught a third. Carissa Ndbele. Did you know her?"

"No." She sniffed. Even that was beautiful.

"We've done a lot of investigating, and we've found that all the victims worked on Coronal shoots, for the same photographer and dressers. Dr Renfrew is an FBI profiler, and he and Agent Bergen" – Allie noticed Bergen for the first time, and gave him a blindingly bright smile. Casey guessed they could mop him up later, but if she caught any of her team melting like that they'd be Dumpster diving till they solidified again – "have found that there have been other, similar cases."

"Like a serial killer? Wow! It's just like on TV! This is so amazing! And I get to help you solve it? It's just like the movies! Jamie, this is amazing! Thank you!"

Casey dug herself out from the haystack of exclamation points with some difficulty, and, much to her surprise, received a look of complete understanding and sympathy from Renfrew. Apparently he did have a single human emotion after all. Irritation. She returned him an equal measure of understanding.

"Miss Despero," Renfrew recalled her attention. "The reason we have selected you is that, in each case, four models have been murdered. One Caucasian, one Slavic, one person of colour, and one Hispanic. Detective Clement's team have found the first three victims, but as yet there has not been a Hispanic victim. Mr Carval was asked to identify a model who would fit the profile, and he considered that you would be suitable, as there are no detectives or officers available who would be appropriate."

Allie looked at Casey. "But...she's really pretty," she said naively. "I mean, she's not a model, but she'd obviously shoot well." She thought for a moment. Despite the voice and thicket of exclamation marks, she wasn't dumb. "With the right make-up and lighting, Jamie could make it look like she was taller. I mean, sure she's got a few more curves than me but I guess she isn't at all fat. She'd do totally great in a lingerie shoot. All the men that saw it would be drooling, like with that old model who did the bra shots and they had to stop putting them near roads..."

"Eva Herzigova," Carval said. "'Hello boys.' That was a classic campaign."

Casey's mouth hung open. Andy and Tyler snickered. O'Leary's belly laugh deafened the room, the bullpen and likely most of Upper Manhattan.

"Unfortunately," Renfrew said, "Detective Clement is well known to Stardance, Coronal's New York agency, and we could not possibly convince our suspects that she was a model. Despite your professional assessment, she is not the correct physical type for the shoot. In particular, she is not Hispanic, and we cannot conceal her lack of height by using Mr Carval as the photographer."

Too damn freaking right they wouldn't. Being photographed on a lingerie shoot was pretty much Casey's worst nightmare.

The three cops spotted Casey's closed, frozen expression and ceased to show any humour at all about the situation as the implications dawned on them.

"We must use Mr Connor Yarland as the photographer, and Mr Severstal and Mr Hervalo as the dressers."

Allie made a face.

"Miss Despero? Is there something wrong?"

"Well, like, not exactly, but you hear things from the other girls, and they're not...um..."

"They get up too close and personal?" Tyler said. "Don't worry, we'll make sure nothing happens."

"Even if it did, we'll make sure they go down for it," Andy added. Allie didn't appear to be reassured. "If they get too handsy. Nothing more than that." Her face cleared.

"You will be in no danger at all."

"We don't know which of those three is involved, or even if any of them are. So we're going to make you the Coronal model – for real" – Allie squealed – "but we'll wire one of the cameras with a tiny extra camera and a mike, and we'll put a tracker chip in you. Bergen swears he can put it in and get it out without leaving a single mark."

"Sure can."

"It's like, totally, Mission Impossible!"

"Yep."

Reluctantly, Casey was developing respect for Allie. Liking was too much of a stretch. She was sure her ears were bleeding from the squeals.

"Okay," Allie said. "When can I start? I've never been, like, a *spy* before!" She bounced up from her chair and hugged Carval enthusiastically. "This is so great, Jamie! Thank you so much!"

"You're welcome."

Renfrew indicated that everyone else should disperse, no doubt while he discussed compensation with Allie.

"When you're done, come out and find one of us, and we'll answer any questions you've got."

"Okay!"

***

"Allie likes you," O'Leary snickered. "What's Carval here goin' to do now you stole his pal? He'll be all on his lonesome."

Tyler shrugged.

"It's amazin'. You been puttin' on a new aftershave or somethin'?"

Tyler had never worn a male grooming product in his life and all of them knew it.

"Must be," Andy chipped in. "Sure isn't his pretty face."

Said not-pretty face scowled.

"Iffen it was pretty faces, she'd'a been lookin' at me."

Andy spluttered with laughter. Even Carval, who'd been pretty quiet, cracked a wide smile.

"You're the biggest teddy bear out, you know," he grinned. "Can't see it myself."

"Bigfoot, teddy bear; teddy bear, Bigfoot – nah, no real difference."

"I got fluffier fur than any bear."

"I could have lived my whole life without knowing that," Casey said aridly, from behind the men. "So how's about you and your fur, woman-magnet Tyler here, and Andy help me and Bergen sort out the logistics?"

"We need Allie to join in, and she's still in with Renfrew."

"Probably tryin' to understand all them long words. I don't get how anyone c'n have swallowed a dictionary, though. They don't taste good an' they don't come with fries."

"Here she comes now."

"I can tell without even looking. Put your tongues back in and stop drooling, guys. I don't wanna swim across the floor."

As Allie undulated closer, it became obvious that she was in shock.

"You okay?" Tyler asked.

"Yeah. I just can't believe how much they'll pay me! I would have done it for free to be on a Coronal shoot! This'll make a real dent in my tuition loans! It's so great! You're all so sweet!"

"Tuition loans?"

"Sure! I'm in senior year at the Steinhardt School."

Andy gasped. "You're a music major?"

"Well, sure I am! I'm an oboist, and I sing."

Casey flomped down at her desk. She hated her. Gorgeous, smart, and musical. Casey sang like a strangled crow. She was probably good at sports too. Why had nobody poisoned her already? Tyler was captivated; Andy was about to start on culture, which should get him shot, but wouldn't; Carval had preferred to shoot and be with her; and the sum total was, it wasn't fair.

O'Leary tapped her shoulder. "C'mon. You could use some coffee, an' so could I." He swept her off. Not one of the others noticed them go.

"She's awful pretty, but she ain't holdin' your boy's attention."

"Yeah, right."

"She ain't. He's lookin' at us. In fact, he's comin' this way."

"He must want some coffee. He's sure not coming to talk to me."

"Had 'nother spat? Boy, you do like to make thin's difficult for yourself. Talk to the man."

"What's the point? It won't cure anything and he'll still be taking his fucking *photos*. This whole case is about fucking photos."

She stomped out just as Carval walked in.

"Waal, look who's here. Seems like a good time to have a nice chat. D'you want a coffee? Casey don't want hers so there's one goin' spare."

CHAPTER TWENTY ONE

"Was it something I said?" Carval asked acidly. "Or something I didn't say?"

"More like someone you brought."

"Oh, for Chrissake. You guys asked me to suggest someone, and now I did you're going to make an issue of it?"

"Naw. But your baby model there just hit Casey square in the gut, sayin' she could model. You remember she hates photos, yeah? An' why?"

"Sure I do. It's not like I could *forget* that bastard Marcol stole *my photo*" –

"You don't have to remind me. I know."

" – so what did you want me to do? Tell the world about it? Renfrew's enough of a vulture without giving him a carcass to pick at."

"Guess not. We gotta fix this, though."

"We?"

"I told you. Everyone in this team gets the same deal. You got told, Casey's been told." O'Leary's sharp eyes watched closely. "Like I said, her dad's been needing a bit of help." Behind his homely face, his brain worked, so that he could truthfully say that he hadn't told Carval anything. "Y'know, Casey don't drink much at all."

Carval gaped at the total non-sequitur. Then he clocked O'Leary's intent gaze, and realised that it wasn't a non-sequitur at all. He'd subconsciously noticed a hesitation when she was offered a drink, and a hint of defiance when she took it. She didn't have beer in her fridge – or hadn't had, the times he'd been there. She'd dashed out of the Abbey after a call, one evening, and the men had made damn sure he couldn't ask any questions; she'd dashed out of the precinct, and the only one who hadn't known why was him.

And O'Leary had just told him why. *Casey* didn't drink much. Casey's *dad*, by implication, drank a lot too much.

"Casey's dad's a drinker," he said flatly. "She has to bail him out. But why the *fuck* couldn't she just say so? It's not like it's her."

O'Leary waited, exuding strained patience.

"What am I missing? Stop looking at me like I'm dumb."

"You're a photographer." The way O'Leary said it reminded Carval that O'Leary might be a mobile mountain but he was also hiding considerable intelligence behind all that bulk. Clearly, he was expected to keep up. He thought hard. Photographs? But his original shot of Casey had nothing to do with alcoholism...oh.

"Panhandlers."

"Give the boy a gold star."

"But I've never met her dad."

"An' if you did? You wouldn't try to shoot them both together?" Carval coloured. "You shoot all the time: when you're allowed an' when you ain't. An' like it or not, she knows it."

"I can't *not* shoot. You don't get it."

"So explain." It was a tone that Casey would have been proud to use. It went straight to the obedience centres of the brain.

"It's like...like *breathing*. I can't not breathe, and I can't not take photos if I see the shot. It would be like not having my hands. I *have* to."

"Seems like you got a problem, then."

"Not if I never meet him."

"True. Anyway, I better go do some work. You better work out how you 'n' Casey fix thin's, cause all this fussin' an' frettin' is rufflin' my fur." He paused. "An' before you get all riled, I told her the same."

O'Leary disappeared before Carval had thought up any answer to his comments. He sipped his coffee, which didn't help, and thought, which also didn't help. With unusual introspection, he realised that no matter what he promised, he'd hardly be able to stop himself taking shots of Casey's blazing personality against the ruin of an alcoholic father.

But. But, just like he'd known that he could never take shots of her against his sheets, and he *hadn't*, he could discipline himself not to take shots of her and her father. He could.

***

Casey had taken one look at Allie captivating her team and the bullpen without the slightest effort and, after finding that there was nothing urgent, decided that she should supply herself with concentrated caffeine in the form of a double espresso from her favourite coffee shop. The few minutes' walk in the chilly November wind wouldn't hurt, either, and it might clear her head. She slipped away without any of her team noticing.

Carval exited the break room, flicked a glance around the bullpen, saw with relief that Allie was deep in conversation with Tyler, Andy, and Bergen, that O'Leary was frowning at his computer screen and the pile of papers on his chaotically untidy desk – but that Casey was nowhere to be seen. Her coat wasn't on the back of her chair, either. He made a rapid assessment of where an out-of-temper Casey might go, and arrived at the answer: to get brain-bendingly strong caffeine. Since she hadn't acquired it from the break room, she'd gone out to buy it. Based on absolutely no evidence, he decided that she'd gone to the same espresso bar in which he'd first cornered her.

He reached the coffee shop just as Casey ordered.

"And an Americano for me, please," he said, and handed over the cash for both their drinks to the barista.

"Thank you," Casey said freezingly.

"Nuh-uh. I wanna talk to you."

"Sure you do. We can talk about the case in the precinct. Thank you for introducing Allie. She'll be perfect."

"I don't want to talk about the case and I sure don't want to talk about a twenty-one year-old with a bad case of squeaky exclamation-itis. I want to talk to you."

Casey stared down into her double espresso.

"Can't you even look at me? I exist, okay?"

"Yeah."

"I'm not going to disappear just because you're having problems. Your problems aren't my problem."

"Oh?" she said sarcastically. "That's a change of tune. You threw your toys out of the stroller when I told you it wasn't your business."

"You made it clear I wasn't important enough to talk to."

"It's not your problem."

"Your team knows all about it."

Her eyes came up. "We've been together five years. You've been here two months."

Carval changed tack before that line of conversation could end badly. "Look, it's obvious it's something about your family."

"Who told you?" she snapped, and before he could reply answered her own question. "O'Leary."

"He didn't tell me."

"Of course he didn't," she said wearily. "He'll have hinted. Plausible deniability so I can't actually shoot him." She returned to staring at her untouched coffee. "So you know. So now you'll try and take photos. The cop and the drunk. Nice segue from the panhandlers to the cops."

"I won't."

"You said *I can't not shoot you.* You said *not when I see something I need to shoot.*"

"I don't *need* to shoot your dad."

Stunned silence greeted him.

"I don't even have to *meet* your dad."

Casey made a noise which could only be represented by *glurp*.

"Uh?" she said, incomprehensibly.

"Why would I meet your dad? You aren't going to tell me if you have to go get him, are you? You already didn't and I don't guess that's going to change, even if I said I wouldn't come unless you asked me." Under the table, he crossed his fingers that his tactic would work. "You don't tell me anything important and then you just assume."

"So we're already back to your hurt feelings," she spat, provoked into angry speech. "I've got more to worry about than that. Dad's been arrested and he's blacking out from drink. He hates that I'm a cop. He wanted me to be a lawyer and I'm not one and now I have to find him a lawyer. He can't remember he needs one. He can't even remember his court date."

Carval stared. That was far worse than he'd thought.

"I've got to get back. We've got work to do. I've been out too long." He watched as every hint of emotion disappeared from her face. "We have to get this op running and Renfrew's not going to be able to persuade Allie properly." She was already opening the door: sharp, hard steps cutting through the whine of the wind; pulling on professionalism like a shell. He'd have put an arm around her; offered comfort; but it was clear she didn't want it. She wanted to do her job. "I haven't got time for any of this."

"Huh?" That sounded far too much as if it included him for Carval's peace of mind.

"I want this perp off the streets. He's killed three girls here, he's looking for a fourth, and if it is the same guy then there are another twelve in the US and more abroad. I haven't time to worry about Dad, but I have to."

Carval reached down and slipped his fingers into hers: finding them cold and unresponsive. He tugged gently, but she pulled them away and jammed them into her pocket. They reached the bullpen without a single word more being exchanged.

Upstairs, the rest of the team, Bergen and Allie were deep in conversation.

"Okay. So we'll inject a tiny tracker behind your ear, where there's no chance of it being spotted."

"That'll work," Carval said. "Anywhere that's going to be shot, it might show up as a bump or shadow with the lighting."

"We'll do it now, so any redness or a little bump will have died down."

Allie didn't look reassured by Bergen's words. "Will it hurt?"

"No. We'll numb it first. You won't feel a thing."

"Then we'll get a tiny camera-recorder on to your purse" –

183

"Why? I thought you were going to put it on the main set?"

"Iffen those dressers are gettin' handsy, we want to have it on tape, whatever else he might be involved in. We'll get him for that, if we can."

"Good plan," Casey said. "Get them for everything we can. Who's going to speak to Selwyn?"

"I believe it would be best if that were you, with either or both of Agent Bergen or Detective Chee to meet with him thereafter to assess the technical requirements. He is already sufficiently intimidated by you that he is unlikely to protest. I will be speaking to Coronal in a few moments. The information Detective O'Leary has provided on the ages of their models should ensure their co-operation. They would not wish to be shamed on social media."

"Do you want to call Coronal first? That way they can weigh in on Selwyn if he gets difficult."

"That might be best. We should not delay."

Renfrew pecked off, resembling McDonald to an extraordinary degree, and leaving behind as much irritation.

"So I don't have to talk to Bothwell?"

"Nope. We'll keep you in reserve," O'Leary told Carval.

***

"That's not a needle, that's a freaking gun!"

"No, no. Look, here's the anaesthetic cream. Let's do that first." Bergen efficiently plastered on the cream. "It'll take about fifteen minutes to work. It's going to be like getting your ears pierced. You didn't feel that, did you?"

"Promise?"

"Promise."

"And you can get it back out?"

"Sure I can. Don't worry."

"What's going to happen?"

Casey stepped in. "What we know is that the victims were dressed and shot for Coronal. We think, but we don't know, that they had to be lured off somehow. But that's why we wanted you. With a tracker, and with a bug in your purse, we can find out exactly what's going on without you taking any risks at all. We'll be all around you, but if you see us don't show it, okay?"

"Okay!"

"Just do everything like you normally would. The shoot's real, but Renfrew'll bully them into co-operating, I guess. I'm leaving that to him."

"But will they use the shots?"

"I don't know," Casey said.

Allie was quiet for a moment. "I guess it's no different to any other try-out," she said, "and I get paid for this one."

"And you actually get shot for Coronal, it's just whether they use them or not. You can still put it on your resume."

"Yeah," Allie said much more happily. "I can!" She looked uncertainly at Casey. "It'll be okay, won't it?"

"Sure. We'll be right there."

"Okay," Bergen said. "Time to put the chip in."

Allie squinched her eyes tightly shut, which meant she couldn't see Carval taking shots. Casey, looking at the injector, was delighted that it wasn't being used on her. That thing would do for elephants.

"Ow!"

"All done."

"You said it wouldn't hurt!"

"Give it a minute."

"Come get a coffee," Carval said to a pouting, cross Allie.

"I don't drink coffee! Bad for the complexion and it doesn't help my singing. *He*" – she gestured at Bergen – "said it wouldn't hurt!"

"Singing?" Carval repeated.

"I'm a music major."

"You are?"

Casey's mood was improving by the word. Carval might have found this model, but he knew absolutely nothing about her. Surely if he'd done anything, um, intimate he'd have at least known her major? The point became moot as Tyler and Andy wandered up, faux-casually, and bore her off, ignoring Bergen's mutters.

"I wanted to check it was working," Bergen complained.

"So check now."

He fussed around for a moment. "Okay. Um...where are they going?"

"Lunch," Carval suggested. He was hungry. "O'Leary, you want some lunch? Bergen?"

"I'll just" – Casey began.

"Come out to get lunch too. C'mon. Before Renfrew spoils the party."

"I don't" – she tried again.

"You should eat. Otherwise you'll get all shaky and won't be able to shoot straight," Carval teased.

"I can always shoot straight," she flipped back. "Shall I show you by piercing your ears?"

"No thanks. They hear just fine without holes in them."

"Aw, now. You could have them pretty dangly earrings with feathers on, like I saw in the store." O'Leary snickered.

"That what you wear off-duty?" Casey quipped.

"Naw. Clip-ons hurt my ears, an' you know fur an' feathers don't mix. All the style guides say so."

She laughed.

"Now, c'mon. It's lunchtime, an' I'm so hungry I could eat an elephant," O'Leary added.

"Don't think they sell those in the lunch bar, but let's go." Carval led them out.

***

Allie was still pouting – which all the men, even O'Leary, seemed to find adorable – as they reached the lunch bar.

"That needle could've injected *dinosaurs*! It was wider than my oboe reeds!"

Bergen cringed under Tyler's condemnatory glare.

"Lunch. Salads there."

Allie went towards the salads. *How surprising*, Casey thought snidely, and herself went in search of chocolate. If she was going to feel short and fat, she wasn't going to deny herself comfort, even if she hadn't wanted lunch or company. A triple chocolate chip muffin and a super-sized coffee later, she was as happy as she was ever going to get next to Miss-Tall-Talented-and-Beautiful; who had three lettuce leaves and two small squares of chicken, without dressing. Allie probably thought that cucumber was dangerously calorific.

"Not much there," Tyler said, looking from it to his own protein-packed plate.

"I don't do lunch."

Of course she didn't. Casey chomped down on her innocent muffin.

"You good with that bug now?" It sounded like if the answer were to be *no*, Bergen's lifespan would be measured in seconds.

"It's stopped hurting."

Somehow, in the scramble of everyone scavenging for their lunches, Carval had managed to end up next to Casey and as far away from Allie as he could possibly be. Of course, that meant that he was in a perfect position for yet more shots: this time of Allie, Andy, and Tyler. His camera was whirring. Casey devotedly addressed herself to her coffee, ignored Carval and his damn camera, and pretended to eat. A small pile of crumbs grew on her plate.

"You okay with the plan?" Bergen asked.

"Ye-es. When will we do it?" Allie sounded nervous.

The team looked at each other.

"We'll know when Renfrew's spoken to Coronal," Casey said. "That'll give us a time. Pretty quickly, I guess. We don't want to waste time here."

"Okay." Her voice wavered. "I could really use the pay-check."

"Thought modelling paid a lot?"

"Only if you're famous. Like Cara Delevingne. The rest of the time, it's

186

not so great as you think. It's better than waitressing, though. And you get felt up less," she added.

"Gotta be an advantage," Andy sympathised.

"*Less.* Not: *not at all.* Selection's a total meat market." Allie's exclamation point overload had disappeared. "The competition's pretty nasty, too. I mean, I've got my major and music, so modelling isn't going to be my career, but if it's their main thing then, like, they get mean. They'll do anything to get one up on the others."

"So," Casey said, thoughts piling up and clamouring to fall out of her head, "if the dresser was handsy they'd put up with it?"

"Well, sure."

"And if someone they thought could get them the next job – like the photographer, or the make-up guy, or the dresser – said 'come for a drink'" –

"And the rest," Carval said cynically –

"or something like that, they'd go along with it?"

"In a heartbeat, sure."

The team paid rapt attention. "Wanna bet that's how they're doing it?" Casey said.

"It would be easy...but" –

"But?"

"But how come Andy didn't catch them on the footage?"

"You wouldn't let the others know!" Allie said. "They'd spoil it and you'd be hated."

"Andy."

"Yeah?"

"Wider footage. We only looked at the entrance. Maybe – couple of streets?

"More," Allie said, bright eyed. "You really wouldn't wanna be seen!"

"Yeah? Okay. Um – three each side – 32nd to 38th and two over – 4th to 8th Avenue. Try one date and see where you get. Carval!"

"Uh?"

"You're a photographer. Would you take them to your studio or to a bar for a drink?"

"Bar."

"Okay. Here's how I think this is going down. They pick the girl up in the shoot, ask her out for a drink."

"Who?"

"Don't know yet. Dressers, photographer, could even be someone we haven't thought of yet. Doesn't matter. They spike the drink somehow, then pretend she's drunk and take her out. Shoot her up with heroin, keep her high, do whatever they're doing" – Andy opened his mouth, and shut it again on Casey's searing glance – "then kill them and dump the body." She took a breath. Allie was pallid. "Tyler. You get over to the dealer in Rikers and find out who he was selling to. Take Bergen, in case he's useful. Move it up the schedule - make it happen this afternoon."

"On it."

"O'Leary. Bars."

"Thousands of 'em. Gotta narrow it down."

Casey grimaced. "Yeah. Start thinking about how. C'mon." She rose. "Let's get moving."

CHAPTER TWENTY TWO

"Ah, Detective Clement. How convenient. I have spoken with Coronal, and they are amenable to employing Miss Despero as their Hispanic model."

Allie squealed: excitement beating out terror. Casey and Renfrew winced.

"They wish to have the shoot within the next day or two. Will you make the appropriate arrangements with Stardance?"

"Yep."

"I've got classes in the mornings, but not afternoons," Allie put in.

"That's okay. If my theory is right, afternoon works far better anyway."

"Theory?"

Casey outlined her thoughts from lunchtime.

"I see. Most logical."

"Allie, I think we're done for now. We'll call you as soon as we know the timing, and we'll do a full briefing then, but there's nothing more to do here. That okay?"

"Sure!"

Allie swayed off, pursued by wistful, lustful, and downright desperate glances. Strangely, Tyler wasn't supplying any of them. As he collected Bergen and departed, his posture was distinctly smug.

"I'll call Selwyn. You guys carry on with the other trails."

She swung off to a conference room to make her call.

"Mr Selwyn. Detective Clement here." She'd have sworn she heard a whimper.

"What can I do for you?"

"We've spoken to Coronal. They have agreed to use a specific model for their next shoot. We want to arrange that as quickly as possible, using Connor Yarland, Jose Hervalo and Kyle Severstal, plus anyone else who habitually works on the Coronal shoots. You are not to mention any police involvement. If you do, you'll be charged with obstruction of a federal investigation."

"Federal?"

"Yes."

"Anything you need. We can set it up for tomorrow if you want?"

Casey contemplated for a moment. "Can we come in tomorrow and set up some tech?" She deliberately failed to specify the tech in question. "Then the shoot could be the day after – afternoon, please."

"Yes. Okay. Whatever you want."

"We'll come in tomorrow after those three are finished for the day."

"They're not due in tomorrow."

"Good. We'll be there tomorrow afternoon. And remember, not a word to anyone. Or you'll be in a cell."

"No-one."

She cut the call, satisfied that Selwyn was so terrified that he couldn't even think about disobeying.

"Okay, that's done." The others nodded as she strode out, already talking. "Tyler gone?"

"Yep. Took Bergen with him."

"Forty-five minutes' drive, minimum an hour inside, forty-five back again – they won't be back till five, earliest." She pondered. "Allie's all fixed up. We can't work out the tech till Bergen's back" –

"I can," Andy disagreed. "I can put it all together and then we'll refine it when he's back. All the footage requests are in, so I'm good."

"Okay."

Andy set to. After a moment or two, he called O'Leary over to talk about layout.

Casey contemplated her empty desk. She'd set everything in motion and, until Berlin's police replied, she had nothing new. She knew what she ought to do: she simply didn't want to do it.

She had to find her father a lawyer. She couldn't leave him to sink: she couldn't let him run the risk of going to jail without lifting a finger to stop it. She'd met plenty of lawyers in her time. She slid away to the break room under the guise of brewing more coffee, and ran through the ones who she remembered for good reasons.

Safely hidden, she downed her coffee and dialled. And if she was only doing it to try to bury the memory of his disappointed, "Should've been a lawyer," she didn't let herself know it.

"Jankel and Jones."

"I'd like to speak to Carla Jankel, please."

"Carla Jankel."

"Hello. This is Detective Clement. Um...I need to hire a defence lawyer."

"What are the charges?"

"Um...it's not me. It's my father. He's got an appearance ticket for Queens County Criminal Court on December 13. Disorderly conduct – tried to take a swing at one of the airport cops."

"I see. Okay. Why are you contacting me, not your father? I can't represent him without his consent."

"I know." Casey swallowed. "He doesn't know anyone."

"But you could simply have given him my details."

She gulped again, and forcibly controlled her voice. "He wouldn't remember to call you. He's...unreliable."

"I see," Ms Jankel said. Humiliation buried Casey as she heard complete comprehension in the lawyer's tone. "Okay. Tell me everything you can, and I'll contact your father. But you'll have to guarantee our fees."

"That's okay."

"Right. Let's get the details, then."

Casey outlined everything, gave her father's contact details, received an assurance that Jankel would contact him before the day was done, and finished the call.

She couldn't move. Laying it all out had exhausted her meagre reserves, already depleted by lack of sleep. Droplets plinked on the table before she could fumble for a Kleenex and pretend they hadn't fallen.

She couldn't pretend about her father, either. She'd had to face the ugly reality behind their facade, and now she couldn't hide the truth from herself any longer. She'd expected the final, fatal knock. She hadn't expected – hadn't wanted to think about – the slow degradation, or the aggressive, angry episodes. Plural. All since she'd been beaten up. The change was her fault. She should simply have cancelled on him: claimed some sickness bug, missed dinner, and not triggered his fall.

The Kleenex squelched in the silence.

***

O'Leary flicked a glance around the bullpen and noticed that Casey wasn't there. For a happy minute, he thought that she'd gone to have a sensible chat with Carval, but then he noticed Carval buzzing around some of the other cops. He decided to let sleeping Caseys lie.

Several moments later, when there was still no Casey, and Carval had dawdled up to fuss over getting shots of his and Andy's hands (and what was *that* about?), he started to worry. It wasn't like Casey to shirk.

"Where's Casey?" Carval asked.

O'Leary shrugged. "Not her babysitter."

Carval opened his mouth again, and then shut it as Casey strode back to her desk as if she'd never been away – at least until the men got a look at her face.

"Uh-oh," O'Leary whispered. "That ain't good." He took a step.

"Where have you got to with the tech?"

"Really not good."

"Halfway. Can't rush genius."

"Did I miss your real name being Bill Gates?"

"I like to keep that quiet," Andy flipped.

"What about narrowing down the bars for Daniela?"

"Likely not popular, busy places. She'd be – they'd have been – noticed. Reckon we c'n eliminate anywhere trendy, an' anyway they got CCTV, all of 'em. Reckon we c'n set the techs to gettin' that, just to make sure, but 't ain't where I'm thinkin' we ought t' look."

"So where are you thinking?"

"Smaller. Mebbe some of those romantic places, mebbe just somewheres dark 'n' quiet."

"It's still too many."

"I know. We gotta rely on that tracker, an' prime our Allie-girl to chatter."

"Shouldn't be an issue. All she'll have to do is be herself."

"Ow," O'Leary chided.

"That's not what I meant. She's naturally bubbly. It'll be natural for her to bubble about where they're going and what they're doing – and who's there."

"Yeah."

"Won't work till she's at the bar, though," Andy said. "She can ask, and maybe we'll get a heads-up, but if I was them I'd be keeping it on the down-low so it couldn't get posted on Facebook till too late – oh my God."

"What?"

Carval was shooting the instant the tone shifted.

"We have to go back to their social media. Now you've laid out how it might have happened, we'd better get someone to re-question the bars we do know about."

"Good thought. Let's find those uniforms who've been involved already"

O'Leary went after Larson and Fremont, the large officer who'd found their third victim, and shortly returned.

"Okay, they'll be on it. Larson for Felice, and Fremont when we pick up where Melissa might've been."

"Good. We should have thrown that in the mix earlier," she said.

"We're picking it up now. We've been concentrating on the main trail."

Casey was already retrieving Melissa's Facebook. When she had a new trail, she needn't think about her father. Right then, she needed not to think about her father. She'd just think about this "van" instead. It had to be a bar.

"Penny for them," Carval said from behind her. She jumped.

"Van. Must be a misspelling."

"Autocorrect strikes again?"

"Wouldn't think so. It's not in any bar name. I just have to think."

"Van," he said aloud. "Van – vin!"

"Yeah. Van."

"No, vin. Like French for wine, vin. Not van. V-I-N."

Casey tapped. There was a Vin sur Vingt wine bar – actually, there were several, and several others with Vin in the name, all over Manhattan. That wasn't helpful.

"Andy, O'Leary, either of yours mention a Vin?"

"Naw."

"Nope."

"Any bar?"

"Only this Felice 83."

"So right now we don't have a clue. I want the rest of that location data."

Carval looked at her white face and the dark circles under her lashes and knew exactly why she couldn't think.

"Okay, Daniela's data was around the Upper East Side."

"Carissa was at Felice 83." O'Leary brought up a picture.. "It's pretty plush."

"Mm. Okay, so reaching, but most likely I can cut this down to the Vin sur Vingts north of Columbus Circle. Let's get Fremont to go to those ones with a photo of Melinda."

O'Leary went to organise that. The others crowded round her desk.

"Those bars aren't full of quiet corners."

"No, but all he – they – would've taken was a minute when she wasn't looking."

"Why'd they change?"

"For my money," O'Leary's bass arrived, "it's 'cause they're tryin' not to have a pattern. Smart," he added, disapprovingly. Casey quirked an eyebrow. "Think about it. Diff'rent colours. Diff'rent cities an' countries. Diff'rent bars. We even got diff'rent partials, so I'm wonderin' if they took turns at being the main man." His homely face became disgusted. "You weren't sayin' in front of Allie" –

"We don't want to spook her. We'll keep her safe."

"Sure we will," the mountain agreed, "but what you weren't sayin' was that they're rapin' those girls."

Carval made a choked noise. He'd known that was likely – he wasn't that naive – but to hear it in that flat tone brought it home right into his sickened guts.

"Most likely. Don't know if McDonald'll be able to confirm it from the kits, but that's my guess."

"Yeah. An' my guess is they're takin' turns to be the star."

Casey's eyes went hard. "Why'd you say that? That they want to be the star?"

He shrugged. "Just words."

"Yeah but" –

"But that would fit" – Carval butted in. "Always behind the scenes, never in front."

"Severstal had tried to be a model and failed."

"Hervalo was always in the background" –

"And Yarland had tried to get with the pretty girls and failed," Casey concluded. "Where's Renfrew? He has to think about this stat."

She surged up, exhaustion forgotten, and, followed by the whole team and Carval, slammed into Renfrew's annexed room.

"What" – Renfrew started, displeased.

"Dr Renfrew, we have a further theory. We hypothesise that our three suspects want to be the star of their own show. And" – Casey's next words were not supported by any evidence at all – "what if they're actually taking shots when they're doing it?"

"Or even filming," Andy added acidly. "Sex and snuff movies."

Renfrew's gaunt face twisted. "How have you come to this conclusion?"

"Severstal tried to be a model and failed. Yarland wanted to get with the pretty girls – and failed. Hervalo's more of a mystery. He's always been out of the limelight. So now they've got a chance to be stars."

Tense silence stretched out as Renfrew thought.

"It is possible. Of course it is possible: indeed, it is likely. However, I could not be certain. It is equally likely that the suspects are not making any permanent records, but are merely living out their fantasies and relieving the frustrations of their youth."

He steepled his skeletal fingers, and tapped the middle fingers together. "If these men are indeed photographing or filming, why would they do so?"

"Because they're perverted bastards," Andy spat out.

"Expand," Renfrew demanded, wholly attentive.

"They'd want to keep the photos. Share them with their perverted pals. Gloat and jerk off over them."

"Have you investigated the dark web for such photos?"

"No. Andy" –

"I can try. We might have to use Bergen, or someone else from the FBI." His voice and face were locked down tight.

"Iffen" –

"I can do it." Andy left the room, rigid-spined.

"Is there an issue?" Dr Renfrew enquired.

"No."

Dr Renfrew did not believe that statement. There, before his eyes, was one of the fragilities of the team, and also one of its strengths. Detective Clement had not hesitated to lie to him to protect her colleague, and her attitude now that Detective Chee had left the room did not encourage further discussion. Her titanic partner was no more approachable.

"Could you keep the idea under review?"

"Of course."

"Thanks."

The detectives, trailed by Mr Carval, exited. Dr Renfrew considered their hypothesis further, and found it to continue to have merit.

Away from Renfrew's penetrating gaze, the cops relaxed slightly. Carval tapped O'Leary's arm.

"Got a sec?"

"Yeah."

Carval led off to the break room.

"So what's this about?"

"We talked about Bothwell, but you didn't need me to talk to him – Renfrew scared them into co-operating without that. But if they're not involved, they still might've heard rumours about where pictures might end up."

O'Leary's eyebrows wriggled thoughtfully as he brewed coffee. "You're suggestin' you might have a friendly chat with your pal?"

"I could, if it helped." Carval took a mug from the machine. "One for Casey?"

"Okay." Inquisitiveness replaced investigation. "You fixed?"

"Don't know. Don't think so."

"But you're tryin'."

Carval shrugged.

"Let's go talk to Casey 'bout Bothwell. Coffee's done. You c'n carry it. Hot mugs burn my paws an' singe my fur."

Casey was chewing a pen as the men approached, and scowling at the screen. Coffee landed on her desk. To O'Leary's worry, she didn't reach for it.

"We got an idea."

"Yeah? I don't, so maybe yours'll help."

"Carval here is pals with Bothwell at Coronal."

"I know."

"Bothwell might have some gossip about where pictures like you theorised might show up."

Casey fired into life. "Yeah? Go feed that into Bergen – oh, he's off with Tyler. To Andy. Bergen and Andy were on to the dark web. Go see if this can help him, and if so let's get on it." The coffee vanished almost as fast as the two men did.

A few moments later O'Leary reappeared, minus Carval. "They're chattin' up Bothwell right now." His teeth gleamed in a swift grin. "Always fun to hear a man grovel. This Bothwell can't do enough for Carval. Reckon he's hopin' for our boy to shoot for him. Spillin' like a toddler tea party."

"Good." Casey glanced at her watch. "Tyler should be back soon." As if she'd conjured him up, he walked in, trailed by Bergen, both sporting identically vicious non-smiles.

"Had a good time?" she inquired.

"Yeah."

"Squealed like a piglet," Bergen added. "Anything to try and get early release."

"Man doesn't like Rikers."

"I hear it ain't popular as a vacation resort."

"Nah."

"So what've you got?" Casey pressed.

"We got some names. Maybe he wouldn't give the main men supplying away, but he told us who bought. I already got a uniform following up. Not one of our names."

"Couldn't be that easy, could it?" she said bitterly, followed by a yawn. Tyler cast her a sidelong glance, followed by a loudly unspoken question, which Casey ignored.

"We won't be gettin' more tonight," O'Leary weighed in.

"Bergen and Andy still have to finish off our tech for tomorrow."

"I'll go see Andy now," Bergen said, and departed rapidly, exchanging places with Carval, who was approaching with a face of deep disgust.

"What'd you get?"

"He knows nothing about anything on the web." He looked like he wanted to spit.

"Do we wanna talk to him anyway? Maybe he's heard some rumours."

"No. Andy grilled him. He knows nothing." He stopped suddenly.

"You've thought of something."

"He might visit the shoots occasionally." Carval shrugged. "It's a long shot."

"I'd take an arrow at two miles right now to get something more. Let's interview him. Not as a suspect." She started to reach for her phone. "Why didn't you think of that earlier?" Carval shrugged again. "We could've interviewed him two days ago." Irritation suffused her tone.

"It wouldn't have made any diff'rence, Casey. The operation's still gonna happen. You c'n interview him tomorrow."

"Now."

"No. Not tonight. Tomorrow." O'Leary regarded Casey. "Home time. You need to get some sleep."

"I *need* to get these slimeballs."

"You won't be doin' it iffen you don't get some rest. Can't do an interrogation with your eyes shut, an' I don't reckon you're fit to drive either."

"I can get myself home."

"Yup, 'cause that's where you're goin'."

Carval watched in admiration as O'Leary squashed flat every objection Casey might have tried to raise. Admiration became horror when he realised that O'Leary was angling for him to take her home.

"I don't want anyone to *see me home* like I'm a grade-schooler. I'll get myself home."

O'Leary gazed doubtfully down at the top of her head. "You sure?"

"Yes. Stop fussing. I'm fine."

It didn't look like the mountain believed her, which was perfectly reasonable, because nor did Carval. Casey was anything but fine. Escorting her home, though, was off the table: Carval liked life, and specifically continuing to live his life.

The point became moot when Casey packed up and stalked out. Even her spine glared at O'Leary, who was cheerfully impervious.

"Are you trying to get me shot?"

"Naw. Not today."

***

Halfway home, Casey's phone rang. She ignored it, and it stopped. Two minutes later it rang again. She ignored that, too. Driving in Manhattan was dangerous enough without answering phones. It rang three more times before she reached her home.

The fourth further time, she answered.

"Dad, what is it?"

"Why din't you answer?"

Oh God. Already drunk again.

"I was driving," she temporised.

"Should've answered. 'M your dad."

"What do you want?"

"Someone called me. Said they were a lawyer. I don' need t' get a lawyer."

"Dad, you have to go to court. If you don't hire a lawyer you'll go to jail."

"I don' have to go to court."

"What did you say to the lawyer?" Dread crept over her.

"She said you'd told her to call me. I said I'd speak to you."

Oh, thank God. He hadn't upset Jankel. Yet.

"Dad," she reiterated, "you have a desk appearance ticket for Queens County Criminal Court at 9.30 a.m. on December 13. You have to get a lawyer. I'll call her tomorrow again, and she'll call you." And she'd call her dad too, beforehand, to make sure he was sober.

"I don' need a lawyer."

No. He *needed* to go into rehab. He *needed* to stop drinking. He *needed* to listen to her.

None of it was going to happen.

"Okay, Dad. I'll fix it."

"Thass my Catkin."

"Bye."

She walked up into her apartment, fell on to her bed and stared, determinedly dry-eyed, at the ceiling. Just like he'd blotted out her mother, he was blotting out his present problem. She set a reminder on her phone to call Jankel the following day, then took a scalding shower and went straight to bed.

Not a tear fell, all that long night. Sometimes, on and off, she slept.

CHAPTER TWENTY THREE

"What did your uniform turn up?"

"Zip."

"Still looking?"

"Yep."

Tyler began to march off, then turned back. "You had any sleep this week?"

"Sure."

"You better tell those bags under your eyes 'bout it. Could get my kitbag in them. Twice."

"Saves checking luggage," she flipped back. Tyler raised his eyebrows, but conceded.

"You were s'posed to sleep," O'Leary began. Casey looked at him. He stopped, quickly, finding something else to do.

Something else resulted in both Bothwell and Carval arriving at the precinct. Carval was as welcome as Bothwell, since his first action was to go straight to the break room and return with a double espresso that would have dissolved granite.

"Let's go talk to Bothwell." The scalding liquid disappeared in one go. O'Leary tailed Casey to the interrogation room, and Carval disposed himself behind the one-way glass. He was really getting the measure of that glass, he thought smugly.

Bothwell hadn't changed much: less hair, which was, a few years on, rather less brunet than it had been; more flab. Fine points of perspiration were on his brow, and Casey unobtrusively wiped her hand down her pants after she'd shaken his. O'Leary wasn't unobtrusive about it.

"Mr Bothwell. You are one of the creative executives at Coronal."

"Yes." His voice quavered.

"Specifically, you're responsible for commissioning the current series of lingerie shoots featuring edgy, late night set-ups."

"Yes." More quavers.

"I have been led to believe" – Carval whistled: that was a stretch – "that those set-ups are being used in videos of women being abused."

"Your detective said that yesterday. I told him I didn't know anything about it. I don't. Why am I here?" His shirt back was darkening.

"The series of shoots all use the same photographer and dressers."

He nodded.

"Yarland, Severstal and Hervalo."

Another nod.

"Why? You use different agencies around the US and the world, so why the same team?"

"Consistency."

"Mmmm?" she encouraged.

"Models we can get anywhere there are beautiful girls, so we can be local – and it adds to our appeal internationally – we're expanding all over the world, so we want customers to relate to the models" –

"That's why you have the spread of ethnicity?"

"Yes. We don't want any ethnic group to feel left out, though we're trying to expand more into the Asian market – we're still planning that out." His eyes blanked as commercial considerations overcame his nerves, and he relaxed.

"Going back to the team…."

"Yeah, sorry. The style they put together is much harder to recreate. I know Carval's shooting you guys, but if I swapped out Yarland for Carval the look and feel of the photos would be totally different. Probably better" – behind the glass, Carval spluttered with indignation: *probably*? – "but it wouldn't be consistent. Not that it matters since he wouldn't come and do it for us." Bothwell was equally indignant. O'Leary didn't conceal a wide grin.

"So you've been using them for a while?"

"Sure. Ever since we began this campaign. It's going to wind down soon – we've been on it for more than a year, and like I said, we need to crack the Asian market and this style isn't going to work there. We need something that's less edgy, more sociable, less overtly sexy." He acquired a wistful expression. "Carval could do it. Life from the streets of those places."

Carval spluttered again. As if he needed Coronal.

"So do you have much contact with the team?"

"I guess so. Times, places, who the models are, any emergencies."

"What do you think of them?"

Bothwell glanced sharply at the cops, suddenly alert. "What do you think they've done? Do you think *they're* responsible for shots on the dark web like your man was grilling me about yesterday?"

Notably, he didn't say *that's crazy*.

"That's an interesting leap," Casey said. "Why'd you assume that?"

Bothwell leaned forward. "Look, I don't want to spread gossip. There's always gossip and bitching and it's always exaggerated."

"Mm?"

"But I often go down to the shoots – make sure it's okay, show the corporate face, remind them who pays the checks, you know? We can't afford for anything to be off. It's why we were so quick to cooperate with you. If something's wrong, we want to have it fixed asap. We can't afford a scandal."

"You go to the shoots," Casey refocused him on her investigation, not his corporate concerns.

"Oh…yeah. Right. Anyway, I was wandering around the set, and it was pretty edgy, but it's what we wanted, and as I was passing the dressing rooms I heard Severstal talking to one of the girls. It sounded like he was asking her out."

"Do you know who?"

Bothwell thought for a moment. "Not sure. It was here in Manhattan, though."

"Did she sound like she wanted to go?"

"She didn't say no."

"Not the same," O'Leary noted.

"She didn't sound like it was the best offer she'd had. More, um, resigned. She agreed, though."

"When was it?"

Bothwell pulled out his phone. His face turned apologetic. "Calendar," he explained. "I travel a lot and I don't remember the exact dates." He tapped. "Okay. I was in Houston then, New Orleans – we like it for a backdrop – the next week, back in New York from September 23… ah, here we are. October 1."

"Was she called Melinda?"

"Yeah, that was it."

It took him a moment.

"Has something happened to her?"

"She was found murdered, nearly four weeks ago."

Casey slid the photos across to Bothwell.

"That's her," he said. "Dead?"

"Yes."

"Fuck. That's awful." His brain caught up. "You're looking into Severstal for murder, aren't you? That's… it's just not possible. Chatting up someone who's not that into you isn't like murdering them." Another catch-up moment. "That's why you're forcing a model on us. You're setting something up. You're trying to trap him."

"I can't comment on the FBI's operations."

"Nor should you," O'Leary grated, staring coldly at Bothwell.

"I got that loud and clear."

"No harm repeatin' it."

"Now, tell us absolutely everything about that visit to the set."

***

"Well, that was int'restin'."

"Not proof, but corroborative."

"Shame he didn't stop 'n' listen a spell longer."

"Yeah. These things they call good manners are a real problem." She smiled sharply. "But now we've got proof that Severstal was asking Melinda out, and she agreed. I really wish he'd overheard where."

"Don't get us out of this sting, though."

"No." She shifted uncomfortably. "I have to make a call. After that, let's go talk to Andy and Bergen about the tech run today."

"Okay."

Casey skulked off to a quiet place where she could neither be overheard nor observed, and called Jankel.

"Ms Jankel, please."

"Carla Jankel."

"Hello. Um… this is Detective Clement. You spoke to my father yesterday, but he said he had to talk to me."

"Yes."

"He has to get a lawyer, whatever he says. Can you help?"

"I think we should both meet with your father. But if he continues to refuse my services after that, I can't act." Jankel became sympathetic. "I'll help if I can, but there are limits. Now, I could meet you both after work next Monday. That'll be time enough. I'll send you the details."

"Please… don't make it a bar?"

"No. If you can get time, we can make it the last appointment of the day at my office."

"I'll make time. Thank you."

"See you then. Bye."

She blanked her face, and concentrated on the discussion she was about to have with Andy. Everything else would have to wait.

***

"Not very glamorous, is it?"

"No." Andy was clipped. Bergen flicked him an assessing glance.

"You don't like this op."

"No."

They fixed a tiny black camera and directional mike to the tripod, then looked around the room.

"Why not?"

"She's not a cop. We shouldn't be dragging her into this." Andy shivered.

"She knows the risks. And your Tyler'll have the guts of anyone who touches her."

"Yeah. How about a camera over the door, pointing at the set?"

"Okay, and another mike, just in case he uses a different tripod." Bergen stuck them in place. From below, they were barely visible.

"How good's that tracker?"

"Best you can get." Bergen looked at Andy from his perch on the stepladder. "What's up? We'll be all over her. We've done this before."

"It's filthy. Bad enough that it's drugged rape and murder, but if they're filming or taking photos beforehand..."

"We haven't found them."

"You missed out *yet*. They're out there."

"How are you so sure – oh. You've seen this before." Bergen descended.

"Yeah."

"It's not in your case files."

"What? How've you seen our case files?"

"Standard. We like to know who we're working with. You're an interesting bunch." Bergen stopped, caught Andy's expression, and changed tack. "Anyway, Allie's tracked, we'll be on site, your team'll be on site and trailing them, and we're going to prime Allie to be chatty. She'll be fine. We'll get her out long before anything can happen to her."

"You'd better be sure about that."

"I'm sure. Now, how about we go wire the dressing room too?"

"Yeah. Let's get them for everything we can."

"Oh yes." Bergen bared his teeth. "Every last thing. I hate these guys."

"Me too. Let's go talk to Selwyn. We don't want him to screw up."

"Mr Selwyn," Bergen began, "we've fixed the tech. You are to ensure that Severstal and Hervalo use Dressing Room Three. If they're messing with the models, we're going to get that too."

"I never allowed that. They all *know* that. No-one's allowed to touch. I've – Stardance has – a really clean reputation and if they're touching they've trampled all over it. We'll be ruined."

Andy's lip curled. Bergen took a different approach. "You've cooperated. I'm sure we can make something of that. But if any of this leaks before we're done, you'll be on the hook. I'm sure Detective Clement won't mind at all if that happens."

Selwyn crumpled. "Anything you ask for. If it's true, I want them in jail. They've ruined my reputation."

They left him to whimper about his reputation and future. It didn't matter to them.

***

"It appears that we are as prepared as we can be," Renfrew pontificated.

"Yeah."

"Detective Tyler, would you be so kind as to contact Miss Despero and brief her? We should do so before her classes tomorrow morning. In this way, should she have questions, we can resolve them before she enters Stardance. The shoot is, I recall, arranged for two-thirty p.m. and will take approximately four hours, allowing for changes in hairstyle, dress, and set arrangements."

"Only four?" Carval asked. "That seems too short. I'd have expected a whole day."

"Miss Despero does not have a whole day: but, should the shoot overrun, that will not be an issue. Now, if we are done, I should like to speak to Detective Clement alone, please."

The rest of the team dispersed, Carval reluctantly following. Renfrew shut the door behind them. Casey had an unpleasant sensation of being summoned by the principal for some misdeed. Renfrew steepled his fingers and pushed up his glasses.

"What is it?" Casey asked. "We've got work to do."

Renfrew regarded her coolly. "I have been observing your team," he stated. "There are some fragilities."

"We're the top team on Manhattan. Any imaginary *fragilities* are irrelevant."

"I do not agree."

If Renfrew steepled and unsteepled his fingers again, Casey was ready to shoot them to stumps. She opened her mouth to argue.

"Detective Chee appears abnormally sensitive to abuse."

Dr Renfrew waited. Detective Clement had not allowed a reaction to appear, which was, of course, a confirmation in itself. He had expected that.

"Before tomorrow's operation, I have to be certain that his reactions will not be compromised by any issues."

Casey stood up, eyes blazing and voice frigid. "Andy is one of the best detectives here. You can't get better on a case like this. If you want him removed from the case, then you can go and tell Captain Kent that. I'll come with you, to scrape up the scraps afterwards. Otherwise, you can accept that we're the best team there is because the only thing we care about is getting the right guy for the murders." She looked challengingly at

204

Dr Renfrew. "Your choice."

"So you are assured that Detective Chee will not be adversely affected?"

"Yes. He'll be as good as any of us."

"Thank you."

Dr Renfrew was impressed by Detective Clement's faith in her colleagues, but he was by no means convinced that Detective Chee would come away from the operation unscathed. Contrary to her assumption, he was not primarily concerned about Detective Chee's behaviour during the operation and subsequent arrests, if warranted; although he considered that there might be some strains which should, if possible, be ameliorated. He was considerably more concerned that Detective Chee would undergo a traumatic reaction afterwards. It was Dr Renfrew's belief that the detective had been himself abused, and that the present case might trigger an unfortunate reaction.

***

"We're going to make this sting *perfect*," Casey spat out.

"Always do."

"How'd he kick your kitty?" O'Leary enquired.

"Damn profiler."

The team needed to hear nothing more. Casey disappeared to the break room. Carval followed her.

"What happened?"

She made herself a coffee, and then one for him. "He's a dumbass," she clipped off.

Carval sneaked a little closer under the guise of picking up the coffee mug. "How d'you feel about tomorrow?"

"I want these guys in Interrogation. I wish we had something so we didn't have to run this operation. Civilians have no place in dicey situations."

"You're worried about Allie."

"Yeah."

"Tyler'll make sure she's okay."

"We all will."

"Allie wasn't what I meant, though. I meant, how do you feel?"

"Fine."

"Liar. You look like death warmed up. You have to get some sleep."

"I'm fine."

"If Kent sees you, he'll bench you. You got sent home last time when he didn't think you were fit. D'you want that happening again?"

"Man's got some sense," said Tyler from just inside the door.

"Sure does," O'Leary added comfortably. "Now, we, um, persuaded Andy to go see some cultural thing, an' now we're persuadin' you to go home an' sleep again, seein' as you didn't take my advice yesterday. An' this time, Carval here's takin' you home. Or you're takin' him home. Either way, you get yourself tucked in all comfy-like" – Casey spat her coffee all over the break room and Carval choked – "an' sleep."

"I don't need to be tucked in like a toddler!"

"Gotcha," O'Leary said. Carval stood, gaping. "You said it, Casey, we gotta make it go perfect-like. You can't do that iffen you ain't sleepin'. So go home, an' take some Nyquil iffen you need to, an' then tomorrow you'll be good."

"We got this," Tyler added.

"You've got this Allie," Casey flipped back with recovered wit. Tyler didn't rise to the bait. "Anyway, I can get myself home."

"Sure you can. An' iffen you're not takin' Carval with you, then he c'n come for a beer with me."

"Doesn't Pete object to all these beers without him?"

"Naw. He's travellin'. Some audit out in Pennsylvania. So what d'you wanna do?" He turned to Carval.

Carval made a snap decision. "Beer," he said, and felt rather than saw Casey's inhalation. Ah. Right. One beer, and then a detour on his way home.

***

Well, that was a peachy day all round, Casey thought, safely at home. Renfrew screwing around with the team, questioning their professionalism, and interfering with their perfectly well-balanced personalities; O'Leary (for whom it was normal) *and* Tyler (for whom it was not) acting like Mother Goose with almost as much squawking and flapping; and Carval first fussing at her and then preferring beers with the men. Which she absolutely didn't mind or care about, because it meant he wasn't trying to take photos or get inside her head or ask questions.

Which only led her back to the real problem: her father, who was falling off a cliff. He'd been – well, maybe not *okay* but certainly not having memory lapses or telling her he was disappointed – keeping it under some control for years. Why get worse *now?* Why take it out on her?

Casey didn't move except to reach for a Kleenex, and then another, and another. She wished, futilely, he'd been kept in a cell. That way, he'd have been forced to stay sober. He couldn't have blocked it out with Jack Daniels and forgotten all about it. She wouldn't have been humiliating herself in front of her team and her boss to fix *his* fuck-up.

She'd still have had to pick up the pieces, but at least he could have instructed the lawyer himself and she'd only have to turn up and try to be supportive. She was beginning to run out of support for him, however guilty that made her feel. She loved her father. She did. But she wasn't sure that he loved her.

When the door sounded, she had a soggy, disgusting mass of Kleenex in the trash can by the table, which, she thought, summed up her entire life. She couldn't be bothered to open it. She hadn't ordered take-out, and she didn't want to see anyone. Another Kleenex splatted into the trash.

The door sounded again. She ignored it, again. Lather, rinse and repeat. Then her phone rang.

Carval, standing outside Casey's door, was some way past wondering why the hell he was bothering and getting well into seriously pissed territory. Only sheer stubbornness was keeping him at her door, and the longer she didn't open it – and he was damn sure she was home – the more riled up he became. He'd had a perfectly pleasant beer with O'Leary and Tyler, who hadn't said anything about anything important, and had therefore been soothingly enthusiastic about sports and gym stats. He'd left with cheerful optimism that a quiet evening with Casey would go some way to fixing things: after all, she'd accepted coffee earlier, and actually told him what was wrong.

However, when the third rap on her door remained unanswered, he was annoyed. He hauled out his phone, and dialled.

"Clement."

It sounded as if she'd answered on autopilot.

"Casey, it's me. Open the damn door and let me in, because I'm staying right here till you do."

The silence of a cut call followed. He was redialling when the lock clicked over.

"What do you want? I'm tired and I didn't expect company."

Carval couldn't see her face, but the flat tone wasn't reassuring. He took a step inside, which she didn't resist.

"I thought you might want some. Company, that is."

"Oh. That another of O'Leary's bright ideas?"

"No," he jabbed back.

"Oh." Pause. "Want a coffee?"

Despite the still-flat tone, and the lack of looking up from her floor, that was hopeful. Carval's natural confidence (Allan would say arrogance, but he wasn't here) bounced back.

"Yes, please." He shut the door and tailed Casey to her pristine kitchen. "Did you have dinner?"

"No."

"Nor did I. Can we get take-out? Chinese? I'll even let you pay half."

"You can't stop me paying my share," she said, with a flick of welcome irritation.

"Lychee chicken again?"

"I like it," she defended herself. She still hadn't turned round.

Carval wandered out of the kitchen to call in the order, and, that done, sauntered to the couch. His eye was caught by a small trash can which he didn't remember being there before: right where he could fall over it. He deftly avoided it, and then cast it a disapproving glare.

Oh. Oh shit.

"What's wrong?" he blurted out.

CHAPTER TWENTY FOUR

She continued to make coffee, and didn't answer. Carval strode back over to her, turned her round by the shoulders, spilling coffee all over the counter, and tipped her face up.

No wonder she hadn't wanted to face him. Her eyes were red and swollen, her face pale, blotched with misery. She wasn't a woman who cried prettily. He stood still for a second, unsure whether to pull her in and cosset her or to ignore her upset as she so clearly wanted. She turned away without a word and began to wipe up the spilled coffee.

He hated crying women. It made him feel inadequate, and he didn't like it. Not that it happened to him much, and it had never happened with his previous girlfriends: they had been as casual as he. It wasn't his fault that Casey was upset, so it was ridiculous that he felt her misery stabbing him in the gut.

It was too much. Carval stepped in, turned her back round to face him and tucked her firmly against his chest, barely reaching his shoulder. There was no sound, and no softening. She simply stood, almost as if she'd been switched off.

Carval dropped his arms, moved around her, and mopped up the rest of the coffee; turned the kettle back on and then filled the French press. He found mugs in the first cupboard he opened, directly above the kettle.

When he turned back, she'd moved to the couch, so that was where he took the mugs and French press. After another uncomfortable moment, he poured. With astonishing self-restraint, he hadn't removed his camera from his pocket, though his fingers itched to do so. Still further testing his self-control, he didn't ask anything. He was pretty sure he knew the answer: another round of her father's issues. She'd mentioned memory loss, and a court date: enough to leave anyone upset.

Casey picked up her coffee mug and wrapped both hands round it, welcoming the heat. She was cold, though the apartment was warm; and bone-deep tired: an exhaustion that sleep wouldn't cure. Her elbows slid on to her knees, and she breathed in the aroma of her coffee and tried not to think about anything.

Carval drained his coffee. "Are you going to talk about it?"

"Nothing to say."

Her voice was dead flat, and she was huddled into a corner of the couch. Hiding, again. He was so sick of her hiding.

"Why can't you just tell me what's wrong?"

"Why is it any of your business? You can't help. I don't want any help." She gulped at her coffee. "I can handle it."

"Yeah, sure. You aren't sleeping, you've used up half a box of Kleenex in a couple of hours, and everyone on your team is watching you like you're an unexploded bomb, but you can handle it."

"If I don't, who will?" she fired back. "There's nobody else. Mom's *dead* and Dad's a drunk. So who else is going to handle it, huh? You can't get day care for drunks."

"I guess not."

"So who else is there? He gets drunk, he gets picked up, who else can go get him, take him home? He hasn't *got* anyone else." She stared bleakly into her black coffee. "I'll just have to do."

"Huh?"

"There's nobody else."

"No. What do you mean *you'll have to do?*"

She stared into her coffee again, and didn't answer, hunching deeper into herself. He'd never seen her so small.

"Doesn't he appreciate what you do for him?" Carval queried.

"Of course he does," but it wasn't convincing. "He's my dad. He loves me." That wasn't convincing either. "Anyway, it doesn't matter." She slugged back the rest of her coffee. "It'll be fine, after the hearing's out of the way."

Carval recognised the close-down. Casey wasn't going to talk, and pushing her had been monumentally unsuccessful every time he'd tried. It didn't mean he had to like it, but – oh. The men had said *don't notice. She won't like you noticing. Don't make a big deal of it, likely she'll say more.* So he'd just pretend not to notice it. Anyway, he was being ridiculous. He barely knew her: two months or so was no time. It was simply fun. Nothing more than that. Fun, and his next exhibition. His own lie squirmed restlessly in his head, but he ignored it.

Instead, he slid up to Casey, and dropped his arm around her stooped shoulders.

"Don't think about it, then," he said, and flirted his fingers over her arm. "C'mere, instead." She didn't resist. She wasn't enthusiastically snuggling in, either. "C'mon," he enticed. "I've got a cure for thinking."

"Sure you have," she said sardonically. "Are you going to pay my medical bills for brain removal too?"

"Doesn't the NYPD plan cover it?"

She huffed out a laugh, though it didn't sound humorous to Carval. "Unnecessary surgery isn't covered."

"So no nose job for O'Leary, then?"

"Nope."

But she'd retreated into herself again as soon as he'd made the joke. He dipped down and kissed the tip of her nose.

"I like your nose. It woffles so delightfully when you're thinking."

"Woffles? What sort of a word is that?"

"It's shorter than scrunches up and wiggles."

"It makes me sound like a rabbit."

"Well, you're soft, cuddly and cute" – Carval oofed. "Ow," he said mildly, and rubbed his ribs.

"I am not cute."

He opened his mouth, ready to receive both feet – and the door sounded. "Dinner," he said, and went to get it.

When he returned to the couch, two plates, two sodas and chopsticks had also arrived on the small table. He cast a sidelong look at Casey, who had perked up at the prospect of Chinese.

Casey wasn't hungry, but she knew she had to eat something. She didn't object to take-out, and she could always minimise the amount she ate and save it for the next day if necessary. She pretended to have more enthusiasm than she did, and did her best to hide the lie. She'd be a lot happier if she wasn't perfectly well aware that Carval's entire life's work centred around observation, and if he weren't observing her now. She turned her attention to seeking out the lychees, which meant she needn't meet Carval's bright blue eyes.

Unfortunately there weren't enough lychees to allow her not to look up again till dinner was done, and every time she did Carval's gaze was on her.

"What is it?" she snapped. "I can't have spinach in my teeth."

"I could watch you eating lychees like that all evening."

"What?"

"Watching you suck them off your chopstick."

"Huh?" she managed, completely blindsided, and took a proper look at his face. He didn't look pitying: anything but sympathetic. She already knew that look: it was quite unmistakable. So many reasons why responding to him was a bad idea: he wanted her to talk about her father; she shouldn't make more of this than it was; she wasn't a gorgeous model, she was an ordinary cop – and one good reason: the lust flaring in his eyes.

Dinner done, and the detritus cleared, Casey sat down, nearer to Carval than earlier. He didn't bother to hide that he was sliding up close, then slung his arm across her shoulders again.

"That's better." He tucked her in a little more firmly. "Much better." His lips quirked. "See, it was a good idea to open the door."

"I was fine."

Carval said nothing, pointedly, and detached a curl from her clip to play with. A few seconds later, bored with the single curl, he let the rest spring loose and ran his fingers through it. She shifted under the touch, but he slid his hand around her nape to turn her head to his.

"There. Right where I want you."

Her eyebrows lifted. "And if I don't want to be there?"

"I'll let go. But you do want to be," he added arrogantly, and ran a finger over her cheek. She leaned into it. Even that small movement was a relief: he'd half-thought she'd back away, again. His arm slipped round her and tightened, pulling her close; his fingers returned to her nape and spread out through the dark curls. Close to, he couldn't miss the darkness below her eyes, the small signs of tiredness and strain. *Don't notice*, he heard again. Previously, he would never have noticed. Previously, he wouldn't have cared, except if it affected his photos.

He didn't have to care about her tiredness now, because the circles under her eyes would add depth to his exhibition: humanity. Except he did care, however much he didn't want to or Casey didn't want him to. The question was whether *she* cared. She'd been off ever since the start of this case, and he had an odd sense that it wasn't all her father. He shook off the thought. Of course it was her father: that was enough for anyone to be off.

It didn't occur to him that a case featuring models and photography might trip Casey's switches. Why should it? She was so perfectly confident in her own skin, and he'd made it clear how much he appreciated her curves. He'd forgotten that he'd thought the models had discomposed her, because he never remembered anything that had, however briefly, insulted him. He'd just thought that he wanted Casey, not the models, and left it all behind.

He leaned down, giving her plenty of time to anticipate, and finally touched down on her lips, slightly parted for him.

He'd meant to be slow and seductive. He really had. But he'd been shut out and away from her for more than a week, and all his frustration with the whole situation simply boiled over into raw heat and hard desire. The instant he'd been given entrance he took it, swung her round and into him and devoured her. He had never thought that he'd react like this, to anyone. His affairs – of which there had been many – had been more casual. Less...emotional. Certainly less irritatingly frustrating.

Dimly, it occurred to him that it might be the first time that he wanted something from his lover, rather than she from him, but then he stopped thinking about anything at all that wasn't Casey's mouth under his and her lithe form in his arms.

Shortly, she was in his lap, where he could take full advantage: the first, frantic raid slowing into a smoother possession; one arm around her, one free to roam. She turned into him: taking as much as she was giving: no-one's doll or toy. His hand slid up under her burgundy top to find the smooth skin of her back, pulling her closer still, plastering her against him so he could sense her speeding heartbeat and know that she was into it. Him.

Her hands slid up to grip his shoulders and then lock around his neck, falling into the tide of desire as quickly and wholly as he could have wanted: heating him up too. He traced her cheek, her ear, but she didn't seem to want slow: taking his mouth hard and giving no quarter, just as he had a moment ago. He shrugged off the thought that she might be using him to blot out reality, and responded in kind.

"Bed," she breathed, as his hands roamed further. He kissed the tip of her nose, and she squeaked crossly.

"It woffled," he said unrepentantly, and stood up, taking her with him. She tugged his hand, leading him to the bedroom. Just inside, he stopped her, and clasped her into his chest, barely shoulder height to him, but fitting perfectly, curved close; ran his hand into her hair and tipped her head back with a gentle pull, meaning to lean down and kiss her again.

Casey didn't want gentle. She reached up to haul his head down so he would kiss her like he meant it, not some half-hearted peck that he'd give any passing acquaintance or photoshoot model. He might have size and width on her, but she wasn't some feeble little girl, naïve and shrinking. Her hands shoved his light blue t-shirt up and he took the hint, whipping it over his head to display that enticing expanse of chest, rough dark hair shading over it with the promise of delicious friction.

"That's unfair," he murmured darkly, and flicked her dark top off in his turn. "There. Even-steven – oh, I do like that."

That was a dark crimson bra. Casey liked comfortable underwear – chasing suspects required decent support for her figure – but that didn't mean it couldn't be pretty. Or, watching Carval's face change, outright sexy.

"That's gorgeous." His long fingers traced slowly along the top edge of the cup, down into her cleavage, up the other side. She breathed more deeply. "Really gorgeous – but not as much as what's inside it." Another slow, teasing trace, fingertips just dipping under the edge of the lace, and she arched towards him as his mouth came down, first to her lips, then, skating over her neck, to the jumping pulse in her throat: not lingering there but grazing her clavicles and descending to the valley between her breasts. His mouth only stayed for an instant, enough to leave Casey more aroused, but not enough to be useful, and he straightened up, stretching.

"I forget how small you are," he grinned. "How about somewhere a little more comfortable?"

"You should be more flexible," she teased.

"And here I thought you liked strength." He swooped her up into his arms, and she laughed and wrapped arms around his neck.

"I could be persuaded."

"Guess I'd better be persuasive."

An instant later she was plopped on to her bed and rapidly divested of her pants.

"Picture perfect," he said thoughtlessly. Casey wriggled under the covers. "Where are you going?"

"I'm cold." It wasn't a lie, but it wasn't the whole truth, either. She didn't want to be reminded of pictures or their subjects, and her chill wasn't only physical.

"I'll heat you up." He stripped, showing off, shivered, and dived in beside her. "You weren't kidding. It's freezing in here." He grabbed her and tucked her in, face to face.

"What are you doing?"

"You're warm. I'm cold. Heat me up." His wicked fingers undid her bra, and shortly it arrived on the floor, with which Casey had had nothing whatsoever to do. She expected him to maraud downwards, but instead he caught her closer, long fingers spreading over her back to cage her, and kissed her seductively.

"There. Warming up."

Casey wriggled against him. "That what you call it?"

"Mhm." He kissed her again, and slipped his hand further down to palm her ass. She threw one leg over him, pressed in – and then there was no talking and no thinking and nothing that wasn't the banked up heat and frustration: he slid her panties off, rolled them and ran a swift line through her damp heat, stopping to play for only a short time as she hauled his head down and dug nails into his back to encourage him home. He thrust in, she opened and sighed, he touched her intimately, and she rose to him over her and gave a soft, sexy noise and was gone as he followed.

He rolled off, caught his Casey and cuddled her in, pillowing her head on his chest where he could nuzzle into her tousled curls and inhale the scent of her hair: some floral mix, almost too feminine for his tough little cop.

His tough little cop? There was the problem, right there. She was, or had been, temporarily *his*. Completely his, and shortly he intended that she should be his again. He simply didn't believe that she really thought of this as a proper relationship, rather than a casual affair, which was both frustrating and irritating.

His arms tightened, unconsciously pulling her closer in body, if she wouldn't be close in spirit.

"Oof. I need to breathe."

"Over-rated."

"Only if you want to be in Rikers for life."

"Nah. The cellmates aren't sexy and they wouldn't let me keep my camera." He mused for a moment. "Though it would be interesting... maybe Allan could fix up a visit for me so I could shoot.... It could be the end point of all the cop work. The murderers in jail: showing the brutality of the outcome... mm, *yes*. And Holding. That's where you put them, too."

He bounced out of the bed and searched his pockets for any scrap of paper and a pen, and, failing to find either, grabbed his phone and texted himself with the idea.

"Great," he said. "That'll be brilliant. I'll really be able to do something with that. If Allan can fix it, then that'll be interesting next time you've got nothing but paperwork."

He slid back into bed, and retrieved her from where she had buried herself up to her eyebrows.

"C'mere." His arms wrapped round her. "That was a great idea. Have you got any more like that?"

"No." He could feel the smirk against his skin. "I've got a better one." He could feel that idea, too, sizzling through every nerve. It was a better idea, for now. Ohhh yes. A *much* better idea. She was wet and warm and wriggling downwards and *ohhhh fuck yes do that again and then lemme do it to you.*

Some time later, all cleaned up, he flung one long arm around Casey, tucked her in like a favourite teddy bear, and fell asleep.

"Urrr... ugh."

The alarm cut through the fog. Casey groaned. Mornings were horrible, and it always took her the full length of her brisk morning routine to put her brain in gear. She tried to get up, and slowly realised that there was a heavy arm over her waist. About the point it dawned on her that it was Carval, it also dawned on her that she'd had a full night's sleep. Again.

She tugged herself out, and forced herself through a shower, dressing and make-up in less than thirty minutes – there was no point delaying: mornings didn't improve until they weren't mornings any more. Running through the technicalities of the sting gave her cold chills, but at least she no longer felt the dragging exhaustion of the previous days.

"Wake up," she said, and followed it by hauling off the cover.

"Wha' – what?"

"Wake up. I have to get to the precinct. Sting op, remember?"

"Yeah... yes! I have to go home. I'll see you at the precinct – when does it all kick off?"

"Be there by lunchtime."

He planted a quick kiss and an enveloping hug on her, and dashed off.

CHAPTER TWENTY FIVE

Carval bounced into his studio in a thoroughly good mood despite the early hour, which wasn't dented when Allan appeared.

"Jamie, I've found a small exhibition room for the shots of hands. I can book it for after Christmas, or wait until after *Murder on Manhattan*. Do you care which way round they are?"

"No, that's what you do." He whistled tunelessly and happily at his uploaded photos.

"Pay attention."

"You'll fix it. You always do."

"I guess you patched things up with your cop," Allan sighed. "At least I don't have to listen to you complaining about everything any more."

"Yep." There was a distinctly self-satisfied tinge to that answer. "And I'll get some really good shots this afternoon because we're going to take down these lowlifes."

"We?"

Jamie coloured. "Okay. The FBI guys and the cops."

"Yes. Try to stay out of their way and confine your enthusiasm to taking photos, please. I can't do exhibitions if you're injured or dead."

"You'd miss me."

"I'd miss your uniquely chaotic approach, for sure."

"You don't sound surprised that there's an operation."

"I already knew," Allan said prissily.

"How?" Jamie turned to goggle at him.

"I happened to be at the theatre last night and I ran across your Andy-cop – the little Chinese one."

"I know which one Andy is," Jamie snipped.

Allan sniffed disbelievingly, having plenty of experience of Jamie forgetting the names of his subjects as soon as he lowered his lens.

"I know all of them. Anyway, Andy told you about an operation? I don't believe that."

"Not exactly. We were talking about the play – he's really well-read and knows a lot about it" –

"It's O'Leary who does amateur dramatics."

Allan goggled. "That monster *acts*?"

"And sings."

"Dear God," Allan said weakly. "How is this possible?" He regrouped. "Anyway, we were talking, and then he said he had to go because tomorrow – today, now – was going to be busy. From which I inferred that there was something more than usual occurring."

"Neat trick, Sherlock."

"And now you've confirmed it. Like I said, don't get injured or killed."

"Aw, you really do love me."

"I like the salary you pay me."

Jamie pouted at him, and then grinned. "Because you're worth it." He turned back to his hi-res screens.

"There's another thing."

"Yeah?" Jamie's attention was already slipping away.

"I got a letter back about that stolen photo."

"Yes?" That had fetched him. Allan had Jamie's full attention.

"About what I expected. Nothing to do with Marcol, couldn't think what was being referred to, don't bother him again."

"But we will." Jamie scowled. "We surely will."

"Is that really a good idea? You're going to stir up a lot of trouble."

"Yes, I am. I want you to find a trail from Marcol to my photo. Or from whoever it was. I'm not dropping this, Allan. Find it."

"It's your funeral. And from what your cops said the other night, when Casey finds out, that might be literally true."

"She's not going to find out. I'll fix it – I'll fix him – and she'll never know."

Allan acquired an extremely sceptical expression, but said nothing. Jamie was already concentrating on his photos, and anyway he wouldn't listen. He never did when he didn't like the conversation. Why he'd suddenly got an itch to go crusading, when he never had before, Allan had no idea. However, he'd never been as desperate for a woman, either, and since the two were intimately connected, that explained everything: though not why Jamie was hankering after a cop who was nothing like his usual run of women. Lust, Allan thought cynically, was an amazing thing. Personally, he preferred a little less high emotion and a little more practicality.

He tapped back down to his own tidy, organised office and began to work on costings and exhibition dates.

***

"So you wired up the studio yesterday?"

"You asked that three times already. Yes, Casey," Andy said with strained patience, "we wired it. We put a camera and mike on the tripod, and another one over the door where it can see everything."

"I've checked all the transmissions and feeds," Bergen added, equally patient, "and it's all working. I've even tracked Allie – she's at West 4th, at the Steinhardt site, so that's working too."

"Stop frettin'. You'll wear yourself out, an' you just got rid of the luggage racks under your eyes. No point getting' tired now. We'll have enough to do this afternoon, an' likely this evenin' too."

"Take a walk, Casey. You're getting in our way."

"I don't like this whole op."

"None of us like it, Detective." Renfrew's precise enunciation didn't improve her day. "However, as we have no better course of action which would prevent further deaths, we have no choice. Let us discuss the logistics of our operation once more."

Casey followed Renfrew into the conference room, overshadowed by O'Leary. Tyler marched in, hard-eyed; Andy and Bergen followed a moment later.

"Detective Tyler will escort Miss Despero to Stardance, and, while doing so, will ensure that she has a small voice detector placed safely in her purse. He will then leave her a short distance from the entrance, to avoid any chance of being noticed by any party." Tyler nodded once, sharply. "After that, Mr Selwyn will ensure that Miss Despero is taken to Dressing Room Three, which has already been wired by Agent Bergen and Detective Chee. Should any impropriety occur, we will not deal with it at that time, but we shall have the evidence necessary to bring charges afterwards."

Tyler's face twisted.

"We'll get them," O'Leary grated.

"Yeah."

"Miss Despero will undergo the shoot. Again, should there be any impropriety, we will collect the evidence and bring charges later. Is that clearly understood, Detective Tyler?"

Tyler scowled. "I know my job."

"Indeed. But you have also demonstrated a desire to further your acquaintance with Miss Despero."

Casey squeaked, despite the seriousness of the situation. O'Leary was suppressing guffaws, and had consequently turned a delicate shade of purple. Tyler's face was also purple, but not with mirth.

"Understood," he gritted out.

"If she is approached by any of our suspects to visit a bar with them, under the pretence that it will further her chances of receiving more modelling engagements, then she will agree. We will be tracking her, and each of you will, separately, have a tracker. Agent Bergen and Detective Chee have confirmed that all are in full working order. An officer" –

"Fremont" –

"will take the glass from which Miss Despero drinks into evidence, with all due care. We will continue to track her from the bar to wherever these men are conducting their felonies."

Renfrew's otherwise even, patrician tones had acquired a steely edge.

"We will then ensure that Miss Despero remains safe, while arresting the perpetrators. Detective Chee will take care of Miss Despero."

Tyler startled. Andy blinked.

"Detective Tyler, you will be required to arrest these men. You and Detective O'Leary are best qualified to do so, with assistance from Agent Bergen. Detective Clement will be in command, however."

A question formed on O'Leary's wide mouth, but he stayed quiet. He met Casey's eyes, and she nodded minimally. Tyler looked from one to the other, and also stayed quiet: realisation spreading over his face. Subtly, the three detectives were closer together, surrounding Andy.

"The exact details of the pursuit and arrest cannot be arranged, of course, as that will depend on the outcome of the earlier actions. However, I think that we are as prepared as we can reasonably be."

"Sounds fascinating," Carval said from the doorway. "Who do I go with?"

"You?" Renfrew queried. He sounded utterly appalled, to the private amusement of the NYPD team. "You cannot attend. This is not a public spectacle."

"I can go with you, or I can follow the team – which I will." Carval wasn't going to compromise. He *needed* the action shots. They'd bring further life to his exhibition – *Detectives going into Danger*.

A tense silence was broken by Tyler. "He can handle himself," he said laconically. "Send him with Casey."

"It'll keep him out of the way," O'Leary added, with a mischievous grin. "Leastways, it's our best chance."

Renfrew's thin face was a picture of distaste, which, naturally, Carval shot. "I cannot approve," he said coldly. "Nor, however, does it appear that I can prevent Mr Carval's presence, authorised or not. It appears that he will cause least disruption if he is with Detective Clement. Make it so."

"Okay, guys," Casey picked up, before there could be any more issues. "Let's get everything finished up and ready to go. O'Leary, will you make sure Fremont is fully briefed? We don't want any mistakes with the chain of evidence."

"Sure," O'Leary rumbled comfortably, and didn't complain at her statement of the blindingly obvious. He ambled off, and shortly ambled back again.

"Let's have a chat – us four. Not the Feds."

The team quietly found themselves a private space, shadowed by Carval, who'd decided that he counted as not-a-Fed. Casey gave him a wry look, but didn't throw him out.

"Okay. So, Andy, you okay with getting Allie out of there?"

"I guess. But I'd rather be taking the bastards down." He surveyed Casey. "Why's Renfrew done it that way? Why not you – I mean, we never normally worry about it but I'd have thought that he'd put the woman with her – female solidarity and all that."

Usually the team would have joked about that comment, but not now. Casey looked Andy straight in the eye.

"Renfrew's guessed enough about your past to be worried" –

"He what?"

"I told him flat out that you were best for a case like this and we were the best team there were and if he didn't like it he could go to Kent himself and I'd scrape up the pieces that Kent left afterwards. Anyway, I think he's concerned about you. I'm not," she added baldly. "But I think, if anything does go wrong, you're the best one to calm Allie down."

Andy's shoulders were tight. Tyler moved to bump his fist, O'Leary clapped his shoulder.

"You're ours. We're a team. Whatever that asshole Fed says, if it starts going to hell the four of us – not the Feds – will make it right." Casey leaned over and took Andy by the shoulders. "Us four, just like it always is. We're going to do this."

"I don't like being side-lined."

"You're not. The big boys here are going to do the physical stuff, just like always. You're going to do the touchy-feely part, 'cause you're good at it, and you know I'm not."

"Too damn right," Andy agreed. The other two men nodded vehemently.

Casey ignored them, and carried on. "You don't *look* threatening, even though you are, and if you're apparently looking after Allie, they won't expect it if you have to get involved." She grinned. "I don't get to beat anyone up either. I get to stay out of the way and give orders."

"Just like usual," O'Leary grinned. "Tellin' us all what to do, even when we know. Typical Casey."

Casey emitted a snatch of *I Wanna Rule The World*.

"*Please* don't try to sing," Andy complained. "You know you can't, and even if that was music" –

"It is," Tyler butted in. "10cc is great music."

"Ugh. Even if it was, which it isn't" – Tyler looked like he would spit – "Casey can't sing. She sounds like a raven with tonsillitis."

"Naw, naw," O'Leary chided. "That's not nice. You're goin' to upset the ravens, talkin' trash like that."

Carval watched the team tighten its bonds, and eased.

"Okay, if you're all finished complaining about my singing, let's get going. Where are these tracker things, Andy? If you've tested them all, we're cool."

"Kent know this is going down?"

"That's Renfrew's problem. He came in and took over, so he gets the fun of telling Kent about it all." They smiled nastily at each other. A job well left to someone else, that, and they had the perfect excuse.

***

"Going to pick up Allie."

"Okay." Again, no jokes were made. The sting was beginning, and the cops only had their minds on the job.

Tyler strode out.

"Agent Bergen and I will take the van to Stardance," Renfrew advised. "I wish to be there in good time." He left, trailing Bergen, whose forgettable face was set hard.

"Okay. Separate cars, spread out north of Stardance. O'Leary, you take Fremont with you. I don't want to have a marked cruiser anywhere near this sting."

"He'll get an unmarked car an' be outta uniform. He'll have to get back with the doped drink pretty quick, iffen there is one."

"Okay. Go up east, if you can. Andy, straight up. I'll go a little west. Carval, you're with me."

The team moved out with purpose. Carval hadn't seen them move like that, as one unit, in the first case, though he recognised Casey's intensity. She'd gone after Merowin like that: fierce and focused; but now the others displayed that same force too. He captured the frightening ferocity through his lens, and then sped after Casey, knowing that she'd leave him behind without a second thought if he were slow.

***

"You okay, Allie?"

"Yes." Her voice wavered.

"It'll be fine."

She touched the chip behind her ear, again, and then the tiny bug in her purse.

"We tested it this morning. It works. We got you." Tyler tried a reassuring smile, which didn't fit his face. "I got you. You'll be great." He patted her hand, and felt the tremor. "We take care of our civilians. It's the job."

"Have you always been a cop?"

"Nah. I was in the Army, first." He wouldn't normally answer, but Allie was trying hard to hide her fears and be normal, and anyway, she was cute and might be interested. Bit more uptown than usually approached him, but…well, she was cute.

"Must have been scary."

All her exclamation points had gone missing.

"Usually it was pretty long-range stuff. Being a cop is better, though."

"I'd rather be a singer."

Singing was something Tyler knew nothing about. He liked rock music, preferably from before the year 2000. The finer points of singing were Andy's thing, not his.

"Okay."

"Guess it's not your thing."

"Can't sing." He flicked a glance at her. Allie's gorgeous face was pale. "How much do you have to exercise?" he tried. Anything so she didn't throw up in his unit through sheer terror.

"I run," she managed shakily. "Five miles on the treadmill daily, but more if I'm going to do a half-marathon. A few different light weights – reps, not mass. I can't afford for my muscles to bulge, but I like to be fit." She half-smiled. "I guess you do a lot more than that?"

"I don't run as far: maybe two, three miles, but I do a lot of weight training. We all spar, though – me and O'Leary, we spar a lot. Nobody else can give him much of a match."

"Wow! You can deal with someone that big? That's amazing! I mean, he's *huge*! A great big sweetie, but *huge*!" Tyler snickered, and preened, and noted the return of exclamation points. Looked like his seats were safe. "Wow! What about the others?"

"Casey and Andy spar. We'd be careful of them, but they might get hurt."

"Casey's in charge, right?"

"Yeah."

"How's that work?"

"She's the best detective, and been detective longest."

"But she looks younger than all of you."

"Yeah, but she's really dedicated. Always gets the guy."

It wasn't wholly true – the team did have the occasional case that went nowhere but the cold-case racks – but Tyler reckoned that Allie needed confidence more than she needed truth right now.

"Always?"

"Yep. We close more cases faster than any other team in Manhattan."

There was a soft sigh, which went straight to Tyler's protective mode. "That's good. But…I'm still pretty scared," she said.

"I get it. It's really good you stepped up. Most people wouldn't."

"Really?"

"Yep."

A brilliant smile burst forth, which should have stopped traffic.

"Okay, we're here. We're going to be all around you, all the time. We'll have everything recorded, so if they do anything at all, play dumb, like you want the next job, and we'll make sure they go down for it. Don't let them catch on, and keep talking once the shoot's over. The more you can pretend to be a bubbly airhead, and chatter about where you're going and what's happening, the easier you make it for us to be close by."

"Sure," she wobbled. "I can do this."

"Sure you can." Tyler got out with her, and to his own horrified surprise hugged her. She sashayed off looking particularly pleased. He sat back down in the cruiser with a thump and wondered what the hell had gotten into him to be hugging pretty girls in the street – or indeed at all. Just good that he wouldn't have to do any more talking. He'd used up more than his year's supply of words in that one car ride.

"She gone in?" His radio recalled him to reality.

"Yeah."

"Okay. Good to go. I'll let Renfrew know. They're coming up around Stardance now."

"She's nervous."

"That's okay. Selwyn's already spread the word that she's nervous because it's such a big opportunity."

"Joining Renfrew," Tyler said, and signed off.

***

"How'd you manage Selwyn?" Andy asked, back in the bullpen.

"It's Casey," O'Leary drawled. "You gotta ask?"

"Nope. She glared, didn't she?"

"I did hear as she" – O'Leary's voice dropped portentously – "*intimidated*."

"Boy oh boy" –

"Are you kids finished yet? We've got an operation running."

"Aww, c'mon. They're goin' to be hours. We don't even get to leave till the Feds give us the nod."

"I know. But...I wanna be ready."

"Are we let in on the recordin's?"

"Yeah," Andy confirmed. "We can go watch what's going on. Bergen's saving the signal they get in the van directly to a server, and I can hook up to that for you, but it's going to be nasty."

"Neat."

"Chain of evidence. All time stamped contemporaneous with the shoot, so there's no question of messing with it."

"They'll claim it anyway."

"Sure, but it'll be easy to disprove."

"I don't want to see," Casey said, "but I have to know."

"You sure?"

"I have to know." She said no more, shoulders set, spine stiff.

"I'll watch it with you," O'Leary muttered. "Shouldn't have to see it all on your lonesome."

"I won't come."

Casey had expected that, and wouldn't push Andy. He went off to work his magic on the tech.

"You okay?" Carval murmured, producing a coffee for Casey.

"Yeah."

Despite her full night's sleep, firmly wrapped up against him, she still didn't look okay: eyes shadowy, face paler than it ought to be. Better, but not right.

"Can you come watch too?"

"Yeah... um... but why?"

"Expert. If something's off, or not what you'd expect, I wanna know about it."

"Do I get popcorn?"

She flicked an irritated glance at him. Humour, it seemed, was ill-timed.

"Only if you want to throw it up. Later isn't going to be pretty."

"You're really sure it's these guys."

"Yeah. I really am. I just wish Allie wasn't involved. I've got a bad feeling about this."

"She'll be fine. Tyler an' Andy'll make sure of that."

"I guess. Not like Andy'll get much of a chance, if Allie's in danger. Didn't you see her and Tyler eyeing each other up?"

O'Leary snickered, rattling the chair. "Sure I did. That's goin' to be fun. Beauty an' the Beast."

"You're the Bigfoot."

"Bigfoots are cute. She said so. Called me a teddy bear. Teddy bears are cute, too."

"If you're six."

"Aw, don't be so cynical. Anyway, looks like Tyler's goin' to have an int'resting time."

"D'you think he'll be watching?"

"Depends if he's joined up with Renfrew or not. He ain't so keen on the man."

"Are any of us?"

"Waalll, you got a point there. Naw. 'Less Carval there's pals with him."

"He's pals with McDonald," Casey said.

O'Leary faked fainting. "You gotta be kidding."

"It's true," Carval said smugly. "McDonald likes me. He was happy to be shot."

"Tell me it was with a .22?" O'Leary wheedled.

"Plain old ordinary camera."

"Like your camera is ordinary."

"It is for me," Carval said unanswerably.

"Anyway, if Tyler's with Renfrew an' he doesn't like how they're behavin', then there's goin' to be trouble."

"He'll keep a lid on it. Don't give a bean for the heavy bag's chances, afterward, though. Or mine."

"I've got it running," Andy said bleakly. "Call me when it's time to go."

Casey, Carval and O'Leary filed into the small room where Andy had rigged the feed. Courtesy of O'Leary's mass, it was somewhat cramped. Casey ended up in between the two men, which was warm but not spacious.

The feed began to run.

CHAPTER TWENTY SIX

Allie tapped the tracker, and ran her fingers over the bug in her small purse. She popped a breath mint, and turned into Stardance.

"Hi!" she said to the receptionist. "I'm Allie Despero. I'm here for the Coronal shoot!"

The receptionist checked her system, and nodded. "Okay, you can go through to Room Three."

Allie sashayed through with the catwalk sway that she had swiftly learned: one foot directly in front of the other, a slight lean back, her posture strutting and confident, her expression a mix of utter delight at the opportunity and a little uncertain whether she could do it right: a woman who knew her next month's tuition payments depended on pleasing the photographer and thus the client. It wasn't totally a lie. She could really use the extra money.

Behind her back, Allie was faintly aware of Bergen's tones, asking to see Selwyn. She relaxed only fractionally, knowing that the team was on the stakeout but wishing it were Tyler, whose brisk confidence had encouraged her. She looked around, and walked through to Room Three.

Room Three already contained the first hair and make-up people, brisk and cool.

"Hi! I'm Allie!" she bubbled. "It's so great to be here!"

"Nice to see a new face. Sit down, and let's get you set."

"This is just so exciting! I never thought I'd get this far!"

"Okay," a twenty-something blonde said over her head. "It's Coronal."

"Yeah? Okay. So, sex hair, just fell-out-of-bed look?"

"Yeah, that's it. Make it look as if there was rough sex, too. Wild night."

"Can't say it's my bag."

"They're trying a new line. Aiming at the Fifty Shades market."

"Oh, I saw that film too!" Allie chattered. "It was totally edgy, wasn't it?"

The hair and make-up artists softened in the face of her apparently vacuous personality.

"I guess so," the make-up artist said. "It's all about sales, anyway. If Coronal think there's a market, they're probably right. They sell enough."

"Anyway, let's get Allie here into shape. You'll be just fine, sweetie, as soon as we're done. You're just the right type."

"Thanks!"

"Now, don't talk till we've done your face. Don't want to smudge you in the wrong places, do we?"

Allie obediently sat quiet and still as she was scrubbed, her hair gelled and artfully mussed, her lips made into a swollen pout, her eyes smudged and a slight flush added to her skin. The make-up was so heavy she wouldn't have recognised herself. She watched nervously in the mirror and hated every dehumanised moment of preparation: turning her into a walking sex doll.

"Don't you look good?"

"Wow!" It sure was wow, but she sure didn't like it, either. Her other shoots hadn't been like this, and she really wondered if Coronal was worth it. She clung to the knowledge that she was helping the cops and that Tyler had said she was brave, and remembered just how much of her tuition fees the money would cover.

"You've really made me look gorgeous!" She produced a stunning, grateful smile.

"You're all done. The outfits are in order. Numbered. Don't get them out of order: it plays hell with the scheduling and you don't want to upset the photographer. He's your route to the big-time: him and the dresser."

"I sure don't wanna upset him, then! I really wanna do more!" She turned to the first set, stripping out of her casual jeans and light t-shirt, then underwear, without embarrassment.

The dresser swished in: a slim, blond man, early thirties.

"Hi!" she tried. He wasn't impressed.

"Stand up," he ordered, in a thin, whiny voice: examining her with hard, critical eyes. He ran his contemptuous gaze over her. "That's wrong. Over here." She did as she was told. She didn't cringe, but she wanted to.

"More tits on show." He moved the cups of the bra so that she was almost exposed, spilling out over the lace edging. "Much better. They want a woman, not a frightened little girl." She didn't comment on the scrape of his fingers across her nipples, or the flare of unpleasantly dispassionate lust in his eyes. He stepped back, and his gaze crawled over her. "That'll do. For now. Follow me." He turned without checking she was following, and opened the door. The make-up artist tossed her a robe, which she rapidly donned and padded after the dresser on to the set.

Her guts twisted instantly; adrenaline kicked up. She'd known what she was in for. She had. But looking at the set, she felt totally out of her depth. She really, really wanted to be out of there.

"Hi," she wavered. She didn't like the photographer or his smile. Both were greasy, slimy and insincere.

"I'm Connor. In you come," the photographer enticed. "No need for fake modesty. You look great: just how we want. Great job, Kyle. Now, we all wanna make this a great shoot for Coronal, so get that sexy ass into gear and come on down."

It was a bedroom set. She'd expected that, but as she examined it, as carefully as she would a new musical score, she was scared. The bed was untidy, a full-length standing mirror was placed close to a vanity; a nightstand beside it. That was okay. She was modelling underwear, after all, and beds weren't uncommon.

The props were uncommon. Allie wasn't as naïve as her voice implied, but she'd never gotten involved with that sort of thing and she didn't want to start on camera. She made a considerable effort not to react.

***

Tyler joined Renfrew in the van, saying nothing.

"Agent Bergen will return momentarily. He is performing final checks."

Tyler merely nodded, once.

"All done," Bergen confirmed, climbing into the van, and adjusted the electronics until the screens and speakers registered. "Good to go."

"Which is which?" Tyler asked, suddenly focused.

"This one is the wire and camera in Allie's purse," Bergen advised, holding up a set of headphones attached to one device. "This one" – he gestured at a larger screen with more headphones – "is the feed on the tripod, and next to it the wire and camera over the door in case this one goes dead." Another gesture. "That's the one in the dressing room."

Tyler looked at the screen where the set was being constructed. For a while, he was interested. About the point they wheeled the bed in, he began to tense. When they positioned the mirror, his fists locked hard. But when they put the props out, he began to swear under his breath: everything he'd learnt in the Army, several times over. Sure, he was as keen as the next straight man on hot women in sexy underwear, but only if they wanted to show it off to him. Those props were only one tiny step from shooting for BDSM Monthly, and he wasn't into that shit.

There was a blindfold on the dented pillow; a set of leather cuffs on the nightstand. The drawer was half-open, showing indications that there might be more toys within. Another set of cuffs was insinuatingly draped at the foot of the bed. The large standing mirror was carefully positioned to

229

reflect the bed and everything on it. This was going to be D/S pornography, or near as dammit.

The set didn't feel like any woman who was on the bed would really want to play with any of it: it felt like force. His Gatorade bottle crumpled in his grip.

And then Allie sauntered in, swathed in a cheap, short, cotton robe. Tyler watched her look around at the set.

"Scared," he said.

"Yes. However, she is not displaying any more nervousness than any model would on receiving an excellent and unexpected assignment. She is performing well."

***

"Okay, beautiful, let's get the robe off and get started," Connor ordered. Allie dropped it, and stood still under his objectifying stare. Despite his smooth tones, she knew that he was getting off on the power to tell her to do whatever he wanted for the photos.

"Sit up on the bed. Turn to me, and smile. Make it sexy. I wanna see that lip pout a little, right there ready to be kissed. Bend your knee. Stretch out: show off those legs. All the way out, and show off your tits too. They're perfect. Imagine your boyfriend admiring them, just off to the left. Give him a come-on smile."

Allie produced her best come-and-get-it smile.

"That's great. You really know how to lead them on. Really hot. You love doing it, don't you? You really get off on them panting after you."

The orders went on. She did as she was told. She exuded sensual enjoyment, and all the while she felt sick. The photographer's oily, sleazy words made her feel dirty, but she didn't lose her focus for a second.

"Let's heat it up. Show your boyfriend what he's getting. You're all excited, totally ready for him. He'll be there in a minute. He's really gonna enjoy that sexy underwear."

She made suggestive gestures on command, changed into ever more erotic garb, and fought back the nausea every time the photographer positioned her, every time the dresser touched her. Both of them were going too far, and she couldn't do anything about it.

The cops would. She clung on to that thought, and Tyler's blunt clarity. *We'll make sure they go down for it.*

***

Bergen had stopped watching after a single, flaring-cheeked minute, scorching his complexion. Renfrew, stone-faced, hadn't missed an instant.

"I shall be exceedingly pleased when these men are arrested."

"Lucky it wasn't Casey," Tyler gritted out, trying to control his fury.

230

"She'd have shot them."

"I entirely concur. I cannot imagine Detective Clement being able to subsume her personality sufficiently to achieve our goal, however motivated she might have been."

The link rolled on.

Now, look a little frightened, but turned on. C'mon, girlie, you know how it feels. Imagine you're pinned down, it's all getting rough. That's it. Pout like you wanna be kissed hard. Open slightly. Mouth and your legs. Lick your lips. I want them wet.

Tyler's knuckles turned bone-white.

***

Back in the precinct, Casey, O'Leary, and Carval were also watching,

"Jesus," O'Leary said, completely outside his usual amiability. "That's disgustin'." His face was impassive, his fingers locked. "This ain't what you do, is it?"

"No. This guy's getting off on talking dirty, and the dresser's getting off on feeling her up. They're scum. They give all of us a bad name and I really, *really* want you to take them down."

"Allie's doing great," Casey said, her own fingers knotted around her shield. "I couldn't" –

"You'd have shot 'em, an' then how'd we get them into Rikers?"

"Cheaper if they're dead," Casey scraped out, "but we can't do that." Suddenly, she smiled nastily. "If they went down in California, it's got the death penalty again."

O'Leary's homely face was equally vicious. "So they do. So they surely do. Wonder if that FBI profiler's thought of that?"

"If not…"

"We'll give him a hint."

All three were still watching, ever more appalled.

***

You want it. Show me how much you want it. Offer up the cuffs, as if someone's there. He's in charge, and you want it. Make me believe it. That's right. Bite that lip.

"Vile."

"She hates it," Tyler bit out.

"Yes. But Miss Despero is doing exactly what is required. Observe Yarland. He is trapped, and revoltingly aroused. He will certainly ask Miss Despero to join him in a bar. As long as she does not break down, the operation should proceed perfectly."

Blindfold on. Cuff round one wrist. Writhe. You love it, don't you? Playing to the camera. Perfect. You're so turned on. Imagine your boyfriend watching you, tied down and ready.

"Filthy bastard. She hates it," Tyler said again. "She shouldn't have to do this," he added.

The oozing tones and slick, soulless voyeurism continued. *Click. Click. Click.*

"Detective, Miss Despero is an adult and agreed to assist of her own free will. I can see as clearly as you can that she is in considerable discomfort, but she is performing her role perfectly. You need not fear for her." Renfrew regarded Tyler coldly. "I assume you wish these persons to be arrested and convicted."

"Know my job. Won't lose control."

"Miss Despero will be protected." Renfrew smiled thinly. "After the operation is concluded, I am sure that she will be happy to see you."

***

Finally, the shoot was over. Allie sagged with relief, but kept her bubbly, happy face intact, even though Connor was crawling around her, oozing flattery, and obviously and unpleasantly aroused. She felt dirty, besmirched. But she'd gotten through it, and the cops would get her out as soon as anything started up.

"Good job, Allie," he said. "You've got a real talent."

"Thank you!" she bounced, and manufactured an appealing smile: a little shy, a little hopeful. "I'm really glad you thought I did well! You made it so easy! I really hope Coronal like those shots!"

"It's telling the right story to get you into it," he murmured. "It felt like you were really getting into it."

"You give good story!" Allie bubbled, flirtation lacing her tone. "I loved hearing it! It was totally real!"

Connor smiled at her, with a hard edge underlying it. "Wanna come for a drink? You really gave out the right atmosphere. Those shots are going to win awards. If I recommend you, then Coronal'll keep using you."

"Wow! You can do that? That's so great! You must be really important to them! Sure I'll come. Where are we going?"

"There are some nice bars up by East 80th. One of them."

***

"That's our cue to start moving," Casey said, disgust roiling in her voice.

"Yeah," O'Leary agreed heavily. "Let's go get these lowlifes. An' if it should happen that they resist arrest, waaalll, I wouldn't mind that one little bit."

"I'd love that too, but we have to keep it clean. No room for them to wiggle out of it." She looked round the bullpen. "Andy, we're go." He joined them. "O'Leary, get Fremont moving. Carval, you're with me."

"Okay." He couldn't say more, still disgusted and shamed: degraded by the actions of a fellow photographer. He couldn't help feeling that Casey was judging him by others' deeds, though nothing had been said.

***

"Let me go change and get my jacket," Allie said.

"Oh, did anyone tell you, you get to keep the costumes?" Connor said smoothly. "Coronal always let the models keep them."

"I do? Wow! That's fantastic! I've never worn Coronal before!"

Connor's eyes flared. "No? Sexy treat for a sexy girl, then."

"Wow!" she bubbled. "That's a totally great perk!" She regarded Connor worshipfully. "Do you do all Coronal's shoots?"

"Yeah."

"Wow!" she repeated, and allowed a tiny hint of calculation to enter her expression. "I'd love to come for a drink with you."

Connor smiled more widely. "Go get your jacket, then, and don't forget the perks. I'll be waiting outside."

Allie took considerable care to bounce off as enthusiastically as if it had all been real. She'd keep the lingerie, though. She couldn't afford hundreds of dollars' worth of sexy lingerie on her own dime, and she'd forget the slimeball photographer pretty fast.

***

"Detective Tyler, I think you should return to your own vehicle and be ready to follow Miss Despero."

Since Tyler was already halfway out of the van, he merely grunted. His cruiser was only a few yards away, but before he started moving he had to check in with the rest of the team.

"Casey."

"Yep?"

"On the move."

"So are we. Let's go get them."

"Fuckin'-A." He cut the call.

Casey drew in breath.

"What's up?"

"Tyler's riled. Really riled. That's not good."

"Huh?"

"You know he's ex-Army."

"Yeah," Carval answered, though it hadn't been a question. "Sniper, he said."

"Yeah. Well. He doesn't usually go back to the language. When he does… it's not good."

"I thought it was Andy that you were all worried about."

"Yeah. We are. But Tyler can do a lot more damage faster, and he's not big on women being disrespected."

233

"He was a jerk."

"Yarland? Yep."

"We're not all like that."

"Didn't say you were."

"We're not," he insisted.

"If we thought you were like him, you wouldn't be shooting us. We don't work with assholes." A razor smile flickered across her mouth. "We arrest them."

She got on the radio. "O'Leary?"

"Yeah?"

"Keep close to Tyler. He's gone all Army on us."

"Shit. Okay."

She dialled again. "Andy?"

"Yes?"

"You better be on Allie like ketchup on fries. Tyler's mad about the whole thing."

"Okay."

She put the phone down.

"Let's go. I'll talk to Tyler again in a minute. Most likely he'll calm down when he's in his car."

***

"Agent Bergen, please ensure that we have the audio feed from Miss Despero's purse, so that we can assimilate all information."

"Yes, Dr Renfrew."

Miss Despero's enthusiastic tones filled the van.

Both of you? Wow!

Yeah. You don't mind, do you?

No! You were both so good, you made me look stunning! I've never looked like that before!

Dr Renfrew's face curdled. He had observed Miss Despero's discomfort. However, she was still performing brilliantly. He wondered, idly, if she was also taking an acting class. If so, he was certain she would be scoring extremely highly. He was certain that few young people could be so convincing.

This is so great! I always go to cheap bars or to Wendy's or Five Guys.

Not too often. You'll lose that figure if you eat too many fries.

No, not often. Don't want to miss out on shoots like this! Where are we going?

The Upper East Side. There are some good upmarket wine bars there. You deserve a treat. Shown off in the proper setting.

I've never been to a wine bar! Wow! You guys really do well! Must be so great, being the main men for Coronal! I'm so lucky to have been picked and to meet you!

We're pretty happy to meet you too. Not everyone's as suitable as you — or as sexy.

Miss Despero giggled. Dr Renfrew's mouth tightened still further. His fingers steepled and unsteepled on his leg, until he became conscious of it and stopped, only to start again as soon as he concentrated on the audio feed.

We're just about there.

I've never been up here! Is this it?

Yep.

Berries? That's a cute name! She giggled again. *Really appropriate. Doesn't wine come from berries?*

Dr Renfrew winced.

Grapes, Allie. Not berries.

Ooops! Another tinkly giggle. Dr Renfrew winced again. Brilliant acting it might be, but if he had wanted to listen to tinkly girlish laughter, he would have pursued a different occupation. He reminded himself sternly that Miss Despero was providing exactly what was required, and concentrated on the feed and locating a Berries wine bar on the Upper East Side.

"Detective Clement?"

"Here."

"The address is Berries Wine Bar, 1372 First Avenue."

"On it. I'll tell the others."

"Thank you. We are recording everything."

"Okay."

"Please be rapid, while maintaining discretion."

"We know what we're doing, Dr Renfrew. We're trusting your tech. Do us the courtesy of trusting our ability."

"I apologise," he said stiffly. "I have no reason to doubt any of you."

CHAPTER TWENTY SEVEN

Allie stared around the wine bar with sincere amazement. Her student budget didn't run to places like this, that was totally for sure. Chairs with cushions, clean tables, the quiet buzz of conversation and soft, neutral music; an atmosphere set firmly to romantic.

"C'mon, sit down."

The men had selected a polished wooden table, discreetly within a half-booth. The bar was artfully lit to suggest intimacy: other tables were occupied by couples, only interested in each other.

Connor slipped into the booth, and beckoned her in. Kyle sat on the far side of Connor, which should have been reassuring. She stared round at the tasteful décor, trying to pick out details in the dim light. Her purse was on the seat between her and Connor, slightly open, as Tyler had told her.

"What would you like to drink?"

"I recommend the Pinot Grigio," Kyle suggested.

"Is that red or white?"

"White." There was the suspicion of a sneer at her naivety. She did know it was white, but her instincts were telling her to play as naïve as she could manage.

"Sounds nice. I don't get wine much."

"You'll like this one. Very light. It won't hurt that lovely figure."

"So, what's your boyfriend think of your chance at the big time?"

"I don't" – she looked down – "have a boyfriend right now."

"Really? Hard to believe. None of them got eyes?"

Kyle's eyes didn't move from her, an unpleasant leer lurking in their depths. The server took the order, and produced three glasses and a bottle.

"Try it. You'll like it."

"Wow! This is lovely!" She took another sip.

"Enjoy it."

"We will too."

"So how long have you been a photographer?" she asked.

"Fifteen years. Started at school, took prom photos, got into the game in Seattle, and then I got the Coronal deal. They love my style. I've been their main man for years."

"And you?" she directed at Kyle, with a wide smile.

"Same for me. I dress you the way they like. I travel, too."

"Where do you get to go to?"

"San Francisco, New Orleans, Paris, London – we fly all over." He watched her carefully as she sipped her wine. "If they like you, they keep you. If they like those photos, likely they'll keep you on."

"That would be great! I've never been out of the States. I'd love to travel!"

"I could put in a good word…"

"I'd totally love that!" She shifted her hand an inch nearer to Connor's, without a flinch. His smile widened, and Kyle's focus sharpened. She sipped her wine again. He hadn't been near it. She hadn't been briefed on what would happen if he didn't dope her drink, and now she was unsure what to do. She didn't want to spend any longer than she had to with these two total sleazebags. She gathered up her nerve, and decided to help the cops along.

She acquired an embarrassed half-smile. "Um… 'scuse me," she murmured. "I need to take a moment."

She left her jacket but took her purse, just like any woman would who was looking forward to the rest of the evening: sending the right signals. This was Connor's chance to dope her wine, and after that, she wouldn't be able to worry about anything. She was totally dependent on the team and the tech, but she trusted them to keep her safe.

***

"Detective Clement?"

"Yes?"

"Miss Despero is accelerating matters. She has given either Severstal or Yarland an opportunity to administer a drug to her drink. They are unlikely to miss that opening. Please would you now ensure that Officer Fremont is inside the bar, so that he may retrieve that glass before the server removes it."

"Sure thing. He's got some evidence bags in the car. O'Leary, you listening?"

"Yeah."

"Thank you." Renfrew dropped out of the channel.

"My turn. I was gettin' bored just sittin' here watchin' the street. Animal Control's been by twice already, an' it makes me antsy."

"Keep your ants in your own pants, Bigfoot. Get Fremont. I'll be on the channel too."

"Fremont, report."

"Here, Detective."

"Where are you?"

"Round the back of East 74th. Out of sight, like you told me."

"Good. Okay, you're a go. You go in, an' sit as close as you c'n manage to Allie an' the two men. Now, Allie's gone off to the restroom, so you'll have to make the two men. You'll recognise them?"

"I guess so."

"Be sure. Or hang out at the bar chattin' till Allie appears. Bet you recognise her."

"Sure will. Can't forget a looker like that."

"Not the point, Fremont," Casey rapped.

"Yes'm."

"Get a drink, but make sure the staff know you'll be takin' that glass soon's the table's clear. An' make sure they don't take any glasses off it, too."

"They've likely doped Allie," Casey said. "Whatever you do, *do not* interfere with them taking her out of the bar, no matter what she looks like. If you do, you'll be off the force as fast as I can arrange it. Then I'll let the Feds have you for blowing their op."

"Yes'm." His tone suggested that he was in front of the Academy drill sergeant.

"Go."

"Yes'm."

They transferred back to Renfrew.

"Okay, Fremont's on his way in. She likely won't recognise him, though she'd react if it was Tyler."

"Good. Thank you, Detectives."

The connection to Renfrew was cut. Casey flicked a fast, unfocused gaze across Carval, barely registering his presence.

"O'Leary, I think we'd better talk to Andy and Tyler now."

"Yeah. Don't want 'em gettin' all fretful-like."

"No. They're both upset."

"We don't want no more upset today. Likely there'll be plenty without addin' to it."

"Patch them in, then," Casey said.

"You still can't do that? Andy better give you another tech lesson."

Carval spluttered with laughter.

"You do it faster. Get them, hm?"

"Aw, sure," O'Leary drawled, and the channel opened up.

"Guys, Allie's taken a hand. She's gone off to the restroom so they get the chance to dope her drink. Fremont's in there" –

"What the *fuck*?" Tyler grated.

"We need that evidence. She's given us the chance."

"Ballsy," O'Leary approved.

"Andy, you good?"

"Yep." His voice was light. "Showtime, boys and girls."

"Okay. Keep the channel clear, and let's do this."

***

When Allie returned – and it hadn't been a lie to take a break – Yarland and Severstal were regarding a big guy, alone, who'd taken a seat nearer their semi-secluded booth than, from their annoyed expressions, they'd liked. When they saw her, they smiled. The hairs on the back of her neck rose.

She smiled brightly and sat back down, heedless of the appreciative glance of the big guy. She got those all the time.

"I really like this wine!" she bubbled, and took another sip. She couldn't taste any difference at all, but her creep-radar was telling her something was up. Their avid gazes didn't waver. "I'm really not used to wine."

"So you said. Stick with us, and you'll get a lot more."

"I'd really like that!" She took another, larger, mouthful.

"We would too. You're perfect. Together, we're gonna make you a star."

The men drank, too.

***

Casey's lips tightened as a sloppy, girlish giggle came from the feed.

Wow! This" – a hint of a slur – *"wine is so good. You guys are so great!*

I think you've had a little too much.

Let's get you out of here, sexy.

I'm sexy?

Sure are.

But I don' like those props.

C'mon. Let's get you out.

"Tyler. Get eyes on them, and follow. Andy, you too. O'Leary, you make sure Fremont gets that glass to McDonald as fast as he can. Wake him up, if you have to. He won't have waited up for us. We need to know what it is in case we have to take Allie to an ER."

"He's a vampire. He don't sleep."

"Just make it happen."

"Okay. No need to snap."

"Then you follow Allie too."

"Not my first rodeo."

"You can't ride. The horse rides on you."

"Easy. We're on it."

You goin' to take me home?

Don't you worry.

Wanna go home. I'm sleepy.

Don't go to sleep, sexy. We've got the whole night.

"Tyler, Andy, you on them?"

"Yep," came in stereo.

You wanna do more, don't you?

Yesssh.

We'll make it happen.

Totally for real?

Sure. You'll be a star.

Wanna be a singer.

You'll sing.

Awesome!

"It all sounds totally innocent."

"Unless you know what's going on."

Where're we goin'? I wanna go home.

Not just yet. Night's not over.

But…

"Got them."

No buts. We're not done yet.

But… don' wanna. Wanna go home.

Not yet.

"Oh, yeah," Tyler grated. "I got you now, motherfuckers."

"Tyler! Tone it down. We're going to arrest them. No more."

"We had a thought."

"You think, Bigfoot?" Andy asked.

"Sure I do. Mebbe it's a little slow, on account of the blood takin' a while to get as high as my head. An' what we thought was that the Feds might be, as you say, *reminded* that California still got the death penalty."

There was a series of satisfied sighs.

"An' you wouldn't want to deny our guys the full experience, would you?"

"No."

"So cool it."

"Andy, you get Allie. Sounds like she's nearly out of it already. Get her out, get her to an ER to be checked over. Fremont should've rousted out McDonald by now."

"Checkin'." Pause. "Yeah. Fremont's got that scared sound. McDonald didn't like it."

"McDonald doesn't like anything. Fremont should find his balls."

"Sounds more like he's worried McDonald will, with a scalpel."

"Focus," Casey rapped.

"They're slowin' down."

Where'sh this?

Our place. You'll like it.

A nasty laugh.

It's dark. This doesn' look nice.

Inside's much better. You'll like it.

Don' wanna. Wanna go home. Don' feel good.

Fuck, she's heavy.

Not! Perfect weight.

Shut up.

Huh? What'ss happ'ning? Did the shoot. We doin' 't 'gain? Thought I did good.

Four cars and the FBI van came to a silent halt outside a run-down office block.

In you come.

Ow!

Stand up, you clumsy bitch.

Wha'? No. No. I don' wanna be here. Lemme go!

"Go!"

Carval started shooting as fast as he could press the shutter: capturing the speed and mass of Tyler and O'Leary smashing through the door as if it were paper; faces grim, muscles straining; power in motion. Andy and Casey were right behind them, tiny in comparison, but the same honed purpose, guns out, the warehouse lights gleaming on the metal.

Yarland had a hand locked round Allie's wrist, pulling her halfway to the bed in the dressed set which filled half the floor space; her face was vacant; much less beautiful without personality; she was sagging. Carval caught the avid lust on Severstal's face, changing to horror as he registered the cops, and then returned to Yarland, appalled to see the object in his hand, far too close to Allie's arm; the sharp needle ominous.

"NYPD! Hands up!"

Shock bloomed on Yarland's face.

"What the hell? This is private property! Where's your warrant?" He'd pulled on indignation, just too late.

"Don't need one. You're abducting this woman."

"Don't be ridiculous. You have no proof."

The big cops held their guns on him, holding his attention: anger tainting the air.

Carval switched focus to Casey and Andy, who were slipping round behind Yarland and Severstal, unseen; Allie still unaware of the situation, Yarland still holding her wrist and the needle within inches.

"Get Allie and get out. She's doped. Get her to the ER," Casey breathed.

"Needle. Can't let that touch her," Andy murmured in return.

"You have to have a warrant. Get out of here." Severstal weighed in, projecting anger but sweat beading on his brow.

"That is where you are wrong," Renfrew's patrician tone cut the air. "FBI. We have been surveilling you since the photoshoot began."

In Carval's viewfinder, Renfrew's skeletal figure became the death of Yarland's game: one thin finger raised for attention.

"How – that *bitch!*" Yarland yanked Allie around, his fury palpable. She shrieked as she stumbled and her wrist bent. Carval was already refocused on Tyler, who had exploded into movement, panning after him.

"Andy!" Casey yelled, already ramming herself in front of Yarland, grabbing for his hand and the bright steel needle. Yarland swung at Allie, and hit Casey instead, as Carval captured Tyler scything in like the wrath of God, flicked back to O'Leary cuffing Severstal, flicked on to Renfrew standing in judgment, flicked back to Tyler, ungently restraining Yarland, whose face was meeting the floor, flicking back to Andy, already most of the way to the door with Allie stumbling beside him, his gun drawn.

Finally, he lowered his camera: tense calm spreading among the cops. Only a minute or two had passed.

"Spread out," Casey commanded. "We have to find Hervalo." She spun to Yarland. Carval raised his camera once more, focused firmly on Casey. "Where is he?" His lips clamped shut. "Severstal. Where is Hervalo?" Equal silence. "Okay." She whipped a glance round the team. "O'Leary, Bergen, you get these guys into Holding. Tyler, you're with me. Dr Renfrew, where do you want to be?"

Carval stayed quiet. Wherever Casey was hunting, that was where he would be. He'd catch the shots in Holding later.

"I will go with Agent Bergen and Detective O'Leary. We shall begin interrogation. I will provide any information on Hervalo to you immediately, and I shall be grateful if you will do the same."

He took a fast shot of Casey's face, utterly dumbfounded by Renfrew's ridiculous formality in the situation, and frowned. Something was off. She rubbed at her arm.

"Okay. Let's do this. Andy, get gone."

Andy walked Allie out, supporting her. "I'll get you to the ER," he managed soothingly, though his eyes were skating all around, looking for Hervalo.

"Don' feel good."

"Don't worry. We got you. You're safe now." Platitudes, but it seemed to help.

"Where'sh Tyler?"

"Taking down the bad guys."

"Said he would."

"We did. It'll all be fine. Let's get you checked out."

"Wan' Tyler," Allie insisted.

"Promise he'll come see you later, but not till you've been to the ER." With a little difficulty, he steered her out to his car, settled her in, and left.

O'Leary, Bergen and Renfrew departed with their prisoners, leaving Casey and Tyler to search the site.

"You okay?" Casey asked.

"Yeah."

"Knew you'd be."

"You?"

"Huh?"

"Rubbing your arm."

"Sonofabitch swung and hit me."

"Uh…" Carval interrupted, "did he hit you with that needle?"

"Huh?" she said again.

"Jacket off," Tyler said, and tugged it. A thin, ominous trail of blood stained the sleeve of her shirt. He yanked the cuff open, and ripped straight up. "Yep. Feel weird?"

"No! That was an expensive shirt," she protested. "And we should be searching for Hervalo, not worrying about a scratch or ruining my clothes. Come on."

She marched off, gun out and ready, pulling her jacket back on. Tyler gazed around the room, scowling ever more blackly at the bed and props, the lights, and finally the cameras.

"Filming. Just like she said." He pulled out his phone. "Toby? Tyler. CSU team to site at the corner of East 97th and FDR Drive. Crime scene for processing. Thanks."

Carval looked at the set, and then looked again. It was precisely the same as the set at Stardance had been… oh. Not quite. These cuffs were metal, not toys. He shuddered.

"Tyler!" Carval could hear Casey's sharp note. "Back here."

"You found him?"

"No. But we should get CSU in right now."

"Already on the way."

"Good. Oh, shit."

"What?"

"That bastard Yarland must've pushed the plunger. Feels helluva good, though… ohhhhh yes."

"Carval!" Tyler yelled, and then swore viciously. "Get your ass over here!"

Carval came racing in and stopped dead. "What the hell?" Casey was sitting down on the floor, a sloppy smile blooming on her face.

"She's high."

"Oh, *shit.*"

"Yeah." Tyler scowled. "Useless for a few minutes 'cause she's high, then she'll crash and be useless for hours."

"Not helpful," Carval said dryly.

"Probably vomit, too."

"Ugh." He looked at her. "Should I get her to the ER?"

Casey giggled, and stripped her jacket off again. "Cosy. Come cuddle me."

Tyler didn't answer, instead pulling out his phone. "Bigfoot? You get that needle? 'Kay. Much left in it?" Unintelligible bass rumbles filled the space. Tyler appeared to understand. "Most? 'Kay. Casey got tagged." Angry thunderous rumbles arrived. "Yeah, yeah. 'Kay. Your call. You get the shit. Back to you soon." He swiped off. "Bigfoot says take her to the ER at Metropolitan, next door to here." Carval stared. "You see anyone else?"

"But..." His photos. He wouldn't be able to take any more photos of the scene or the hunt if he were taking Casey to the ER. But there was no other cop to search the place. He put away his obsession, and accepted reality.

"Take her keys and car. Likely they'll do nothing, but if Bigfoot says so..."

Casey was abruptly violently sick, fortunately to one side.

"ER," Tyler repeated. "Move!"

Carval's feet moved without any input from his brain. He hauled Casey away from the mess and into standing.

"Keys likely in her jacket."

They were. He took them, wrapped an arm round Casey's waist, and marched her out. Her stumbling and giggles were disturbingly reminiscent of Allie. Knowing his luck, they'd end up at the same ER. Behind him, Tyler was back on the phone to O'Leary, demanding back-up to clear the premises.

***

Carval arrived at the Metropolitan Hospital's ER only a few moments later. Casey was still giggling and euphoric, but at least she hadn't vomited again. Cleaning out her car wasn't on the to-do list. He steered her in, and explained, stressing *active cop attacked on duty*, to the triage nurse, who took the few details Carval could provide. Casey giggled, and was no help.

"Are you next of kin?"

"No," he admitted. He gave the nurse O'Leary's number, which was all he knew. She raised an eyebrow. "He's another cop."

"Best friend," Casey interjected, and yawned. "Sleepy."

"Okay, let's take a look," the attending doctor said, after Carval had repeated the story. She put Casey in an examination room, and turned round. "You can't stay. The waiting room is right over there."

He retreated, but didn't leave, texting O'Leary to let him know the situation. Faintly, he could hear the unusual sound of a totally unstressed, relaxed, happy Casey answering the doctor, interspersed with muzzy yawns. It would have been great, if she hadn't also been slurring her words.

The doctor emerged after an objectively short time which apparently lasted several hours.

"She's responded well. We'll keep her under observation for a short time, maybe an hour or two, and then she can be discharged. She was lucky." Her tired eyes flicked over him. "You her boyfriend?"

"Yeah."

"Stay with her. Bring her back if you're worried about anything. You can go in now." Her pager sounded, and she dashed off.

In the examination room, Casey was lying on the bed, fully dressed, and dozing. There was nothing to do but hold her limp hand, and wait.

CHAPTER TWENTY EIGHT

It wasn't long before Carval was bored. Holding Casey's hand was fine, but he preferred her to be awake and capable of making conversation. The room was uninteresting, the machines were chirping regularly and tediously, and the trace on the screen wasn't changing, which was excellent, but also boring. If he tried to take photos, he'd likely be evicted. He'd been lucky to get away with it last time. He had a sudden thought, and pulled his phone out.

"Andy?"

"Yeah?"

"Where are you? I'm in Metropolitan ER."

"What! Why?"

"Casey got a scratch with that needle. O'Leary said get her checked."

"That's his evening ruined."

"Where are you?"

"Probably two doors away. Waiting for Allie's mom to turn up."

"Is she okay?"

"Yeah. Still coming out of it, but McDonald said it was a roofie and the doctor agreed. Nothing to do but wait." Andy paused. "What's Tyler doing?"

"Still at the site. With Casey out, he had to call in for some help and wait for CSU. Why?"

"Allie asked for him."

Carval grinned. "Really? There's a picture. I didn't have him down as a ministering angel."

Andy snickered. "Guess the perps are in Holding?"

"Yeah, but they hadn't found Hervalo."

"We will."

"No' found him?" Oh. Casey was awake. "Gettim. Tell Tyler t' gettim." She started to sit up.

"Uh-uh. You get to stay till they discharge you." A snicker rose from the phone. Carval swiped it off before Andy could say anything. "They said an hour."

"Why'm I here?" She was still slurring.

"O'Leary said to do it. Tyler's clearing the crime scene with CSU."

"Didn't need hosp'tal."

"Maybe not, but I'm not tangling with O'Leary and Tyler. You wanna have that fight, go ahead."

She subsided with a disgruntled mutter which boded ill, though Carval didn't feel that either man would be in imminent danger. Before she could reconstitute her semi-scrambled brain, there was the sound of a brisk stride and Tyler appeared.

"Down?" he inquired. Casey attempted a growl, and managed only a half-yawn-half-growl. "Not yet."

"Perps?" she tried.

"Holding. Renfrew had a go. No luck."

"H'rvalo?"

"In the wind. BOLO's out. Hunt's on. He won't hide long."

Tyler turned sharply by the right, and left without farewell or fuss.

"Guess he's going to visit Allie."

"Din't you?"

"Nope."

Casey looked at him with the most peculiar expression on her face. Shorn of her normal control and cynicism by the after-effects of heroin, Carval could actually see something more than the casual façade.

"Never thought of it," he said truthfully. He stared at her as, finally, cogs turned in his head. "You've been upset about the *models*? Why?"

She turned away.

"No, you don't. Come back here." He gripped her shoulder and rolled her back. "If I wanted models I'd have them. You saw how Allie reacted. I don't want them."

"I don't wanna talk about this."

"Well, I do. You can't run away and you can't shoot me and if you stick your fingers in your ears and sing la-la-la I'll go down the hall and get Tyler and Andy in here to pull them out. And even if you close your eyes like that your ears are still open so just *damn well listen to me*. If I wanted to date a model I'd date one. I don't. And I don't cheat either, so you can drop that thought right now too." His angry breath sliced the air. "I *thought* I was dating you. Am I?"

Slow hand-claps came from the door. "Just as well I'm examining Miss"
—

"De'ct've!" Casey complained –

"Detective Clement to see if she's fit for discharge. You can fix your relationship issues elsewhere. This isn't a hospital soap opera, it's a place to treat the sick."

Carval reluctantly stood up and left, before he was dismissed. From the waiting room, he thought he saw Andy's slim form whisk by, but he couldn't tell and wouldn't go after him. Shortly, Tyler passed by, smiling like the lion who'd got the best bits of the zebra. Carval didn't call out to him, either, though after Tyler had gone he thought that a hard sparring session might have been a better plan than sitting stewing.

He didn't get much time to stew. Casey was deposited at the waiting room with a small sheaf of paper and a muzzily annoyed expression. The doctor made a sharp *come-on* gesture to him.

"Take her home, and stay with her tonight." She smiled sardonically. "You can try to fix whatever's bugging you, though likely she won't remember much of it tomorrow."

"Will," Casey said. Carval thought she looked like a cross, ruffled cat, and grinned.

"Whatever. C'mon, time to go home."

"Precinct."

"No. Home."

"I wanna 'terrogate those bastards."

"Tomorrow. Tyler said they're in Holding. It's after nine. Tomorrow."

"Now."

Exasperated, Carval tapped O'Leary's number, and when he picked up, tersely explained, and then handed the phone to Casey.

"Naw, you're not comin' in."

"But" –

"But nothin'. No-one's interrogatin' anyone tonight. An' after that last trick you pulled, Kent's watchin'. You come in against advice again, you'll be benched, bet on it."

"But" –

"No buts. You ain't comin'. Go home, sleep it off, an' start clean" – Carval snickered at the inadvertent pun – "tomorrow."

"Hate you," Casey sulked, sounding like she was four and missing a treat.

"Naw, you love me. Always have, always will."

Casey blew a raspberry at the phone.

"That's not nice," O'Leary chided. "See you tomorrow." He cut the call before Casey's befuddled brain could answer.

"Home time," Carval said briskly, taking advantage of the moment and the opportunity to put an arm around her to steer her to the car. She complied, still sulkily. The pout was adorable, but drawing attention to it might be fatal.

***

Once they had reached Casey's apartment and Carval had made sure she was both inside and sitting down resting, he made coffee, which, even in their two-month acquaintance, he had discovered could never be wrong. Fortunately her machine was simple (if expensive), because aside from camera equipment and the associated programs, he wasn't particularly tech-savvy.

When coffee landed under her nose, Casey inhaled, but didn't spark into life. Carval took the easy option, sat down next to her, sipped his own mugful, and put an arm back round her shoulders. Astonishingly, she snuggled in without any hesitation. He didn't like that she'd been hurt, again, but he surely liked her snuggly.

"Why were you so uptight about the models?"

"That's what you like," she said, still sloppy and slurring. "All over Google. Always a pretty girl. Tall and beautiful."

"You Googled me?"

"Be benched if I ran you."

He goggled. "Do you run all your boyfriends?"

"Wha' boyfriends?"

He was dead sure she hadn't meant to say that.

"Anyway, you weren't my boyfriend then."

He couldn't believe the relief that flooded through him. He was *never* worried about not being someone's boyfriend. Never. Sometimes the reverse, but he'd never *wanted* to be a boyfriend before. "But I am now," he said firmly. "So forget the models. If I wanted them, I'd have them. I want you, and I've got you."

There was no answer. He looked down, and found she was asleep, coffee untouched. He sighed, untangled his fingers from her hair, and carried her through to her bedroom, reflecting that he couldn't and wouldn't have done that for any of his previous lovers. Small had advantages. There was a sloppy t-shirt under the pillow, so he delicately undressed her, slid her into the t-shirt as best he could and then tucked her in.

And then he went back to his coffee, a book he borrowed from her shelves, and wallpaper TV, until he was tired enough to curl around her protectively and sleep too.

***

She felt *vile*. It was the worst hangover she'd ever suffered, by far. Casey groaned, and only realised she wasn't alone when there was an answering grunt. Phew. Carval. She didn't remember how he got there...oh.

"Urrgh," she managed, and tried to sit up.

Sitting up wasn't the best idea ever. Unfortunately, it was required to choke down two Advil with water, and keep them in her stomach. She staggered to the shower, turned the dial to scalding, and stood under the water until her skin felt clean. It didn't help her thumping head, but it didn't make it worse. Possibly that was because nothing could have made it worse. Amputation at the neck seemed infinitely desirable.

She staggered back out of the shower, and tried not to stab herself in the eye with the mascara wand. It was a major triumph that it went on her eyelashes, not her teeth.

"'Lo." It escaped the smothering bedcovers.

"What the hell happened last night?" she asked the mirror.

"You got stuck with a needleful of heroin," Carval said baldly, "went to the ER, and I brought you home."

Blurred memories fuzzed into her mind as he spoke. The takedown, the scratch, Allie being saved, harsh words in the ER, and, much later and only half-heard, *I want you and I've got you.* She'd think about that later, when she might be able to think.

"Ugh."

"Yep."

"Work." Suddenly her face flashed into life. "Yarland and Severstal. Interrogation. I better get going." Carval blinked. "Lock up. Here's the key." He plucked it out of the air. "See you later," she said over her shoulder, and was gone.

On the way to the precinct she avoided the potholes as best she could, in case her head fell off, and parked with extreme care. She wasn't quite sure where the edges of the world were if she wasn't concentrating with all her might.

Coffee helped, and the third double espresso, all downed as fast as her throat could take them, left her feeling almost normal.

"Mornin'," came from behind her. "Feelin' okay?"

"Advil is a blessing."

"Sure is."

"Have we found Hervalo yet?"

"Naw. Everyone's lookin'. But we got the other two in Holdin', so if you wanna cheer yourself out of that there hangover of yourn" –

"Going too far. Even you don't say *yourn.*"

"Woke you up, though. Anyway, if you wanna have a little fun" – they smiled viciously at each other – "we got the other two."

"Better wait till Renfrew arrives," she said. "Manners, and all that."

"Ain't inter-agency co-operation a bitch?"

"I do not find it so, when those co-operating are sufficiently talented," Renfrew intervened. "May I have a coffee from your excellent machine?"

"Sure." O'Leary wasn't embarrassed in the slightest.

"I infer that you wish to interrogate our perpetrators?"

"Yes."

"We have not yet located Hervalo."

"Let's start with Yarland."

"I shall observe," Renfrew said.

"We'll let you know when he's in Interrogation."

Casey sent Carval a quick text to let him know that there would be interrogations of suspects, and began to plan her strategy in a beautifully quiet conference room. She started with O'Leary.

"Tell me what happened last night. Everything after we went in."

O'Leary complied. Casey cross-questioned him relentlessly.

"I ain't your suspect," he complained. "Stop rippin' into me like I was." He tried a scowl, which had no effect, and continued. "An' then I took the suspects off with the Feds, put out a BOLO for Hervalo, an' Renfrew had a go-around in interrogation an' didn't get anywhere. You c'n interrogate Tyler."

Casey poked her pounding head out of the conference room door, spotted her prey, and summoned Tyler and Andy.

"Both of them?"

"I want to know what happened to Allie after Andy took her to the ER. Make sure she's okay too."

"Dead easy," Andy said. "They called her mom, checked her out, McDonald confirmed it was a roofie – though it was all dressed up in medical-speak" – suddenly he smiled nastily. "That was fun to listen to. McDonald had a go-around with the doctor, with his biggest stick up his ass, and turned them inside out – so they kept her till her mom turned up, I guess."

"I guess?" Casey repeated, unimpressed.

"Well," Andy drew out, "about that point Tyler here turned up, and she seemed pretty pleased to see him, and I'm not keen on playing third wheel, so I left them making eyes at each other."

Tyler ignored the snickers with magnificent disdain.

"Yarland got you with the heroin when you got between him and Allie," he said to Casey. "Few minutes later, you got high, vomited, so Carval took you to the ER."

"I knew that," Casey said impatiently. Behind her, O'Leary gave Tyler the thumbs-up for skirting the details. "What about the site? CSU report? Where's Hervalo?"

"Searched and CSU swept it. All sorts of cameras and laptops. Clear they were filming. CSU have the tech. Fingerprints of all three all over, but no-one else found in the tech room."

"Good. Last thing we want is an unknown criminal mastermind."

"Forensics are running all the other prints, hairs, blood, DNA. Nothing back yet, but they'll cross-match against our vics."

"Follow the money," said Andy.

"What do you mean?"

"They were filming. Tyler's search confirms it. CSU have the laptops from the site, but they don't even have to get into them for me to know what they were doing. Those films were uploaded and people paid to watch them. *Subscribed*," he spat.

"Easy," O'Leary rumbled, and touched Andy's shoulder.

"Is Bergen here?"

"Yes," the man said. They hadn't noticed his entrance, and yet he had a cup of coffee already. Renfrew had followed him.

"You and Andy get up to CSU and take those laptops apart," Casey commanded. "Trace their site and bank accounts from there. Soon as you get something, we'll get warrants on the accounts and trace that through to their own money. Dr Renfrew, I assume you can arrange for an account freeze when we get warrants?"

"We only have to show probable cause. That will not be a problem, once Agent Bergen and Detective Chee have done their work."

Bergen threw his coffee back in a way Casey appreciated, and the two of them departed. Renfrew exited, and Casey was left with O'Leary and Tyler.

"Anything else I should know before I take these men apart?"

"Naw."

Tyler merely shook his head.

"Okay. We'll talk about how I got to the ER later," she said ominously. The men quivered. "I'll just think through all of this before we get started. O'Leary, you're in there with me."

The interrogation was too important to rush. Casey took time to structure her thoughts and tamp down her revulsion and anger at the perpetrators, ignoring the fuss and bustle around her and the remnants of her headache. When she looked up, Carval had arrived: some time ago, judging by the almost-empty coffee mug. There was another mug in front of her, which she automatically drained, even though the liquid was lukewarm, and returned to her tactics.

A few moments later, she was done. Her face was set, her full lips pinched tight, and her brown eyes were cold and focused. Carval took a few shots, but she didn't notice anything except her goal.

"Bring Yarland up to Interrogation," she ordered, and the uniform jumped to it.

"Right," she snarled, when the officer returned. "Let's go make Yarland's day *hell*." She picked up her pen and pad with her notes, and was halfway across the floor with O'Leary before Carval had blinked.

***

Yarland obviously hadn't appreciated the sting operation. It appeared that he must have tripped and fallen while in Holding, too, or possibly there was honour among thieves, so to speak. She'd hear that story later. She read him his rights, and began.

"Connor Yarland," she said coldly. "Fashion photographer, rapist and murderer. Quite a sheet you've got. They'll have fun with you in Rikers. The boys in there don't like rapists much…but they're quite keen on sex."

"You lying bitch!"

Casey's expression remained utterly bored; O'Leary impassive next to her.

"I've never been convicted of anything. I haven't done anything wrong. You entrapped me and my lawyer will make sure the jury knows it. I'll be free."

She held his gaze. "You've done plenty of things wrong, and we didn't entrap you. You chose to spike Allie's wine, and you chose to try to inject her – and did inject me – with heroin."

"You won't have a minute's credibility when my shots of Allie get into evidence. She loved it. She wanted the next job and she came with us willingly."

"Really? Because I've got lots of discussions with the FBI in which it's clear that she only took the role to give you enough rope to hang yourself. And Selwyn knew all about it, too."

That rocked him.

"And everything was recorded from the moment she walked into Stardance. Including her requests to go home, that you ignored. She didn't consent, Yarland, and we've got it all on tape. We've also got you and Severstal assaulting her. On film."

Carval was impressed. Casey hadn't turned a hair about the idea that Allie would be trashed in evidence: she'd thrown Yarland's behaviour right back in his face. He had seriously underestimated his mark here, and it was about to bite him on the ass.

"And you assaulted me, too, with that needle of yours, and I've got all the evidence for that. So I can hold you as long as I like. Slam dunk into jail, assaulting a cop. You won't like Rikers, Yarland. Of course, you'll only be in Rikers if the San Francisco PD don't claim precedence. They're aiming for Death Row for you, and if they want you we'll happily wave you bye-bye, *baby*. The needle's much cheaper than putting you in jail, and it's on California's budget too. Win-win, from where I'm standing."

Yarland's colour drained.

"The only way you might get out of that was if you give us *everything* on the other guys. Severstal, Hervalo – and where is he, by the way, because if you don't help us find him we'll regard that as non-cooperation and you'll be straight off to San Francisco."

"I don't know anything."

"Liar," Casey said. "I've got plenty of evidence all three of you were in it together. You know all about him. You've been working together for years." She shrugged. "Still, have it your own way. You're going down. It's not my problem." She stood up, and left, ignoring his incoherent desperation. O'Leary followed her, having not said a single word.

"That was short," he said. "What about Hervalo?"

"Yarland's got no chance. I just want him to roll on the other guys. We could use getting more on everyone, and when they roll on each other it's always better." She led the way into Observation. "Now we'll let him sweat. He's going to be really unhappy for a while. He didn't expect to be facing the death penalty. He'll spill."

They wandered into Observation.

Carval slid up to her, and loosely wrapped her into the crook of his arm, ignoring Renfrew's presence. "It was fun to shoot, too. He's not very happy, is he?"

"Nope," she replied, popping the P with a plosive snap of satisfaction. "The less happy he is, the happier I am."

"Most impressive, Detective Clement."

"I'll go back to him later."

She stared through the glass at the revolting, pathetic figure of Yarland, twisting his hands as if was the upset one here. He'd made his own bad choices: she had only had to do her job professionally, no matter how much she disliked the perps. It had left her with a dose of heroin and the hangover from hell, and a wasted evening in hospital. But sending them down for life – or death – would make up for all of that. Oh yes. She was going to be right there to see it.

CHAPTER TWENTY NINE

"Now for Severstal," Casey said. "Bring him up to Interrogation Two. We'll leave Yarland to work himself up."

A few moments later – no-one was dumb enough to hinder a hunting Casey – she and O'Leary faced Severstal. He wasn't nearly as pretty after a night in Holding, but he was just as angry as the first time they'd interviewed him. Casey read him his rights, each word precisely enunciated into his flushed, snarling face.

"Do you understand?"

"I want a lawyer."

"Do you understand?"

"Yes. I want a lawyer," he spat.

"Sure. But just to tell you, we've got everything on tape and film since Allie walked into Stardance, and by lunchtime your bank accounts will be frozen. So how're you going to pay for a lawyer, huh? Not that a lawyer can get you out of this. We've got you all wrapped up. Assault, attempted rape, actual rape, and murder. Oh – and assault on a cop. All because you wanted to be the star of a movie."

Her tones dripped bored contempt.

"Couldn't make it for real, could you?"

"Not enough talent," O'Leary dropped in.

"But never mind. The only acting talent you'll need in jail is pretending to enjoy it when you bend over for the big boys. Not that you'll have to do that for long, because you'll be on your own in Death Row."

"Dumb bitch. New York doesn't have the death penalty."

"California does. San Francisco want you. I'm happy to give you to them."

"Closer to Hollywood, I guess."

"That's what he wanted."

Severstal's angry face had paled in a few short sentences.

"But you want a lawyer, so that's what you'll get."

"Some fresh-faced public defender."

"No! I got enough money for the best."

"Didn't you listen? Your accounts will be frozen. You can't use the money from your crimes to defend yourself."

"You can't do that!" But his voice quavered.

"The FBI can. They're in this too."

She stood. "Now you've asked for a lawyer, we're done." She paused. "Hervalo's still out there: probably emptying the accounts and flying down to Rio. He'll be living the high life and you'll be on Death Row."

Her hand was on the door. "We'll send a lawyer in."

"Wait!"

She raised an eyebrow.

"You got to give me time to think."

"Think?" She cast a glance upward at O'Leary. "I guess we can do that." Disappointment laced her words. "I wouldn't want him to have any complaints. Do your thinking," she directed to Severstal, and left.

"Waal, that was fun. Still, it didn't take long. You gotta drag it out. Build dramatic tension, ain't that what they call it on TV?"

"We're not on TV. You've been doing too many am-drams or talking to Andy too much. We just want to send them down." She smiled. "So let's let them stew. D'you want to bet who rolls first? I'll pick Yarland."

Her voice was light, but her eyes were hard and cold. Her suspects made her sick: nauseated by the knowledge of their actions and their self-centred arrogance. She wanted them to be as terrified as their victims. Some killers at least had a shred of humanity left, but not these men. She pushed down her emotions.

"No bet. You always win. 'S not fair."

"When do you think Andy'll be back?"

"Before lunch."

So it proved. Andy and Bergen whisked back in, exuding smug satisfaction.

"We cracked the laptops right open," Bergen enthused. "Their security was no match for us."

"So our good friends Yarland and Severstal are going down for life, if California don't call dibs and give him the needle instead."

"Mm," Casey mused. "Life in Rikers as a rapist and murderer – of youngish women, which I'm sure nobody would *deliberately* let out... or Death Row in California, which would be drawn out too. Mmmm. What a lovely choice. Let me think about that." Her expression was as vicious as Andy's. "Okay. Get me up to speed with everything you found at CSU."

Andy and Bergen started talking. Thirty seconds later Casey's eyes had glazed.

"I don't want to hear the details. Tell me you got the laptops open and the evidence of the sites and account numbers."

They presented identically disappointed expressions at not being able to show off their brilliance. "We got them."

"Okay. Warrants time. One for searching the apartments, one for financials, and Bergen, you do whatever you have to do to freeze these accounts. We'll get Hervalo when we've got the damn address."

Forty minutes later Casey had her warrants for Yarland and Severstal. The less said about the way she had forced them through, the better, and it was entirely possible that the judge's clerk was still shaking. Renfrew had been perfectly formal.

"Andy, Tyler?" Casey waved the paper at them.

"Yeah?"

"We've got our warrants, so we can search Yarland and Severstal's places, but we don't know where Hervalo lived so I can't get one for him yet. Can you go rip their apartments to shreds? Take CSU with you. They might find some other useful stuff. Some more evidence would be good."

"On it. See you later."

"What else was there?" Casey asked, as the other two left. "I thought we were getting prints, DNA, hair, all from Forensics? And *why* don't we have an address for Hervalo, huh?"

"Still waiting for anythin' useful. We got Hervalo's old address. He moved."

"So why don't we have the new one?"

"Databases not up to date," O'Leary said world-wearily. Casey made an intemperately furious noise.

"How long's it going to take?"

"'Nother day, minimum." There was a sound of small avalanches from O'Leary's stomach. His prairie-sized cheeks turned a pretty shade of pink. "Guess that means it's lunchtime," he said. "C'mon. Let's get some food, an' then you can rip them apart in Interrogation. You won't be no good iffen you're faintin'."

Casey didn't want food: her stomach roiled and cramped at the thought. But O'Leary's gaze was just a little too sharply enquiring for her to make an excuse. He knew her too well.

"Okay." She turned. "Carval, you want some lunch?"

"Works for me. I'm hungry too."

Casey sighed. "Okay."

"Let's go to Dinosaur Bar-B-Que," O'Leary decided.

"That's so you can have their roast brontosaurus," Casey snipped.

"Naw. I do like their pulled pork, though. Just like my ma makes."

The three of them ambled out. Well, O'Leary ambled. The other two were forced to a brisk pace.

"We got time. Andy 'n' Tyler won't be back for at least a coupla hours, an' we ain't got Forensics before tomorrow. I'm hungry."

The booth was a little over-full with O'Leary in it. Casey was tucked in between Carval and the side partition, with O'Leary occupying the whole of the other side of the booth. Carval was quite happy with this arrangement, since it enabled him to stay firmly in contact with Casey.

He was unnerved by the way she'd behaved earlier. She'd been cruelly terrifying with Yarland, and then more so with Severstal, and while they both deserved it, Carval wasn't sure that she'd been acting.

When she ordered, he was more worried. She had soda, but only wanted a solo BBQ pork slider and fries. She ate a lot less than half of her meal, sluggishly. Most of it was scattered around the plate, picked apart and dropped. He suspected that had O'Leary not suggested lunch, she wouldn't have bothered. Neither man commented, though they had both noticed, and knew that the other had noticed too.

Too soon, Casey was jonesing to get back to the case, and had hustled everyone into finishing and leaving, though O'Leary's dark mutterings about the lack of opportunity for dessert meant that leaving was delayed till he could get pecan pie to go. Carval sulked all the way back to the Thirty-Sixth, because he hadn't thought of that and O'Leary refused to share. Casey sighed all the way back to the Thirty-Sixth, which changed nothing about Carval's disgruntlement or O'Leary's smug grin.

On the way back, it was Casey whose fast steps left the others struggling to keep up. When she found that Tyler and Andy weren't back, she was unreasonably annoyed, scrabbling all the other evidence together, drawing the spaces in their case on her murder board. She glared at the board till it should have shrivelled and burned, and all the time her fingers knotted and twitched, as fidgety as Carval had ever seen her.

Fortunately, before Casey's restless fingers caused a friction-lit fire, Andy and Tyler reappeared, stony-faced.

***

"You okay?" Tyler asked.

"I guess." Andy closed into himself. "Glad I'm not the one interrogating."

"Too close to home?"

"Yeah. They were filming, like I said." Tyler nodded. Andy scratched in a harsh breath. "I guess it wasn't pretty. It never was."

Andy stayed silent as Tyler negotiated the traffic to Yarland's New Jersey apartment, in a high-end area. Yarland might have claimed to be a top-class photographer, but if Andy was any judge – and he knew more about money than the rest of the team – Yarland couldn't have afforded that location without some serious extra-curricular earnings. It was pretty clear where those had come from.

CSU arrived right behind the detectives, and the apartment was taken apart. There were photos in a smart album, barely hidden in among several others containing ordinary shots.

"Fuck," was Tyler's only comment.

Andy nodded: lips clamped shut, bloodless; his face tight and pale.

Tyler moved a little closer to him. "Need a minute?" he murmured.

"That sonofabitch took them as *souvenirs*," Andy forced out. "Mementoes." He swallowed convulsively, choking back words. "I'm okay," he managed, belied by the greenish tint to his skin and his dead eyes, looking a million miles and many years away.

"Not okay. Take a minute." It was an order, but Andy wasn't receptive.

"No. We're *doing* this. I can do it. I'm not a rookie."

"Sure," Tyler appeased. "Let's do it."

They finished the search, leaving the CSU team to do their thing, and moved on to Severstal's apartment, not far away, taking the revolting photographs with them. Another CSU team was ready and waiting when they arrived.

Severstal had his own collection of depravity, even more vile than Yarland's. Tyler had thought himself inured to inhumanity, after his Army days, but he recoiled after the first page was turned.

Andy... didn't. He gazed at the shots, inscrutable.

Abruptly, he jerked out words, inaudible to anyone but Tyler.

"He tried... they wanted to do that to me. Wanted me in photos like that. Every time I said *no*, he beat me, but they couldn't if I had bruises..."

"Hear you." It was an acknowledgement. Tyler knew the story.

"Till I ran. That was the choice. Do *that*, be beaten – or the streets."

"Twelve," came softly.

"Twelve. Yeah."

"Fuck."

"Yeah." Andy hunched: slim, fragile, defensive; old pain crawling through his eyes. "They...once, they did. That... that was when I left. Ran," he added bitterly. "The cops wouldn't have listened, then."

Tyler nodded, just once, another acknowledgement. He felt the same, for his own reasons. They'd agreed on this before.

"Just a disrespectful young nephew, such a bad boy, not respecting his elders like Confucius taught. They had all the right words, for all the right people. Child Services, doctors, nurses. Always the right words to cover up, and nobody listened to a child. So I ran. Even the streets were better than that. I...never again. Streets, or..." Tyler heard *suicide*, though there was silence between them.

Andy turned away, shuttered and cold.

"Easy, man. Our team now."

"Best thing that happened."

"We all got demons. We're with you. Team, all the way. That won't change." Tyler touched Andy's shoulder: swift reassurance. "Let's get back. CSU can finish up here. Finish shift, get a beer. You can have that green tea piss-water you like."

"It's healthy," Andy forced back, "not like that stuff you drink, full of E-numbers and artificial colours."

"Seen my gym stats?"

"Seen Bigfoot's, too."

Nothing more was said on the way back, but, cop-like, the tension was eased by the banter.

***

"What have you got?" Casey asked, immediately the two men reached the bullpen.

"They kept photos. *Souvenirs*, like holiday snaps, in albums."

"Show me." There was no room for argument in her tone.

Renfrew and Bergen appeared on her words. Tyler spread the photos out on Casey's desk and everyone looked at them. There was a horrified silence.

"Nothin' like bein' caught on Candid Camera," O'Leary said heavily: no humour whatsoever in his tone.

Carval watched from a slight distance, shooting the protective circle around Andy, Renfrew's sharp eyes flicking from something on the desk to Andy, to Casey, back down to the desk; capturing the expressions of disgust on the faces of hardened investigators. Satisfied, he drifted over to them, and looked down at one of the photographs on the desk.

He almost vomited on the spot; dashed to the restroom and threw up: sure that it was everything he'd eaten for the last week; retching till his throat was raw and only thin bile was left. Shooting the panhandlers hadn't shown him that side of life, and now he'd seen even that single photo, he couldn't erase it from his mind. He retched again.

"You okay?" The chinaware trembled. "Mebbe you shouldn't've looked?"

"If I'd known, I wouldn't have." He spat, and retched again, exited and rinsed his mouth over and over again, under O'Leary's watchful presence. "How can you?"

"First time, I couldn't. Threw up on the spot. Leastways you didn't make a mess in the bullpen. Seen that, too. 'T ain't no shame. You get... not used to it, but harder 'bout it." He extended a paw, and clapped Carval gently on the back. "You'll be okay. C'mon. Casey's goin' back in on Yarland, an' she's out for blood."

260

They walked back. Casey's command tone was in sharp conversation with Renfrew's patrician suavity.

"So are the accounts frozen?"

"Yes, but Mr Hervalo's had two major withdrawals last night: one in cash. We are tracing the bank transfers, and will have the recipient account frozen as soon as it is found."

"If it's freezable. What if it's offshore?" Andy tapped his fingers restlessly.

"We shall do our best."

"With that cash, he could already be gone."

"He has not used his credit cards, and you have had a BOLO out since last night which has not identified him as passing any airport or border security. Therefore he is still most likely to be in the USA. We are also searching. Should he be identified, we will arrest him."

***

Yarland was an unpleasant shade of green-white: as if he was about to vomit, or had.

"Contemplating the needle?" Casey jeered before she was fully through the door. "I'll be watching. I'll enjoy it as much as you enjoyed taking those photos and dreamed about filming rape and murder later on."

Carval had already started to shoot. He'd not heard that sneering, taunting tone from Casey before. He thought she was acting. He *hoped* she was acting. The air of the room was cold, heavy, claustrophobic, palpable even through the glass. O'Leary stood massive and motionless behind her.

"You can bring the photos of Allie into evidence if you like. I've seen them. They're nothing special." She was contemptuous. "Any two-bit tit photographer could manage that."

"You lying bitch!" he howled. "Those photos take *talent*. No-one else could have done it. No-one could have turned those sluts into great art. They didn't deserve to be made famous."

"Sluts?" Casey said coldly.

"Yeah. Worthless trash. *I* made them gorgeous. They owed me everything."

"So you played them. Took them out and drugged them, then raped them on film so you could sell it to people as depraved as you are, all for the three of you to make money and get your rocks off."

"We deserved it. No-one else could have done it."

"Lots of scumbags have done it. You're not even original. You're just another boring porn merchant."

"Those films are *brilliant*."

"And yet we caught you."

"You can't keep me here."

"Oh, I can. We've got enough to send you down for life. Or to California for death. You and your pal Severstal. Hervalo was smarter. He's disappeared. But you and Severstal? We've got your *mementoes*. All in smart albums. They'll finish you, as if the films weren't enough."

She paused, and then began again.

"You and Severstal are the ones who're going to die in prison while he walks free. You all roofied the girls. You all injected them with heroin, raped them, killed them and beat them up after to try to hide the evidence. But we've only got you two."

Her voice fell to a menacing whisper. "I only wish you could die *once for every one of them*." She bared her teeth. "It'll feel as if you do, though. Did you know that? They make believe you won't feel a thing. You will. You'll scream with the pain. You'll void your bowels and bladder and then lie in your own piss and shit screaming and humiliated, and then you'll die slowly. And I'll watch. Every. Single. Second. For all of them."

Carval's fingers were gripping his camera so tightly that they hurt, but he couldn't stop shooting, the click continuous. She was using words like a scalpel, flaying Yarland to the bone without a touch, Nemesis with a gun and shield.

He was terrified.

This was not his Casey. This was Justice, blind to human frailty, blind to anything except cold, cold results. He didn't know this person at all.

"You're going to die screaming, down in California," she whispered, and smiled horribly. "And I'm going to watch."

And he broke.

He spilled everything: account numbers, the sordid, appalling details of the deaths – all those they had identified, and more besides.

"Your website?"

"Hervalo did all the tech."

"Where is he?"

"I don't know."

"That doesn't cut it." Intimidation suffocated Yarland. "Tell. Me. Everything." He gulped, searched for a water cup that wasn't there. "Tell me."

"He has a house. Larchmont."

"Pretty fancy for a dresser," O'Leary noted.

"Address."

He gave it. O'Leary exited for a minute, and returned, giving Casey a nod. Carval assumed that meant cops were already on their way to Larchmont.

"Anything else?"

There was a pause.

"I told you everything. I want a deal."

Casey's face was at absolute zero. "There are no deals. You helped him. If they want you, they'll have you. Connor Yarland, you are charged with multiple rapes, murders, assault, and assault on a police detective. O'Leary, get him taken away."

"Noooooo!" he screamed. "You promised."

"I promised you *nothing*." She stood. "Rikers or the needle. Either way, you'll *suffer*."

She walked out, as cold as the Antarctic winter, leaving Yarland begging behind her.

Carval followed from Observation, slowly, appalled and awed in equal measure. He found that his own hands were shaking, now he'd stopped shooting. He'd never seen anything like it and he never, *ever*, wanted to again. He could hear Yarland through the shut door: reduced to grovelling terror and shreds, pleading for his life and mercy.

There was no mercy. There was only Casey, and blind Justice.

CHAPTER THIRTY

Carval returned to watch from Observation as Casey tore Severstal to shreds just as she had eviscerated Yarland: equally glacial, leaving him equally shattered. Nothing new arose from that interrogation, but his shots would be astonishing: the power and the fury, the quivering terror and the sense of doom.

He exited Observation. Casey had disappeared. Carval looked around, and saw only Renfrew and Bergen, exiting Observation.

"That was scary," Bergen said.

"She assumed the role perfectly," Renfrew added.

"Are you sure she was acting?" Carval asked. "It didn't feel like it."

"Mm," was all Renfrew said, and steepled his fingers.

***

In the restroom, Casey was losing everything from her stomach down to its lining: a painful, unproductive retching that burned her throat and ripped at her abdominal muscles. She wasn't throwing up at the memory of what she had just said.

She was throwing up because she had meant every last word of it.

She'd never been unable to detach, before. She'd always maintained a distance, kept herself apart. This time, she couldn't. It was all too real: it *could have been Allie* if the team and the FBI hadn't been right on her tail. If the locator hadn't worked... if they'd hit traffic... Death was a matter of microscopic margins.

She retched again, painfully, and sat on the floor, because she couldn't summon enough energy to raise herself up. The undercover op, the interrogation, and the results – none of it was who she thought she was. It had tripped some switch deep within her.

None of it was who she *was*.

And yet it had all looked and felt so convincingly real: and could she be that person? Was she that person?

She *wouldn't* be that person. She *wouldn't*.

She cleaned up, dusted herself off, and walked out into the bullpen, to all appearances her ordinary self.

Carval's expression when he caught sight of her was not normal, nor was it comforting. He looked worried, and somehow frightened, and his smile was uncertain. She was about to sit down when Renfrew annexed her in a swift cut-out and conveyed her to the agents' conference room. A rapid jerk of his head removed Bergen, who did a half-decent job of pretending that he was leaving to talk to Andy about tech matters and the laptops.

"Yes?" Casey queried. "I'm done with Yarland and Severstal."

"Yes, you are," Renfrew agreed, slowly. "That was an impressive performance, with both suspects."

"We do what it takes."

"Yes. And sometimes it takes more from you than you believe could be taken."

"Meaning?"

"I observed the entire interview. You were completely convincing." His eyes were piercing, and Casey remembered that Renfrew was a qualified psychiatrist as well as an FBI profiler. "One might almost have thought that you had been sincere, and not bluffing to obtain a confession."

"Might one?" Casey stalled.

"Detective Clement, you are clearly under some strain. Whether that relates to this case or other matters is not clear" –

"Are you telling me I'm not fit to do my job? Go tell Kent, if you think so."

"Your aggressive response is not necessary."

"You taking pot-shots at me and my team is *not necessary*," Casey bit back. "I'm fine. I'm going to put those slimeballs where they belong – jail. What happens to them there isn't my call. And I'm going to put their pal in there with them."

"Mm," Renfrew emitted.

Casey turned away towards her desk, unwilling to expose herself to Renfrew's dispassionate scrutiny.

"Who went out to Larchmont?"

"Fremont an' Larson."

"None of us?"

"Don't think Andy's up for another one."

"Guess it's you and me, then. We can't leave it to Fremont or Larson."

"They're just holdin' the fort till one of us shows up."

"We'll both go. C'mon."

"I'm coming too," Carval said.

"Oh?"

"Sure he can. Comp'ny for me while you're givin' orders an' scarin' the uniforms an' CSU."

"Okay."

***

"Captain Kent?" The captain looked up, and nearly concealed his irritation. "A word, if I may." Dr Renfrew closed the office door, and smoothly took a seat.

"What is it?"

"I consider that Detectives Clement and Chee are in danger of over-stretching themselves in pursuit of the current case."

"Do you." It wasn't a question, nor was it friendly.

"Captain Kent, you may dislike me, but you cannot deny my experience and qualifications. Your team may be the best, and I have seen nothing to contradict that view – indeed, I should be exceedingly happy were they to work with me again" – Kent choked – "but Detective Chee has, I believe, been exposed to abuse in the past, the memories of which this case has re-opened, and Detective Clement is in a fragile position, for reasons which are unclear but appear to relate to a combination of her dislike of glamorous photographs, the stress Detective Chee is under, the introduction of Detective Marcol of Narcotics" – Dr Renfrew sent a sidelong look at Captain Kent, who most regrettably failed to react by look or movement – "and matters in her personal life."

"Really." Another non-question.

"Both detectives are treading a narrow line to maintain their control. It would take very little for either of them to lose their head."

Kent's control cracked. "Dr Renfrew, I will deal with my detectives as I see fit. I have complete confidence in their professionalism and if any of them had needed a break I would have ordered it. That team has been completely stable for years and you are not to poke at it to see if you can find any holes. They support each other. I suggest that you leave them to it until they invite you to help." His tone indicated that that would come some time after a frigid winter in Hell. "Now, if you have finished?"

Dr Renfrew exited, dissatisfied. He foresaw difficulties for both detectives, and he was seldom wrong in his predictions.

***

"Casey and O'Leary went up to Larchmont."

"Yeah?" Tyler blinked. "Not us?"

"Guess they thought we'd had enough fun for the day."

"Paperwork."

"Let's get this case into order. When we're done, I could really use a drink."

"Sure. Others?"

"The team." Andy's lips thinned. "Not the Feds."

"Poke-nosing?"

"Yep."

"Carval?"

"Yeah. Bigfoot said he didn't deal well with the souvenirs. Likely he could use a drink too."

"Man's one of us now."

"Guess so."

"What've we got?"

Scrawls joined the existing scrawls on the murder board. Paperwork became organised into a neat file. Tyler unobtrusively dealt with the appalling photographs, and Andy slowly eased back to his normal sharp-witted, quick-fire self.

From his conference room, Dr Renfrew watched in astonishment. He had expected Detective Chee to exhibit a desire to see the perpetrators or to leave. Instead, he was working with Detective Tyler, to all appearances perfectly relaxed.

If Dr Renfrew could have seen Tyler's tight shoulders, or the blankness in Andy's eyes, he would not have been nearly as chagrined.

***

"That's interesting."

"Huh?"

"Hervalo did some technogeeking. His laptop – the one at the scene – was full of podcasts and discussion groups about it. I guess he was the one who set it up."

"Huh." Tyler wandered over to see.

"So – I have to get with Bergen. If Hervalo was the technogeek, then he could already have diverted everything to a different IP address and accounts. We gotta go after that. Cloud storage. VPNs. Bergen!"

Andy dashed off to find Bergen, leaving Tyler to listen to the unintelligible sound of tech-speak at a thousand miles an hour.

***

In Larchmont, there was no trace of Hervalo, but plenty of traces of his complicity. CSU were busy: blue-gloved fingers turning over every last object and finding enough evidence to make Casey happy. What they couldn't find, however, was Hervalo himself, which did not make her happy.

"Gone." Casey's face twisted. "In the wind."

"He can't hide forever. We got a BOLO out, we got his face plastered all over the news. Someone'll spot him."

"He even left his phone."

"No laptop, though."

"No-o – no!" She was dialling in an instant. "Andy?"

"Yeah?"

"Andy, Hervalo hasn't got a laptop here at his home. You got one on site, yeah?"

"Yes."

"Would they link up?"

"A network? They might – he might be running a VPN, someone would host the site" –

"No tech-speak. I don't understand it when you do that. How about cloud storage, or the like? Separate access from a different laptop? You and Bergen take all that and run with it."

"Already on it."

"Great. Ask Tyler to chase down the money, with Renfrew. Me and O'Leary'll finish up here."

"What'cha thinkin'?" O'Leary asked when the phone went down.

"Long shot. If Hervalo had a back-up, or the cloud, or something like that, he might be accessing it from somewhere else. There's no laptop here, but he left his phone. So we could've tracked him by his phone, he thought, but he doesn't think we can track a different laptop." She showed white teeth, which wasn't much of a smile. "He's going to find out he's wrong."

"Neat. Anythin' else to be done here?"

"I don't think so. D'you think we've missed anywhere?"

"Naw. It's up to CSU to find trace evidence. We can't do that."

"Let's get back, then."

***

"Have we got anything more?" Casey wasn't even fully through the door before she started.

"No. Andy's off being technical with Bergen. Hervalo's money was routed through a Cayman account. Trail's gone dead. Nothing from the BOLO."

Casey scowled. "Nothing?"

"Nothin' yet." O'Leary lumbered up behind her. "Forensics tomorrow, like they said."

"Beer. Andy wanted one. Just the team." Tyler turned. "And your boy. Take his mind off the souvenirs."

"He didn't take them well? I didn't see what he looked like."

"Yeah. Bigfoot went after him. Not pretty."

"Naw. Man was real sick."

Casey filed that for future thought, alongside *I want you and I've got you*. It was too difficult to find headspace outside the job for complicated concepts, when her suspects weren't all captured. Carval being complicated was…well, *complicated*. She'd have thought he was…um…well. *Not* inured to it, but certainly not likely to be that badly upset by it. She shrugged the thought back into its box. She didn't have time for it now.

"Beer, then. I could use one too."

She unenthusiastically pulled herself together. There wasn't much spark left, and her eyes were tired and dull. As soon as her hunt had been halted, everything had stopped.

"We all could."

"Guess that means the Abbey."

"Sure does."

"Beer?" Carval, for the first time anyone could remember, didn't have his camera out. "I could really, really use a beer." His face was drawn, indefinably older.

"Where's Andy?"

"I'll tell him. Go down. Get them in."

"Okay." O'Leary heaved himself to his feet. "Let's go. 'S been a rough day."

The three cops and Carval reached the Abbey, annexed their favourite corner, and lined up the beers. A few moments later, Andy joined them, took a bottle and downed it without pausing for breath. No-one commented. Each of them had done the same.

O'Leary downed another beer in two huge swigs, and ran a sharp glance around the group.

"Difficult day."

Nods, and more beer being swallowed, greeted his opening. No-one took him up on the open offer to talk. He shrugged, not accidentally moving Casey closer into Carval.

"A little room here, Bigfoot."

"All cosy-like here. You c'n relax."

"I'd relax better if you gave me some more space."

O'Leary's china-blue eyes twinkled, and he didn't move. "Anyway, drink your beer. You c'n use somethin' after that show." Casey buried her nose in the bottle. "You were pretty scary in there."

"Mhm?"

"Sounded a lot like you meant it."

"What did I miss?" Andy's fingers locked around his beer.

"Casey put the frighteners on them. Never seen anythin' like it." O'Leary shuddered. "Broke 'em in bits." He finished his beer in one huge draught, and picked up another. "They sure thought it was real. I ain't sure it wasn't either. So was it?"

"Yeah." She set her beer down hard, shoulders tightening and her fingernails white with pressure. "I meant every single *fucking word of it* and I hate that I did. I don't *get* involved. I take them down. After that they're not my problem. But I meant every word and I want to see those sleazy bastards *dead*." She turned away from the team's eyes, curling into herself and her small form becoming even smaller.

"Guess they got that." Tyler pushed another beer into Casey's ambit. "Good. No place for those motherfuckers on this planet."

O'Leary shifted, and Casey was forced even closer to Carval, who took the hints O'Leary's movement was dropping and slid an arm around her shoulders.

"All friends here. No-one's goin' to tattle on you."

"You brought them down. No more sick photos and films from those bastards."

Carval said nothing. It wasn't his place: the team was dealing with its own. He petted fingers at her shoulder, and drank his beer.

"They're never going to see daylight again, because of it. It's okay."

"It's not *okay*. It's not okay to let your feelings into it like that." Her white-knuckled fingers knotted.

"The only people who know that it was real are us. We ain't tellin'."

"That stick-up-his-ass profiler knows."

"He suspects. He doesn't *know*."

"He ain't goin' to know, neither."

Casey wasn't obviously reassured, but she wasn't curling into herself any further. O'Leary swung towards Andy.

"That's Casey. How 'bout you? This case ain't great for you either, an' the Feds've been pryin'."

Silence fell. Andy's gaze flicked from O'Leary to Carval: back and forward, back and forward.

"I hear you didn't handle the photos so well," Andy challenged.

"No." Carval swallowed back bile. "As you keep reminding me, I'm not a cop."

"Enough," O'Leary growled. "No fightin' here."

"Team." Tyler punctuated his single word with a firm clonk of his beer bottle on the table.

"We don't want the Feds poke-nosin'. We fix ourselves, just like we always do. No trouble. No gettin' at each other. One team."

Casey roused herself. "You all know how we roll. We're tight. We solve the hardest and the worst cases *because* we're tight. I'm with Bigfoot. No fighting, no sniping. Let's fix it all now, and wave the Feds bye-bye as soon as we can."

"What she said," Tyler added.

"'Kay. So let's get this on the table so there's nothing left poisoning us. I've said my piece. I'm still standing. So will you be."

"An' if you ain't, we'll hold you up till you are."

"I threw up," Carval said, after a short silence. "They were vile. I'm not naïve, and I know some people use working with models to, um, harass the girls. But... nothing like that." He hunched defensively. "I never knew anything about anything like that."

"Naw. Iffen you did, you'd not be here. We're cool."

"My family died," Andy said. "Ended up with relatives. They" – he gulped, and stopped, flicked a glance at Carval.

Tyler touched his back. "Team," was all he said.

"They... they were into that." Dead silence greeted him. Three people already knew. One had his lips clamped tight shut, and unconsciously bit his fingers into Casey's shoulder. "I ran. I was twelve."

"Twe" – Carval *oofed* as a sharp elbow hit his ribs, and shut up, shocked cold.

Andy stared at the table, and said nothing more.

"We got it all out. Ev'ryone's here. We don't need to talk about it no more."

They all drank to that.

"You cleared for sparring yet?" O'Leary directed at Casey.

"Yeah."

"Mebbe you 'n' Andy should have a go-around tomorrow. Do you both good."

"Typical big man. Hitting things – or people – makes everything right."

"Naw, that's not true. But a good hard spar c'n deal with a lotta tension." He smirked widely. "Of course, so would" – he waggled his eyebrows.

"Finish that sentence and I'll finish you, O'Leary!"

"Chocolate," he continued.

She groaned.

"That expensive chocolate you said you liked."

"How would you know?"

"You wouldn't share." His lower lip protruded, toddler-like.

"I never share my chocolate. It's mine. Not for you bottomless pits. You'd eat it all and then I'd be angry, and" –

"We won't like you when you're angry," they chorused, and everyone laughed, and drank their beer.

***

A while later, the party broke up.

"Want a ride home?" Casey asked Carval.

"I thought you might want some company, and some dinner."

"I can cook."

"Take-out's easier. Do you want Thai? Sushi?"

"Mexican," Casey said. She didn't say *comforting carbs*. Strangely, Carval heard it.

"Okay. Anything you don't like?"

"Nope. You choose. I've got soda at home."

"Sounds good," he said, and hoped that dinner would ease the last of the strain around her; give him the chance to make sure that she really was okay. He maintained a demeanour of amiable warmth all the way to her apartment, all the way up, and all the way until dinner had arrived and been eaten – Casey didn't want much, and most of hers ended up in the fridge for, he assumed, tomorrow. She sipped at her soda, until he finished and tidily put his plate away by the sink.

"Shall I wash up, and you dry?" he suggested.

"Just leave it. I'll get there later."

He returned to the couch, and dropped a comforting arm around her shoulders, implying without quite encouraging that she should snuggle into his broad frame and be easy with him. She moved closer, which was both delightful and astonishing, and then reached up to pull his head down and kiss him. It wasn't an invitation he'd decline; and he didn't: responding in kind. With her, he could try to forget the depravity of the crimes; with her kissing him, her hands around his neck and his arms enfolding her, he could almost forget her earlier ice-cold fury, her destruction of the two suspects. When she was lax against him, he didn't remember the hard cruelty of the interviews, or worry about which was the real Casey.

He dived in, frantic to forget: to have his soft, responsive, cuddlesome Casey back; but she wasn't soft, but raiding, desperate, seeking forgetfulness for herself. He gave up, and gave in.

But afterwards, he nestled her in, playing with a rioting curl of her hair.

"Today..."

"I don't want to talk about it." She closed her eyes. "It's over. I don't want to think about it." Suddenly she turned into his chest, shivering. "I really don't." Typical. Shutting him out before he'd even knocked on the door.

He stroked down her back, long fingers spanning wide to warm her, and pulled the covers close in.

"I never do that."

His arms tightened round her: an inadvertent jerk of surprise.

"Do what?" Encouragement slid through the words, enticing more of the unexpected speech.

"Get involved. You can't get involved. You have to detach."

"Or?"

"Or you burn out, or go rogue. You can't get involved."

"But you left at the end of the day. You and Andy. You put it down, and we all went for a drink."

"I shouldn't have needed to put *anything* down."

"How couldn't you be affected by that? It was *vile*. I" – he stopped, shuddered, and turned firmly away from the memory of the photos and the aftermath.

"I'm a cop. We have to be detached." He heard *you don't*.

"You did detach. You didn't shoot him on the spot."

"Brains on the wall isn't a good look," she flipped, but her hands curled around his biceps. "We can't go shooting suspects who don't try shooting us."

"I guess." Carval's own hands slid back to press her in. "But see, not shooting him means you were detached."

"Until I ripped him apart in Interrogation and meant every last word of it." She'd tightened up again, closing off.

"And walked out without punching his lights out."

"True…"

"So you did detach," Carval pointed out. She didn't answer, and he didn't press, because she'd actually opened up a little: a rare insight. "You okay now?" Her head nodded against his chest. "Good. C'mere."
Shortly, there was no more talking.

CHAPTER THIRTY ONE

"We got a hit on the BOLO," Andy announced.

"Where? When?"

"Now, at LaGuardia."

"Did they pull him in?"

"Yeah. Seems he's not happy about it. Yelling and hollering in a very uncivilised fashion about his rights."

"No harmonious chi, that man."

"Oh? That the rights he didn't care about for those girls? What are the words? Oh yes. Life, liberty and the pursuit of happiness. He didn't pay much attention before now. Funny how he's worried about them now that he's the one losing them."

Bright, predatory smiles illuminated the bullpen.

"They'll be bringin' him in soon's they c'n get there an' back."

"We have found Mr Hervalo?"

"Yep. Picked up at LaGuardia."

"Money don't buy brains."

"Indeed not. If I were being pursued by Law Enforcement, I would certainly not be so unintelligent as to take air transport."

Somehow, everybody else heard the words *if only you were being hunted* hanging in the air. Even Bergen smiled.

"Detective Clement, do you intend to interrogate?"

"Yes." It didn't admit argument. Renfrew didn't argue. "O'Leary will be with me." Renfrew was transparently *not* saying anything of the order of *Good*. "We'll use the same tactics as yesterday. They worked then."

Renfrew's face positively yelled his belief that it had been anger, not analysis, yesterday. Fortunately, he still didn't say anything.

"Let's get it all wrapped up by the end of the day. Have we got Forensics yet?"

"Just coming through."

"Money trail?"

"Told you. Stopped at Cayman."

"However, all known US accounts are frozen, and should you identify further accounts from your interrogation, we shall freeze those as well."

Casey's scowl would curdle milk. "Okay," she eventually said. "What else do we have to get in order to close this off?"

"Not a lot," Andy confirmed. "Tyler and I got most of it done while you were off searching houses and not finding laptops."

"You did paperwork? Wow."

"I'm a tidy, organised person."

"Had to be tidy, in the Army."

"So we're in good shape?"

"Yeah. Add Forensics, add Hervalo's interrogation, all done by the end of the day."

"Perfect."

"If you're that far through, Clement, then you and Chee can provide me with a proper report." What was Kent *doing*? She partnered with O'Leary, not Andy. That rat *bastard* Renfrew. He'd tattled. "My office."

"Yes, sir."

"Report, Clement."

She did, standing at parade rest: logical, organised, and emotionless.

"I see. Chee, inform me about the technology which was used."

Andy did, also at parade rest, also emotionless.

"Thank you. At ease." Neither detective noticeably eased. "How have you found working with the FBI?"

"No issues, sir."

"None, sir."

Kent regarded them beadily. "I see," he said again. "So there were no tensions?"

Hell. Kent knew something. Or Renfrew had told him something. Or both. Captains shouldn't interfere in the team. Hadn't he got reports of his own to do, or a meeting at 1PP? Casey bit the bullet.

"Dr Renfrew seems to think that we were more affected by the case than we are, sir." There. Truthful and tactful. Okay, so it might not have been true yesterday, but it was true now.

"Mm." Kent was thinking. That was always worrying. "Why might he think that?"

"I don't know, sir. He watched me interrogate yesterday, so maybe he thought that was a little full-on."

"Did he think you'd crossed the professional line?"

"Not to my knowledge, sir."

Kent desisted. "Chee."

"Sir?"

"Why would Dr Renfrew think you might be affected by this case?"

"I have no idea, sir."

Kent pinned him with a penetrating stare. "No idea?"

"No, sir."

Casey remained as inscrutable as Andy blanked the question. Kent's own brand of interrogative silence filled his office, but failed to make any impression on his two obdurate detectives.

"Chee, dismissed. Clement, stay."

Andy escaped. Casey wished that she could too, since being ordered to stay was never a good sign.

"What's really going on here?" Kent rapped. "Something's up with this case and your team. What is it?"

"Nothing, sir."

"Clement" – oh, God, he'd used her name: that meant trouble coming head on down the track – "the most respected profiler in the FBI has twice arrived in my office to raise concerns about the mental state of members of your team. Are you seriously trying to tell me that he's got no grounds?"

"No grounds at all, sir."

"Mm. Would you care to explain why Dr Renfrew believes Chee to have been abused?"

"No idea, sir." That wasn't a lie. Casey had no idea how Dr Renfrew had arrived at his conclusions.

Kent favoured her with an exceedingly sceptical glance. "I see." Casey disliked that piece of verbal punctuation more with every repetition. It was wholly possible that Kent did see, which she had been praying could be avoided. "In that case, perhaps you would like to explain why he believes that Detective Marcol had caused tension?"

"Marcol was here to provide information for our case, sir, but then asked me on a date. Totally inappropriate when we're working a case."

Kent blinked, slowly. "And your previous acquaintance with Marcol?"

"We were in the same class at the Academy. I hadn't seen him since until Narcotics sent him over."

"I see." No, Kent, *don't* see, Casey thought. The less *seeing* he did, the better.

"Sir, it's all irrelevant to this case."

Kent gave up. He didn't have time for a chess game and Clement was blanking him at every turn.

"Okay. Dismissed."

"Sir."

She outright fled, straight to the break room for tooth-dissolvingly strong espresso. Behind her, Kent considered whether he should exercise his interrogation skills on the whole team at once, to find out what they were hiding. He knew that they were hiding an awful lot of history. Oh, for Chrissake. He'd asked the wrong question, too. He'd asked how Renfrew had concluded Chee had been abused. He should have asked straight out if Chee'd been abused, to confirm his information. Call himself a Captain? He had to sharpen up. Did it really matter, though? Just because an FBI profiler thought they were on the point of snapping, didn't mean that he had to believe it.

He peered out of the window of his office and surveyed the scene. Clement firmly in control, as ever, and the team looked perfectly normal to him. He'd leave it – for now. He had a drink lined up with Garrett of the Third soon, and after that he was going to get some answers. He wasn't having his best team falling apart, if he could help it.

He had a look at leave taken, and overtime worked. Hm. Maybe a little enforced leave. He could afford to give them all an extra couple of days at Thanksgiving, if this case was closed. It was only a week or so away, so they'd all be back in time for the Christmas murder rush. Done. Kent made a few small notes on their files, and turned to the rest of his work.

***

"Is Hervalo here yet?"

"Naw. An' he has to go through Bookin', so it'll be an hour. Go play with what Forensics sent us, an' stop fidgetin'. Or go make coffee an' drink it, to calm down."

"Coffee. You've already dealt with the Forensic information."

"How'd you know?"

"You're all looking smug."

"Yeah. Proves all three of them were there – and that they didn't change that bed too often."

"Eurgh. Too much information." She disappeared to concoct a cleansing coffee, though brain-scrubbing would have been more effective.

An hour or so later, a burly uniform appeared. "Hervalo's in Interrogation, Detectives."

"Playtime."

"I want a go at bein' bad cop this time," O'Leary pouted. "You've been bad cop all case an' it's not fair."

"You look like the bad cop even when you aren't. Just loom menacingly. No effort required."

"Awwww."

"And if you want to be worse cop, go ahead. Last one, and we'll have them all wrapped up like a pretty present for the prosecutors."

"They'll be givin' us thanks. Appropriate to the season."

"Yeah. Right now, let's go give Hervalo our thanks for him being here."

They strode off, O'Leary matching his steps to Casey, then dropping behind as they entered. The effect was just as they planned. Hervalo showed no fear of Casey, but his jaw dropped as O'Leary entered. The big cop's sheer scale intimidated without requiring anything else. Sadly for Hervalo, he'd concentrated on the wrong cop.

"Jose Cerrado Hervalo. You've been arrested for the rape and murder of Daniela Petrovich, Carissa Ndbele, Melinda Carnwath, and the attempted rape of Alejandra Despero. I hear you've been hollering about your rights. So I'll read you them."

She read Hervalo his Miranda rights slowly and with emphasis, letting the gravity of the words and the ice in her tone work on him.

"Those are your rights," she finished. He was pale under his swarthy skin, staring at the Formica table. "Is there anything you'd like to say?"

"It wasn't me. I wasn't involved."

"Don't lie. Your fingerprints, DNA and hair are all over the scene. The arresting officer says that they booked $9,000 in cash from you – conveniently under the reportable limit, that. Funny, we can see that you withdrew $9,900 yesterday. Cash for a hotel, cash for a cab, cash for dinner and breakfast, cash for the air ticket to Albuquerque. About right to leave you $9,000." She caught his eyes, and he couldn't look away. "Why'd you need that much cash if you weren't trying to run?"

Silence.

"Okay, let's try something else. Why'd you rape and murder those girls on film?"

"I didn't."

"I already told you not to lie," Casey bit. "But let's be clear. Your next stop is jail. The only question is whether it's life in Rikers or Death Row in California."

Hervalo gulped, loud in the suffocating silence. Casey and O'Leary exchanged glances.

"I think we'll keep this one in NY. Death Row would be solitary. In Rikers, he'll have lots of friends. Pretty boy like him, they'll all want a piece. I mean, he won't be filmed, but he'll find out how the girls felt." Her smile was stiletto-sharp. "Poetic justice, hm?"

"I dunno. I think Death Row's the right place. Plenty of time to consider his failin's, as you might say. An' I'm sure he'd be in the general population sometime. Like you say, he's a pretty boy. Sure to make a lot of friends, while he's waitin' for the needle."

Hervalo's eyes skittered from one cold cop to the other.

"I guess. On Death Row, he'll have plenty of time to think about what's coming. No dope to soften the blow. He won't be able to escape that way. Nothing to ponder except when he'll be taken out, strapped down on a gurney, and injected. He can wonder if it hurts or not."

"I'm told it does."

"Me too." Their voices were light, conversational, and ice cold. Not a hint of anger or revulsion appeared. It was as if they'd forgotten Hervalo was there. "Hurts like hell, they say."

"An' then they're gone."

"Yep."

"Easy way out."

"Except for the waiting, and the pain when they stick the needle in and inject."

"Guess so."

The tension grew as the conversation continued. In Observation, Carval kept shooting, oblivious to Renfrew's concentration and Kent's fierce attention to the scene inside. Tyler and Andy had slipped in, too: still and silent, not drawing attention to themselves. Bergen peered from behind them all, as forgettable as ever.

"You can't do that!" Hervalo exploded. "I didn't kill anyone."

"You were part of it. That's conspiracy. You all get the same punishment."

"Just think, they'll all be in the same place. Ain't that sweet? They c'n keep each other comp'ny."

"Tell each other bedtime stories, before they go back to their cells."

"An' their cellmates."

"Yeah."

"You... I...."

"Tell us everything. It's your only hope."

Just as the others had, Hervalo broke and began to talk.

"I see," Casey said. In Observation, Kent's lips twisted in recognition. "But you've forgotten something."

"No! Nothing!"

"Oh, yes. Who hosted the site you were uploading the films to?"

Bergen gasped. "How did she know?"

Renfrew stilled his steepling fingers. "Shh. This could be extremely useful."

Hervalo paled still further, shaking.

"Who hosted it?"

"I...I don't know!"

"Liar." She turned to meet O'Leary's light, hard eyes. "Guess he's for California. No loss." She started to stand.

"No! I don't – I – not California! Please!"

"The girls said *please*, too. Didn't help them."

"I'll tell you. Please, I'll tell you!"

And he did. Another full ten minutes. In Observation, Bergen and Renfrew stood, transfixed. Kent's stony face gave away nothing, but his body language exuded pride.

"Take him away," Casey said coldly.

"But…"

"There are no deals," she said, and stalked out.

When she reached her desk, she could faintly hear Bergen and Renfrew's rapid, commanding discussion. Shortly, that conversation ceased, and Renfrew emerged, his skeletal face smiling.

"That was extraordinarily effective," he said. "What prompted you to that line of questioning?"

"Andy's work," Casey said. "He mentioned that someone would host the site."

"The films would be uploaded to a site on the dark web. Whoever was running – hosting – that site might be running more of them," Andy explained.

"Ah. A team effort."

"We are a team."

Renfrew blinked at the force of her statement.

"Anyway, it's done now. Just the paperwork to do. You'll go after the web host – it's out of our jurisdiction – so we're finished."

"It has been a pleasure" – Renfrew began, and Casey's phone rang.

"Clement."

"It's Carla Jankel. Look, I'm really sorry, but something's come up and I can't make Monday. Can you get yourself and your father here by four?"

"Today?"

"Yeah."

"I'll see what I can do. I'll call you back, okay?"

"Thanks."

"Bye." She swiped off. "Excuse me," she said to Renfrew, and made for the door.

Some moments later, she returned, grim-faced, and unwillingly trudged to Kent's office.

"Sir? May I speak to you?"

Kent smiled widely, an expression so unusual that Casey almost fell over. "Yes. Come in." She closed the door. His eyebrows lifted. "That was an excellent performance by you and your team," he said, before she could open her mouth. "Even the Feds are impressed. It's been a difficult case. I want you all to take a proper break over Thanksgiving, and I am ordering you all to take two extra days, from Thanksgiving to the following Monday."

"Thank you, sir." What else could she say? She didn't want the extra days now – she would need them, she thought sadly, to deal with her father.

"Now, what do you want?"

"Uh, sir, I have to go see the lawyer about my father's court hearing. It was supposed to be after work but she can't do that any more and please, sir, may I have leave this afternoon, after lunch? I'll come back after and make the time up, or tomorrow, or use that extra day you just gave me" –

"Stop." Kent's smile had vanished like the proverbial snowball in Hell. "Why can your father not deal with his lawyer himself?" Unpleasant silence fell. "I require an answer, Clement."

She brought her gaze up to meet Kent's stern look. "He...doesn't remember why he needs a lawyer."

"I'm sorry?"

"He doesn't remember the arrest, the desk appearance ticket, the hearing date, or why he needs a lawyer at all." Her mouth twisted, sour bile at the back of her throat. "If I don't fix it, who will? He's my dad. I can't let him go to jail without trying to help." She stopped, conscious that she'd blurted out far too much.

"Astonishing. An explanation which I haven't had to extract with a pry bar." Casey winced. "And you actually came and asked for leave. Equally astonishing." Another wince. "You may take your leave. You will make the time up over the next two days you are on shift. Before Thanksgiving. You will still take the leave days I have given you over the Thanksgiving weekend."

"Thank you, sir."

"Dismissed."

She trudged back out, and disappeared to call Jankel and confirm that afternoon's appointment, after which she put her head down to move on with completing the paperwork. The one bright spot was that the Feds were packing up their equipment and departing.

"Detectives?"

"Yes, Dr Renfrew?"

"May I see you all, please?"

Nobody *actually* sighed as they trailed into the conference room, now denuded of almost every trace of the FBI team.

"I have been most impressed by your work. I wish to thank you, and to assure you that, were we to require the help of the NYPD in future, I should request the assistance of this team."

Four jaws dropped. Bergen, behind Renfrew, stifled a laugh.

"Thank you," Casey choked out. None of the others could manage more than a nod.

"Good working with you," Bergen added. "Andy, you've got some nice tricks there. I might call you for a proper download, sometime when we've got some space."

"Sure." Andy's answering smile was genuine.

"Many thanks. Good bye."

And Renfrew was, thankfully, gone. They watched, not subtly, to make sure that he did, in fact, go and didn't lurk around or, worse, go and talk to

Kent again. Bergen, by contrast, got a friendly wave.

"Phew," Casey said, summing up the team's feelings. "Now, let's get this wrapped. And" – she paused enticingly – "Kent's given us all an extra couple of days over Thanksgiving."

"He what?"

"Wow."

"I c'n have more time with Pete an' the family."

"Let's get this *done*," Andy enthused.

"An' then let's go for a beer." Three men nodded firmly. "We'll get your boy along too."

"I'll pass."

They stared. "Pass?"

"You ain't had another fight already?"

"No."

"No," Carval repeated, wandering up. He'd managed to avoid the whole FBI circus's leave-taking, Casey noted.

"So why?"

"Dad." Bitterness spilled out. "I have to deal with some stuff. Captain gave me leave to go early, as long as I make it up later."

"Okay. Well, when you're done, iffen you want, we'll be in the Abbey. Give me a call, we'll get your drink in."

"Thanks." Which everyone there knew wasn't agreement. "Now, let's finish. Can't keep Bigfoot from his beer."

CHAPTER THIRTY TWO

"Thanks for rescheduling, Detective Clement, Mr Clement."

"Call me Casey."

"David," Casey's dad said, enunciating carefully. Casey cringed.

She'd gone to pick him up, and found him, despite her earlier call, with a glass in his hand and an open bottle. "Come to take me to the airport?" he'd said. "We're going to DC, to see the new museum." She hadn't argued: simply put him in her car and driven: explained – again – when they reached Jankel's offices.

And now, here they were, sitting in a stark conference room: chilly pity in Jankel's face which Casey could hardly bear to watch. She put a coffee under her father's nose, and didn't get one for herself.

"So. There's a hearing on December 13. That's your desk appearance. That's *not* a trial. It's just to enter your not guilty plea and receive a date for the trial. Sometime in January, most likely, you'll have a trial date."

Jankel carried on explaining. Casey, who was familiar with the whole sordid process from her uniformed officer days, pretended to listen, and wondered how on earth her father would fare if he couldn't even meet his lawyer without having a drink beforehand.

Finally, it was over. Her father hadn't asked a single question, but at least he'd agreed to retaining Jankel. Casey had noted a few key points down, and had agreed to provide (knowing her father wouldn't or couldn't remember to do so) the information the attorney needed.

"Thank you," Casey said. Her father shook Jankel's hand, and repeated the courtesy.

He was silent as he sat down in the passenger seat, as he had been silent through the meeting, and silent through most of the journey home.

"Catkin?"

"Yeah?" Her eyes were firmly on the road. If she concentrated on the traffic, she couldn't be thinking about anything else.

"You will be there at the hearing, won't you?"

"Yeah. I already booked leave."

"You have to be there."

"I'll be there."

"I know I messed up. I just… I don't remember any of it. I just wanted us to go see the museum, like we talked about. I forgot we hadn't agreed."

Her heart clenched. "It's okay." But it wasn't okay. It would never be okay.

"You're a good kid, Catkin."

She could have cried. If she were such a good daughter, why was he still drinking to the point of blackout? If she were such a good kid, why wasn't she enough for him? Now she knew that he was disappointed in her, being a *good kid* didn't help. She was just useful, when there was no-one else to help him out.

He didn't say anything more as she dropped him off, just *thanks, bye, see you Sunday as usual?* That hurt, too. On her way home, she paid strict attention to the road again. It was better than letting her misery escape.

At home, she didn't bother with dinner, pacing around her cosy apartment: sitting down for a few moments: picking up a book, turning a page, putting it down; channel surfing, but nothing held her interest. She wanted…she wanted someone who'd simply hold her. She didn't need to have her tears dried: her tears for her father had dried up long since, she told herself, and knew that she lied. She didn't need anything but some comfort and someone who seemed to care. Carval seemed to care. At least, he'd certainly said that he wanted her. That… that would do.

She tapped out a text to O'Leary, telling him she wasn't going to join the team, and then one to Carval, simply asking him to come over. Then she waited, and waited; went to take a shower, and waited. There was no reply. She curled unhappily into her comfortable sweats, and decided that she'd got it wrong. She was surprised just how much that hurt, for a supposedly casual liaison.

It began to dawn on her that she wasn't as casual as she'd thought. She'd been downright jealous of Carval's history, and that he was shooting Allie, and she'd hidden it in work and more work, just as she always did. Well, hell. Now what?

Now nothing, that was what. He hadn't texted back, well over an hour later, so clearly he wasn't coming. She sent another text: *don't bother, it's too late now, see you in the precinct.* If it weren't so late, she'd have gone out running, but it was dark and cold, and the tip-tapping drops on the window were more sleet than rain. She stared out into the bleak November night, and wondered how she'd become involved without even noticing.

***

"Casey ain't comin'." O'Leary waggled his phone, miniscule in his huge paw, to prove it.

"No surprise."

Carval simply shrugged, under the knowing eyes of the three cops. His phone buzzed. Depressed, he ignored it. Most likely it was Allan, fussing.

He didn't think about it again till the beers and camaraderie were done and the group dispersing, without a single word being said about Casey's absence. Unreasonably, he was cross with her. He'd wanted to see her without the damn case and his history of model eye-candy getting in the way, and she hadn't come.

He flicked through to the text.

Oh, *shit*. It was from Casey, and it had been sent immediately after she'd texted O'Leary. He goggled at it, not believing the words in front of his eyes.

Would you come over?

She'd wanted him to go over. She'd wanted *him*. Not the team, not the team with him, but simply him. And he'd missed it. The message had been sent nearly two hours ago, and he hadn't seen it. By now, she'd have given up on him. Even as he thought that, another text buzzed. *don't bother, it's too late now, see you in the precinct.* No, no, no. She'd actually asked him to go over, straight after a difficult meeting involving her dad, and he'd missed it because he'd been pissed that she wasn't coming for a drink with them.

"You okay?"

"Yeah," he managed, distracted.

"Move out the doorway, then."

"Prob'ly seen the perfect shot. Betcha it's me."

Andy blew a raspberry. "Whatever it is, I wanna go home. C'mon, stop staring at your phone and shift."

Carval shifted. Andy and O'Leary moved past him and away; Andy staggering slightly, O'Leary protectively close. Andy had downed more beers than Carval had ever seen him drink, even on the previous night when they'd all had plenty, and they'd hit him hard.

Tyler paused. "Go see her," he said.

"Have you taken over from O'Leary as Cupid?" There was no real bite to the words, though.

"Team."

"Tag team, more like. What about Andy?"

"He'll be okay. Been tough, but he 'n' Casey'll have a session on the mats and he'll be good. Knew when to talk, needed some drinks, blur the past."

As far as Carval had known, Andy had been as close-mouthed as Casey. He deduced that Andy had talked to Tyler, and understood another thread weaving the team together. It wasn't just O'Leary who provided stability.

They all did, in different ways: so maybe they all needed support, in different ways?

He put that aside. "Night."

"Go see her."

"I am."

Tyler nodded approvingly. "Good."

Carval hurried off. Casey had wanted him, and now she was backtracking. No way. He picked up a cab to avoid the sleet and for speed, which deposited him at her block in short order.

***

Casey was still staring mindlessly out of the window when there was a determined rapping on her door. She supposed it might be O'Leary, as she padded over to look. He had a habit of turning up if he thought she needed a friend, and no matter how she tried to dissuade him, he was too big to be dissuaded. She checked through the peephole, and was utterly astonished to see Carval.

"I didn't expect you."

"I didn't look at my phone." He stepped in and hugged her. "Sorry. I would've texted if I'd seen it earlier."

"'S okay." She pressed closer, head tucked against his chest. "You came." She didn't care if it sounded needy. She simply wanted him to cuddle her in and surround her: big, warm and comforting.

"C'mere." He petted over her hair, loosely confined in a messy bun, and down her back. She breathed him in: no cologne, the slight hint of beer, and his own male smell. Her arms slid round his waist, holding on. In bare feet, she barely made his pecs, the top of her head against his collarbone. Imperceptibly, she eased, softening into him as he leaned down to pillow his cheek on her hair, and then didn't let go when he straightened to walk them both to her couch.

"There." She merely curled in, bonelessly flexible and smaller. "Wanna talk, or just stay here?"

"Stay here." She took a breath. "Just be here." Her head fell on to his shoulder, a stray curl tickling his neck.

"Sure."

She relaxed further into him, quiet and still, enjoying the gentle petting of his fingers; a hand on his knee to keep herself close. He didn't speak, and somehow, enclosed in strong arms and silence, it was easier to talk.

"We went to see the lawyer. Dad and me. He didn't remember why. He'd had a drink." She relapsed into wordlessness. Carval dropped a tiny buss on the top of her head, and still said nothing, conveying comfort in his quiet. "He could go to jail, if this goes wrong, and he couldn't be sober. Couldn't face it without a drink." She tried to turn away, but he turned her back, and further round, till he had swung her legs over his and cradled her against his chest. She didn't protest: she had quite enough to do to control her face and emotions. Her hand crept to his shoulder, her cheek rubbed against his cotton button-down.

"You're crying," he said in surprise.

"I'm not."

He tipped her chin up, gentle but brooking no resistance. "My shirt's damp. It wasn't me."

"I'm not crying. There's no point crying."

"Well, stop not-crying into my shirt and crumpling it. I'll get a cold and I can't take photos if I'm sneezing. It ruins the centring, and you don't want your head chopped off, do you?"

"I'll settle for chopping off Renfrew's."

Carval laughed. "He took some getting used to."

"I'd rather not get used to him."

"He gave good shots, though. Like McDonald. Perfect contrast to you."

"Me?"

Carval thought swiftly. "The team." She settled again. His undisciplined mind flitted sideways. "I'd have thought you'd have wanted to be with the team tonight."

Her shutters instantly dropped: her shoulders stiffened and her spine locked. "No."

And then, quite suddenly, she braced further. "I" – she stopped, gulped, took a shallow, hasty breath. "I just needed to be held."

His arms dropped in shock. Casey started to scramble away, and he grabbed her back. "Don't run away." She couldn't. He'd made sure of that – well, unless she protested, in which case, since he was a decent man, he'd release her. He wasn't into force. Especially after this particular case, he wasn't into anything that wasn't complete consent and utterly clear signals about what was liked, wanted, and sought.

"I can do that," he said, and simply did, waiting for her to relax into him again. He could wait, because for the first time in weeks – maybe the first time ever – he was sure that she was in this with him.

Their peace was interrupted by the shrill of Casey's phone.

"Clement – Dad? What's wrong?"

"Nothing's wrong. I just... well, I got to thinking, and I thought you were unhappy, and I just thought, well, maybe I should call and make sure you were okay."

"Everything's fine."

"Katrina Anne Clement" – Carval startled, listening in without compunction – "that line didn't work on me when you were a teenager and it isn't going to work now."

She pulled out of Carval's arms and began to pace. "Nothing's wrong. It was a difficult case, but we solved it. I'm a little tired, that's all."

Her father made a sceptical noise. Carval could clearly see Casey's desire for her father to stop asking questions. It wasn't an evening where pushing her would be well received (he'd gained far more ground by *not* pushing, he realised), and he thought that this would go wrong almost immediately.

Automatically, he reached for his camera, and had it halfway out before he realised how extraordinarily destructive taking shots would be. It took some effort to put it away again.

Casey continued to pace. "It's fine. I'll go to bed early." Which said nothing about sleeping. Carval couldn't hear the other side of the conversation any more, but the lemon-sour twist to Casey's pursed lips didn't give him confidence that it was going well.

"Dad, it's *fine*. Stop worrying. I'm tired, that's all. You don't have to worry about me."

"Look, I'm all grown up. I don't need you to tell me how to relax. I know how to deal with a rough case."

"Yes, I've eaten." Her fingers crossed behind her back, which would have been amusing were it not for the note of stress rising in her voice. "Stop fussing."

And then it exploded. Only God and Casey knew what her father had said to her.

"You're my dad. Yeah. Sure you are. When you're sober and watching your words so you don't tell me how disappointed you are with me. How I should have been a lawyer and shouldn't be a cop because it's no job for a woman. You don't have the right to tell me how to live my life when you're the one who's blacking out drunk and you're the one being arrested for disorderly conduct. You couldn't even show up sober to meet the lawyer who's going to try to save you from jail. I had to organise all of that because you were too drunk to do it yourself and you didn't even pay attention. I'm not taking advice from you on my life because you don't understand it and you don't approve of it, and your life's not a good example anyway. This conversation is done. I'm done. I can't fix you and you can't help me."

She gave her phone a vicious swipe to cut the call, threw it down on the couch and, entirely oblivious to Carval's horrified presence, fled for her bedroom and slammed the door shut. The phone rang again, until it went to voicemail; repeated itself twice more, and then stayed silent.

Carval had precisely no idea of what to do.

He sat uselessly for a moment, then engaged his brain. The best option seemed to be to go after her, since she wasn't mad at him. Leaving, which had crossed his mind, felt cowardly. He tentatively tapped on the bedroom door, and, receiving no response, carefully turned the handle and padded in.

Casey was face down in her pillows, shoulders shuddering but making absolutely no noise. He plumped down on the bed next to her, instinctively picking her up and cradling her into him. She didn't resist.

Her face was ghastly, but her eyes were completely dry.

"I guess that's that," she said. "I can't fix him. He won't fix himself." She manufactured a rictus expression that might have been a distant cousin to a smile. "Wanna go for dinner on Sunday? My plans just fell through."

"Sure," he placated. He had no idea how to deal with this shell-shocked-but-hiding-it Casey. Play normal, and see where they went, he supposed.

"After all, last time you asked me out to dinner I was multi-coloured so we had take-out. We can make up for it." Another ghastly not-smile.

"Sure," he said again. "Where d'you want to go?"

"Somewhere."

"That doesn't narrow the options much. Smart, casual, European, what?"

"Somewhere that'll give us a Thanksgiving meal. 'Cause my plans for Thanksgiving just fell through, too."

She began to cry, evidently trying not to but failing, as if reality had finally pierced the shield. "He might as well be dead."

"He might stop."

"He never has before. He always goes back to it. He can't cope with her being gone." She reached for a Kleenex, and blew her nose and dabbed at her eyes. "It was nobody's fault. Brain cancer, caused a traffic accident. One of those things." She dabbed and blew. "But he can't deal with it." Dab, blow. "I've never lost it with him before. He's my dad. I can't... if he's gone, I've no family left."

He didn't know where the cliché came from. "You've got the team. They're like your family. Not family, but close."

"It's not the same. Even the best friends aren't family."

Carval shrugged, out of ideas. "Well, someone's tried to call you three times, and likely it's your dad. So you can talk to him, or stay right here, or leave everything till tomorrow."

"Called? Why didn't you say? If it's a case, I have to go."

She whipped away from him before he could say that all of them had been her father, scrubbing the back of her hand across her eyes and catching a Kleenex on the way. Her phone was still where she had thrown it, half under a cushion. She snatched it up, and checked the screen.

"No case. Just Dad." The phone clacked down on the table.

"Don't you want to listen to them?"

"No." It fell like a rock, but she dabbed at her face again.

"Okay. C'mere, then." She stared at him. "Come here," he said, and then impatiently pulled her down anyway.

"Uh?"

He didn't bother with talking, but simply cuddled her in.

"What are you doing?"

"You said you just wanted held. You're being held. Snuggle in, and enjoy it."

"What?"

It probably wasn't fair to do this now, but…Carval believed in winning, and right now he was intent on winning over Casey. She'd asked him to come, she'd opened up…and now he wanted her to admit that that meant that it was more than a series of casual evenings. Nothing too intense, of course. He didn't do intense.

"You asked me over to cuddle you. Have you changed your mind?"

She sniffed. "No." Her bedraggled form curved into him, though it couldn't have been a conscious act.

"I give good cuddle," he smirked.

"If not good modesty."

"Why be modest when you're the best?"

"Do they send photos of your ego from the International Space Station?" she snarked. Carval heard normal-level snark with more relief than he'd have cared to admit.

"Yep, right along with all the other wonders of the natural world." The menacing growl was even more of a relief.

"More like a natural disaster."

"That's not nice. But if we're talking about natural disasters, then I'm pretty keen on earthquakes."

"Huh – oh. That's so lame you need to use a walker for it. Next you'll tell me you're going to make the earth move, just in case I didn't get it the first time."

"Actually," Carval oozed, "I'd rather show you." He dipped his head, tipped up her chin, and indulged in a lengthy, leisurely kiss which left her breathing a little more deeply. "That's better." He kissed her again. Her hands curled around his neck and pulled his face closer.

And then she simply invaded: taking full control and leaving Carval in no state to do anything but respond to her lead. He could taste desperation on her tongue, a frantic desire to forget, but once her small hands slid under his t-shirt he stopped thinking. All he could do was let the fire take him.

Instinct undid her shirt, instinct loosened her pants' belt and button, and instinct lifted her and discarded them all. She wasn't behindhand: tugging his t-shirt over his head, skin meeting skin; slipping away only to pull him up and to her bed, stripping him as soon as they were there, falling back and bringing him over her: no teasing, no play, only the clash of bodies and hard, fast satisfaction.

After, she lay pillowed against his chest, over his heart, limp and exhausted. That hadn't been lovemaking, but oblivion. He peered down, and found her eyes shut. She'd fallen asleep, or as near as made no difference, without any admission at all. He rearranged them, laid an arm over her to keep her near, and followed.

He was woken by Casey's phone ringing. She staggered out of bed, but it had gone to voicemail before she'd reached it. Following her, he heard the message as she replayed it, automatically on speaker.

Catkin, I was thinking. You were right. I'm going to rehab again. I'll do better this time. Don't give up on me. I don't think any of what you said. I'll call you.

She stood, staring down at the phone on the table. "Rehab?" Hope lit her face. "He last went three years ago. I never thought" – she flung her arms round Carval.

"It's going to be okay."

Fin.

ABOUT THE AUTHOR

SR Garrae grew up in Scotland and then worked in international finance in London until her retirement. She lives in the UK with her family, who are somewhat bemused by but supportive of her complete change of career.

She always loved books, but didn't start to write original fiction until after she retired. She now balances writing with travel, reluctant but very necessary gym visits, and designing her own book covers.